CW00410391

UNDISCLOSED CURIOSITY

UNDISCLOSED #2

CARLY MARIE

CHAPTER 1

LOGAN

MY EYES CRACKED open when the evening sun filtered through the blinds, and I felt the cold spot next to me in bed. That spot had been occupied by Trent Sylvan, my very naked best friend, when I'd fallen asleep. I kept the sad sigh of frustration to myself. This was what we'd agreed to when we accepted that a relationship between the two of us would never work. Post-sex snuggles were no longer in the cards. Well, maybe extended post-sex snuggles were no longer in the cards, because Trent never left me before I fell asleep.

No matter what I said and no matter how well my brain understood that we weren't still in a relationship, I missed it. At least, I missed it with him. We'd been a *thing* so fleetingly that we hadn't even told our closest friends. To everyone we knew, we were still and only ever had been best friends. Hell, I was pretty sure no one in Kingston Springs even knew I was bisexual. Why would they when I didn't bring guys around?

Then again, why would I bring guys around when I'd already met the perfect man? I had no reason to bring a guy around when I knew I'd never find another man like Trent. I had to accept that best friends with benefits would have to do, at least until he found his Mr. Right and not just Mr. Right Now. Unfortunately for me, I was Mr. Right Now. It would happen eventually. He was too good a guy to stay single forever. The thought sat heavy in my stomach and I struggled to brush it away.

The delicious tenderness in my ass that only came after being fucked long and hard reminded me of why I was in bed to begin with. And the feeling reminded me again that there was only one man who could make me feel so thoroughly used that I didn't want to move for hours.

The one man I couldn't have.

I knew we needed different things out of a relationship. It didn't matter how off the charts our sexual chemistry was or how deep our friendship ran; I wasn't submissive, and Trent needed a submissive.

On paper, our relationship should have worked beautifully. I was a puppy, and Trent was a Dom. In practice it wasn't so simple. Even as a pup, I wasn't submissive. In that headspace, I liked knowing someone was there to make sure I remembered to take a drink or help me keep track of time, but I didn't like being spanked or doing tricks for a Master. Outside of puppy space, I couldn't stand someone—even my best friend—keeping tabs on me or trying to set a schedule for me.

Trent thrived on control—he needed it to be truly happy. It took less than a month to figure out that we couldn't be what the other needed long term. In order to preserve our friendship, we agreed to not date.

I hadn't told Trent how painful the split was for me, and I didn't plan on it. Two years later, it sometimes still hit me hard that I couldn't make it work with my dream man. The last time I'd ghosted him for a couple days—no small task when we lived together and worked in the same office—was because I'd seen him flirting with someone at the bar and it had nearly ripped my heart out. Jealousy at seeing him with someone else turned me into a green-eyed monster, and I didn't like it.

Despite confusing both my brain and heart, despite knowing what we were doing was making it harder to separate my best friend from the love of my life, we still fell into bed together. Boyfriends or not, once we'd learned how good we were together in bed, our sexual chemistry couldn't be ignored. I usually fell asleep faster and slept better after a round of sex with Trent than I did with anyone else, but he always slid out of bed before I woke up. If I really analyzed his motives, I would have to admit it was likely his way of trying not to confuse me. While logically I appreciated it, I still hated it. I missed waking up warm and cozy and wrapped tightly in his arms.

A clattering in the kitchen brought me out of my thoughts. My heart pounded in shock for a moment before I realized it was probably Trent making dinner for us. I had plans to go to DASH, the BDSM club in Nashville, and Trent had a late shift at work. We both needed to eat before we left, and Trent would make sure we both got food.

There were still times he'd go to DASH with me as my handler when I wasn't in the mood to play with someone else, but usually we tried to avoid going to the club at the same time. Seeing your best friend nearly naked, or in my case watching my best friend punishing a naughty sub, wasn't something we preferred to see on a regular basis. Our schedules at work usually aided in our ability to avoid each other fairly well.

I dressed quickly, doing my best to ignore the tenderness in my ass, before heading to the kitchen. Trent greeted me with a big grin and his sexy as sin wire-rimmed glasses. "Hey, sleepyhead."

Pretending to be unaffected by Trent was getting harder and harder as time passed. Part of me had even begun to wonder if I could find some modicum of submission in me. Would a little submission be enough for him? I shook my head to clear the thoughts. "First of all, haven't I told you not to wear your 'please fuck me' glasses when I don't have time to drag you back to bed? And second, how long have I been asleep?"

"Sorry, my contacts are bothering me. Besides, I figured they could help Curious get all horny before going to the club." He winked. "You never know, you may meet a sexy guy that checks all your boxes."

I rolled my eyes. The only man for me was Trent. Going to DASH had never been about finding a man, whether he accepted it or not. "You're seriously messed up. And don't call me Curious. Jesus, when you do that, you make my dick all confused."

Curious was the name I'd chosen for myself when I'd first gotten into puppy play over five years earlier. It might have been unconventional to choose my own puppy name, but I'd known that the odds of me finding a handler that could accept I didn't want to submit were slim. When I sank into that headspace all I wanted was to not think for a while. I'd jumped into puppy play after discovering a book about it. The first thing I thought of to describe myself was curious, and with that, Curious was born.

Trent let out a full belly laugh that had me chuckling as well. When he finally stopped, he slid a bowl of spaghetti and a side salad toward me. "Eat—you need your energy for tonight. You won't be able to give some poor unsuspecting Master a run for his money if you don't have food in you."

I ate a few bites of spaghetti before I spoke up. "Not looking for a Master. And I'm just going to chill tonight. No scene play for me. I may hit up the littles' room, find that super-soft beanbag thing and people watch, for all I know."

Trent snorted. "Logan, you can't sit down for more than five minutes without going stir-crazy."

I can when there's a certain cute little who likes to cuddle. I wasn't willing to tell Trent that. He was convinced I needed someone less controlling than him but still more kinky than vanilla. Aiden, the sweet little who I'd been meeting up with more often than not in recent months, was about as far from a Dom as someone could get. He wanted a Daddy to take control. I couldn't do that. I was too damn distractible to be a decent Daddy for anyone, but especially someone as sweet as Aiden. We'd met at the club earlier in the year, shortly after I'd sworn off all relationships, male and female. Our almost-relationship, paired with the sex Trent and I shared, is what had kept me from looking for another relationship. That was for the best anyway —every one I'd had ended in disaster.

Aiden and I had made it a point to not allow our relationship to develop into anything more than some frotting or a hand job, usually in one of the BDSM club's private rooms. But we texted frequently between meetups. A strong friendship had formed between the two of us, and yes, even sexual attraction was there too. I'd already learned my lesson about letting sexual attraction and friendship morph into a relationship with someone I couldn't meet the needs of. I wasn't going there again.

When Aiden was diapered and in his little headspace and I was in my puppy gear, I could cuddle with him for hours and never get antsy. I couldn't even do that with Trent unless I was falling asleep. The only time I ever got restless around Aiden was if someone I didn't have a good feeling about tried to engage with him.

Just the thought of seeing Aiden again had me ready to rush through dinner.

I must have made a face because when I blinked up, Trent had his eyes squinted, examining me closely. "What's that look about?"

I shoved a bite of food into my mouth. "What look?"

"Don't talk with your mouth full."

I forced myself to swallow, but I flipped him off at the same time. "You're not my Dom—you can't tell me what to do."

"If I were your Dom, you'd never be able to sit down. Now, why did you get that dopey smile on your face?"

I wiggled slightly in my seat. He wasn't even my Dom and I was hardly able to sit after he fucked me earlier in the evening. I had no desire to have him—or anyone else—redden my ass. Then I remembered Aiden and his cute smile. Too bad Trent wasn't looking for a little. If I allowed myself to go down that rabbit hole, he ticked every box Aiden was looking for despite Trent being too stubborn to realize it. My best friend had the potential to snuggle the hell out of someone like Aiden. Trent still swore he was the big bad Dom type, but I could see the super-soft teddy bear lurking right below the surface. The older he got, the more apparent it became to me. He wasn't playing as hard at the club from what I'd heard. Actually, the last munch I went to I'd overheard a few of the Doms saying that Trent hadn't had more than a spanking scene in over a year.

But it would be weird to introduce Trent to Aiden—the man I'd accepted I loved despite not being able to do anything about it, and the man who had quickly become an important person in my life. I wasn't ready to say I had feelings for Aiden, but I knew if we spent more time together feelings could easily develop.

It was all sorts of fucked up and, selfishly, I didn't think I was strong enough to survive the two of them together.

I shook my head to clear the thoughts because, thankfully, it didn't matter. Trent still tried to go for the brats, even if they were all wrong for him. Sure, he wanted more of a lifestyle relationship, but he'd shut down the idea of being Daddy. The last time we'd talked about it he'd told me it was because all the boys looking for a Daddy at DASH associated him with discipline, so it didn't matter anyway. He was so oblivious.

It didn't change the fact that I could see the giant teddy bear who would snuggle a sweet sub to death. I didn't like going to bed at a certain time, and I didn't want to have to check in with him multiple times a day. I also didn't like punishments. Trent needed someone who craved the love, doting attention, and punishments he loved to give and I wasn't that person.

But where would that leave me?

Yup, I was a selfish asshole.

"Logan..." Trent's tone had taken a hard edge that made me squirm again. Dammit, he was a good Dom.

He only got growly like that when I wasn't paying attention. Shit, he'd asked me a question. What was it? I replayed the conversation we'd been having. Friends with benefits, sexy times, awkward to introduce them, funny smile. Oh! "It wasn't a dopey smile!"

Trent raised an eyebrow at me and inclined his head. "Really?"

"Really. I was just thinking of a... friend."

The disbelieving look Trent gave me said I probably wouldn't be able to avoid the question forever, but I didn't know if I was ready to share Aiden with him yet either. Aiden and I had something special. Almost as special as the decades-long friendship and bond that Trent and I shared, only ours was much newer. I shoved a bite of salad in my mouth in the hope of deterring Trent from asking more questions.

He shook his head at me but changed the subject. "Okay, well, I need to get to work. Finish eating, then have a good night at the club. Promise me you'll text me when you get home? I'll worry about you otherwise."

The lump I felt in the back of my throat was easier to ignore when I swallowed the bite in my mouth. It wasn't so easy to ignore when I spoke. "Promise. I'll even text you when I get there."

The promise made Trent relax. I might not have been a

submissive, but I liked making him smile. Knowing I'd done something to put that smile on his face made me happy. He deserved all the happiness in the world. He kissed the top of my head on his way to the steps. "I need a shower before work. Have a good night. And Logan?" He waited until I looked up. "Please remember to text me when you get home."

I nodded. He'd worry about me all night if I didn't.

"Have fun. Love you."

"Love you too." The words were so automatic by that point it felt weird if we left each other without saying them. The habit had started sometime in our late teens or early twenties. I'd been in the Marines, and as we said goodbye, we'd say it when we hung up the phone. I'd not felt romantic love for him at the time, but over the years those feelings had changed. Now it was so ingrained in us we didn't think about it. Well, I thought about it, and the words always made my heart race a little. I absolutely loved Trent Sylvan, and I knew without a doubt I always would.

When I was done with dinner, I packed up my bag. I didn't plan on jumping into a scene and a mosh wasn't scheduled for the night, so instead of my sexy harness and leather jock, I grabbed a pair of well-fitting sweats, a snug T-shirt, and my show tail. I wasn't going to be putting a plug in—even my smaller one would be uncomfortable after Trent had fucked me so well. I had a number of leather jocks that would allow me to attach my tail directly to them. But I decided to go more simplistic—and more comfortable—and chose a leather belt instead. Not that Trent would believe me, but a hookup at the BDSM club was not what I was looking for.

Until Trent met his forever guy—whether he knew it or not —I was his. All I wanted to do was curl up with Aiden while he played and gave me belly rubs.

On my way out of my room, I grabbed a package of teething cookies from the box I kept hidden in my closet. It would be too hard to explain to Trent why a box of teething cookies had suddenly appeared in our kitchen, but Aiden had let it slip that he liked them one evening while we were having dinner and since then I never went to the club without a package of them. The smile Aiden gave me each time I handed them over made it totally worth the extra few bucks I spent at the grocery store every once in a while. He'd shared a packet with me and, while they weren't terrible, I definitely didn't enjoy them the way he did. *Seriously, just give me a real cookie and I'd be happy.* Then again, the little graham cracker dog bones Trent bought for me from time to time probably had the same effect on me. I chuckled at the thought as I tossed my bag into the passenger's side of my truck.

There was something about knowing Aiden would be little at the club without me around that always made my stomach uneasy, so I made sure to be at least ten minutes earlier than we'd planned on. As long as I'd known him, he was the most punctual person on the planet, making it far easier for me to plan my arrival time.

The club didn't allow electronic devices in the main play areas—privacy reasons—so I always made sure to have a paperback book with me when I went to hang out with Aiden. I spent a moment texting Trent to let him know I'd arrived safely, then dug my book out of my bag and settled in to read until Aiden inevitably knocked on my window. Ten minutes later, at exactly eight p.m., I heard his knock.

Aiden was contemplative as I exited my truck. "Why are you always early?"

I tried to give a casual shrug—I didn't want him to start arriving earlier than me. "Trent made dinner tonight, so I was running a bit early."

Aiden gave me a hard look like he didn't quite believe me, but then he inclined his head toward the door. "Shall we?"

I grabbed my bag and stuffed my book inside. "Let's go." I was normally on the go, but after Trent had fucked me so well, I couldn't wait to curl up and cuddle for the night. Maybe I could sink far enough into my puppy space that I'd be able to push thoughts of Trent out of my head for the evening. For whatever reason, they were invading my thoughts more often than normal. I planned on ignoring the part of my brain that swore I was cheating on him, telling me I shouldn't be at the club without him despite us agreeing to give each other space at DASH. This was why it was a bad idea to mix pleasure with friendship. Trent and I worked hard to not let our sexual relationship be anything more than sex, but my brain still didn't seem to get the memo. There was part of me that had fallen in love with my best friend back in high school and I just had to keep reminding myself that we wanted very different things out of a relationship.

Different, and what was beginning to feel impossible for either of us to find. Unfortunately, unmatched chemistry between the sheets and a lifelong friendship didn't always mean we'd be compatible in base desires.

And now I had put myself in a bad mood to be entering the club.

Alice sat at the registration desk, just like always. As the mother of Master Zachary, DASH's owner, Alice had been integrally involved since the inception. I couldn't imagine sharing kinks with my parents, but Alice wasn't like any other septuagenarian I'd met. She'd also been the receptionist since the day the club opened, and I was sure Dom And Sub Haven wouldn't be the same without her. She gave us a bright smile, scanned our ID cards into the computer, and let us back into the club.

Aiden's butt was rounder than normal, telling me he'd changed into a diaper before he'd left the house. Yes, I was inspecting his ass. It was a perfect bubble butt in just a pair of jeans, but when he put a diaper on it was rounder. With him walking toward the locker room in front of me, thoughts of Trent drifted away. The amplified bubble butt and his unstyled brown hair that flopped into his face paired well with his little side. Of course, the dark scruff on his face was decidedly *not* little and I enjoyed teasing him about it.

We made our way to the changing room and Aiden began shimmying out of his fitted jeans and sweater to reveal a onesie with puppy prints all over it. For the first time, I was jealous of his attire.

Even jealous, my dick reacted to him. If I thought he was sexy in a onesie and a thick diaper, I could only imagine how Trent would react. *Fuck, I was not going back down that track.* I focused my brain power on his shirt. "Where'd you get that?"

Color filled his cheeks and he ducked his head. "Umm, someone I know online made it for me."

"That's so cool!" It was cute and bright and the aqua-colored paw prints matched my puppy gear perfectly. I forced myself to focus more on getting ready than his shirt, but it was hard. My puppy gloves, tail, knee pads, collar, and finally my hood went on and we were ready to go.

While I'd focused on getting myself ready, Aiden had clipped his binkie to his shirt and dug his favorite stuffed animal, Hedge, out of his bag. The old hedgehog looked kind of sad, and despite him insisting it was clean, its fur was matted. The last time I had teased him about it he'd insisted it wasn't dirty but well loved.

I made sure to grab the cookies from my bag and pushed them into the pocket of my sweats before I got on the floor. We'd done this routine so many times in the past few months that it had become second nature to me. Aiden got his sippy cup from his bag, then picked my leash up and clipped it to the D-ring on my collar. "Come on, Curious. Let's go." He didn't sound like the man I'd walked into the club with. His voice had softened and there was an excited tone that hadn't been there before. I didn't normally like a leash, but with Aiden it didn't feel like a submissive act. With him, I was simply a little boy's puppy, nothing more, nothing less.

As we made our way to the playroom, the few people at the club that evening smiled at us. We had to look like quite an odd pair—a little and his puppy strolling through the club with no Dom in sight. Even when I glanced up, I could see the fullness of Aiden's diaper through his onesie. I got a few pats on my head from people I knew, but we were mainly left alone.

CHAPTER 2

AIDEN

THE WORLD WAS FUZZY. I hadn't slipped fully into subspace, but I was in a place where background noise sort of faded away and the only thing I was focused on was the puppy beside me and my toys in front of me.

Until I'd met Curious at the club, I'd never been able to find any sort of little space on my own. I'd always worried about letting go and leaving myself vulnerable. There was something about the puppy that made me relax. I knew he wouldn't let anything happen to me.

At DASH, Curious was my shadow. Since I met him late the previous winter, I hadn't been at the club alone. He was more of a guard dog than playful pup, at least around me. I'd seen him roughhousing and playing with other pups at a few moshes the club had held, but that wasn't his normal state with me. He'd even scared two potential Daddies away over the course of our friendship. As soon as they'd approached me, he'd begun to growl and forced himself between me and them. The first time, I'd been shocked because he'd never done anything like that before, but afterward, Logan held me close as he patiently explained that he'd seen the Dom around the club and always got a bad feeling about him.

Over the course of our friendship, I'd learned that I trusted Logan's gut instinct. When I discovered a few months ago that he was a deputy sheriff, that trust made a lot more sense. I'd also noticed I sank even deeper into little space since I'd learned what he did for a living. His gut never seemed to turn off, no matter if he was pup or human.

Despite having great chemistry and my level of comfort around him in general, he wasn't looking for a relationship. Correction, he was looking for a relationship, but his heart was already spoken for. He'd talked about his best friend a number of times, and I knew he wished there could be something there, but he'd also told me he knew they couldn't work. Something about his friend being too dominant and him not being submissive. Then again, according to Logan, it hadn't stopped them from still sleeping together. I couldn't imagine sleeping with my best friend or a man I had feelings for, and not getting my heart broken. Whether he said it or not, Logan's heart was already broken, so maybe it didn't matter to him. I couldn't figure their relationship out, but thankfully it wasn't my relationship to decipher.

Our incompatibility in the kink department hadn't stopped us from falling into a bed—or floor, or even an arm chair in the playroom once—a number of times since we'd met. We'd both agreed it was nothing more than casual sex, but sometimes it was hard for me to remember that. I clicked with Logan, and Curious, in a way I'd never clicked with anyone before. But I respected that Logan wasn't a Daddy, and we both knew he couldn't give me that. In the end, I wouldn't be truly happy without it, and Logan would feel terrible for being unable to give me what I was looking for. There was a chance we could make it work for a while, but long term the odds of a relationship ending in any way but flames were slim to none.

While I respected Logan's position on not being either dominant or submissive, on a personal level I couldn't relate. I would be happy handing my phone to a Daddy and telling him he could have complete control over my calendar.

I'd worked my entire adult life to make a name for myself as a photographer. There had been years of barely scraping by with rent money. I'd even lived in my car one spring and summer to save money between leases. At twenty-seven, I made enough money to have a nice life, but my schedule tended to be erratic at best, chaotic at worst. There were weeks on end where I might only have one session and others where I was booked for days on end with almost no downtime.

I wouldn't change what I did for anything. I loved my profession and I'd met the most fascinating people over the years, from actors to musicians to billionaires and socialites. I loved what I did but I also had a hard time saying no for fear that I'd get a reputation for being unavailable, and as a result would overbook myself.

For the night, though, I had Curious curled up beside me, soaking up every belly rub and pet I was willing to give. I swore he'd make a good kitten because he practically purred with every touch, but he didn't like when I told him that. If I didn't pay attention to him for too long, he'd reach over and bat down the tower I was building... like he just did.

"Curious, no!" My scolding didn't sound severe, even to my own ears. I'd sunk further into little space than I'd realized. He had his favorite rope toy beside him, so I tossed it across the room and watched him scamper after it as I started to rebuild my tower. The reprieve didn't last long and he was back, dropping his toy in my lap and nudging at my hand for pets.

The process continued for a long time before Curious rolled over on his back for belly rubs. When he rolled over, a packet of cookies fell out of his pocket and landed on the floor. I felt my eyes widen and my legs bounced with excitement. "Cookies!" My voice might have been almost a squeal, but I couldn't help it. He'd brought me cookies. *Again*. I didn't know why that surprised me as much as it did. They were always in his pocket for me, but for some reason little me always thought it was the most novel, sweetest thing anyone could do for me. "Thank you!" I bent down and gave him a kiss on his muzzle, and even though his hood covered most of his face, I could see color rise in the skin below his eyes.

I curled up so my head was resting against his chest as I ate my snack. I had only found the vanilla-flavored cookies at the store, but Logan had managed to find banana, blueberry, vanilla, and even a ginger-flavored one. Logan turned his nose up at them, but I thought it was sweet he always had them with him.

By the time my cookies were done, I wasn't as little as I had been earlier. Logan had spent the last ten minutes alternating between rubbing my thigh and rubbing my tummy. If I was little, the touches would have been nothing more than comforting. Out of little space, however, the touches were erotic, bordering on maddening. Especially when my cock started to fill within the confines of my diaper.

When had I peed? I didn't remember doing so, but it was heavy between my legs, and with my cock pressing persistently against it now that it had woken up, it was impossible to ignore.

"Not nice." My voice was no longer soft or gentle; little space had been replaced by arousal.

I heard Logan's deep chuckle and knew he could tell I was once again adult Aiden. Then his fingers snaked down past my belly button and glided over my diaper. His touch was barely enough for me to feel it through the thick padding, but just knowing it was there had me arching my back.

"Stay still."

Fuck. Why had I volunteered how much I liked to be controlled? Logan knew all my buttons, and when we started to play like this, he pushed them all perfectly. I moaned and my muscles shook in an effort to stay still. It worked until his lips wrapped around my earlobe and he sucked gently. I ground my hips upward, my diaper pushing against the palm of his hand and in the process rubbed over the sensitive underside of my cock.

"Brat," Logan teased.

"Asshole," I shot back. I had fantasies of being edged or denied when I pushed too far, but that wasn't the way Logan and I operated together. Instead, I let myself sink into the feelings while trying to remain still. I could at least pretend that I was being a good boy for my Daddy—big brother, maybe—while Logan took his sweet fucking time getting to the point where he was ready to let me cum.

He found every tender, sensitive erogenous zone on my body. My ears, my neck, my nipples, my inner thighs, and he rubbed, nibbled, nipped, bit, and sucked everything he could reach. Sometimes his thumb and forefinger would pinch my nipples through my onesie with one hand while his other explored the crease of my leg, and he pushed his muzzle lightly in the side of my neck. The man was magical. I struggled to rub my belly and pat my head, yet he could pinch, massage, and even with his hood, lick at the same time.

"You wanna cum?"

My head bobbed up and down and I panted out a reply. "Y-yes. Cum."

Logan chuckled and I knew I wasn't going to get the friction I desperately desired even before he spoke. "Soon."

He ran his thumbnail over the peak of my hardened nipple, and even through the cotton of my shirt, the sensation made me call out. It didn't matter that we were in a BDSM club and my moan might have attracted attention from those in other areas. I just wanted release.

Logan, the stubborn asshole that he was, didn't seem to care that I was aching and sore and just wanted to cum. He wasn't providing any more stimulation to my cock than gentle grazes across the front of my diaper as he passed it on a search for his next target. Apparently getting frustrated with his hood, Logan pulled it up so it was resting on the top of his head. It looked comical, but when teeth clamped down on the flesh of my neck and I felt Logan latch on, I didn't care how funny he looked. There would be a mark there for days to come. My chest rose, and I wasn't expecting the hand that pressed down over my diaper and began to rub right where the head of my cock was resting.

"Fuck," I bit out between clenched teeth.

Logan released the suction on my neck and spoke directly into my ear. "Cum for me, Aiden. I know you want to."

My orgasm crashed over me as soon as the words were out of his mouth. When my lips parted to grunt out my pleasure, my binkie was shoved in. He held it there while I rode out the waves of orgasm that racked my body while I worked the binkie furiously. By the time the last aftershock subsided, my diaper was sticky and warm, but I knew the blissful feelings wouldn't last long.

"All better?" Logan's question was sweet and quiet.

I nodded and hummed around my binkie. He was no longer holding it in my mouth, but it felt like it would take too much effort to push it out.

Logan gave me a push. "Come on, you need to clean up your toys, then we need to get to the changing room. You're going to be miserable in a few minutes."

I pouted but knew the puppy was right. I hated that he was right. This was why I needed a Daddy.

I must not have kept that thought fully in my head because Logan laughed a bit too loudly for the space. "Dude, any Daddy would make his boy clean up his toys, post-orgasm or not. Come on, I'll help."

Just because he was right didn't mean I had to go without a fight. So I sighed dramatically as I forced my limbs to start working with my body. "Cleanup before orgasm next time."

Logan laughed again. "I'll try to remember that. You were just too cute."

As the last bucket was put back on the shelf of the playroom, my dick shifted slightly. "Eww, it's sticky."

"Come on, let's go get changed. You can shower before we leave." He pulled his mask back down, mumbling something about it squeezing his brain but needing hands to help me clean up.

CHAPTER 3

LOGAN

WE FINISHED CLEANING up and Aiden headed for the door ahead of me, anxious to get his wet and sticky diaper off. I'd just gotten onto all fours to stand up when two figures filled the doorway. It was a Tuesday night, and the littles' room was quiet even on the weekends, so I was surprised to see others coming in. I didn't have to see their faces to know it was a little and his Daddy walking in. The boy's feet were covered in footed pajamas with dinosaurs, and a blue dinosaur hung by his side.

"Daddy, do you think—?" The boy, whose voice sounded familiar, stopped speaking abruptly. His feet started to turn the other way as I began to sit back on my heels so I could look at who was joining us.

"Whoa there, sweet boy." The other voice, one I knew almost as well as Trent's, said in surprise. I finally looked up in time to see Travis grab on to his boyfriend's hand just as Caleb had almost disappeared down the hallway.

Aiden looked between me, Travis, and Caleb in confusion, quickly picking up on the change in the room at their appearance. Caleb wasn't my biggest fan. I might have made a fool out of myself shortly after he and Travis got together. From everything I'd gathered about him in the last eight months, Caleb was shy. Almost painfully so. And I... well, I wasn't. I was loud and opinionated. And when Travis and Caleb had gotten together I'd instantly picked up on how much they adored one another. It was through watching them across the table when our group of friends got together that I had realized, no matter what I told myself about moving on, that I was still in love with Trent.

I'd been casually seeing a woman—Erica—for about a month at that point. We were so casual we hadn't even had sex. Truth be told, I hadn't had sex with the last handful of women I'd dated since Trent and I had broken up. When our relationship ended because I could not convince myself to sleep with Erica, I'd accepted that it was pointless to even try to date. It wasn't just that Trent was the only man for me, he was the only person for me.

I'd gone out that night with one goal in mind—drink enough that I could no longer feel feelings.

Of course, one of the hazards of having a close-knit group of friends is that, when you invite one out to drink your pain away, you invite all of them, whether you know it or not. I'd invited Dean, who had proceeded to invite the rest of our group of friends. I'd made it three drinks in when Merrick, Larson, Travis, Caleb, Dean, and much to my chagrin, Trent had all shown up. I'd drunk even more when I saw Trent. The evening had left me with a hangover from hell, Trent dragging my drunk ass home and taking care of me for the next eighteen hours, and Caleb seemingly scared of me.

I'd been on my best behavior around him since then but he still seemed leery of me. As if things couldn't get more awkward, *little* Caleb walked into the BDSM club to find me more or less in my puppy gear, with a little. I saw the way his eyes had lasered in on the giant dream catcher tattoo on my back. He didn't have to see my face to know who was under the puppy mask. He'd been around enough that summer to have seen it on more than one occasion. I bet the aqua-colored paw print in the center of the dream catcher made a lot more sense now. Everyone was curious as to why it was there, but I'd been cagey at best with answers until that point.

Thank fuck they hadn't walked in while I was jerking Aiden off. I resisted the urge to fall backward and groan.

Caleb was standing in the doorway with Travis, clutching both Travis's hand and his dinosaur, trying to look anywhere but at me.

I ducked my head, not wanting to make Caleb even more uncomfortable. "Hey, we were just leaving," I explained.

Travis was studying me carefully, but I couldn't figure out why. "Don't rush out of here on account of us."

I focused more on Travis than Caleb. "We're not. I promise. We were getting ready to leave."

Aiden spoke up like he needed to confirm what I was saying. "Curious and I have been here for a while. I just cleaned up my stuff so we could get going."

Travis's face softened. "Okay. As long as we're not running you out of here." He turned to Caleb and gave him a little push. "Go on, Cal, go find the dinosaur book. I'll be right there to read it to you." Caleb looked hesitant but finally nodded and headed over toward the bookshelf where I often found books to read to Aiden.

We waited for Caleb to make it to the shelf before we started to walk toward the door. "Hey, Trav, make sure he knows I won't tell anyone."

Travis smiled fondly at me. "I know you wouldn't, Logan. I hope it could have gone without saying that we're not going to share anything about you either."

"Thank you. It's, it's not really a secret." I stumbled, uncharacteristically shy. "I just don't tell many people about this. It's hard to explain." I chewed my lip as I looked over at Caleb. "Will, uh, is he going to be okay with me knowing?"

Travis chuckled lightly. "He's going to be embarrassed for a while. Are you okay with him talking to Dexter about seeing you here? I'm sure Dexter will be able to assure him better than even I could that he doesn't have to be embarrassed."

Dexter was Caleb's best friend. They were about as oddly matched as two people could be. For all of Caleb's shyness, Dexter was as loud as his bright red hair. For whatever reason, it didn't shock me that he would know about Caleb. Dexter had become a staple in our group since just about the time Travis started bringing Caleb around. I'd never gotten the impression that they kept much from one another. If talking with the guy would help Caleb not avoid me forever, I'd gladly let him talk about what he'd seen.

"That's fine." I looked over at Aiden, who had begun to watch Caleb intently. I could almost see the gears turning in his head—he wanted to go meet the shy boy across the room. He would love to have a playmate that understood being little. Despite his curiosity, he'd begun to wiggle slightly and I knew that he not only wanted but needed to be changed. "We really should get going. Maybe we could introduce them at some point? Obviously when Caleb's ready." I tried to shrug casually, but I had a feeling I looked anything but relaxed.

Travis gave me a warm smile. "I think when he processes everything, he'd like that."

Aiden walked out of the room at that point and I had started to follow when Travis caught my elbow. "Thank you," he said quietly into my ear.

"Huh?"

Travis looked over at Caleb, who still refused to look our way. "For handling this so well. He's only just started coming here with me. His biggest fear was seeing someone we knew."

I almost laughed but caught myself. "I just hope we haven't ruined his night. He already doesn't like me much." *Oops, I hadn't meant to say that part out loud.*

Travis narrowed his eyes. "What do you mean he doesn't like you?" He looked over at his boy in confusion. "He likes you just fine."

"I intimidate him something fierce, and I know that." I flicked one of my neoprene ears. "This allows me to... escape my head, I guess you could say. I know being little helps Aiden a lot. The club is his safe space, so to speak. I really hope that you guys coming across me here doesn't ruin it for Caleb. This place..." I gestured around the room but meant the club in general. "It's one of a kind."

Travis smiled. "Thanks, Logan." His eyes fell on my collar. "Or should I thank Curious?"

It meant a lot to me that Travis had taken my presence that evening so well. "We're one and the same. Have a good night."

"You too."

I hurried down the hall to catch up to Aiden where he'd stopped to wait for me. "Friends?"

I rubbed the back of my neck. "Travis, yes. I've known him since I got out of the military. Caleb is his boyfriend. They've only been together a few months. Caleb is scared of me."

Aiden stumbled from the shock. "Why is he scared of you?"

"I may have gotten a little too drunk at the bar shortly after he and Travis got together. Long story short, he wasn't entirely sure what to make of me before then. He's definitely not rushing to be my friend after that."

Aiden looked thoughtful. "I see. When I'm little, I have a tendency to block out most stressful things. That's why I never really came to the club much before I met you. I kind of shut down and I didn't want to leave myself vulnerable like that. If it helps, I think he kind of shut down when he saw you. I saw it in his eyes. He sank really far into his little space really fast."

I winced because I'd seen it too. I hoped he didn't have a rough time coming out of that space later that evening. I'd feel bad if I was responsible for it.

"Stop it," Aiden scolded me as we made it to the changing room. "You're worrying too much. His Daddy—Travis—he'll take care of him and you know it."

I did know it. I just needed to make myself believe it, and I needed to stop feeling guilty about being in there when they showed up. "Go get a shower. I'll wait for you."

Aiden didn't often take long in the showers, so I focused on changing out of my gear. I was pushing my gloves into my bag when Matt, a Dom I'd known for years, approached me. "Hey, Matt," I greeted him warmly.

"Hey, Curious. I was hoping I could get your help with something this weekend."

That was a new one. "Sure, what's up?"

Matt fiddled with a length of rope he had in his hand. "Would you mind terribly doing a shibari demo with me this Saturday?"

In general, ropework wasn't my favorite kink. I would not be the guy tied to a bed during sex. However, Matt and I were friends, and he'd used me as a prop a few times in the past. Never in a group setting, but he'd done some work on me to show someone who was interested in learning rope play or working on a complicated knot.

"No suspension, right?" Matt knew that one of my hard limits was suspension work.

"No, no suspension. Just some ropework."

I heard the shower kick off. "I think that's fine. We can grab a coffee later this week to discuss the details."

Matt looked relieved at my response and it made me feel

good to know I'd helped. "Thanks. I would normally reschedule, but my partner is going out of town on business and this was kind of late notice."

Aiden came out of the shower area with his hair slicked back and wearing a pair of sweatpants and a sweatshirt. Matt saw the way I watched Aiden and nodded once. "Great, I'll call you later this week and we can talk specifics."

"Thanks. Talk later." With that, Matt squeezed my shoulder and walked away.

Aiden wasted no time in questioning what he'd walked in on. "What was that about?"

"Matt's doing a shibari demo over the weekend. His normal partner just got called away on business, so he asked me to step in."

A muscle in Aiden's jaw twitched. "I thought you didn't like being restrained." We'd had a conversation about that a few months back, so he knew I didn't like being tied up. But I always had my safeword if things got to be too much.

"I don't normally. But Matt's a good guy. I've let him practice knots on me in the past. He likes using me as a guinea pig because he doesn't have to worry about me falling into subspace. It lets him focus more on the skill and less on being a Dom, if that makes sense. I just tell him if something makes me uncomfortable."

"Oh, okay. That makes sense. As long as you're okay with it. When is it?"

"Saturday evening, I think Matt said. I'll figure out the time later this week."

"Mind if I come?"

"Of course not. Why don't you let me pick you up this time? I drive by your house on my way to the club. It's going to be busy that night—no reason for both of us to have cars."

CHAPTER 4

TRENT

ONE OF THE hardest things I'd ever done was let Logan go. I'd been more than half in love with him since our football teams played against each other in high school. At the time I'd only recently come out to my family, and my dad was having a hard time accepting it. I'd felt so alone back then. Then this blond-haired monster of a guy who looked like he could take on the entire team shows up on the fifty-yard line bitching about his school's homophobia and how he wouldn't go to another school dance until a guy he knew and his boyfriend could go as a couple. I'd stood there with my mouth hanging open in shock.

Fifteen-year-old Logan Caldwell had rendered me speechless in under two minutes. He'd been a voice of acceptance in a time where the most progressive areas of the country were just beginning to hear the rumblings of marriage equality. Logan proved right there on the football field, of all places, that he was an ally that I had desperately needed at the time. That night he became the first non-family member I came out to, though I still wasn't entirely certain if I'd come out to him or if I had simply outed myself to him.

My flapping mouth and bright red cheeks and the stammering I'd done at his rant had given me away. When we bumped into each other outside the locker rooms later that evening, he'd handed me a piece of paper with his phone number—home phone number and instant messenger name because we really were that old—and a friendship was born from that.

It really couldn't be considered a friendship, though. That would be selling what the two of us had quite short. We were inseparable through the rest of high school. Even when he went into the Marines after graduation, we'd stayed in touch. I was the first one he told about discovering he was bisexual in our twenties. He was the first one I told about discovering I was a Dom.

When he came out as bisexual to me, part of me selfishly saw us together forever. Fast-forward nearly fifteen years, and sharing a home for over six of them, we'd both known that something had been simmering between us for years. A late-night conversation had led to us both admitting we wanted to try a relationship. Even knowing everything we knew about one another, we'd naively thought that we could find a happy balance. For a month I thought it would work out, that we'd manage to come together and find happiness despite having such different desires. Unfortunately, reality never quite matched fantasy. It didn't take long to see that we each had baggage, not bad baggage but baggage made up of emotional needs that neither of us was able to fulfill for the other. Logan couldn't submit to me the way I needed to be happy. I couldn't shut off my Dom side in a way that he could be happy. Faced with the option of keeping my best friend or losing the man I thought I was destined to spend the rest of my life with, I chose my best friend.

There were days I didn't know if I'd made the right choice. Maybe I should have fought harder to find a way to make it work. Two years later and I still felt like I'd left my heart on the couch the night we both admitted it would never work out. I still didn't sit in that spot.

The hardest thing I'd ever had to do was kiss him on the head and send him out to DASH while telling him that I hoped he found a guy to hook up with. I'd done it countless times since our relationship ended and my insides twisted each time. At least I'd solidly disproved the old taunt *Liar, liar, pants on fire.* I would have combusted on the spot if there were even a shred of truth to it.

The thing that always surprised me was Logan never did find a guy to hook up with. He talked about a mutual hand job here or there, but he'd never talked about having sex with anyone, and before we dated, he'd talked about it all the time. Not that I had room to judge—I hadn't either.

Maybe if we'd stopped falling into bed together it would have been easier on my head. Except we did keep landing in bed, and for those moments in time it felt like my soul was whole again. I had the man I loved more than life itself in my arms. Then I'd lie there with him until he fell asleep before forcing myself to leave another piece of my heart next to him as I got up.

I was fucked up.

That could have been why I'd been so on edge for so much of the last few days. I hadn't asked Logan about his night, and he hadn't volunteered information. He always told me that he didn't go to DASH for the hookups, but why else would he go to a fetish club every few weeks?

When he'd woken up and was cagey but had told me he'd seen someone he wasn't expecting at DASH, it had thrown me for a loop. When I pressed, Logan told me he couldn't betray a confidence because he'd promised he wouldn't talk about it, but I could see it was weighing on him.

For the time being, I'd dodged a bullet since Logan hadn't found a guy at the club. But it was a temporary reprieve at best and I knew it. One day Logan would find someone to settle down with—man or woman—and I'd have to act happy while my heart broke. I didn't have to experience it to know what it would feel like. It was going to be awful, yet I knew that as long as there was hope that Logan wasn't going to settle down, I'd never truly look for another guy.

My slightly raw emotions were probably what led to the current argument Logan and I were having in my office as he got ready to leave for the night. To go to DASH. To do a *shibari demo* with a Dom. A well-respected Dom whom I would trust with my life.

But it was Logan.

And *shibari*.

I couldn't contain my groan. "What the hell do you mean you're doing a shibari demo with Matt?" Okay, I might have been a little worked up, but I knew Logan hated being restrained.

"Jesus, Trent, go ahead and tell the entire department what I do on my downtime!" He threw his hand toward my closed office door. He was right—I didn't need to rip him a new one in the middle of the office. Our front desk officer, Tammy, would have a field day if she knew what either of us did when we weren't on duty. Cheatham County did not need to know the sheriff's—or the deputy's—kinks.

I took a deep breath, trying to get myself under control. "You hate being restrained, Logan. It freaks you out. Why in the hell does this sound like a good idea to you?"

Logan threw his head back and studied the ceiling like he was praying for patience. I knew my patience was gone at that point, but hell, maybe he could find some of his own. "I haven't had a reaction to Matt practicing ropework on me before. He's in a pinch. It'll be fine." He shrugged, and if I didn't know Logan almost as well as I knew myself, I'd have missed the slight hesitation in the gesture.

Famous last words.

How many times had I heard Logan utter those words in our lives? And how many times had they ended in disaster? Too many to fucking count, that's how many. Ice skating on old man Thompson's pond? "It'll be fine!" And it was fine, until he ended up in chest-deep ice cold water in the middle of the pond because the ice wasn't thick enough to support his weight. Jumping off the roof onto a trampoline? "It'll be fine!" Except he hit the trampoline with so much force it launched him into my mom's rose bushes. The idiot had needed stitches after that one. Confronting a hostage situation? "It'll be fine!" Once again, the man ended up in the emergency room. That time we'd both ended up in the emergency room, me for stitches and him for a bullet that had to be removed from his thigh.

Of all the stupid plans Logan had made over the years, this could have been the most idiotic. And I couldn't be there to make sure he didn't have a panic attack because I was scheduled that night. I was going to kill him if he didn't kill me first.

Holy hell.

Shibari.

Logan had a panic attack shortly after he'd joined the sheriff's department when he'd been handcuffed during a training drill. I'd been the only one who knew Logan was in the middle of a panic attack, and the instructor thought I was insane when I screamed at her to get the cuffs off him. He didn't outwardly freak out; he inwardly panicked and totally shut down.

Matt was a good guy. I was glad Logan trusted him enough to let him practice knot-work on him, but I wondered if he'd really thought this through. However, Logan wasn't even going to talk to me about it more or give me a chance to talk him out of it. "Listen, you ask me to tell you when I'm going to DASH, so this is me telling you. I appreciate that you're worried about me but it's needless. I trust Matt to not do anything that will make me uneasy."

I'd known Matt for damn near a decade. I knew he wouldn't do anything to intentionally make Logan uneasy, but if he didn't know what he was doing was triggering Logan, he wouldn't know to not do it.

"I'll be fine. I can do this. It's not a suspension demo or anything like that. I made sure to clarify that with him beforehand." Logan leaned forward and kissed my cheek. "Thank you for looking out for me, Trent. I appreciate it. But I'm not some fragile little flower you need to keep safe. I'm also not your submissive and you can't make decisions for me. You're my friend, and as such, I respect that you'd like to know when I'm heading to DASH, so I gave you the heads-up. But I need to get going if I'm going to do everything I need to get done before I have to leave. Love ya."

"Love you too," I said automatically as he turned on his heel and left my office, leaving me staring after his denim-clad ass. It was a nice ass and felt great around my dick, and usually watching it walk away would send all the blood in my body rushing south. That night, it just left me pissed off.

As soon as I heard Logan call goodbye to Tammy, I hurried to my desk to start making calls. I called four of my officers before I finally resigned myself to calling my third in command. I hated to have to bother James since he'd already worked overtime that week. He'd recently gone through a nasty breakup, had just moved, and I knew he needed some time to decompress. With my other options exhausted, and given I was the fucking sheriff of Cheatham County, I knew I needed to bite the bullet and do it. I couldn't just leave work and I'd worry myself sick if I wasn't at DASH that night.

I tapped James' phone number into the antiquated desk

phone. One, two, three rings, and finally there was an answer. "Hey, boss man."

"Can you do me a huge favor?" I asked in lieu of a greeting.

"I'll be there in about a half an hour."

I blinked. "I didn't even ask anything."

"You're calling from work. You sound panicked. Oh, and you're scheduled until tomorrow morning. Something's got you in a tizzy, and I'm guessing you need to leave right the fuck now."

I huffed, but inwardly I was saying a thank you for every good deed I'd ever done to have a man like James working for me. "I owe you." He hung up and I started to pace my office. Logan Caldwell was going to drive me to an early grave. I tried to take the time to make sure all my work was wrapped up well enough that I could easily get back to it the next time I was scheduled. I made sure to tell Tammy about the change, and I put my stuff in my bag. Then I paced more.

My best friend was an idiot.

When James showed up thirty-six minutes after I got off the phone with him, I was still pacing and still thinking about what a moron Logan was. James took one look at me and shook his head. "Get out of here. You look like you're somewhere between puking and exploding with rage." Yeah, that just about summed up my internal turmoil perfectly.

"Thank you. I owe you. I'll make it up to you." I grabbed my bag and ran toward the door. Logan had to be at DASH at nine. It was quarter to eight. That would give me time to get home, change so that I wasn't still in my uniform shirt and didn't look like I was there to arrest someone, and maybe grab a quick bite to eat before I'd need to get into the car and hightail it to Nashville.

My goal was to stay completely under the radar. If Logan saw me there, he'd get pissed that I left work. He'd also be pissed that I didn't trust him. And I knew my hovering had a chance to piss him off no matter what the outcome of the shibari demo was. But I'd never forgive myself if something happened and I wasn't there. Logan being pissed at me for a few days was worth the risk.

I made it to DASH mostly by rote memory. I'd been going with friends for almost fifteen years, basically since I'd been old enough to gain access to the club. A few of us met up one or two times a month, usually just to sit in the scene area and chat while we watched everything going on around us. Sometimes one of us would pick up a scene, but lately scenes hadn't been interesting me enough to go out of my way to join. As I got older, I felt like my interests were beginning to change. The bratty subs begging to be bent over a spanking bench while I worked a flogger or a crop across their backsides weren't doing it for me. The problem was that I hadn't figured out what it was I was looking for. I'd begun getting more and more frustrated with every visit to the club that ended with me leaving without participating in any scenes.

It didn't really matter what I wanted long term. I only had one goal in mind as I drove to DASH that night—make sure Logan was okay. My truck had barely come to a stop when I slammed it into park, tossed my cell phone into the glove box, locked up, and stalked into the building.

Alice was behind the desk as always. She seemed rightfully surprised at my sudden appearance, maybe because it was five minutes after nine and if I was going to be at a demo I was always there early. Maybe it was the mutinous expression on my face.

"You okay, Sylver?" she questioned carefully.

A smile tried to tug at my lips at the name I'd been going by since I started coming to the club. Sylver was just as much a part of me as Trent Sylvan, and it always felt like I was coming home when I heard someone call me that. I gave a curt nod but had to force myself to soften my features. "Yeah, better now that I'm here." It wasn't even a lie. I was so much better now that I was there. I could hear the group just behind the heavy black curtain, and from the looks of the parking lot, a nice crowd had shown up. Hopefully, the crowd would give me the ability to hide in plain sight. With any luck, I'd be in and out without ever being noticed. As soon as the rope demo was over, as long as everything went well, I planned on heading right back to work.

Matt was standing on the slightly elevated stage when I walked in and tried to blend into the background. Logan wasn't looking at me, thank god, so I settled in to be a silent observer. Matt already had rope around both of Logan's legs in an intricate pattern. It was sexy, there was no denying that, and for the time being Logan appeared relaxed. Despite not being able to see more than his eyes with his hood on, the lack of shirt allowed me to see any tense muscles, and there were none. His body language helped me relax. Finally laying eyes on him and being able to see for myself that he was fine had a weight lifting from my shoulders. I took a few deep breaths and calmed my racing heart.

Matt continued to talk to the group, discussing what he was doing while Logan stood still. He crossed and flipped the rope in various ways to create the most ornate-looking knot I'd ever seen across his chest and around his back. Logan was even laughing at some of the jokes Matt was making. Maybe Logan had been right. Maybe this would be fine and I'd been overreacting all along.

I finally let my guard down some, preparing to head back to the office when this was done, apologize to James, and get back to my work, when Matt took Logan's arms. The hairs on the back of my neck bristled and my muscles tightened. I felt a twitch start in my jaw. Had they talked about this in scene negotiation?

Not that I needed the reminder that Logan wasn't a sub—I got one every time I looked at him—but he'd always been good with scene negotiation. Even just volunteering for something like this, he had no problem talking about hard and soft limits. Those he did scenes with always knew his safeword. I had to assume they'd talked about this scene. Matt had to have told Logan his plans, and Logan would have had to agree to them. Logan understood the importance of both parties being on the same page.

My eyes flicked from Logan's arm up to his face. As soon as I saw his eyes widen that fraction of an inch, my body went on full alert mode. I was already getting up, completely ignoring my desire to stay undetected.

Matt tied one arm from shoulder to wrist, then started in on the other side. Logan was doing all right, all things considered. A little tenser than he had been a few minutes before but nothing near a full-on panic attack like I'd expected. I inched closer, not significantly but enough that I'd closed a few feet of distance between the stage and me. The entire time I watched him far more carefully than I normally would in a situation like this. What was going on in his head? Was he okay?

One minute, Logan was fine as Matt worked the ropes down his left arm. The next, as Matt began securing the ties so that his arms were immobile behind his back, I saw Logan's eyes change. It must have been imperceptible to the rest of the crowd because no one said anything, but I saw the exact moment his eyes became unfocused. Matt couldn't have made more than a few twists of the rope behind him, but Logan was gone.

"Llama!" I yelled as I dodged my way through the bodies standing around. How the hell could it take so long to make it thirty feet? Was I being held back by something?

I'd known Logan's safeword from the moment he chose it. I'd told him to make sure it wasn't something he'd have a problem yelling out in the middle of a club or even during sex, but he'd insisted on it being llama. So I yelled "Llama" in the middle of the club.

I heard someone yell "Curious!" at the same time I'd called his safeword. Matt stopped what he was doing. Thank fuck he knew Logan's safeword, but when he looked at Logan, he seemed confused because Logan clearly hadn't said anything and he wasn't resisting in any way.

Then I was on them. "Untie him," I barked at Matt, who already had the safety scissors in his hand. I reached Logan at the same time Matt started cutting the rope away... and the exact same moment another guy arrived, looking panicked.

"I've got you, pup," I said to reassure Logan as the ropes loosened around his body. His hands fell to his sides as the rope was cut, and I knew the panic would subside quickly. I looked over at Matt. "Sorry. I know that look. He was starting to panic. You don't have to cut the rest. He'll snap out of it soon, now that his hands are free."

The guy beside me looked gutted. I didn't know who he was or how he knew Logan, but I could tell he cared about him a great deal. And he'd known as well as I had that Logan wasn't all right. With that, a pit formed in my stomach. Was he the reason Logan had been coming to the club every few weeks? I pushed the feeling of jealousy away and focused back on Logan.

Matt continued to cut the ropes from Logan's body. "No way in hell am I going to keep him bound any longer than necessary. I can replace the rope easily."

"Thanks."

Matt looked more shaken than the unknown man, who was holding Logan's hand. I saw Logan's fingers wrap around the other guy's and give them a squeeze. Yeah, they knew each other well. The familiarity between the two both made my heart soar and my stomach twist. Had Logan found the person for him? It should have made me happy, but it hurt to know I couldn't be that for him.

Matt's voice brought me back to the moment and saved me from my own thoughts. "We talked about this beforehand. I told him exactly what I had planned. We even practiced it."

I tried to smile at Matt as I supported Logan's weight. He was beginning to crash, the panic finally subsiding enough that his muscles were relaxing. "To that I have no doubt. As soon as he told me his plans for tonight, I knew this had the potential to go badly. He trusts you; I know that. But I knew the combination of restraint paired with a group setting could be a trigger for him. I think it's what triggered the last panic attack he had like this."

I didn't even know if Logan realized that his trigger seemed to revolve around being restrained in front of a group. I didn't know what had happened to him in the military that caused that reaction, but something did, and we were going to have to talk about it sooner rather than later to avoid a third situation like this. "Thanks for stopping when I yelled."

Matt forced an uneasy laugh. "Sylver, you know me well enough by now. When I hear a safeword in the middle of a scene, you can bet your ass I'm going to stop. I had no idea he might have reacted like this."

I squeezed Matt's shoulder with the hand I wasn't using to support Logan. "You're good, man. You're going to need some aftercare after this one too."

The statement caused him to laugh, but then he nodded. "I think you're right. I'm going to go find a bottle of water and a quiet corner."

The brunette beside me was rubbing his thumb over Logan's hand, seemingly unsure of what to do next. I smiled over at him. "Hey, I'm this big oaf's best friend. Thanks for watching out for him tonight."

Brown eyes blinked up at me like he'd just realized I was

standing there. A flash of something I couldn't make out crossed his eyes. "He told me he had issues with being restrained sometimes. I didn't think it would be like this. I'm glad you remembered his safeword because my brain went totally blank. I knew it, but I never thought I could have used it. I just knew something didn't look right."

Zachary appeared through the dispersing crowd. "It's going to be fine," I assured the younger guy at my side, taking control of the situation since I could see Matt was crashing just as hard as Logan and the friend I still didn't have a name for. I turned to Zachary. "Can you get someone to sit with Matt? He's dealing with some Dom-drop. Curious shocked the hell out of him. And maybe someone to clean this stuff up? I don't think Matt's up for it."

Zachary brushed the scraps of rope off like they were no big deal. "Fuck the rope. I'll sit with Matt for a while. You got Curious and Aiden under control? Or do you need help too?"

Aiden. I had a name to go with the face... a name that fit the man well. I looked over at the spooked guy clutching on to Logan's hand, looking scared and uncertain of everything happening, and smiled softly.

He adjusted himself and I caught a glimpse of his name tag. The dots on it told me he was submissive and not there to play that night. With that knowledge, I was sure I could handle the two on my own. And while I knew it probably made me a bad person, I was relieved that I likely wasn't standing next to the man who would replace me in Logan's life. "I've got these two."

Zachary nodded and waved me away as I began leading them down the hallway. I needed to make sure to check in with Matt later. I'd give him a call or a text when things quieted down, and I'd make sure Logan did the same. They were going to need to talk that scene out like rational adults, but they both needed to be in a better headspace first.

CHAPTER 5

LOGAN

I'D BEEN FINE.

I kept replaying what had happened and I couldn't figure out where it had gone wrong.

I'd been just fine.

Matt had followed the script to a T. Hell, we'd even done a trial run before the actual thing. No, the knots hadn't been elaborate, but he'd weaved them around each of my legs, my chest, my arms, and had even tied them behind my back. I knew exactly what to expect. I hadn't freaked out. I'd been calm and confident.

So then what the fuck happened?

Why was it that as soon as I was up there and he started securing the ropes behind my back, my vision went dark and I couldn't seem to make my mouth work. My head was screaming *Llama, llama, llama,* but my mouth refused to move. And when I finally did hear the word, I'd known it wasn't my voice. Two bodies had appeared in my fading vision—one grabbed onto my hand, the other stood in front of me and supported my weight as I slumped against him. At first I had no clue who they were, but as soon as my arms were loosened from behind my back, my senses began coming back to me.

I didn't need to open my eyes to know the scent of my best friend. My face was pressed into his chest so hard that it would have been impossible to miss. Once I knew Trent was there, safety and comfort washed over me. I cracked my eyes open and saw Aiden holding my hand. He looked scared to death. In a few minutes, or hours, once the fog had cleared, I'd feel like the biggest asshole ever for scaring him—and likely Matt—like I had, but for the time being all I could do was squeeze his hand tightly to try to let him know I'd be okay.

Trent was talking to someone, someones maybe, but I couldn't make my brain focus on what they were saying no matter how hard I tried. Then we were moving. All three of us. Though Trent seemed to be doing most of the work, at least for me.

I was thankful he was as take charge as he was because, at the moment, I wasn't ready to take charge of anything, walking included. Though my brain was coming back online enough to know that one, Trent was at the club when he should have been at work—I already knew I was in for an earful when I felt better. And two, Aiden was holding my hand so tightly I could hardly move my fingers. At least Aiden would be easier to deal with than Trent; he needed Hedge and he'd calm down a lot.

With my brain still hazy and my movements uncoordinated, I couldn't seem to grasp where Trent was leading us. With my brain struggling to keep up, my brain-to-mouth filter went from on the fritz to completely nonexistent. "Where are we going?"

Trent continued to walk down the hallway and toward a door I was beginning to recognize. I was finally putting everything together when Trent spoke. "The locker room. You need to get ready so I can take you home. You're in no condition to drive. And I bet you don't have your stuff with you."

I hated when Trent was right—I didn't have anything with me. It wasn't that I'd ever considered it aftercare, but I had a routine I followed after a mosh. I'd never felt the need for it after a scene, so it hadn't crossed my mind as I left the house. That meant I didn't have my favorite weighted blanket in the car. The *Scooby-Doo* movie was on my phone at least. It was on Trent's phone too, since he was normally with me when I sank fully into my puppy headspace at the club.

But I couldn't watch the movie and drive at the same time, and according to Trent I couldn't drive at all. "I drove Aiden here," I blurted out when I remembered Trent had every intention of driving me home.

He muttered a curse word under his breath and shook his head. I shrank into myself slightly knowing that I was the reason Trent was upset. Correction, Trent wasn't upset, he was pissed. As much as I hated to admit it, he had every right to be. He slowed his pace as we got to the changing room and began talking to Aiden. "You don't know me from Adam, but you're welcome at our home. If you're not comfortable with that, I can drop you off if your place is on the way, or I can call you a ride. I'll happily pay for it."

Aiden's eyes darted frantically between Trent's and mine. His house was close, basically halfway between our house and here, but I'd freaked him out and didn't want him to be alone. "Our house has a really comfortable bed in the spare room. Or you can sleep in my room."

Aiden nibbled at his lip while he thought. "Um, would it be too much trouble if I spent the night?"

I couldn't decide how I felt when Trent responded to Aiden with a light, patient tone. That definitely wasn't jealousy... right? "Of course not. I'm not about to drop someone off somewhere if they aren't ready to be alone. Especially after that." I flinched slightly. I'd made a royal mess of things. Trent had a need to control and protect that went far deeper than his job. There was no way in hell he'd be letting me out of his sight until he was certain I was okay. Right then, I was fine with that. Usually, some quiet time in the car with my favorite movie then my blanket when I got home was enough. I wasn't sure they would be enough this time. It was the closest I'd ever felt to understanding how important aftercare was.

Aiden's head finally bobbed up and down. "Yeah. I'd rather make sure he's okay. As long as you don't mind..." He looked at Trent's name tag and the series of dots that noted Dom but unwilling to play before he finished the sentence. "Sir."

Trent tipped his chin downward once in a curt nod. "Thank you. I will feel much better knowing you're both okay." He directed us into the locker room. "And where are your lockers?"

I patted the pocket of my jeans with my free hand and produced my locker key. "Number twelve. We shared."

There was no hesitation in his movements as Trent plucked the key from my hand and deftly worked the lock open. The stupid thing stuck like a motherfucker, but it opened with no problems for Trent.

I watched as he grabbed my heavy gym bag out first, then reached to grab the smaller bag behind it. His hand halted for a brief moment before he looked over at Aiden. Aiden's bag was a well-packed diaper bag covered with hedgehogs. Inside of it, there would be a change of clothes, a few diapers, a bottle, a pacifier, and Hedge.

Trent's eyes softened as he grabbed the bag, then they hardened in an instant when he looked back at me. He had a lot of thoughts about what had happened, and they would come out eventually. Even through his frustration I could see how his eyes creased at the corners with worry, and the light pulsation in his temple that I knew meant he had a headache. I felt bad for being the one who did that to him, as unintentional as it might have been. He sighed like he'd made up his mind about something. "Come here, pup. You need that hood off before we can leave."

I took three steps toward him and leaned forward. Trent's hands reached out and pulled my hood off gently. I hadn't realized how much the panic had dampened my hair with sweat until I shivered when the cool air made contact with my overheated head. Trent didn't hesitate to pull me into a hug, rubbing his hands up and down my bare arms and around my back.

"You need to get dressed, then we'll get out of here." He was in caretaker mode. There were times I would fight it—most of the time I'd fight it—but that night I needed it as much as he did, so I stood there and let him do his thing. He started by putting my hood in my bag, then he pulled my T-shirt out and held it open.

I bit back the urge to tell him I could do it myself. Caring for me would help assure him that I was fine—hell, maybe it would assure me in the process. Besides, my legs still felt a little wobbly and my hands were still shaking as I raised my arms to slip into the shirt.

Once I was layered in both a T-shirt and sweatshirt, I was ready to go but Trent wasn't at that point yet. He turned his gaze to Aiden. "Do you have a sweatshirt in your bag?"

Aiden shook his head. "I just came in my T-shirt. I'll be fine."

Trent shook his head and began to shrug off his flannel shirt. It would swallow Aiden's frame, but Trent had that look in his eye that said he wasn't going to take no for an answer. "It's cool in the evenings now. You need to have a coat or a sweatshirt with you when you leave the house, especially in the evenings."

Pink rose in Aiden's cheeks but he allowed Trent to help him into the shirt. The shoulders hung halfway down Aiden's upper arms and the bottom hung to his mid-thigh. It was comical and Trent was going to be cold in just his short-sleeve undershirt, but he wasn't going to care and I wasn't going to be the one to point it out.

He grabbed both bags, tossed them over his shoulder, then held out a hand. "Come here, pup." I reached for his hand automatically. It had been a long time since he'd held my hand leaving the club, probably since we'd accepted a relationship would never work between us. When my hand slipped into his, it felt like a missing piece of me had been slotted back together.

His large warm hand wrapped around mine and he held it securely. Some of the unease in my belly started to loosen its grip on me. I held my other hand out to Aiden and he gripped it tightly. It didn't escape my notice that I was providing the same comfort to Aiden that Trent was providing me. I squeezed both hands gently and smiled to myself when I felt two squeezes back.

As soon as we were in the truck with me sandwiched between Trent and Aiden in the front seat, Trent fished his phone out of the glove box. He tapped on the screen for a few seconds before turning the phone on its side and handing it over to me. I sighed as the opening credits of *Scooby-Doo* played. I didn't know when the movie had become my happy place, but it had and I was thankful Trent knew exactly what I needed at the moment. I angled the screen so Aiden could also see it and we settled in for the half-hour trip home.

Ten minutes in, I felt Trent rest his arm behind my back and I leaned into him. Aiden's weight pressed more firmly against my side, and when I looked over, Trent's hand was resting on his shoulder.

By the time we made it home I was exhausted. The excitement of the club, the crash of adrenaline, the comfort of two warm bodies pressed against mine, and it was all I could do to stay awake. Trent pressed a kiss to the top of my head. "We'll talk tomorrow. Right now, I need to get you to bed. I have a feeling you're going to be out the rest of the night."

It was half past ten, earlier than I normally called it a night, but I had a feeling Trent was right. We filed into the house with Trent still holding both our bags. He placed mine on the ground by the door. Then he helped Aiden out of the shirt, handed him his bag, and pointed us both to the steps. "Go upstairs and get ready for bed. Your eyes are drooping shut."

I almost told him he wasn't my Master, but when I looked at him, he was looking more at Aiden than me. *Interesting.* Then he turned his gaze to me. The frustration I heard in his voice was nothing compared to the disappointment and stress in his eyes. "Upstairs. Brush your teeth and get ready for bed."

That time I did open my mouth to protest but all that came out was a giant yawn. Fuck my body and its willingness to defy me. Aiden gripped my hand. "Come on, Curious. Maybe we can finish the movie when we're ready for bed?"

My eyes automatically flicked toward Trent, who gave an almost imperceptible nod. At least his voice was softer when he said, "Go."

"Come on. I'll show you where we can get ready." I glanced back at Trent. Would he come up like he normally did after a night at the club? Did he think Aiden and I were dating? I should have told him about Aiden before, but it hadn't seemed important until then. We didn't tell each other about every person in our lives, and Aiden really wasn't a person in my life. He was just part of my life, but now that Aiden was there with me, I had a nagging feeling that I'd fucked up.

Aiden nodded and followed me up the steps with his bag in his hand. "Do you need help getting ready?" I'd never asked him that question before, but I felt like it was only right. My freak-out was the reason he was here anyway.

He shook his head. "I'll be fine. Thanks, though."

After showing Aiden where the bathroom was, I stripped down to my underwear and slipped under my weighted blanket to wait for his return. As I was waiting, Trent appeared in the doorway. "Mind if I come in?" His deep voice was soothing, and I felt my body relax.

"Please." That definitely was not a tremble in my chin at knowing I hadn't pissed him off so much he didn't want to see me.

He came over and climbed into the bed beside me, allowing me to snuggle into him. We'd cuddled like this since we were teenagers. Even before I'd realized I was bisexual—before sexuality, professions, and life complicated our relationship. Trent had always given the best cuddles. I'd loved being able to have them anytime I wanted when we'd dated, and I'd missed the easy affection since we broke up.

Snuggles allowed my brain to settle, which was probably one of the reasons I was able to lie next to Aiden at the club for hours. He gave cuddles and snuggles, pets and belly rubs so freely that it was easy to lie beside him while he played.

Trent rubbed at my scalp with his fingertips. "Do you two want to watch more of your movie? I brought the tablet up so you've got a bigger screen."

Best best-friend ever.

"Let's wait for Aiden to get in bed. He likes it too."

Not even two minutes later Aiden came out of the bathroom. Hedge was gripped in his hand but hanging by his side. Even from the bed, I could tell he wasn't wearing a diaper under his snug pajama pants, but a bright red waistband peeked out above the top of his shorts. The outline of thick padded briefs as well as a pacifier in his pocket showed through the thin material as he headed toward us. He looked confused as he approached, like he didn't know if he'd be sharing the bed with me now that Trent was there. I didn't want there to be any question in his mind about where I wanted him, so I patted the bed beside me. "Here."

Aiden slipped into bed and I gripped his hand.

Trent hummed beside me. "Ready for the movie?"

We both nodded and Trent hit play. He'd taken enough time downstairs to find the place we'd been at on his phone so it picked up right where we left off. I didn't remember much of the movie after that because I was asleep minutes later.

CHAPTER 6

AIDEN

LOGAN'S BREATHING evened out not even five minutes after the movie started. I felt his hand loosen on mine, and he was out. It didn't surprise me. He'd had a long night, and I could appreciate how exhausted it had made him.

As his breathing turned deeper, I felt Trent's hand squeeze my shoulder. I looked over in surprise to see the big man smiling softly at me. "You doing alright?"

So many thoughts were racing through my head. I'd spent most of the time we'd been here trying to ignore how awkward the situation really was. I trusted Logan completely, both as Curious and as Logan. He'd talked about his best friend a few times in the past, but meeting him so unexpectedly had thrown me for a bit of a loop. I hadn't been ready to go back home and spend the night worrying about Logan and how he was holding up. But at home I wouldn't have been left spending the night in the home of a man I didn't know while the man I did know slept soundly beside me.

Awkward.

Tall, dark, and handsome on the other side of Logan was wet dream material. Broody and muscular with a no-nonsense demeanor, I would be putty in his hands given half a chance. Even if I hadn't seen the Dom designation on his name tag at DASH, every part of him exuded Dom.

I took a moment to remind myself that it would be an exceptionally bad idea to try anything with Logan's best friend. Not only did I have a relationship with Logan, but Logan was still very much in love with the man gripping my shoulder. That was a messy situation all around, so I forced myself to focus on his words. How was I doing? Overall, I was okay. Still a little confused about what had happened at the club, but I was okay. "I'm alright."

"You sure?" Trent wasn't going to be easily convinced that I was, in fact, fine. That deep, confident voice that seemed to look into my soul wouldn't have let me lie, even if I'd wanted to.

I decided to tell him the truth. "Really, I'm fine. I'm a little confused about what happened at the club. It spooked me to see that look in his eyes. But knowing that he's sleeping comfortably right now is helping a lot."

Trent rubbed my head. When he'd been running his hands through Logan's hair when I came out of the bathroom, it looked like he was petting him. On me, it didn't feel like a pet. It felt more protective and calming. Thankfully, the words must have convinced him that I wasn't lying because he hummed something that sounded like acceptance. He was definitely a Dom. Too bad he wasn't a Daddy. Logan had only mentioned a time or five about how Trent wasn't.

"I'm sorry you had to witness that. I'm not entirely certain what causes that reaction in Logan, but I've seen it happen one other time. As soon as he told me what he had planned tonight, I had a bad feeling about it."

"Is that why you were there even though he told me you were at work?"

Trent's eyes widened. Was I not supposed to tell him that

Logan had mentioned him working? Looking back on the evening, I should have taken it as a bad sign when he'd so casually mentioned that Trent was at work and wasn't amused that he couldn't be there. How was I supposed to know that Trent had been upset because he thought something bad might happen? Had I known, I wouldn't have let Logan do it.

"Yeah, that's why I was there. I called someone to come in and cover for me. I couldn't risk Logan blacking out without me being there. He wouldn't have been able to use his safeword if that had started to happen."

I felt my head nod. "That was scary."

"Scared the hell out of me the first time I saw it happen in training. He totally blacked out. He just stood there with this vacant stare and I couldn't figure out what was going on. The woman in charge of the demonstration was pissed as hell when I started barking at her to uncuff him."

"Uncuff?" My voice squeaked as I got the question out.

"It was an apprehension demo. The instructor used him to demonstrate on. He completely shut down as soon as his arms were behind his back. I'm pretty sure something happened to him when he was in the Marines. I don't know what—he's never told me. I don't push much for the specifics of that part of his life. Tonight made me see that it's time for me to get more details."

That sounded terrifying, but Logan knew he didn't like being restrained, which was part of the reason I'd been so nervous about him doing the demo with Matt in the first place. All of the random pieces that made Logan an intriguing puzzle began coming together. "Wait, you're the best friend Logan works with."

"Guilty."

"So you work at the sheriff's department too?"

He laughed gently while amusement danced in his eyes. "You could say that. I'm the sheriff."

Logan didn't budge at my gasp of surprise.

"I don't know if I'm surprised or not that Logan hasn't mentioned anything to you about my job. He's great at keeping confidences. That's probably why he hasn't mentioned you to me, but I can also see how much you mean to him."

My brow furrowed in confusion. We were play partners who happened to fall into bed sometimes. Hell, we didn't even have penetrative sex, so why would I warrant telling? "We don't even hang out outside of the club unless we're having dinner together. I don't know how I could mean much of anything to him."

Trent's hand worked slowly through my hair. "You could see there was something wrong with him before I even had his safe-word out. I saw the way he reached out to you. He trusts you."

I snorted, then remembered Logan was sleeping and made sure to watch the volume of my voice. "He's my protector."

"Your protector?" Trent sounded genuinely confused by my words.

"He doesn't leave my side at DASH."

A scritchy sound came from across the bed as Trent scratched at the stubble on his face. "Not your Dom?"

I covered my mouth with Hedge to keep a bark of laughter from escaping into the quiet room. "Oh god, no. Not my Dom. Not anyone's Dom. Logan isn't a Dom. He's just... he's my guard dog."

Trent moved his hand down to Logan and carded his hand through Logan's thick hair. Years of tenderness and love showed in both the touch and the softness in his eyes. Until then, I hadn't seen that tenderness toward Logan from him. Trent had been angry at him, I'd thought, but maybe it was that he was concerned? "Yeah, he's not a Dom."

I shook my head.

"He's not a sub either." I didn't have to know Trent to know how much those words hurt him to say. His eyes spoke volumes.

Logan's inability to submit to Trent had come up in a number of conversations. I already knew how much it bothered Logan that he couldn't be what Trent needed, and I was quickly learning it hurt Trent just as much. The two shared a love I couldn't begin to understand, and they'd accepted that they couldn't be what the other needed. They were both trying to encourage the other to move on, yet their hearts were still intrinsically entwined.

I shook my head again. "If he could be, there's no question in my mind he would be one for you." Reaching over, I took Trent's hand in mine and squeezed. It was so much larger than my own that it looked funny.

Trent ran his free hand over his beard again. "Fucking shibari. What the fuck were you thinking, Logan?" His words were quiet but laced with frustration. It had to be eating up the Dom inside of him. He continued to talk to Logan like I wasn't there, like the only time he'd be able to say these things was when Logan was sound asleep, so he needed to say them right then. "You didn't even give me warning. Jesus, what would you have done? You can be so thickheaded sometimes."

Sometimes? Logan was the most stubborn man I'd ever met. Silly and playful and serious and stubborn. Yeah, Logan was an interesting combination of things. I bet thickheaded wasn't the worst thing Trent had called him over the years.

I was witnessing something happening between the two men. I couldn't help but wonder if Logan had a clue how much Trent still cared for him. Then again, I didn't know if Trent knew how much Logan cared for him, either. These two were a mess, yet in my gut something was telling me they would never figure it out if someone didn't show them. Snuggled next to Logan, with Trent rubbing at my head, I couldn't shake the feeling that I had somehow become entangled in the mess they'd created. Maybe I could show them they needed one another once and for all.

My eyes became heavy and I snuggled closer to Logan. He let out a little sigh that caused Trent to hum. "He loves to snuggle. I swear, it's the only time he stops. Sometimes I wonder how he sleeps if someone isn't holding him."

I blinked over at Logan. He'd always been affectionate with me; it was the only way I knew him. From the day he'd knocked into my tower the first time, he'd always been cuddly. He'd helped me rebuild my tower, then curled up next to me, and I'd adopted a puppy. But I'd never seen him sleep before then. Logan definitely looked peaceful.

Trent wrapped his arm around Logan and Logan burrowed into the blankets. He mumbled something that sounded an awful lot like, "Turn off the lights," then fell back to sleep. Trent reached over and flicked the lamp off, then settled his arm back around Logan so it was resting on my hip. "Goodnight, Aiden."

I pulled Hedge so he was between me and Logan. "Night."

CHAPTER 7

TRENT

I WAS up at seven staring at Logan and Aiden. Something had happened while Aiden and I chatted quietly the night before, but I couldn't figure out what it had been. There was a connection or a friendship or something that was pulling me to him. I'd watched the two men sleep for almost an hour before finally drifting off myself. The last thoughts I'd had were about how sweet the two men were together and questions about how deep their friendship ran.

Then I'd woken up early and was back to staring at them. God, the two were adorable. Logan had rolled over and attached himself to me at some point throughout the night. He'd grabbed on to me, his face burrowed in my chest and his arm draped over me. It was easy to forget how affectionate he was when he wasn't going a million miles an hour. On the other side of him, Aiden had an arm and a leg tossed over Logan's body and was sharing Logan's pillow.

The initial shock of Logan's friendship with a little had begun to wear off. I was still struggling to figure out *how* their friendship worked—Logan was so wiggly and Aiden didn't seem like a wiggly or hyper boy—but it did. Admittedly, it had taken me longer than it should have to process what I was seeing after I'd removed Logan's bag from the locker. I saw the diaper bag, I knew what it was, and after seeing his name tag, it shouldn't have been as shocking as it was.

Then at home I'd seen how connected the two were. It would have been hard to miss. I most certainly hadn't missed the way Logan's body sagged in relief when Aiden came out of the bathroom or how he'd reached for him as Aiden approached the bed. Just like I hadn't missed the outline of thick briefs beneath his snug pajamas or the stuffed animal in his arm. I'd actually been more surprised that he hadn't come out of the bathroom in a diaper.

As I looked over the sleeping men, the blue binkie with a hedgehog on it caught my eye. I didn't know where it had come from, but it was suctioned between his lips and didn't appear as though it was going anywhere in the near future. I'd never been attracted to a little before, but Aiden was intriguing and something was pulling me to the boy. That in itself was strange.

I had over fifteen years in the BDSM community, and I'd been drawn to the more controlling aspects of the lifestyle. At DASH, I was the Dom subs came to for a hard flogging or a whipping. I needed to control every aspect of the scene. Knowing what I did about myself, I should not have been thinking of ways to make the little in Logan's bed happy. In all honesty, I should have been getting up and heading to work—I could always find something to do at the office. Pursuing Aiden would be stupid. Not only did he and Logan have a connection, so in my mind he was Logan's already, but I'd end up hurting him. I didn't know enough about the boy sleeping to know what he liked, but I couldn't see him being into hard impact play or wanting to hand complete control over to me. I needed to get over those thoughts.

But I couldn't shake wanting to see the boy smile. To give

him something to smile about. That was a dangerous path to go down, but I couldn't seem to stop myself.

I slid out from under Logan's grip and helped roll him so he was snuggled into Aiden, then headed for my bathroom to shower quickly before getting breakfast ready. My thoughts focused more on what to make for the puppy and the boy sound asleep down the hall than my shower.

Yes, I needed to have a conversation with Logan. I knew that, but I wasn't going to push first thing. He was going to need to get food in him and Aiden didn't need to be witness to the argument that was bound to occur. No matter how badly I wanted to keep my anger in check, Logan had scared the shit out of me the night before and my emotions would come out in some way. They likely wouldn't be in a way I wanted Aiden to see.

It wasn't even eight when I was making my way to the kitchen to figure out breakfast. A quick check of Logan's room told me that he and Aiden were still sleeping soundly, so I had time to get breakfast started, whatever that might be. I grabbed my phone and sent a text to the only person I knew to ask.

Hey, what's Derek's favorite breakfast?

My phone rang in my hand not even a minute later. I knew who it was before I saw the caller ID.

"Hey, Colt."

He charged right in without a greeting. "Derek would eat the sweetest, sugariest cereals known to man if I didn't put my foot down."

I snorted. "Not your husband Derek, your boy Derek. When Derek's little, what does he like to eat?"

"Easy. Pancakes. He likes to dip them in the syrup. But nothing can touch. Oh, and he likes two different dipping sauces. He has these really cute divided trays with cartoons all over them. Makes it much easier to keep things separate. I've never figured out why it's so important to him that nothing touches since he uses his fingers and dips the pancake pieces into each one and they mix up anyway. And he always needs a bath afterward. Wait. Why are you asking me about my boy's favorite breakfasts?"

Pancakes with two dipping sauces, nothing touching, in special plates. This was more complicated than simply making pancakes. This was exactly why I wasn't a Daddy. This shit didn't come naturally to me. I could handle teasing and sass from a brat, but I didn't have it in me to think about how a little would want his food on his plate. Then I thought of the sweet guy curled up with Logan and knew I'd end up figuring out a way to make it happen, even if only so he had a good memory of the last twelve hours. Logan scaring the shit out of him, then ending up in a stranger's house for the night couldn't have been easy on him.

"Long story. Let's just leave it at a bunch of shit happened last night that led me to having a sweet boy spend the night. We were all stressed and I suspect I didn't give him the best first impression of me. I'd like to make it up to him."

Colt was silent for a moment. "We all? How many people are there?"

Fuck, I'd said too much. Not only was Colt a friend of mine, he was also a sheriff in a nearby county. Of course he'd pick up on anything remotely vague I might say. "Just me, Logan, and Logan's friend."

"Logan's friend. Who is a little. How do you know he's a little?"

I chuckled as I thought about the hedgehog-covered diaper bag, the cute pajamas, the well-loved hedgehog, and the binkie. The boy loved hedgehogs. "It would be impossible to miss."

Colt grunted. "You're not going to give me more, are you?"

"Not a chance."

"Okay, well, my answer stands. Pancakes, lots of syrup, and if

Derek's little, he always has a sippy cup of milk with breakfast. Sometimes juice, but only one cup. My husband doesn't need that much sugar first thing in the morning... or any time throughout the day. The man is hard enough to manage when he's not on a sugar high."

"Thank you, Colt."

"No problem. Lunch sometime this week? Then maybe you'll tell me more about this mysterious boy you had spend the night."

I rolled my eyes. "Lunch, yes. No promises on telling you more."

"Oh, and if he's little, have a washcloth ready for after breakfast."

"Huh?"

"You'll figure it out. I hear movement—I better get going."

What the hell would I need a washcloth for? Colt sounded like he was already shifting gears, so I said goodbye and hung up.

After we ended the call, I was left searching through my kitchen for what I might have for Aiden's breakfast plate. Logan loved pancakes and I made them frequently for breakfast, but Logan had always taken care of plating his own food. We didn't have much in the house for a little. Why would we?

I dug to the back of the cupboard we kept random plasticware in. There was a nagging memory of divided plastic trays that we'd gotten for a barbecue once. They weren't bright or patterned, but if they were still there they would probably work. By the time I found them buried in the back, I'd already decided it was past time to clean the kitchen cupboards. The number of unmated lids and containers was staggering, but I'd found the red divided tray. That one find had me far more satisfied than it should have.

I didn't bother looking for an appropriate cup for a little.

There was no need. There never had been a sippy cup or bottle in the house. Ever. Hell, my siblings didn't even have kids and Logan was an only child. I would take the small victory of having the rectangular divided plate.

Twenty-five minutes later, there were three pancakes left on the griddle and sausage finishing in the frying pan on the other side of the stove. I had a stack of pancakes on a serving platter for Logan and me, but the last pancakes were going to go on Aiden's tray.

As I'd searched for the maple syrup I knew was in the back of the fridge, I bumped into a bottle of strawberry syrup. I pulled it out and examined the bottle, trying to remember where or when I'd gotten it. Then I remembered Logan coming home a few months earlier with a bag of groceries and insisting that we needed strawberry syrup. By we, he really meant that he needed it for when I made him breakfast because Logan didn't make breakfast.

I stared at the bottle of syrup for entirely too long. The glass bottle made me think about my relationship with Logan and how our friendship could have gone to shit after we broke up. Except it hadn't—he still came to me with problems, still came home to our house every night, and still curled up with me if he thought he could get away with it. That last one made me smile because, whether he knew it or not, he never needed an excuse to snuggle with me. But I liked the excuses he came up with and seeing the look on his face when he thought he'd gotten something by me. The fact that he was usually asleep within minutes instead of tossing and turning for hours ensured I'd never turn him down.

It took the fridge dinging its disapproval at being left open for me to come out of my thoughts. I grabbed the maple syrup from the bottom shelf and bumped the door shut with my elbow before heading back to the stove to finish up breakfast.

In small bowls, I warmed up both the maple syrup and strawberry syrup in the microwave while I finished the sausage. Even once I got pancakes and sausage onto the partitioned plate, something didn't feel right. Despite staring at the plate hoping it would tell me what was wrong, nothing came to me. I'd just gone to the cupboard to grab plates for Logan and me when it came to me.

Aiden's plate, despite being divided, looked too adult. I hadn't cut his food up. *Duh.* It was apparent that I'd not spent enough time around littles, or at least I hadn't paid enough attention to the ones I had been around. As I grabbed a fork and knife to slice up the food on Aiden's plate, I remembered Colt doing much the same thing for Derek no matter who was around.

When the food was in bite-sized pieces it no longer looked like an adult's plate. A sense of pride washed through me that I'd figured it out. As I was pouring the warmed syrup into the wells, I heard footsteps on the stairs. I looked up from my spot with just enough time to see Logan and Aiden walking down the steps holding hands.

In the light of day, without the chaos of the club or the stress of the aftermath, I took in Aiden's body in a new way. He was young. Not college young, but he was at least a decade younger than Logan and me. Even his dark beard didn't hide his youth. "Morning."

Aiden yawned and for the first time I noticed his binkie had been clipped to his pajama shirt. Pink tinged his cheeks but he didn't seem uneasy about being in the house. Logan's eyes fell onto the kitchen island and the pile of pancakes and our plates stacked beside the platter. Then he saw the divided tray and his eyes widened in surprise. "I'll be right back." He dropped Aiden's hand and hurried back up the steps before Aiden had even made it all the way down.

Aiden looked up to where Logan had disappeared, confusion written all over his face, then back to me. "Thank you for letting me spend the night." His fingers worked the fur of his hedgehog as he made his way toward the island. He'd just begun to examine the breakfast when Logan returned with a light blue sippy cup in his hand and a triumphant grin on his face.

Logan made his way over to me while Aiden was still examining the island. The way he was studying what I'd done made me self-conscious. Had I read him wrong? Had I overstepped? Logan didn't seem to have the same concerns. He got right beside me, leaned over, and kissed my cheek. "You are so sweet," he whispered into my ear. "Here's his cup." Logan pushed the blue cup into my hand and I looked at it in confusion. What was I supposed to do with it? "He really likes milk," Logan supplied with a light chuckle.

Oh. *Ohh.* Oh, right. By the time his cup was filled and the lid secured, Aiden had found words again, though his cheeks were flushed red as he spoke. "Thank you for breakfast. It looks good."

Logan tugged Aiden down to the seat beside him at the island. "Trent makes the best pancakes. And I picked out the strawberry syrup."

Aiden nodded as he stared at the plate in front of him. "It looks good."

I slid a plate and fork toward Logan, but I didn't feel right doing the same for Aiden. Instead, I picked his plate and cup up and walked the few feet around the island to place them in front of him. My hand ran through his hair without input from my brain. "Thank you. I hope you enjoy them."

When silverware was passed out and I'd put a cup of coffee in front of Logan and me, we all began to eat. At first, Aiden was quiet while he focused on his meal, but Logan's wiggles from beside him soon had him grinning.

I growled low in my chest when I saw Logan reach over and swipe a bite of pancake from Aiden's plate. "You have your own."

Logan shrugged innocently. "But Aiden's are cut already."

"Eat *your* breakfast, Logan."

Logan stuck his tongue out at me in response. "Aiden shares." He reached over again but Aiden smacked his hand.

"Bad puppy. These are good, and you have your own." He pointed to Logan's plate with his fork. "Either cut your pancakes up or ask..." Aiden's voice trailed off and his brow furrowed as he thought. "Uh, Master? Sir?"

"Either is fine. Or you can call me Trent."

Aiden's cheeks turned pink but he nodded. "Thank you, Sir."

We fell silent as we ate. Not surprisingly, Logan ate more than his fair share of the food. I had made extra because I knew after the crash of the previous night he would probably be starving. As breakfast finished, the light mood evaporated. I gathered our plates to take them to the sink, but I could see the tense set of Logan's shoulders. Confrontation was unavoidable by that point. He wouldn't want to go to work without clearing the air—it wasn't how he operated.

I didn't want to have the argument while Aiden was in the house. I didn't know if Logan was ready to hear how much his stunt the night before had not only scared me, but hurt me as well. I'd never had Logan dismiss me like he had the night before, and as a result I was still working through some of those feelings.

Logan blinked up at me from his coffee cup. "I'm sorry. I fucked up."

The anger I'd felt the night before was nowhere. A strange feeling of betrayal I'd never felt with him had replaced it, and it was a lot harder to process than anger.

CHAPTER 8

LOGAN

"You damn near gave me a heart attack last night." Trent's words weren't aggressive, they weren't barked, they sounded... fuck, they sounded hurt. And was that a tremor I saw in his hand as he took a sip of his coffee?

Trent gave up on the coffee and placed it on the counter beside him. "You... you pop into my office and tell me you're going to do a rope demo when, when you *knew* I couldn't be there." His voice cracked as he spoke. This was a side of Trent I'd never seen before, and I wasn't sure what to make of it.

He pointed to me, then to Aiden. "You scared the shit out of both of us. You'd told Aiden you didn't like being restrained. And I was the one with you the last time you blacked out like that. Jesus Christ, Logan, do you have any idea how that made me feel the first time I saw you panic?"

I shook my head. I had no idea. I just knew that Trent had been there. He hadn't let me out of his sight for the rest of the day and had curled around me in bed when we got home that night.

Trent paced, and I ventured a glance over at Aiden who looked just as upset as Trent. Anger directed at me was an emotion I could handle, but the look of sadness and disappointment—that was enough to have me nearly in tears.

"I really did think it would be fine. We talked about it. We practiced. It was fine."

Trent leaned against the counter, his entire body sagging against where he rested his hands. "But then you were in front of a group of people and it didn't go so well."

"Well, yeah."

Trent looked like he was praying for patience. "Logan, why don't you like being restrained?"

That was an easy question to answer. "Have you ever had your arms and legs bound and been tossed into a pool?"

Trent and Aiden both shook their heads and responded in unison. "No."

"I can't think of many people who went through that who would enjoy being tied up."

Aiden spun his blue plastic cup around on the counter. "Why didn't you tell that to Matt? Or Trent?" He looked over at Trent and my eyes followed. A muscle twitched in Trent's jaw.

Why was it that every excuse I came up with sounded shallow and like, well, like an excuse? My shoulders sank. Everything I wanted to say *was* an excuse. I settled on the truth. It wasn't a fear I had ever voiced aloud and it took more effort than I felt it should have to get the words to come out. "Because I don't want to be defined by my past." Arms wrapped around me from either side in a tight embrace.

Trent's lips grazed my temple. "You, Logan Caldwell, will never be defined by your past. Our pasts shape us to the people we are today, but they do not define us unless we let them." His thumb wiped below my eye and it was then I realized I'd been crying.

Aiden kissed the opposite side of my face. "You're really brave."

I scoffed. I didn't feel brave as I sat there with tears running down my face.

"Logan," Aiden said, his voice firm and steady. He hooked his finger under my chin and pulled it so I was facing him. "Logan, listen to me. You've faced that fear over and over again. You conquered that fear. You beat it."

"I panicked."

Aiden's eyes narrowed. "You've let Matt tie you up a number of times and not freaked out. So there is something about doing it in front of a group that you can't do. But your fear of being tied up? You've beaten that."

I opened my mouth to protest, then played Aiden's words back. He was right. I had beaten it. Well, mostly at least. I might never be able to do ropework in front of a group, but I could let someone I trusted tie me up and not have a panic attack. "I owe Matt an apology."

Trent's arms tightened around my body. "Yeah, you do. May want to go out to lunch with him or something so you can talk it out. He was really shaken up."

"I'll give him a call." I would, just not right that second. Not while I was still emotionally drained.

Trent hummed in approval. "Thank you." He squeezed my shoulders again then stepped back to finish cleaning up the kitchen.

Aiden placed another kiss on my cheek and for the first time I noticed how sticky he was. He'd started eating his pancakes with his fork, but I'd looked over a few times to see him picking at them with his fingers. Now I could feel where sticky prints dotted my temple, cheek, and under my chin from his lips and fingers. Before I could say anything to him, Trent was standing beside Aiden. "Now I know why I needed a washcloth handy. Let me get you cleaned up. You're a mess, and you've made Logan messy too."

Who told him to get a washcloth?

Aiden's face turned pink as Trent gently took his face in his hands and wiped the syrup off, then took each of his hands and cleaned them with the rag. I almost laughed, but when I saw the tender smile on Trent's face and how careful he was being with Aiden, there was no way I could make light of the moment.

Trent looked at peace. Content in a way I'd never seen him. The big burly, firm-handed Dom was being tender and sweet with my friend. Instead of being happy for them, my heart clenched in my chest. Sure, he'd sworn he wouldn't make a good Daddy and he didn't have experience with littles, but I'd always suspected this would happen if I introduced him to Aiden. Trent was a nurturer. Always had been, always would be. I was certain I was witnessing something happening between the two. I'd never seen him with that look on his face before. Something as easy as wiping Aiden down after breakfast made him happy.

Not only could I not be submissive to a Master, there was nothing in me that wanted a Daddy either. Much like the end of my relationship with Erica, I was getting the distinct feeling that a door was closing on whatever was still between us. It hurt like hell, but there was no way I could give Trent that. I couldn't ever be as submissive as Aiden. Maybe it should have made me feel better to know that there was no way I could personally make Trent happy, but instead it made me feel worse.

Then Trent was in front of me. "Look at me, pup." His voice was filled with amusement and his attention had focused completely on me. There wasn't the same tenderness in his eyes that I'd seen when he was focused on Aiden, but it didn't feel awkward. The humor of my sticky face tugged at his lips, and when I didn't immediately pull away or tell him I could do it myself, his touch became softer. "You're a mess."

The thought of pulling back had crossed my mind for a brief second, but this was something that didn't feel odd to me. It didn't feel like a Dominant caring for a submissive. It felt more like a casual act between lovers. I wasn't ready to let my brain go down that path, so I shut it down quickly. Not after I'd just thought that whatever might be between us had evaporated, maybe forever.

Trent stepped back and ruffled Aiden's already messy hair. "Are sticky fingerprints normal while you're around?"

"If you feed me sticky things."

How did Trent move between being so dominant with Aiden but so casual with me? It was almost fluid. If letting Trent wipe my face was all there was to submission, I could handle it, but it was the rest that was too much. I glanced over at Aiden to find him finishing his milk.

My brain was ready to move on from the last five minutes and I searched for something to talk about. Something tickled my brain about Aiden's work schedule picking up soon. "When's your next project?"

Aiden tensed as he set his cup down. "Just about three and a half weeks from now."

Trent must have noticed the tension in Aiden's voice because he was suddenly paying a lot more attention to our conversation than wiping the counter down.

"How long is it?"

"It's scheduled for four days. But I finish that and go right into two more projects. I'm booked solid for almost three weeks, and I have to work editing in there too. Well, not for the first shoot, they are paying someone else to edit those. It's a swimsuit shoot. The director is known to be an absolute nightmare to work for."

Trent gave up all pretense of cleaning the counters. "What is it that you do exactly?"

Aiden's face lit up as he started talking about his job. He would talk about his work for the next hour if given half a chance, but I also knew the schedule wore him out. "I'm a freelance photographer. I do a lot of work around the Nashville area. In the coming weeks, I have a variety of projects going on. The easiest is the home tour. It's like ten different houses in the area. I just have to go in and take pictures. Those will be easy to edit as long as I take my time setting up. It will be a few long days, but the pay is great. Then one of my old clients is shooting an album cover and asked me to do the photography for it. That's going to take longer. But like I said, the first one is that swimsuit shoot. It's going to be a tough job but it pays really well."

"All of those are going on at the same time?" Trent had heard everything Aiden had said but also everything he hadn't.

Aiden shrugged like it wasn't that big of a deal. "It will take about three weeks total. I'll have to sacrifice some sleep in there, but it will pay the bills for a few months."

Trent bristled. I could see the overprotective Dom struggling to stay under the surface. "Down, Dom," I teased, trying to lighten the mood.

Out of my peripheral vision, I saw Aiden glance over at me, but I was looking directly at Trent. When his head followed my glance, his eyes widened.

Trent cleared his throat. "Don't kill yourself for your work."

Aiden smiled bashfully. "I'll try."

A brilliant idea hit me and was out of my mouth before I could stop it. "We should go to the club before your schedule picks up. You won't be able to go in the middle of all that work."

Aiden's eyes sparkled. "That sounds perfect. I'd love to do that."

A few minutes later, Aiden asked to use the shower. As soon as Trent and I were alone, he leveled me with an icy glare. "Does he work too much?"

Depends on your definition of too much. "His work isn't consistent. Though I get the impression that his downtime is less common than it once was."

Trent growled, displeased with my response. "He said you're his protector."

I couldn't help the flush or the embarrassed grin that crossed my face. "Something like that, maybe. The first time I saw him at DASH, he was playing alone in the playroom and he looked lonely. I may have knocked my toy into his block tower, but then he played with me for a long time. We went to a diner afterward to talk. He told me he went sometimes to decompress because DASH had a great toy room and he liked hearing people because his house was always so quiet. When he told me he didn't have a boyfriend or a Dom or a Daddy, even at the club, it made me uneasy. I didn't want him there alone—it would be too easy for an asshole to bother him. I just started planning my visits around his." It was a bit more complicated than that, but not much. And I wasn't going to be the one that told Trent that a few of the bigger assholes at the club had approached him since I'd been hanging out with him.

Trent's fingers carded through my hair, and a happy growl escaped me. I couldn't help it. When he did things like that, Curious came to the surface in the blink of an eye. "Good pup." Praise didn't normally do much for me, pup or not, but when Trent praised me for looking after Aiden, I felt my chest swell. Another kiss was placed on the top of my head. "Keep him safe."

I nodded. "Of course."

CHAPTER 9

AIDEN

So, this is kind of an odd request. Would you want to come down here tomorrow afternoon? I'm off and Trent works. I could use a puppy day after last weekend.

I read the text from Logan at least five different times. It sounded like he was inviting me to his house. It would be kind of fun to have a playdate at someone's house. And Logan was safe. Also, not having to travel to the club would be a nice change of pace.

That would be fun.

The text was sent with almost no conscious thought on my part. My brain was already trying to plan what to bring with me the next day.

My phone rang and I looked at it in confusion. Why was Logan *calling* me? When was the last time I'd talked to a friend on the phone? Didn't everyone text now? "Hello?"

"Hey. I was going to go to the grocery store in the morning. What do you want for lunch and dinner?"

"I'm not picky."

I could almost see Logan's eye roll as easily as I could hear his exasperation. "I know you're not picky, but I want to make sure we have stuff here you like."

I thought for a minute. "Chicken nuggets and macaroni and cheese." My stomach rumbled, reminding me I hadn't had dinner yet.

"Okay, that's a good lunch, but what about dinner?"

I'd thought chicken nuggets for lunch and macaroni and cheese for dinner. But I'd forgotten that Logan was so much bigger than me. I'd seen the man eat before—he would easily make that lunch. "Uh, what about peanut butter and jelly sandwiches for lunch and chicken and macaroni and cheese for dinner?"

"I can work with that. Any other snacks you like?"

"You know most of what I like."

I heard clicking on a keyboard. Logan was probably making a list because he'd end up forgetting what he'd gone to the store to buy without it. "I should probably pick up a cup and bottle. What about plates?" Logan had mumbled the words, so I expected he was talking to himself, but I jumped in.

"I'll bring my stuff. Don't worry about getting stuff for me. It's only a playdate." But it was a playdate. With my puppy! I needed to go get him a new toy before I went over the next day. After I just told him not to buy stuff for me, I was turning around to do the same thing.

Logan huffed his displeasure. "What about toys? Can I buy you some blocks or something at least? I don't want you to have to bring toys here too. That's a lot."

There went my protector again, and I relented. "I love blocks."

"Great. I'll see you tomorrow." Logan hung up before I could say goodbye, but that was how I found myself standing on his front porch at quarter to ten the next morning with three bags in hand: my diaper bag, a bag with a few new puppy toys, and a bag containing meal accessories.

I'd barely rung the bell when the door flew open and I came face-to-face with a very excited half-Logan, half-Curious. He was quite distracting wearing only an aqua blue singlet with the outline of his half-hard cock restrained only by the thin spandex.

"Hi!" Logan practically vibrated with excitement.

My eyes had yet to find their way from his crotch, though my brain was beginning to scream at me that I needed to look at Logan's eyes, *not* his dick. I finally pulled my eyes upward to his face. "Hi." Logan was smirking at my reaction, so I didn't feel too bad about gawping at him.

With my eyes away from his dick, I saw he already had his gloves and collar on, and a quick scan down his body—pointedly ignoring his midsection—proved he already had his knee pads on. The only things he was missing were his hood and his tail. I knew that because when he turned around to usher me in, his muscular butt was very devoid of a tail.

At least some of that thought process must have been vocalized because Logan began to talk. "I thought about my tail, but I didn't want to be hard as a rock all afternoon. Walking upright to cook or go down the steps isn't easy when my prostate is being nailed constantly."

Logan took the shopping bag I'd packed my lunch and dinner stuff in, then looked at me with confusion when I refused to hand over the one with the new toys I'd picked up for Curious. I'd show him those later when we were playing. "You don't have to cook for me. I can cook."

Logan shook his head as he removed the plates, cups, silverware, and one of the bibs I'd brought with me. "My house, I cook. Go get ready. Remember where my room is?" He gestured toward the steps.

I remembered and headed that way. In the future, I'd remember to order food to be delivered instead of making one of us cook.

In his room, I opened my diaper bag. Since it was just the two of us that day and the house was plenty warm, I decided to just wear my diaper and the cute cover I'd bought on Etsy a few weeks earlier. I had a matching bib that looked like a bandanna that I could clip my binkie to. Getting changed didn't take more than five minutes, and then I was heading back down the steps in just a pair of socks, a thick diaper and matching diaper cover, and the bib with my binkie clipped to it. In one hand, I held tightly to Hedge and in the other, the bag of toys I'd bought Curious.

Logan had pushed the couch and coffee table out of the way while I was upstairs, and he already had his hood on and was pulling blankets out of the storage ottoman. In the middle of the room, a large rubber tote sat, and I couldn't help but be intrigued by it. As soon as Logan noticed me at the base of the stairs, he hurried over and took my hand.

"Come see!" He was so excited he practically vibrated out of his skin.

I found myself kneeling beside the tote a few seconds later. Logan pushed at my shoulder with his. "Open it. Open it."

I worried that if I didn't open it quickly, Logan would explode. When I pulled the lid off, my eyes widened in surprise and I found myself shaking my head. "This is too much. You shouldn't have!"

Even around his hood, I could see a blush creep up his upper cheeks. The tote was filled with toys. He'd bought the promised wooden blocks, but there were also soft blocks and wooden race cars, even a toy that shot soft balls out of it that looked ridiculously fun. I tossed my arms around his shoulders and squeezed him. "Thank you, puppy!"

When the happy whimper came from his chest, I knew playtime had begun. Reaching into the bag I'd brought with me, I felt the adult world slip away.

Curious barked and jumped about each time I pulled a new toy out of the bag. Watching him so excited about his toys made me happy too. I liked knowing that I'd done something to bring him happiness.

As I started pulling toys out of the tote to play with them, Curious chased after every ball, rope toy, and squeaky toy I tossed his way. He'd never been so free and uninhibited around me, and I suspected I was only just seeing his true pup for the first time. I was beginning to understand why Trent had been so confused about my saying that Curious was my snuggly guard dog at DASH.

At one point, one of the balls from the toy Logan bought me flew higher than I'd expected, and before I could crawl over to get it, Curious found it. I laughed as he pounced on it, doing a somersault as he grabbed it. The soft ball popped out of his grip and Curious chased it until it slipped under the couch and out of reach. I crawled over to where he was growling at the ball that was just out of reach of his big hands and the padded gloves that, while protecting his knuckles from the floor, only served to make his hands bigger.

My hands and arms were smaller, so I lay on my belly and slid my hand under the couch, easily grabbing the ball. "Mine." I held it to my chest, ready to crawl back over to my toys, when Curious whimpered and batted at the ball. "Puppy, you have toys." I pointed to the toys scattered around the living room. His toys had started out in a little box but had been strewn from one side of the living room to the other. A rope toy had been left on the couch after he'd rolled off it while he wrestled the toy a little while earlier. A rubber ball he'd chased tirelessly for a long time had been left by the front door when a squeaky toy had caught his eye. And now, he was after my ball.

Curious whimpered again, this time giving me his best puppy dog eyes, and I gave up any pretense of telling him no. I handed it over, and to my surprise, he batted it toward the toy and used his snout to push the ball into it. He watched with excitement as the ball shot out the top, then fell back, bouncing off his head before rolling back to where I was still sitting. I rolled the ball back to Curious, who repeated the process, both of us having fun with the toy until I heard a loud rumbling in Logan's stomach.

Like a switch had flipped, Logan stood up. "Time to make lunch, and you probably need a drink." He headed to the kitchen, muttering something about being an idiot, and returned a moment later with my sippy cup filled with apple juice. "Sorry, I forgot to give this to you earlier."

I followed him back to the kitchen area and climbed onto the bar stool. When I took the first pull of the drink Logan had handed me, I noticed just how thirsty I was.

"This is why I usually have Trent around when I really submerse myself in puppy play," Logan was saying as I drank greedily. Logan pulled a bottle of water from the fridge and downed half of it in one gulp. "I get so wrapped up in playing I forget to take care of myself. Trent makes sure I drink and eat enough."

That all made sense. I was pretty quiet when I sank into my little space. Maybe it was because I never had other littles to play with, or maybe it was just who I was when my little side came out. Playing with Curious was the most interaction I'd had with anyone when I was little, and Curious at home was totally different than Curious at DASH. Logan slid apple slices across the counter toward me. "I can see why that's important. You play really hard."

Logan moved around the kitchen effortlessly. I was more of the prepared meals, frozen dinner guy. I could cook, but it wasn't a natural thing for me. I much preferred to bake. Seeing a puppy comfortably moving throughout the kitchen was making me smile.

"I didn't work out this morning." He sounded a bit uncertain of himself as he spoke. "Am I too intense?"

I shook my head, my mouth too full of apple slices to speak for a moment. When I forced the bite down, I elaborated. "Not at all. I like seeing you having fun. It's different than when you're curled up at my side."

"Great." Logan slid a pack of crayons and a coloring book over to me. "Lunch will be ready soon." Reading between the lines, I could tell Logan didn't want me pulled too far out of my headspace, so I focused on my coloring and before long I heard a plate being slid across the counter.

Logan had left no detail overlooked. A peanut butter and jelly sandwich—the crust cut off perfectly—sat in the largest divided section. The three smaller ones contained grapes, yogurt, and celery sticks with peanut butter. I turned my nose up at the celery, but the stern look coming from behind the puppy hood told me I'd be wise to eat what was given to me.

"Celery is good for you."

"It's green," I protested.

Logan tapped my peanut butter-covered celery with a long stalk of his own. I looked up to see him take a bite off the end, and my face pinched like I'd eaten a lemon. "What is that look for? I put, like, half a jar of peanut butter on your celery—you won't even be able to taste it! It's gonna be like crunchy peanut butter."

I poked at the offending object on my plate. "Yeah, if by crunchy you mean stringy. It's like eating a peanut butter-covered G-string." I did feel a little bad when Logan inhaled a chunk of the celery stick he was eating and began to cough.

"Eat it," he gasped, trying to sound stern and failing.

I picked the piece up with trepidation and took a bite. It took way too long to eat the chunks of celery he'd put on my plate, but eventually they were gone and I could focus on the actual food in front of me.

Logan finished his lunch well before I finished mine. I'd totally missed him taking off his hood as he ate. His short hair was plastered to his head, and he had cleaned up most of the kitchen.

"You are a super messy eater."

I wasn't that bad, though at the time I probably resembled that remark a bit too closely. There had been a reason I brought extra bibs with me that day. For some reason when I was little, my fingers were just as likely to be used as a fork or spoon, usually more likely. It wasn't even a conscious thing on my part. Logan approached with a washcloth and began wiping me down.

"How did you get yogurt on your belly?"

I couldn't help but laugh as he wiped me down then looked at the bib around my neck and shook his head. "There's yogurt on this too." He unclipped my binkie, then stuffed the nipple into my mouth. "Don't lose this while I grab you a new bib."

With my new bib in place and the kitchen clean, Logan directed me back to the living room. While the toys looked fun, a morning of playing, then a bigger lunch than I'd had since the previous Thanksgiving had me very tired.

"Get Hedge. I'm gonna go make you a bottle, then we can go upstairs and read a book before nap time."

Nap time? I didn't think the day could get more perfect. I headed over to where I'd left Hedge and made it back to the kitchen before Logan had milk in my bottle. "Warm or cold?"

He'd asked the question so casually there was no reason it should have embarrassed me the way it did, yet my cheeks turned pink. "Warm, please."

"Go on up to my room. I'll be there in just a minute."

I headed upstairs, taking the opportunity to change my diaper while he was downstairs. We'd never discussed how he felt about my diapers and I didn't want to do anything to make things awkward. Logically I knew he was fine with me wearing them, but I didn't know if that also meant he'd be fine seeing me change a wet one. If we were going to spend whole days together now, it was something we needed to talk about.

I yawned again as Logan entered the room. "Trash can's in the bathroom," he mentioned as he headed over to his side of the bed.

I still felt awkward as I returned to the bed after washing my hands, but Logan patted the bed and waved the bottle in front of me. Curling up while he held my bottle felt a lot like it did when we were at DASH. He found a picture book beside his bed and opened to the first page. I was asleep well before the end of the book.

CHAPTER 10

TRENT

JAMES CAME into the office three hours earlier than he was scheduled, mumbling something about his crazy neighbor. I wasn't sure what was going on there, but since he'd moved into a new townhouse a few months earlier, he'd been working extra hours frequently and telling me it was because his new neighbor was driving him up a wall. Right then, I'd take the distraction. The station had been slow that day, so I'd been using the time to catch up on my never-ending piles of paperwork. When I dreamed of being sheriff as a child, I always dreamed of catching the bad guys and helping people. Stacks of reports, backlogs of paper trails stretching back before I was elected sheriff, and then adding to the paper by my own report generation had never crossed my mind.

The pile was threatening to swallow me whole if I didn't get my head out of the gutter. To say my mind had been preoccupied the last few days would have downplayed the chaos in my brain. I'd spent one night with Aiden—not even *with* him, we just shared the same bed—on the other side of Logan, and something had been tickling the back of my brain ever since. Maybe it was just that hanging out with him for those few short hours had made me feel a lot like I'd known him forever. Which I knew was ridiculous because I couldn't know even a fraction of who he was. He made Logan so happy it was hard to ignore and hard not to like him.

I didn't know what was the most confusing to me: still thinking about Aiden or the fact that no matter where my thoughts drifted, Logan was still there. It hadn't helped that Logan had been off when we finally got Aiden to his house on Sunday morning. Snippy and short wasn't normal for him. Logan had been adamant that there was something between Aiden and me. He wanted to know what I thought about Aiden, and he talked Aiden up the entire ride home. But just behind his excitement, unmistakable worry pinched the corners of his eyes and kept his chin just a little stiffer than was natural. He wanted me happy. He wanted me happy enough to push me toward someone it would pain him to see me with.

Would there ever be a man I could settle down with that wouldn't hurt him? We were great at not talking about our feelings, but I'd seen him studying me over the years, the gears in his brain working double time to figure out if he could be that man for me. I knew the look because it was the same one I gave him when I thought he wasn't looking. Was there a way I could make him happy?

Then Logan met Aiden, the sweet boy I knew next to nothing about but couldn't get off my mind. All I knew for sure was that Aiden was a little and he worked a lot. I also knew he made Logan happy in a way I hadn't seen before. And Logan was acutely aware of every move Aiden made.

Thanks to our conversation on the way to pick up Logan's car at DASH, I knew Aiden was looking for a Daddy. Logan was convinced Aiden was exactly what I needed, but I wasn't so certain. Sure, Aiden had been sweet and caring, and he seemed to know exactly how to calm Logan down. Those things were great, and he'd be perfect for *some* Dom, just not me. I'd fuck up and hurt him. I'd be too harsh and it would kill me if I upset him. Logan needed to get those thoughts out of his head fast so that I could get them out of my own head.

Sitting alone in my office all day had caused my thoughts to begin to swirl into a tornado, and if I wasn't careful, they'd be causing me nightmares of unfinished paperwork, and Logan and Aiden together. James' issues with his neighbor, however trivial they seemed to me, were a welcome distraction that evening.

"What's going on this time?" I questioned, rocking back in my desk chair.

James collapsed dramatically into the chair across from me. "He keeps coming over. Yesterday evening, I came home from the grocery store and he was coming out of his house. Trent, he wouldn't stop talking to me! He followed me into the house while I was unloading groceries, and he just kept talking. And the guy practically vibrates energy. He was telling me about some fucking dodi tree in the backyard. *What the hell is a dodi tree?* He talked about the damn thing for, like, five minutes."

"Didn't you say that he was close with the old tenant?"

James nodded. "He's said something along those lines about twenty times now."

"Maybe he's lonely."

"But I'm not!"

I rolled my eyes. "A friend who isn't between your sheets would be good for you. But, since you're here three hours early, I'm heading home."

James waved me off as he headed out of my office. "Later, boss."

It wasn't often that I got to go home on a late day in time to actually have dinner at a decent hour and get to sleep before midnight. I hightailed it out of the office before James could change his mind.

As soon as I pulled into the driveway, I knew something was off. A car I wasn't familiar with was parked behind Logan's truck in the driveway. Walking in the front door, I was even more confused. Curious' toys were strewn all over the place, the couch was moved, and a giant tote was in the middle of the living room. Had Logan had a playdate with a friend while I was at work? It wasn't like him to leave things out like this. He was scatterbrained but not usually messy. Actually, Logan lived by the motto, "A messy house leads to a messy mind." According to him, he didn't need to risk a messy mind.

Looking around again, I could see he'd tried to clean up some. I could smell that he'd had dinner, but as I put my gun away, I noticed that at least the kitchen had been cleaned up. Heading for the steps, I began to unbutton my shirt when I heard giggles upstairs. I felt a growl deep in my chest. It wasn't like I had a claim on him, but I hadn't slept with anyone else since we'd broken up. While I wasn't sure Logan hadn't slept with anyone else, I was certain he hadn't brought someone back here.

I turned the corner into my bathroom to find Logan and Aiden splashing in my tub. Logan knew he could always use it if he wanted to since my bathtub was a lot larger than the one in his room, but this turn of events was not what I'd expected.

Bubbles were practically spilling out of the tub, and Logan and Aiden were both blue as Smurfs, not from cold, but from... was that *paint?* What the hell were they doing? The laughter definitely wasn't sex, but they were too far gone in their play to notice me for the moment. Logan still had his hood and collar on, but Aiden was finger painting on his chest with what I was becoming more certain was blue paint. The same shade of blue coated Aiden's ears and the back of his shoulders and neck, and I suspected his front was just as blue.

Logan's eyes were creased with laughter and he looked like he was having the time of his life. Aiden's giggles as he traced Logan's pecs, occasionally allowing his fingers to flick over Logan's pierced nipples, were pure joy. Did Aiden have any idea how much that turned Logan on? Or was it simply something that drew his attention? I could understand both. I'd been drawn to those nipple rings so many times over the years. They were there, begging to be touched and played with, but there was basically a connection wired directly between the piercings and his dick.

Logan reached over to the side of the tub and picked up a yellow squeeze bottle, then poured more of the blue gloop into his hand. When he set the tube down, I looked at it more carefully. Colorful letters spelled out Bodywash Paint. It was quite clearly made for children, but the two men in my bathtub seemed to be having a blast with it.

Aiden giggled again at something Logan had done and the sound wrapped around me like a blanket. I was starting to see what Colt found cute about Derek's little side. Aiden was carefree in a way I'd never seen another adult be. I'd seen some of it on Sunday morning when he'd reacted to everything I'd done for him at breakfast. Having a boy with so much happiness and love to give could be addicting—I was seeing that now. Even I could enjoy the peals of laughter emanating from my bathtub for a little while.

I must have made a sound because Logan and Aiden both looked over at me. I could see the twinkle in Logan's eyes from beneath his hood, but as Aiden swung his body around, all that was visible beneath the blue paint on his face were two impossibly wide eyes staring at me in shock. Blue paint... everywhere. I couldn't see his cheeks. Even the dark scruff I remembered from the weekend was hidden beneath a layer of blue.

Now that they knew I was there, there was no reason to continue standing in the doorway like a statue. I took a few steps forward and could see the bath water had also turned blue. They would never get cleaned off sitting in that. I could already see a persistent ring of blue on the white porcelain soaking tub and was cringing inwardly.

"Do I even want to know?" I asked slowly, careful to not sound frustrated or upset.

Aiden looked back at Logan, who just started laughing. "Arts and crafts time."

I felt an eyebrow creep up my forehead. "Arts and crafts?"

Logan bobbed his head. "It's part of a well-structured day." He lifted his hand from the water and started ticking items off on his fingers. "Playtime, lunch time, story time, nap time, cartoons and playtime, dinner time, arts and crafts! But it was kinda needed. Aiden was covered in ketchup and cheese sauce after dinner." He pointed to the counter where a scrap of fabric I assumed was a bib was in fact covered in food. I fought a shiver but found myself thankful Logan had cleaned the kitchen as well as he had.

Instincts kicked in. It was exactly how I would have responded to Logan if I'd found him in this situation without Aiden. I lined the floor from the tub to the shower with dark-colored towels from my closet and turned back to the men in the tub. "Okay, both of you out of there and into the shower so you can actually get cleaned off."

Logan whimpered a protest but stood up. Blue dripped from him, and even trying not to, I winced. What sadistic bastard had come up with body paint and slapped the label bodywash on it? Fuck. My. Life. There was a chance I was mourning my once-pristine soaking tub. As he turned around to extend a hand to

Aiden, I got to see Logan's very round ass. All those squats he did definitely showed in his naked backside.

My jeans were nowhere loose enough to accommodate the effects of me staring at his ass. To distract myself, I turned to my walk-in shower, turned the water on, and adjusted the temperature.

When Aiden was out of the tub, I ventured a glance at his chest. Logan had been more purposeful in his coloring of Aiden's torso because he looked like a toddler had put war paint on his chest. I was pretty sure there was a puppy's head around his nipple, and that was definitely an arrow pointing directly at Aiden's dick. I forced myself to look away before I got caught staring at it. I was not going to look. After I'd spent nearly eight hours of what should have been an eleven-hour shift thinking about how perfect the two were for each other, I did not need to be getting aroused by Aiden's naked body. Had I mentioned fuck... my... life yet?

"Shower. Both of you." While I tried to save my tub. Even as the water drained in the tub, I could see my suspicions were correct. There was a ring of blue that stretched three-quarters of the way up the sides.

Aiden rolled his eyes, though mischief and playfulness showed through the action. "Yes, Daddy." The words had been so dryly delivered that even I couldn't mistake them for anything but playful, and he and Logan dissolved in a fresh round of giggles.

Speaking of this dissolving, it looked like the two were melting before my eyes as blue paint rolled off their bodies in sheets, running down their legs and soaking into the bath towels that lined the floor.

Sadist fuck.

"You're terrible. Both of you. In the shower."

Logan still had his puppy hood and collar on as he entered

my walk-in shower. Thankfully he'd fallen in love with the neoprene hoods and not the leather ones, but he was still going to need to take it off at some point so he could wash and dry his hair.

I knelt beside the tub, feeling my half-hard dick pinch slightly in the snug confines of my jeans, and hissed out my discomfort. At least that would keep me from getting any harder while I worked on scrubbing my tub. Aiden seemed to forget about me being there as he and Logan washed the remaining blue suds from their bodies. I looked over at one point to see the floor of my shower foamed up. *How much of that shit had they used?*

The only saving grace to the blue tub was that the soap did come off with minimal scrubbing, though it had taken enough effort that my back had gotten sweaty. Of course, that could have been because I was still wearing my polyester uniform shirt. I rolled my eyes at myself and stood up to remove my shirt and dump it into the basket to be cleaned. I turned around to find Aiden staring at my undershirt-clad torso. I became acutely aware of my slight love handles that were obvious beneath the formfitting shirt.

Logan elbowed Aiden playfully, and even from beneath the shower head I could hear his words. "He doesn't think he's sexy."

Aiden's mouth hung open for a brief second at Logan's words. I turned my back to make sure the tub was fully cleaned and heard his response. "How can he not think he's sexy?"

I fought the blush creeping up my face and focused too hard on my already clean tub. Did I leave? Did I stay? What the hell was the protocol for this situation? I couldn't be the only man who had walked in on his best friend and his friend taking a totally platonic bath together while painting each other, then spent the next ten minutes cleaning the tub while they showered.

Right?

Okay, I probably was. So that left it up to me to create protocol. In that moment, I decided the best plan was to play turtle, so I scooped up the towels, deposited them into the hamper, and headed to my room to get changed and then go find myself dinner.

Thirty minutes later, Logan came down the steps alone, looking confused. When he found me on the couch—the couch I'd pushed back to its rightful spot in the living room—he padded over and took a seat. "Why'd you run off?"

I looked over at the steps, expecting Aiden to come down at any second. "He's asleep," Logan answered the unasked question.

"What was I supposed to do? Stand there and watch you two shower?"

Logan huffed but slid closer, forcing my arm around his shoulders. "You could have gotten Aiden ready for bed."

"Ready for bed? Logan, why would I do that?"

"He needs someone like you in his life. All take charge and dominating. He'd be putty in your hands."

I kissed Logan's temple. I could appreciate what he was trying to do, but it wasn't going to work. "I'm not a Daddy." Even if I was, I couldn't pursue him because I cared too much about the man beside me.

"You're going to miss out on a great thing. You've got to take the chance. I'm not the one for you." His voice broke on the last sentence and I felt tears prick the backs of my eyes.

"You don't know I'm the one for him either. Pup, I've never had a little. I haven't had luck with any D/s relationship outside of a scene. Being a Daddy to a little is a big responsibility. I'm the sheriff of Cheatham County." I was going to ignore the part of my brain telling me that Colt had made it work with Derek and their lives were even more insane than Aiden's and mine.

"You'll make a great Daddy if you give yourself half a chance. You're a much better teddy bear than you are an ironfisted Dom, even if you don't see it yet."

I rubbed Logan's shoulder and changed the subject. "Let's watch Scooby. It sounds like you've had a busy day, and I bet you could use the time to relax."

Logan didn't protest. Instead, he adjusted himself so his head was on my lap and let me turn on the movie. Twenty minutes in, he was sound asleep on my lap with my hand still petting his head. There was no way I could do anything to mess *this* up. I didn't even know if *this* had a name, but I knew it was something.

CHAPTER 11

LOGAN

"Hey, Cur-Logan." Matt's voice caused me to jump far more than his nearly calling me Curious in public. I was sitting at a back table at Beans and Brew Thursday afternoon. I'd called him the day before and asked him to meet me for coffee. We still needed to work things out from the club, but my brain seemed to be stuck on how much fun I'd had with Aiden on Tuesday.

When my heart stopped racing I smiled up at Matt, who was standing awkwardly by my table. "Thanks for meeting me today. Take a seat." I tried to flash him a reassuring smile, but I suspected it looked a bit pinched. Once he was seated, I charged in, ready to say what had been eating at me since the incident at DASH. "I'm really sorry for Saturday night. I hadn't put it all together until Trent and I talked it out Sunday morning. When I was in the Marines, I, uh, had a guy tie my hands up and throw me in a pool. He was an asshole and thought it would be funny. I guess the SEALs do something like that in training too, and he thought it would be *fun*. Except I damn near drown. The only thing that saved me is that I can't sink for anything. My body popped up and I managed to flip myself onto my back, but without my hands to stabilize me, I was wearing out fast. An instructor and a group of new recruits came across me and got me out as I was starting to give up."

Matt's eyes widened in shock. "Jesus, you never said anything about it!"

I ducked my head and ran my hand nervously over my neck. "The guy got kicked out of the program, but those scars ran a bit deeper than I care to talk about. The first few times you did ropework with me it made me nervous but not uncomfortable, and nowhere near a panic attack like I had at the club. I thought I'd be fine. I hate feeling like a fear has gotten the best of me. So instead of talking about my fear, I ignored it. For that I can't apologize enough."

Matt blew out a breath. "I really wish you'd said something before Saturday night. I'd never have asked you."

"It isn't the first time I've had a panic attack while being restrained. I hadn't put two and two together until Trent pointed out that I freaked out a few years back during an apprehension demo at work when the instructor used me to demonstrate on. I seem to have a trigger around being restrained in a group setting."

Matt looked pained. "I'm sorry that happened to you. God, I feel terrible that it triggered you."

I winced. "Please don't beat yourself up. This is definitely on me. I didn't tell you some important pieces of information."

"I appreciate you sharing that with me. I know it couldn't have been easy. So thank you. Are you doing okay now?"

I nodded slowly. "Yeah, a lot better. I feel like a bit of an asshole, but yes."

Matt took the information in stride, and I was thankful that he didn't press any further. Instead, he changed the topic to the next mosh at the club. By the time we were done with our coffees, I felt like we'd both managed to move past Saturday night, and I felt better. I could only hope Matt felt better as well.

Matt stood up and offered a hand. "I'll see you at DASH soon."

I shook his hand and stood up as well. "Absolutely. See you soon."

As I threw away my trash, I decided to grab another coffee and got back into the line.

I'd been in line for about two minutes when the door opened. The chimes drew my attention up from my text with Trent, and I was surprised to see Caleb standing in the doorway. He'd been focused intently on his phone, and I found myself surprised to not see Dexter with him. Dexter had volunteered that they worked together, and from what Travis had mentioned, Dexter and Caleb were basically attached at the hip.

Caleb looked frazzled, then I heard him mumbling to his phone about Dexter being even more impossible when he was sick than healthy. That explained where Dexter was, or at least why he wasn't with Caleb. Would it be strange to try to duck out the door before Caleb saw me? But what if he saw me disappearing and thought I was avoiding him? Shit, where was Trent? Though it wasn't like I'd told Trent I'd run into Travis and Caleb at DASH. I might not have had much of a filter, but I knew not to talk about what I saw at DASH, so Trent really couldn't have helped me. And truthfully, having an overprotective Dom there wouldn't have helped much.

Shit.

Caleb jumped and his eyes flicked up to meet mine. Apparently, that thought hadn't been all in my head. *Think, Logan, think.* I didn't know what the right answer was, but I felt bad enough that the guy looked like he was about to run at the sight of me. Caleb's eyes were as big as half-dollars when he looked up at me. *Say something, Logan.* "Um, can I buy you lunch?"

Caleb took a step back and bumped into the specials sign. It swayed precariously and I reached back to stop it from falling, but that put me right in Caleb's space. "I, I... uh." He cleared his throat. "I'm supposed to be getting lunch for Dexter. He's sick today. I think it's just allergies, but maybe it's an actual cold. But I haven't seen him today, so I'm not entirely sure. I'd be able to tell one way or another if I saw him."

He was rambling nervously. I really hated that I made him that nervous just with my presence. "I'm sorry. I know I'm hard to handle, but I don't want you to be scared of me."

My words drew Caleb up short. "I'm not scared of you. Maybe just a bit intimidated?"

I winced. I didn't like that feeling any more than making him scared. Caleb softened. "I really do need to get Dex lunch, but he can wait a little bit. He's a pain in the ass anyway."

"I'll buy his lunch too, as an apology for making him wait."

Caleb smiled at that and I relaxed some. Neither of us knew what to say while we waited in line, but once we got to the same table I'd sat at with Matt, I at least felt like we were far enough away from people to talk openly. Much like always, I said the first thing that came into my head. "I won't tell anyone."

Caleb froze, a bite of salad halfway to his mouth. "Oh. Uh. I."

"I haven't even told Trent. I may be loud, but I know how to keep my mouth shut."

That time, Caleb winced. "I never thought you would tell anyone," he told the table more than me. "No one ever has anything bad to say about you. Even when you were so drunk I don't know how you were standing up, you were still nice. Stubborn as a mule, but polite. You're just loud, and I'm not."

"I know I messed up that night, and I am really sorry. I was going through a lot of shit." That was an understatement that I wasn't even willing to sort through all these months later.

Caleb gave me a weak smile. "You don't need to apologize. I'm best friends with Dexter. Believe me, I've seen and heard things from that man that would probably make even you blush."

I chuckled. "That would probably be hard, but I'm glad I'm not as scary as I could be."

Caleb ate three more bites of his salad before he spoke again. "So you're a puppy?" Then his eyes widened again. I was starting to think that everything spooked him. "Shit. I shouldn't have just blurted that out. Daddy would tell me that it isn't my business to ask, especially after you've assured me you won't tell anyone about me." Then he groaned. "And I just called Travis Daddy. Holy hell." His head hit the table.

"Whoa. Caleb, it's okay. First, I think I figured out that Travis was your Daddy as soon as you two walked into the room. And it's okay to ask about my pup side. By the way, his name is Curious."

"He was cute." Caleb turned red and groaned. He must have been experiencing a brain-to-mouth filter malfunction for the first time. Thankfully, he was talking to the king of brain-to-mouth filter malfunctions and I wasn't easily embarrassed. Though I thought it was sweet that Caleb thought I was cute as Curious.

"Thank you. What can I say? It just comes naturally."

"And you're full of yourself."

Ah-ha, there was a little bit of a bite to Caleb. I loved it. "Honestly, I think Curious is adorable. He's the cute side of me that doesn't have to worry about saying something wrong because I don't talk when I'm in my headspace. And it's a lot easier for a pup to be hyper and adorable than a thirty-six-year-old sheriff's deputy."

Caleb nodded as he took in what I said. "That makes sense in a weird way."

"When I go to DASH with Aiden—the guy I was with—I'm

actually not hyper at all. He doesn't have a Daddy to take care of him, and I don't like him to be alone there."

"Is that why you don't mind being a member at DASH?" Caleb asked.

I didn't understand the question. Why would I care if I was a member at DASH? "Huh?"

Caleb flushed but plowed ahead with his question. "Dom And Sub Haven is a *gay* BDSM club. You're not gay."

My eyes widened. How had I overlooked that fact? "I'm not straight either. I'm definitely bisexual."

His eyes widened slightly, but he schooled his features quickly, then nodded slowly. "So, are you and Aiden together then?"

I appreciated how easygoing Caleb was about the admission. "Nope. Aiden's a little." I didn't feel bad saying that because Caleb would have had to be blind to not already know that. "And I'm a pup. A very hyper pup who's not submissive or dominant." I held up my hand when Caleb's brow turned down in confusion. "It's a headspace, not a domination-submission thing for me. It's complicated. But I'm not a Dom and I'm not a sub. Which is why we're friends but not boyfriends."

"Oh. Interesting. It's cool that you're such good friends."

I smiled, thinking about Aiden. "If we could make a relationship work, I absolutely would. He deserves to be happy. Unfortunately, I'm not someone who can make him happy."

Caleb nodded in understanding. "That's hard. Dex and I were the same way until I met Travis. I'd spent a lot of nights thinking about how much easier it would be if I could just be attracted to Dex. The one time we tried to kiss in college was enough for us to know it would never work. That and I'd probably kill Dexter."

I liked hearing Caleb open up some. His shoulders had come down from his ears and he was smiling brightly as he spoke. I'd talked things through with Matt and managed to mend fences with Caleb all over the course of a lunch break. He'd almost finished his lunch when the radio on my hip pinged with a call. "Well, I better get going. I should have known that my extended lunch wouldn't last forever."

Caleb forced himself to swallow. "Have a good one, Logan. Maybe... maybe you and Aiden would like to come to dinner with Larson and Dexter and I sometime?"

I blinked in confusion. We all met up every other week for dinner at Steve's Tavern. Caleb read the confusion on my face and smiled. "Um, Larson and I get dinner together every few weeks. We... we *get* each other. Maybe you'd have fun joining us? I bet your friend—Aiden—would like it too. As long as he doesn't mind the two of us being kind of shy at first."

I thought about what he'd said for a few moments. Was he insinuating that Larson was submissive? Larson was at least six foot six of quiet, muscled bear and a lieutenant with the Nashville Fire Department. Well, at the very least maybe another meal or two with Caleb would break the layer of ice that had formed on our relationship months earlier. "I'd like that. I need to get going but go ahead and text me details. I'll pass them on to Aiden."

Caleb smiled. "Have a nice day, Logan. And thanks again for lunch."

"Anytime." I grabbed my hat off the booth and hurried out the door to my SUV.

CHAPTER 12

TRENT

I'D BEEN LOOKING at the damn budget proposal from the mayor's office for the last four hours, trying to make heads or tails of it. I probably would have been able to had it not been for the constant distractions rolling my way. It started when my phone rang twenty minutes in.

"Sheriff Sylvan," I growled into my cell phone, not taking my eyes off the report on my computer screen.

"Bad time?" The voice on the other end of the line had me confused for a brief moment, and I pulled the phone from my ear and looked at the screen. *Dean.*

"Hey, man. Sorry, I was looking at a budget proposal."

Dean's laughter filled my ear. "Seriously? I've seen your budgeting spreadsheet. You have no business looking at a budget proposal for the department."

"Fuck you."

Dean laughed harder. "Seriously, Trent, you need someone else to look that over. You'll miss something. Remember I'm the one who balances your accounts. It's a damn good thing you let me pay most of your bills or you'd bounce checks."

I rubbed the bridge of my nose. "You're the numbers guy. All I ever wanted to do was catch the bad guys. This shit is stupid."

I hated this shit. Dean had taken over paying everything for me shortly after we'd graduated college. I'd shown up at his apartment one night with circles under my eyes and my checking account so fucked up I couldn't figure out which end was up. He'd sighed, huffed, and grumbled, but within three hours had my account figured out. I had paid my rent twice, written a check to the gas company for my water bill, and sent my water bill to the gas company. At least I'd sent my electric payment to the right place. From that night on, he banned me from ever touching the bills again. I put all my expenses on a credit card that he then paid every month.

I wouldn't have trusted just anyone with that information, but Dean was a math whiz, an accountant, and he dabbled in the stock market. He'd set Travis, Larson, Merrick, and me up with portfolios in college. Thanks to his money sense, we all had a nice nest egg to start our adult lives with. He'd even set up an account for Logan when he'd retired from the Marines. I was the only one who had turned over all my bills to him and gladly paid him every month to handle them for me, though.

"I'll keep it quick. I think I want to move some of your stocks around, sell a few and buy a few that I think are going to go up soon."

My eyes glassed over at that point and I interrupted him. "Man, just do your thing. I trust you."

I could hear a smile in Dean's voice. "That's what I thought you'd say. Anyway, good luck with your budget. Ask Logan if you need help. He's actually pretty good with deciphering those things, believe it or not."

I growled. I knew Logan was good with it, and he did help me frequently, but he'd been in a mood all day. Not a bad one, he just hadn't been able to focus on anything for more than thirty seconds at a time. I heard a crash at the other end of the hall. I instinctively knew it was Logan and called out the doorway to see if everyone was okay. All I got were good natured moans and a few laughs. I sighed. It had been a long fucking day already. "Thanks, Dean. I gotta go."

And I had no idea where I'd left off or what I'd read. *Fuck.* I started over again. An hour passed with only a few outbursts from the office, and usually it was Logan who cursed as he tripped over something.

When Merrick's head popped around the doorframe at eleven thirty, I almost jumped out of my skin. "What the hell are you doing here?"

He sank into the seat across from my desk like he owned it and propped an ankle over his knee. "Can I help with anything?"

"Budgets. I fucking hate budgets."

Merrick opened his mouth to say something when a football flew down the hallway followed by a crash, and Logan's deep voice yelling an apology to Tammy. I picked my hat off the desk and used it to cover my face. "I may kill him today."

Merrick's rich voice was full of amusement as he spoke. "He was practically vibrating when I walked in here. What did you feed him this morning?"

"I made him an egg-and-cheese bagel and he had a cup of coffee. Some days, he's just like this. Thank fuck they are few and far between now."

"Logan! Go play basketball or something. Jesus." That was definitely James' voice. I didn't even know when James had gotten there.

"Can I help you figure this thing out?"

I threw my hands in the air. Merrick was a restaurant consultant who worked all over the country. He was rarely in Tennessee anymore, and under normal circumstances I'd be curious as to what he was doing here. As it stood, I was happy to have the help. "Do your thing!"

Merrick cracked his knuckles and motioned for me to hand him the laptop. I gladly passed it across the desk. "I'm going to go get a coffee and some Advil. I'll be back in a few."

Merrick pulled a pair of wire-rimmed glasses from his suit coat and waved me off. I didn't know what I'd do without my friends. The relief lasted until I saw a football sticking out of an overturned trash can with papers and debris strewn across the floor. "Logan!" I bellowed and watched a few of my officers sink into cubicles.

Logan's head popped out of James' office with a faux-sheepish grin on his face. The man was trying to look innocent as could be, but he was failing miserably. "Yes?" he questioned, batting his eyes.

"I swear, Logan Caldwell, I will lock you in the holding cell if you don't get that shit cleaned up."

Logan bounded out of the office he was hiding in and made a show of cleaning up.

I looked around the room. "Next football that flies through this office, you will all be on walking parking duty for the next week!" It was getting cool out and no one wanted to be outside more than necessary. Hell, I didn't even know if we had that jurisdiction, but I was willing to find a loophole if they pushed my buttons enough.

Tammy gave me a sympathetic look and handed over a bottle of Advil from her desk drawer as I made my way to the front of the station. "Sorry, Sheriff. Logan's got more energy than the Energizer Bunny today and I think he's rubbed off on the rest of them." I grumbled as I swallowed a handful of pills without water. "Drink, Sheriff. You're going to give yourself an aneurysm if you keep this up."

Merrick took that moment to call from my office. "For as

serious as this man is at work, would you believe he's about as mature as a thirteen-year-old boy when we go out?"

I pinched the bridge of my nose. "Fuck my life. Tammy, I need new friends."

Tammy patted my arm. "Sheriff, I think they are exactly what you need... even Deputy Caldwell."

I grumbled, took the water Tammy held out to me, then stalked back to my office. In the ten minutes I'd been gone, Merrick had made more progress on the budget than I had in hours and had begun making color-coded notes in another sheet.

I sank into my chair and started to aggressively sort through files on my desk. I'd nearly broken the pencil I was holding in half numerous times before the Advil started kicking in and the tension in my body eased. By the time Merrick shut my laptop an hour later, I was feeling guilty about the way I'd snapped at the guys, though I suspected Logan had deserved the frustration.

"Okay. It's not as bad as it could be. I highlighted places where I think you need to look harder, and they didn't give you enough in the budget to hire any additional officers. You're going to have to bring that up with the powers that be. It's not terrible, it's not great. You've seen worse. Seriously, Trent, instead of nearly stroking out, call me. Christ, I do this for you every year."

"Is that why you're here today?" It hadn't occurred to me until that moment that it was strange for Merrick to show up at the station in the middle of an afternoon during a normal workweek.

"Dean called me. Gave me a heads-up. Said you sounded like you were about one budget line from a coronary."

"I should be pissed that you all gossip like a bunch of hens, but right now I really just want to kiss you."

Merrick smiled and stood up. "Well, my work here is done.

See you guys on Thursday. Also, go get some fresh air. You're wound tighter than a ten-day clock. I think this place will survive without you for a little bit. Hell, maybe take Logan and go on a run. I think the man could use some fresh air as much as you could."

That didn't sound like a half-bad idea. I had some of Logan's toys in the cab of the truck. It might have been weird, but tossing a ball for Logan was centering for me, and it let him run out some energy. "I think you're right."

Merrick headed for the door. "I know I am."

I heard him bid goodbye to Tammy on the way out the door, and I turned the opposite way out of my office to go find Logan. It wasn't hard to find him. He was finalizing the schedule for the next week while bouncing on the ridiculous dinosaur "chair" he'd bought online a year earlier. It was a cross between a bouncy toy and a balance ball chair, but Logan swore it was better than any desk chair he'd ever had. I was pretty sure it was because it shocked the hell out of people who walked into his office.

"Come on, let's go get some fresh air. We've been inside too long."

Logan looked up at me and grinned. "I played basketball earlier. And James and I threw a baseball back and forth for a while. Tammy wouldn't let me have my football back, though."

"Probably for the best."

Logan bounded to my side not even five seconds later. "Where are we going?"

"I figured we'd head to the park." If Logan had his tail in it would have been wagging.

CHAPTER 13

AIDEN

Fall was finally touching Nashville, meaning I'd been able to turn the air-conditioning off in my house two days earlier and the evenings and early mornings were cool enough for a heavy shirt or light coat. All the kids were finally back in school, and the moms and dads who normally filled the parks walking or taking their younger kids to the park seemed to be at Parent and Me classes or whatever it was that parents did with toddlers. I didn't really know, but I'd heard clients talk about them before, and each fall about this time the parks cleared out during school hours.

All in all it was a perfect day to go to the park to take some pictures. I grabbed a long-sleeved shirt in case the wind picked up, grabbed my camera, and headed toward the car. If I wanted an unpopulated park, even in fall, I couldn't go toward Nashville; I had to go away from it. There was a cute park with some soccer fields and great trees a fifteen-minute drive south of my house that I'd always enjoyed taking pictures at, and it had a great playground with swings. If it was empty, I usually spent a few minutes on the swings before I headed home.

I spent over an hour at the park walking the trails and snapping pictures of leaves and trees and even a few animals that had been brave enough to stay around when they saw me. When I made it to the end of the trail I was on, I had yet to see another person at the park and decided to swing for a few minutes before heading home. I was already cutting through the soccer fields when I caught sight of two men walking toward the center of the field.

One was wearing a ball cap and a baggy gray sweatshirt and the other had on a cowboy hat and a bulky long-sleeved shirt. The one with the cowboy hat had his hand resting at the small of the other guy's back. The one in the ball cap leaned against the other one and love radiated from their body language. I started snapping pictures of them without much thought. Then I felt creepy taking pictures of the men without their knowledge, but thought I'd approach them and ask them if they'd like copies. If not, I'd delete them and move on. It wouldn't be the first time I'd done something similar and it probably wouldn't be the last.

The man in the cowboy hat leaned over and pressed his lips to the side of the other one's head, then dropped his hand. As he stepped back, I saw him reach into a bag I hadn't noticed in his hand before and pull something out. A few seconds later, he cocked his arm back and threw the item. From across the field, I could see a red ball go flying through the air, then the guy in the ball cap took off after it. He reminded me of Logan chasing after the ball in the living room the week earlier, just on two feet instead of four.

Ball Cap ran back toward Cowboy and tackled him in a hug. In the blink of an eye, they were rolling around on the ground. I could hear the laughter and barbs from across the field. "Ouch, my dick." One guy groaned—I assumed Ball Cap since he was on the ground with Cowboy on top of him. Cowboy was laughing uproariously, but his face was hidden by his hat.

Ball Cap reached up, and his hand disappeared beneath Cowboy's shirt. As I took the next picture, Cowboy yelped and grabbed at the right side of his chest. "Ouch. That hurt!"

Ball Cap cackled. "Serves you right!"

They rolled around on the ground for a while more, Ball Cap ending up on top once, then rolling over as Cowboy pinned him, both of them still laughing. Even I was laughing while taking the pictures. I knew these would be great; I didn't have to see them to know that. The shadows over each of their faces didn't matter —their body language spoke volumes.

Eventually, they both got up and Cowboy picked up the ball and chucked it as far away as he could. Ball Cap took off after it, long, powerful legs eating up distance quickly. When he caught up to the ball and turned around, I snapped a picture of his bright smile as he tossed it back. I'd been so focused on capturing the moment that I'd taken four pictures before I looked at the guy's entire face.

Logan.

My finger stopped snapping, but I kept the lens focused on him. He was gorgeous, and each time his eyes flicked to whom I could only assume was Trent, love radiated off him. These two were idiots if they ever thought they'd be happy without one another.

I must have gotten lost in my thoughts because I jumped when the ball came flying toward my camera. The long lens made the ball look like it was going to hit me in the face and I squeaked in surprise, especially since Logan came barreling into the frame a half second later. I was lens-to-sweatshirt when the figure stopped moving. I dropped the camera from my face to find Logan looking at me, his head cocked to the side in curiosity. Between the hat, gloves, and the camera that had been covering my face, it took Logan a moment to recognize me. I knew the moment it clicked into place because Logan's blue eyes lit up. "Aiden!" He turned to the guy in the cowboy hat and motioned him over to us. "Trent! It's Aiden!"

The guy I'd been photographing slipped away before my eyes as he started to walk toward us looking more like a cowboy than a sheriff. Laughter and playfulness had been replaced by a seriousness and intensity that made my insides turn to Jell-O. As he got closer, I saw a smile begin to play on his face. "What are you doing here?"

I dug the toe of my Converse into the grass, inexplicably uncomfortable. "Taking pictures."

"Just happened to be taking pictures in Kingston Springs?" Trent questioned.

I looked around, for the first time thinking about where the park was. Mentally pulling up a map, I saw the sheriff's station only a few blocks from where we stood and felt my cheeks flush. "I've always loved this park. It's quiet and the trails are great."

Logan looked over at the playground. "And it's got a cool playground." He winked at me, as if he knew exactly where I'd been heading when I got sidetracked.

Trent glanced from the playground to me, then the playground again, and smiled. "Is that where you were heading to?"

I tried to seem casual as I shrugged but I could tell neither man believed me. "I don't know."

Logan bent down and grabbed the ball that had rolled about five feet from me and held the ball out. "Play?" The sincerity in his voice had me beginning to nod my head before Trent spoke up.

"That's really sweet of you, pup, but I think Aiden wanted to play on the playground."

"Just swing." The words were out without input from my brain and I mentally kicked myself.

Logan reached out and took my hand that wasn't holding my camera. "Come on. We're not ready to leave yet." Then he got a puzzled look on his face and glanced over at Trent. "We're not leaving yet, are we?"

Trent shook his head. "We just got here, pup. And you're driving everyone at the office nuts. You need to run some more energy off."

Now that he mentioned it, Logan was basically vibrating. "What did you have to eat today?"

Logan thought for a moment. "Normal stuff. I think it must be a full moon or something. I just have a lot of energy today."

I looked over at Trent, who shrugged a shoulder. "I mean, this happens from time to time with him."

"Great. Come on." Logan pulled me ahead and directly toward the swings at the far side of the playground. Trent walked behind us, and when I glanced his way, he was shaking his head in amusement.

We made it to the swings and Logan began pushing me toward one. "Wait, my camera."

"I'll keep it safe," Trent assured me as he took it from my hands and set it on the picnic table that sat near the swings. He sat back, tossing the ball Logan had discarded in the mulch.

"What do you think you're doing?" Logan questioned as he climbed onto the swing next to mine.

Trent blinked over in confusion. "I'm relaxing. I'm here to let you burn off energy. *I* wouldn't have a problem curling up on this bench and sleeping."

Logan shook his head. "You have to push us."

Trent blinked. "Logan, I've known you since we were fifteen. You know damn well how to push yourself on a swing."

I pushed off, letting the two argue, quite happy to be able to swing. It was peaceful, always had been. Moving without touching the ground allowed my mind to drift and calmness to settle over me. I zoned Logan and Trent's bickering out and had even managed to ignore how damn sexy Trent was just tossing the ball up in the air. If I focused on his arms moving beneath his shirt, I'd have never been able to relax.

Logan's voice brought me out of wherever I'd zoned out to. "You're supposed to push him. That's what Daddies do." My feet had been tucked under me as I'd come down in my swing and the words surprised me so much I toppled forward and landed straight in Trent's arms. When had he gotten there?

"Jesus, Logan, are you trying to kill him?" Trent growled with me sitting on his lap where we'd landed on the ground.

Logan was still swinging and laughing hysterically at our predicament. "Well, at least you caught him. You're halfway there."

"Logan," Trent warned, clearly frustrated with him. His voice softened when he turned back to me. "Okay, boy, up ya get. You know what they say. When you fall off, you got to get right back in the saddle again."

"Well, Daddy knows best." The word slipped out effortlessly and I couldn't help but chuckle to myself.

Trent's answering laugh told me I hadn't overstepped. "Exactly, baby boy. Just remember that." There was just enough humor laced in his words that I knew he was playing along with Logan's insane pushiness.

Trent gave me another push, and I was on my feet and heading toward the swing. When I climbed on, Trent stood behind me. "I'll push you this time, just so Logan doesn't say anything ridiculous again to make you fall and get hurt."

And Trent did push me. It felt different than doing it myself. I couldn't remember the last time someone had pushed me on the swings, but it was nice. I felt safe and my little side was dancing dangerously close to the surface for being in public.

Of course, Logan tired of the swings before long, getting to the apex of his swing and launching himself halfway across the playground. "Logan Caldwell! You are not a bird!" Trent scolded as he landed and rolled a few times.

"I'm good!" He bounced up on his feet and held his arms out in a ta-da motion and I couldn't help the giggle that came from me.

"Oh, you think that's funny?" Trent questioned, squeezing my sides lightly when I came back down to his arms. Uncontrollable laughter spilled from me, but Logan was already after the ball in Trent's pocket.

"Please?" Logan could pout better than I could and part of me felt like it wasn't fair.

I figured that was the end of him pushing me, but the ball flew across the park and the next time the swing came down, Trent was there to push me upward again. I had no idea how long Trent repeated the same actions, pushing me until Logan got back with the ball only to throw the ball again. He had to have been exhausted by the time Logan came back, finally out of breath. "Done," he panted, sounding far more like an actual dog than he probably realized.

Trent sighed in relief. "Thank fuck. My arm is about to fall off. What about you, baby? You about done swinging? The wind is picking up and your nose is red." I liked the way he called me baby. Sure, it was playful, but it was fun and I felt like I'd made a new friend. It was nice to feel included with Logan and Trent.

For the first time I noticed that my nose was, in fact, cold and my cheeks felt windburned from swinging so long. When had the nice fall day turned cloudy and cool? While I didn't want to stop, I couldn't deny that I should. "Yeah. I am getting cold, Daddy." If he could tease me, I could tease him as well. Logan seemed ridiculously happy with himself, but I ended up rolling my eyes at him. He was either oblivious or refusing to acknowledge that the two of us were only teasing.

Trent slowed the swing gently and I hopped off, heading to pick up my camera from the picnic table.

"Can we stop at the coffee shop on the way back to the office? I want hot chocolate." I worried that Trent was going to throttle Logan when he asked the question.

"No, no chocolate. Jesus, we just spent forty-five minutes running your ass out. You can get a hot tea—no sugar!" he added quickly before Logan could even open his mouth.

Logan scrunched up his face. "You're mean."

"I live with you, I'm working the same fucking shift as you today, and I can't get away from your ass if you have too much sugar or caffeine."

They were funny.

"Come on, we'll get Aiden something before he has to leave, though. He looks about frozen."

What could I say? I didn't have as much muscle as either of them did. I was downright scrawny compared to them.

Logan rolled his eyes as we started to walk. "I bet you'll get *him* hot chocolate."

"I don't live with Aiden. I also don't see him bouncing off the walls like you've been *all day long*."

Logan huffed as we walked into the coffee shop and up to the counter. Trent didn't even give us a chance to look at the menu. "Baby, do you like hot chocolate?"

If he was going to keep up the teasing, I had no problem keeping it up too. "Yes, Daddy."

Logan giggled like a child and Trent and I both rolled our eyes. Thankfully, the line in front of us cleared and it was our turn. "Afternoon, Sheriff." The lady behind the counter greeted him. "What can I get for you today?"

Trent pointed to Logan. "Hot tea with honey and milk. A coffee, splash of cream," he pointed to himself. "And a hot chocolate for this one," he pointed over to me.

She tapped a few buttons on the computer screen. "Whipped cream?"

Trent nodded and Logan narrowed his eyes. "Dammit, A, you have him wrapped around your little finger. I *never* get whipped cream when I come here with him."

I snorted a laugh and Trent shot us a look that told us to behave. It did the trick for me, but I had a feeling it would take more than an icy stare to get Logan to behave. Somehow, I'd gotten stuck with this crazy duo and I didn't see myself getting away from them easily.

CHAPTER 14

LOGAN

I WAS one eye roll away from putting Trent in a sleeper hold. He'd been weird since Monday when Aiden had left us after the coffee shop. The damned budget had been completed, I didn't throw a football into anything, and I'd even had a breakthrough on a cold case that led to an arrest. Seriously, the man should have been on top of the world, but he was an insufferable ass.

My money was on his head and heart being torn about Aiden. I saw the way he looked at Aiden. I'd also heard him on the phone the night before. I'd been going to sleep when Trent came home talking to someone. It probably wasn't okay to eavesdrop, but it wasn't like I'd been trying to.

"It was a nice morning but nothing more. I am not looking for a boyfriend."

What? Yes, you are!

"No, seriously. I don't need someone in my life in that way. He was sweet and he loved the pancakes. He and Logan have even played here a few times, but I'm not looking to date."

Liar, liar, liar! He really was delusional.

"Fuck, Colt, you're as bad as Logan. He keeps trying to push me toward him too. But I'd never be a good Daddy."

There was a pause while Colt spoke.

"No, Colt. I'm serious. I don't want a little. I'd be a shit Daddy. I work too much. Even if I *was* interested in him, I couldn't do that to Logan. The man cares about him way too much."

What?

"Besides, there's no way I could keep up that level of attentiveness you have."

Colt was a Daddy? My mouth flapped open. I definitely shouldn't be hearing this conversation. But what was I going to do, knock on the wall and tell Trent I could hear them? *Fuck.*

"He's a cute guy, yes. He's started playfully calling me Daddy. It's cute, but there's nothing more than play to it."

And you call him baby, asshole. Goddammit, the man was oblivious! I was just going to have to try harder. Trent was compassionate and caring and had a controlling streak that Aiden would love.

"No. A little is not going to want me to micromanage everything. I'd run him off so damn fast my head would spin."

I had *not* done a good enough job proving to Trent that he was exactly what Aiden needed. Or maybe Aiden just put off too much of a sweet, innocent sub vibe for Trent to pick up on easily. No matter what, I needed to rectify this problem. The question was, how?

"Logan doesn't seem to realize it, but they are perfect for one another. He told me that Logan is his protector. How sweet is that? Logan's got a heart of gold. I could never do anything to jeopardize his happiness. He just needs to see that they're perfect together."

First, *wrong.* I wasn't a Dom, and Aiden needed a Dom. But second, well, second, Trent sounded gutted to say those words. I could hear the pain in his voice even through a wall. We'd already accepted we couldn't make each other happy, so as much as it sucked, I'd have to find some inner matchmaker with my two best friends. I needed them to see, without a doubt, that they were meant for one another.

That was where the idea came to invite Aiden to dinner at Steve's Tavern the next night. Our core group met up every other Thursday for dinner at Steve's. It was a bar owned by Travis's dad. Trent had met Travis, Dean, Merrick, and Larson in college. Dean was the uber-genius who started college at sixteen and had somehow managed to help the various guys pass classes along the way. Trent had met him in a required business accounting class and—surprise—Trent had been failing miserably. Dean had somehow managed to pull his grade up to passing, though only by the skin of his teeth by the way it was told. There was a reason no one let Trent near a checking account.

When I retired from the Marines, the group accepted me with open arms. Travis eventually met Caleb, who introduced us to his best friend, Dexter, and one of Travis's coworkers had started to join us with his boyfriend from time to time. The group was growing, so adding someone else wouldn't seem weird.

Besides, it would give Aiden a chance to meet Caleb outside of DASH and give Trent more time to spend with him and see that they were perfect for one another. It was a win-win situation for everyone. Okay, maybe it was a win-win for Aiden and Trent, but eventually it would be a win for me, once I got over the sour pit in my stomach from pushing Trent toward happiness that wasn't with me.

And that was how I ended up in the garage at six Thursday morning running myself damn near to death on the treadmill and trying to avoid Trent. The knot that had formed in the pit of my stomach had kept me up most of the night and had grown to something between guilt and grief. I lost the tank top I'd been wearing at mile five. By mile ten sweat was pouring into my eyes, my loose gray sweatpants were stuck to my legs, and my lungs felt like they were going to explode out of my chest, but that fucking ball in my stomach was still there. I slowed my pace down to a jog for a few minutes before finally killing the machine and heading over to the weights. I couldn't let Trent see me before I got my emotions under control. He'd take one look at me and know something was wrong.

The more time I spent with Aiden, the more I knew in my gut that they'd be perfect for one another. The more I realized that, the more I had to face the fact that I was going to lose Trent sooner rather than later. Until that month, this was an inevitability I'd understood would happen but had been able to ignore. Since the first time Trent saw Aiden's diaper bag and I saw the hard lines of his body soften, I knew he'd found the one who could give him what I couldn't.

I pushed the free weights harder than I should have. My arms would be dead for the next two days, which would only serve to piss me off more because I wouldn't be able to work out. On the bright side, the pain in my muscles had pushed the pain in my stomach away, and between the aches and the sweat dripping from every surface of my body, I was pretty sure Trent wouldn't want to look at me long enough to see that something was up.

Turned out, my worry was for naught when I got inside to find I'd killed so much time in the garage, Trent was already at work. I took my time showering, then eating a late breakfast before finally texting Aiden. I had to find a way to get him to Steve's Tavern tonight.

I spent ten minutes figuring out how to accomplish my goal, then decided it was best to simply invite him over and hope he hung out long enough that it was time to go to Steve's.

[Me] Want to come over?

The response was almost immediate.

[Aiden] I'm bored to death. Yes! Wait, come over for what?

The sentence probably wouldn't have made much sense to most people, but I understood what he'd meant.

[Me] If you want little time, you're welcome to be little today. Or we could just hang out.

Aiden took a minute to answer.

[Aiden] Would it be okay if we just hung out? I'm not feeling all that little today.

I sighed in relief. Curious didn't feel anywhere near the surface with all the crazy thoughts swirling around in my head. The fact that every muscle in my arms and legs ached didn't help matters.

[Me] Perfectly fine.

[Aiden] I'll be there in about twenty-five minutes. Want me to bring lunch?

[Me] I'll make you something, don't worry about it.

By the time Aiden got to the house, I'd put together a filling lunch for him and a smaller one for me since I'd eaten not long before. I hadn't gone full little lunch for Aiden, but I'd still cut the crust off a cold-cut sandwich, and made sure his popcorn, carrots, and cheese cubes didn't touch. I'd also cut up an apple and set it to the side of a brighter-colored plate I'd found in the cabinet. Judging by his smile, I figured I'd gotten the presentation right. Little Aiden was never far from the surface, even when he wasn't little.

Once I had lunch cleaned up and the dishes put in the dishwasher, I grabbed two beers out of the fridge and passed one over to Aiden. "So, what should we watch?" I asked as I eased myself onto the couch, my breath catching as my thighs struggled to support me on the way down.

"What the hell did you do to yourself?" Aiden questioned,

tucking his knees under his body but still closer to me than was strictly friendly.

"Pushed it too hard working out this morning."

Aiden shook his head but took my sore, slow-moving muscles as an opportunity to lean over and snatch the remotes off the coffee table before I could. "Victory is mine!"

I groaned, but there was no malice behind it. "What are you going to torture us with?"

Aiden tucked his knees under him and curled up into my side, his beer resting on the side of his knee. "*The Knight Before Christmas*. I've been dying to see it."

"Like the poem?"

Aiden laughed, not the giggle he had when he was little but an adult laugh that stirred things deep in my belly. I tried to remind myself that I needed to keep this platonic because the end goal was to get him and Trent together. My thoughts threatened to sour the light mood we'd had between us, but the next words out of his mouth made me forget all about the bitterness in my stomach. "No, puppy! The Christmas movie on Netflix. With Vanessa Hudgens."

My mouth flapped open a few times. "We're watching a romantic comedy?"

Aiden's smile widened. "Yup! And you can't do anything about it."

I would let him think that I had a problem with it. Romantic comedies were my weakness and I'd been trying to find the right mindset to sit down to watch this one for weeks now. I just hadn't been able to sit still long enough. So I huffed like I was annoyed while trying to hide my smile behind my beer bottle.

We settled into the movie, and aside from a few breaks I had to take to move, despite my sore muscles protesting heavily, we managed to finish it in under two hours. Aiden had watched me in amusement as I'd paced and bounced when I could no longer sit still, but he never got frustrated. This was why I didn't go to the theaters to watch movies. The thought of sitting still for hours on end was enough to make my skin crawl. Trent had made the mistake of taking me to the movies once and I'd wiggled like there were ants crawling on me. I'd felt bad that I'd been such a distraction throughout the movie, but even at sixteen, Trent had simply shrugged and told me we would watch movies at home from then on.

I'd never met a person other than Trent who would simply pause the movie and wait for me to be done moving before starting it again. Everyone else just kept watching the movie and ignored my bouncing. Aiden never complained, never rolled his eyes, and didn't sigh in frustration when I started to wiggle. At one point, I hadn't even realized I was wiggling until he paused the movie and pushed at my upper arm. "Go walk around. It's like sitting on a vibrating couch." He was smiling as he said it and had used the time to get up to grab another beer for himself like it was completely normal that we had to take a break not even halfway through.

The movie ended and Aiden looked at me with big eyes. "Want to watch something else? Or we could go outside and throw a ball around for a bit?"

I moaned because the idea of throwing a ball hurt. "Normally I'd love to throw a ball back and forth, but there's absolutely no way I can do that right now."

Aiden looked at me thoughtfully, then started pulling pillows off the back of the couch and throwing them on the ground between the couch and coffee table. "On your stomach," he demanded, pointing at the pile.

"Only Trent can get away with demanding me on my stomach." *Dammit, I had not meant to say that.*

Aiden threw his head back laughing. "Get your ass on the pillows. Well, not your ass. I want your ass up."

My cock twitched. I doubted he had any idea what he was doing to me, but it got me to get on the pillows before my dick made itself known. I needed Aiden and Trent to see they needed each other. If he was still thinking about my dick in his hand or my hand on his dick, that would muddy the waters.

"Good puppy." Then Aiden straddled my ass, a knee on either side of me, and his hands began kneading sore muscles in my arms and shoulders.

"Holy shit, Aiden, where'd you learn this?"

"I have a few friends who are massage therapists. They've taught me a thing or two over the years. Being a photographer doesn't sound all that stressful, but holding up a camera and squatting into weird positions for the perfect shot can play hell on muscles. My shoulders hold tension like you wouldn't believe after a long shoot."

Actually, I could believe it. I'd taken crime scene photos one time to help one of our techs out and my shoulders ached for two days after holding the stupid camera for six hours. It wasn't that the camera was heavy or even awkward, it was just holding my body in that position for so long killed my muscles. I would not make a good photographer.

Aiden dug his thumb into my shoulder and I moaned loudly, my back arching automatically. My ass ground against his cock, reminding me instantly what a bad idea it was for him to be straddling me. "Fuck." His dick was hard in his jeans and I could feel it through the thin sweatpants I was wearing. Then my cock rubbed against the pillows as I came back down. My dick began filling rapidly, instinct taking over for logic.

Aiden's voice was filled with mischief when he spoke. "I had no idea you could be such a demanding bottom. You always seem so in control."

He didn't know how amazingly well Trent could work my ass. And with Aiden straddling me, demanding my ass up, he had no idea how much he sounded like Trent at the moment. I enjoyed sex any way I could get it, but for Trent, I was almost exclusively a very needy and usually bossy bottom.

Aiden slid down so his ass was straddling my thighs and his hands moved to the globes of my ass. When he squeezed down, I let out a breathy gasp. I had no idea if it was from the pain of my sore muscles being kneaded or from the possession my brain put into the touch. I had a feeling I was reading too much into every one of his movements, but my resolve about not getting off with Aiden was forgotten. His thumbs were dangerously close to my hole, and even through the fabric of my pants, I wanted more.

I rocked my hips over and over, grinding my cock into the pillows while Aiden squeezed and massaged my ass. Aiden's own grinding over my thighs was only vaguely registering in my brain. "Oh, oh, oh shit. Aiden. I'm..."

My words trailed off as Aiden skimmed his fingers over my hole. The soft, fleecy material of my pants combined with the firmness of his fingers sent electricity through my body. Gentle and rough, soft and firm, it was all too much and my body tensed, protesting muscles and all, and I came in my pants like a teenager. Aiden played with my hole through my orgasm, only releasing his grip on my ass when my body sagged into the pillows with a giant sigh.

I hadn't even realized Aiden had come until he snorted a laugh. "Ugh. It's a good thing my bag is in the car—my underwear has cum in it."

I craned my body around to see Aiden. His cheeks were flushed and he was breathing just as hard as I was, but looking down at his crotch, there was no sign on his pants that he'd cum. I knew as soon as I stood up the wet patch would be noticeable in my own pants. As though he could read my mind, Aiden smiled bashfully and unzipped his jeans to reveal a thick pair of padded briefs. His hand ran along the back of his neck sheepishly. "I, uh, don't wear regular briefs very often."

I didn't know what I found so funny, but I began to laugh. "Well, in this case, it worked out well. Far better than it worked out for me. Trent's going to kill me if I get a cum stain on our couch cushions, so I'm going to get up and get changed before this soaks all the way through. You can go get a new pair of undies and change." A yawn escaped me, my orgasm taking more out of me than I'd realized. "Then you can pick out a new movie. I think that orgasm just ensured I'll be able to sit through another one."

Aiden cackled as he wiggled off my legs. "Success!"

"Oh, you're a brat!" I called after him as he scurried toward the door. "One day, a Daddy is going to have his hands full with you!" I winced, remembering my entire goal of the day was to get Aiden and Trent to see they needed each other. *Fuck*. I had likely just screwed that plan up. Though it had felt so good that I was struggling to convince myself it hadn't been worth it. The drying cum in my pants ensured I didn't overthink for much longer.

My muscles ached as I stood up and I felt far older than thirty-six years, but I forced myself to throw the pillows back on the couch, then climb the steps to my room. After a quick trip to my bathroom to wipe down, I found another pair of sweatpants to slip on, then headed back downstairs with a load of laundry. Aiden was just stepping out of the bathroom and I held the basket out to him. "Toss your undies in here. I'll wash them with my stuff." He flushed but did as I requested.

The brightly colored alphabet blocks on his thick briefs made me chuckle as I tossed them into the washing machine. They stood out against my basket of gray, black, and tan cloth-ing. Though my underwear was decidedly brighter than my clothing—because solid underwear was boring—they had a very different feel than Aiden's thick training pants.

With the laundry started and a bottle of water in hand, I sank back onto the couch. "Okay, next movie."

Aiden grinned like he was getting away with something devious and turned on *The Devil Wears Prada*. I smiled to myself and settled back into the couch with Aiden at my side.

CHAPTER 15

TRENT

AT LEAST I knew who the car belonged to when I pulled into the driveway at four thirty. James came in early, but only by twenty minutes. It had been just enough for me to sneak out a few minutes before the end of my shift so I could get home to pick up Logan. Seeing Aiden's car in the driveway told me why Logan had been suspiciously quiet all afternoon but didn't bode well for us getting to Steve's on time, if ever.

Over the last handful of months, the group had gone from mercilessly teasing Travis over being continually late to our dinners to teasing Logan and me. It wasn't like we were as late as Travis used to be, but for some reason, the two of us could never make it to Steve's on time. No one needed to know that it was because we had Thursday evenings off and oftentimes ended up getting distracted before we got on the road to the bar.

With Aiden at the house, all pretenses of making it on time went out the window. I wouldn't know how late we'd be until I got inside, so I turned off the ignition and headed for the house. To my surprise, I didn't walk in to find toys across the living room or to hear Logan and Aiden playing in the tub again. The two were on the couch. Logan had what appeared to be a half-empty beer on the end table next to him and Aiden had his own beer bottle in his hand. A movie was playing on the TV, and Logan was sound asleep with his head resting on Aiden's shoulder.

Aiden looked over and flushed slightly as I walked in the door, but I was too shocked at seeing Logan asleep in the middle of the day while one of his favorite movies was on to immediately react to him.

"Hey," I whispered to Aiden, who raised his hand in greeting. I made my way to the kitchen, locked up my gun, and walked toward the couch. "What did you do to him?"

Aiden's laugh was richer than I remembered it being, quite a bit more masculine than the first few times I'd heard it. "He'd been complaining about overdoing his workout this morning and being sore, then we started the movie and he was out not even halfway into it."

I shook my head. Part of me was envious of Aiden—Logan struggled to sit still so much that he normally ended up shaking from the effort to not move. Aiden got a marshmallowy sweet guy who could sleep just about anywhere. Part of me was annoyed that Logan would never sleep now that he'd been napping for over an hour. "We're supposed to be meeting some friends for dinner tonight." Before I could continue and ask him if he wanted to go with us, Aiden paled.

"Oh shit. Sorry, I had no idea."

I held up a hand. "It's okay. I was going to see if you'd want to go with us." I began to rub Logan's head and he hummed, burrowing into Aiden's side a little more deeply. "Pup, you need to wake up."

"Sleep," Logan mumbled.

Aiden's brain had gotten stuck on me inviting him to dinner

with us and didn't register Logan's mumbles or deeper snuggles. "I should probably go home."

Logan's eyes popped open. "No. The movie."

"It's over," Aiden chuckled. "And you and Trent have plans tonight."

Logan blinked in confusion. "But I wanted to introduce you to Caleb."

Caleb? Why did Logan want to introduce Aiden to Caleb? And why was Aiden turning bright red?

"Oh. I, um, is that a good idea?"

Logan leaned his head into my hand and I knew he was nervous that Aiden would say no. Aiden wouldn't have been hesitating if he'd known how much Logan liked him. They were a cute pair and Logan had fallen for him harder than he was letting on. It sucked that neither of the two people Logan was willing to trust with his heart could be the person he needed. Well, maybe that wasn't it—*I* wasn't the person Logan needed, and he was convinced that *he* couldn't be what Aiden needed. In twenty-one years of friendship, I'd never seen Logan like this with anyone but me.

"I think the guys would really like you. Please? I'd meant to ask you, but apparently I fell asleep before I could."

Aiden looked up at me, like I needed to give him permission. That wasn't my place, unfortunately, but I nodded just the same. "We'd love to have you. Logan's right. The guys would love meeting you, and I think you and Caleb could easily be friends."

Aiden flushed at Caleb's name and I got the distinct impression I was missing something, but he nodded slowly. "Yeah, okay. Dinner would be nice."

"Yes!" Logan jumped up, then winced. "Fuck, I hurt everywhere."

I'd popped my head in the garage to tell him goodbye earlier that morning, but he'd been running full out on the treadmill and it looked like he'd been trying to outrun a demon. The look on his face had haunted me all day, and at some point I'd need to talk to him about it, but with Aiden there it wasn't going to be now.

"I'm going to go change my shirt. You may want to get changed too," I mentioned to Logan. He looked comfortable in his loose tank top and oversized sweatpants, but I could see the outline of his cock through them and they really weren't dinner-appropriate attire.

Logan hobbled up the steps in front of me, cursing each step. At the top of the steps, he hesitated for a long moment, looking me up and down slowly before he turned and headed to his room. I really wanted to know what that pained expression was on his face and why he looked like he was walking to the electric chair.

Logan slid into the passenger's seat of my truck and Aiden climbed into the backseat, sitting in the center so he could lean forward and talk with us easily on the way to the bar. "So, why are we rushing to get there?"

Logan slowly angled his body so he could see Aiden better. "Travis's dad owns the bar we're going to. Travis was always a workaholic and never showed up on time. To the point that some weeks, he would forget to show up at all."

"Then he met Caleb and all of a sudden his world revolves around Caleb and the man is working a steady nine-to-five Monday through Friday and not a minute more."

Logan nearly cackled beside me. "Trav's world revolves around Caleb. The two are head over heels in love with one another. Travis will do anything for Caleb. He's a lot like Trent... except maybe not as controlling."

Aiden's face flushed deep red and he tried not to look me in the eyes.

Logan continued like he hadn't noticed Aiden's reaction... or my low warning growl. "Trent needs someone who *needs* him. I think Travis is more like the super-sweet, spoil-his-boy-rotten Dom. Trent would definitely do that too, but he needs an additional level of control."

Aiden's breath hitched and I watched him in the mirror as closely as I could while still keeping an eye on the road. Thank fuck for quiet, mostly untraveled country roads. "I-I... huh?"

"Looogan," I warned, drawing out his name and not bothering to keep my annoyance out of my voice.

I should have known it wouldn't matter because Logan plowed ahead with his *matchmaking* ploy. "You always talk about having too much on your plate and juggling too much at times but not being able to say no. Trent would thrive on giving you boundaries and limits. He *needs* that." There was a short pause, and he added so quietly I barely heard him. "That's why we can't work. That's why he needs a boy who needs him. He can't be happy with an overly excitable pup with more energy than he knows what to do with."

My heart clenched and every fiber of my being itched to reach out for him. "Logan."

He forced a smile that didn't reach his eyes. "Aiden's what you need."

Aiden flushed, but I noticed he didn't deny Logan's words. "I can manage. I've been doing it for years now."

That didn't sound promising, but I also wasn't about to pursue Aiden. Logan would be crushed if the two of us got together, and truthfully I'd seen the way Logan could relax around Aiden. There was a good chance that if the two of them figured out their differences they would make each other very happy. However, if Aiden needed help with his schedule, I could always be available to gently guide him in the right direction.

I tried to meet Aiden's eyes in the mirror. "If you need someone to help you set a work-life balance, I'm happy to help you as a friend. Just because you may need someone who is more take charge unfortunately doesn't mean I'm the right man —Daddy—for you. It isn't as easy as Logan wants it to be. I have no experience with being a Daddy." I gave Logan a pointed look. "You need to let Aiden figure out what's best for him. You don't need to be so in his business."

Logan sighed and rolled his eyes.

I flicked my eyes back to Aiden. "Logan's a steamroller. Don't let him force you into something you don't want." I could see the blushing photographer would be a sweet boy for his Daddy when he found one. He was also able to be the perfect boyfriend for Logan.

"Thank you." He blushed and ducked his head again. He struggled to find a new topic and finally asked about the rest of the guys we were meeting. Thankfully, it was a much easier conversation that lasted until we pulled into the parking lot at Steve's.

We made it there on time, three minutes early to be exact, but of course, Travis was already there, as were Merrick and Dean. I didn't see Ben and Asher, but they weren't always with us. Dexter's fiery red hair was visible across the crowded room. I didn't see Larson yet, but that wasn't surprising either. He worked crazier hours at the firehouse than Logan and I did.

Seeing the guys at the table, I saw Logan's face light up. Had he been feeling better, he likely would have bounded across the dining room, but as it was he was walking like he'd been riding a horse for a month straight.

"Fall on a cactus?" Dean snickered as we walked up.

"Fuck you," Logan shot back with no bite in his words. "I ran, like, ten miles today and lifted weights. My muscles are pissed."

I took a spot by Dean. "I know you swore off dating eight months ago, but maybe you need to get laid. You've packed on even more muscle since you swore off women."

My back stiffened at the comment and I looked over in time to see Logan practically fall over his feet. "Not looking for a girlfriend," he almost spat out, causing Dean to hold his hands up in surrender. His reaction lent credit to my assumption that he was feeling something toward Aiden. It only solidified my resolve to not touch the situation with a ten-foot pole.

"It was just a suggestion."

Logan looked more mutinous than I thought the situation warranted, but I brushed it off as him being in pain. My attention was drawn from Logan when I saw the way Caleb's eyes widened when he saw Aiden, but then a shy smile crossed his face and he motioned him over to where he was sitting. Aiden and Logan had a whispered conversation in which it seemed they were debating where they were going to sit, but then Aiden took the spot next to Caleb, leaving Logan to sink into the seat beside mine, looking more than a little frustrated at something.

Logan sulked for a few minutes before whatever Aiden and Caleb were talking about drew him in. With so many people around the table, it was nearly deafening, but as Logan relaxed, his voice could be heard over everyone else's.

With the chaos of conversations and so many men, I almost missed Larson sliding into the seat beside Dexter. A few tattoos peeked out of the bottom of Larson's sleeve and his face was mainly hidden behind a full beard, but his expressive eyes were never able to hide his feelings. Right then, Larson's eyes were a mixture of confusion and amusement as Aiden and Logan chatted. Larson had always been a man of few words, though he'd gotten close to Caleb over the last handful of months and seemed to come out of his shell, at least around Travis and Caleb. That night, I was watching Larson smile more easily and laugh more freely, even with Logan and Aiden in the mix. My curiosity was high and I was dying to find out.

"No way!" Logan laughed, slapping the table with his hand.

Instead of jumping or flinching, Caleb was giggling uncontrollably while nodding his head.

I glanced over at Travis with a furrowed brow, trying to figure out what was going on between the four men. Travis offered a lazy smile and a wink, like he wasn't surprised at the turn of events. *What had happened between these men in the last few weeks?*

Even Aiden was giggling and I was certain I was seeing his little side coming out slightly. I couldn't hear a damn thing they were talking about, but his eyes were bright beneath his big plastic-rimmed glasses and he was bouncing slightly in his seat. Logan had placed a hand on his thigh to calm him, much like I often did with Logan. I looked down to see my own hand on Logan's thigh, squeezing gently in a subconscious gesture to remind him to keep his voice down. Logan glanced over at me and flashed me the brightest smile before returning to his conversation with the guys next to him.

Weirdest. Dinner. Ever.

"You keep staring at that boy like that and you're going to bore holes in the back of his head," Dean smirked.

My head shot over to him. "What?" *Who was he talking about?*

Dean nodded toward Aiden. "Mr. Too Adorable."

I glanced over at Aiden and felt a small smile spread across my lips and my pulse quicken. *What the hell was that about?*

Then Dean glanced over toward Logan. "And maybe this new guy will help you move on from Mr. Unattainable."

My mouth fell open. "What?"

Dean rolled his eyes at me like I was a moron. "Oh, come on, Trent. We've all known you've been gone for Logan since the first time we met him. You look at him like he hung the moon and stars, and he's slept his way around the whole of central Tennessee."

"You may want to watch what you say about things you don't know."

Dean cocked an eyebrow, almost daring me to prove him wrong. "Maybe I'm wrong, but from where I sit, Logan's not going to settle down."

A hand cracked Dean on the back of the head and for a moment I worried it had been me. "You sound like an asshole." Merrick was rubbing his hand from the force of the slap he'd delivered to Dean's thick skull. "I love you, man, but Trent's right. You don't know what you're talking about. Just because *your* crush isn't here doesn't mean you have to be insufferable to be around."

Dean dropped his eyes to the table and rubbed his head with one hand while he pulled at his oversized shirt nervously. It was a tick he'd had for years, and he did it so frequently that his shirts had stretched out awkwardly at the hems. "You're right. Sorry, Trent. I'm in a pissy mood. Your feelings toward Logan and Logan's love life are none of my business."

"Thank you." I managed to get it out, surprising even myself at how sincere the words sounded. After a few minutes of deep breathing, I felt my muscles begin to relax. So what if Aiden was cute? He was Logan's, not mine.

Dean pointedly ignored me for most of the rest of the night, and by the time we left, I could tell some of the others had picked up on the odd tension between us. Dean hadn't said anything that wasn't assumed by everyone else, but I knew Logan's love life better than any of the others around the table.

Part of me wished Logan would come out as bisexual, but he'd steadfastly maintained that he'd tell them when he had a guy to introduce to them. I ignored the memory of him admitting he was excited to tell the guys we were dating, but we'd realized it wouldn't work before he ever could. If he did come out, I suspected the comments would only get worse and the guys would push us to get together. Looking at it from the outside, we'd make a good couple: best friends, housemates, coworkers.

If we could survive all that and still be best friends, dating really shouldn't have caused a problem. What really got to me was that I *knew* how amazing we could be, and would be, if we could just find a way to make it work.

I'd never left a dinner feeling so out of sorts.

CHAPTER 16

AIDEN

LOGAN TURNED weird when we arrived at the bar. He'd been quiet and broody, but the storm cloud cleared a few minutes after we joined a conversation. I was quickly learning that Caleb had a tendency to be painfully shy. Dexter and Travis had a way of pulling him out of his head and getting him to talk more, but when we'd first arrived, I'd thought he'd never say anything to me on his own.

By the end of the evening, Caleb hadn't been leaning into Travis as often and had offered smiles more easily. I could tell Logan was still on edge, but it wasn't from whatever was going on between him and Trent. No, the tension in his shoulders and the steel in his eyes had softened, but he was choosing his words carefully and speaking more quietly than usual and it was damn near killing him. Logan was definitely on edge. Everything from the slight tension he held in his jaw to the fact he'd been nursing the same beer so long it had to have been warm told me so. It had started the first time Caleb had ducked his head when Logan had teased me about watching how much I drank that night.

Twenty minutes into the evening, Larson, a giant of a man,

arrived at the table apologizing about being caught at a fire until after his shift should have ended. I'd had to work to school my surprise when he sat down at the table. He was so tall and broad the chair barely looked like it would support him. But then he settled into the conversation, and I was shocked to find his voice was quiet and he shot tentative smiles my way.

For the most part, Larson didn't speak unless he'd been spoken to and seemed to take in everything going on around him. In that way, he reminded me of a quiet version of Logan. Caleb came out of his shell a little more when Larson arrived at the table, and from their easy conversations I knew they were close. Unfortunately, the more easily conversation came between Larson, Caleb, and me, the more uncomfortable Logan became. I kept shooting him questioning looks and tried to elbow him subtly in an attempt to get him to loosen up. All I got from him were uneasy glances.

Finally, Larson leaned across the table and spoke into Logan's ear. Had I not been sitting right next to Logan, I never would have heard the words.

"Listen, I know you're nervous, but acting like you've swallowed your tongue and are sitting on a bed of nails is only going to make this more uncomfortable. He told me about you guys running into each other at Beans and Brew. He's more worried that *he's* going to make things awkward. Be yourself."

Logan's eyes widened as though he hadn't considered that some of Caleb's awkwardness was his own making and not because of Logan trying to be included in the conversation. It went a long way toward helping Logan relax, and the more he let his guard down, the less bashful Caleb was. By the time our dinners came, conversation was flowing far more easily. I suspected it had helped that Logan had steered far away from any topic that might have even come close to what we'd seen at DASH.

Dinner dishes had been taken away when Dexter's eyes widened and he smacked the table. "Oh my god, Cal, the guy that moved into your old place is so fucking gorgeous."

Caleb smirked and I saw him roll his eyes. "So you've said."

Dexter sighed, throwing his arm over his forehead and fanning himself. "So sexy, but he has the personality of a wet mop."

Larson narrowed his eyes in thought. "What exactly does that mean?"

"It means that he won't talk to me unless I force him to!" Dexter was clearly frustrated by this information. I felt for the neighbor. I didn't know any of my neighbors and I was totally okay with that. "But he's got these biceps that are bigger than my thighs! I saw him the other day with his shirt off and he's got tattoos." Dexter was practically drooling. "And I swear to you, Cal, I have no idea how he gets his jeans on. They are like a second skin!"

Caleb leaned back and looked down at Dexter's outfit. "I think the same could be said about you."

Dexter stuck out his tongue. "I look fabulous in these. Thank you very much."

"I never said you didn't. I just said they look like they're painted on you and I can see your butt crack when you bend over."

I would have been mortified if someone had said that to me, but Dexter just grinned wickedly. "Cal, you've seen so much more than just my ass crack. Besides, it's a great ass."

Logan snorted and shook his head. "I thought Trent and I had no boundaries in our friendship."

"You guys don't," I responded dryly. "Do you forget that I've seen you two together?" My words had Larson, Logan, and Caleb laughing loudly enough that a few tables around us stared.

Dexter waved his hand in front of his face. "It's not like I'm trying to jump him! I think he's straight anyway." He paused and his eyes went far away while he got lost in thought. "If he ever wanted to experiment, I'd totally be down for the job, though."

Caleb's mouth hung open in surprise and his eyes widened. "Slut."

"Hey, my dick wants what it wants... and believe me, that man..." He waved his hand in front of his face. "But he doesn't seem to have any friends. He works at the weirdest hours and no one ever comes over. He didn't even have help moving in! I try to be friendly, but he gets all weird with me." Dexter let out a long sigh. "Did I mention the six pack and beard? *He's sex on legs!*"

"But you definitely don't want to climb him like a tree," Logan snorted.

"I'd have to be blind not to notice him! Hell, Logan, even you'd think he was gorgeous. He'd put your muscles to the test."

I rolled my eyes. Dexter was being ridiculous, but from the reaction of the men around him, I suspected this was nothing new. "So, why is he so standoffish?"

Dexter threw his hands in the air. "I wish I knew! He walks around like a storm cloud with this perma-scowl on his face. He's going to get wrinkles! No man that gorgeous should have scowl-lines! I keep trying to take him drinks and talk with him, but he grunts and only gives me one-word answers. It's infuriating." Dexter went quiet for a moment. "He's sexy, but I really just want to be his friend. Even if he *was* into men, I'm sure he couldn't handle me."

Caleb let out a bark of surprise that made Travis look over at him to make sure he was okay. When he saw he was fine, Travis returned to his conversation and Caleb adjusted in his seat to pat Dexter on the arm. "Dex, I love you, but I don't think any one man, no matter how sexy, tattooed, or muscular he may be, would be enough to handle you."

Dexter stuck his tongue out at Caleb. "I just want to be his friend, dammit."

Before the conversation could finish, Trent leaned over and placed a hand on Logan's forearm to let him know we were leaving. I was shocked to find that three hours had passed in what felt like the blink of an eye. Larson, Caleb, and Dexter all exchanged numbers with me, then to my surprise Logan asked if I minded him adding me to their ongoing group text. At first, I'd thought he meant one between him and a few of the guys, but when unfamiliar phone numbers started blowing up my phone two-thirds of the way back to Logan and Trent's house, I figured out he meant the *entire* group.

[Unknown] Shit, I was supposed to mention that I have a time conflict next meeting. I'm going to have to skip.

[Unknown] Yeah, right, time conflict, *just tell us you have a hot date.*

[Unknown] I wish. I've got a new business consult lined up.

[Unknown] So we won't see you for another two meetings at least.

[Unknown] Actually, I'll be around here, it's a local bar.

Okay, that was Merrick. I'd learned he was a highly sought after restaurant consultant who traveled the US. From what Logan had mentioned, it was rare for him to be at the bar more than once every three or four meetings. I entered his contact info.

[Logan] Do I want to know what bar?

[Merrick] Probably not.

[Unknown] Not like he'd tell us anyway.

[Caleb] Should we actively avoid any bars in the area?

[Merrick] Probably that dive over near Fairview... That place scares me, but they haven't contacted me... so I'd stay well away from there.

[Unknown] ~shudder~ That place has been shut down by the health department more times than I can count. They're beyond help.

*My office was near there. I ate there right after they opened and got
food poisoning.*

[Logan] *Don't text and drive, Dean!*

Okay, so I filled in another blank and added Dean's name to
my phone.

[Dean] *I had to get groceries. I'm in the store. Thank you, Dad.*

Christ, if this was their conversation all the time, I didn't
know how any of them got work done. My phone had vibrated
more in ten minutes than it had in the last month.

[Merrick] *No one die please. Oh! Avoid that place up in Nashville
near the arena. The place with the creepy deer decor. I swear, I think
it has fleas!*

I knew that place.

[Me] *It got shut down for good last month. It's vacant now.*

Three texts came through in rapid-fire succession.

[Unknown] *Wait, who's this?*

[Dean] *New person in the group chat?*

[Merrick] *New person, or new phone number?*

[Me] *Uh. Sorry, it's Aiden.*

[Logan] *I added him to the group chat.*

[Merrick] *Welcome.*

"Jesus, Logan, what the hell is going on? My phone is like a
fucking vibrator right now."

Logan laughed. "Want me to put it in your lap?"

"You're an asshole. You know that, right? Is there an emergency or something?"

"Merrick's going to miss next dinner because he's got a bar
consult somewhere nearby. But he says there's nowhere we
should avoid eating except that dive down between home and
Fairview. But we avoid that place already."

"How the hell is that place still open?"

"Beats me."

We pulled into our driveway and Trent parked behind Logan

so he didn't block my car. Logan turned around to face me, wincing slightly at the sudden movement. "You staying the night?"

I shook my head, though I was disappointed. "No, I really shouldn't. I have some actual work to do in the morning. Gotta finish dotting the I's and crossing the T's on this next shoot plan." I groaned. It was going to be days of hell and I knew it.

Logan and Trent both got out of the cab. Before I could reach for the door handle, Trent had my door opened. I glanced over to where Logan stood and saw him watching with a sad smile on his face. When he noticed me watching him, he forced the smile to look more genuine. Really, it just made him look like he'd swallowed a lemon.

Saying goodbye to Logan wasn't easy. When I went to hug him, he held on tight. I felt myself wanting to curl up and stay with him longer, but I'd seen the bright, color-coded schedule on their fridge when I'd gotten a beer. Logan worked at six in the morning, and Trent had an appointment at eight and was scheduled in at noon. Personally, as much as I loved cuddling up with Logan to sleep, I liked sleeping in more.

"Text me when you get home. I'll worry."

I smiled and gave him a quick peck on the cheek then turned to leave. Trent had come up behind me and I could see the intensity in his eyes as he focused on me. Despite the twitch in his arm as though he was restraining himself from reaching out, he kept his face neutral and nodded to me. "Please, text Logan. We'll both worry until you do."

"Promise." I smiled and headed toward my car. The two of them watched from the front porch until my car was on the street.

I didn't look at the shoot plan at all that night. Instead, I spent hours editing the photos I'd taken of the two of them at the park. They were gorgeous—very little editing had been required for any of them. I had taken so many, and they were all so perfect I hadn't wanted to skip any. I tried figuring out a way to help them see how much they needed each other while I worked. Sadness sat heavy in my stomach at the thought. I'd miss them when they figured their shit out—both of them.

CHAPTER 17

TRENT

My alarm rang at six fifteen, and as soon as I opened my eyes I knew something was wrong. My throat was raw, I was chilled despite being under the blankets, and my eyes burned. Not just the normal morning, barely awake dry eyes but a burning heat that felt like my eyes were hot. It had been a long time since I'd felt anything like this, but I knew what it was.

I had a fever.

I shivered with every step from my bed to the bathroom to pee, then to Logan's bedroom door. The door was open and Logan was buried under the blankets in what looked like a tiny ball, his nearly buzzed hair stuck up at odd angles from his head. I felt bad waking him up, but there was no way I could go to work and James was already at the office, having pulled the night shift. The only option was to wake Logan up.

"Hey," I croaked as I knocked on the doorframe.

Logan mumbled something I couldn't understand and burrowed farther under the covers.

"Logan," I tried again, this time moving closer. When he didn't move, I sat at the foot of the bed and squeezed his foot.

He buried his head in the pillow and shook his head. "Don't want to let him go."

"Logan…" The poor guy was so out of it he was dreaming.

"… know you need Daddy." His words were mumbled and hard to understand but they were there. "Mmm, love him."

I rubbed Logan's leg. Even with being sick and my brain not working right, I knew I was hearing something I shouldn't. "Logan, wake up, pup."

He whimpered, a sound I associated much more with Curious than Logan. "Hurts. 'Sokay. I love Trent."

Shit. My heart clenched at his words. We told each other we loved one another frequently. Nearly daily. For me, I'd meant the words every time I spoke them, and deep down, maybe I'd always suspected Logan did too. My brain definitely hoped that they were just words he said to me out of habit and that they didn't mean anything. Of course my heart had always hoped he meant them.

Now my brain was trying to remind me it was only a dream, while my gut told me that I was hearing his true feelings. I was way too sick to be processing what that meant because my heart was telling me to curl up with Logan and tell him how much I still loved him. I forced myself to focus on why I'd been in his room in the first place. "Pup. Wake up." I managed to force my voice to sound stern enough that Logan drew in a sharp breath.

"Trent?" he questioned sleepily, confused by my presence in his room.

Even fevered and tired, I found myself smiling down at him. "Hey." My voice cracked, the effort of being stern to wake him up having caught up with me, and my throat hurt worse.

Logan's eyes cleared in the blink of an eye. "What's wrong?" He was sitting up and looking me over, his hand instinctively going to my forehead. "Jesus, you're burning up."

I found myself only able to nod in agreement. "I know. I feel like shit."

"Have you taken anything for that fever yet?"

"Not yet. That was next on my list of things to do. But I'm scheduled at seven and there's no way I can go in like this."

Logan was already climbing out of bed, completely naked. The sight was too much for my body after having heard what I just had. Despite feeling like I'd been hit by a truck, my cock began to fill in my underwear. The thin cotton of my briefs was not enough to hide my arousal, and I pinched my eyes shut, focusing on the pain. I instinctively swallowed hard and the pain that radiated down my throat was enough to get my cock in check. I took the opportunity to head out of his room and toward the kitchen to find some Advil.

With painkillers in my system and a glass of water in hand, I headed back to my bedroom. I'd barely curled into my blankets, shivers still wracking my body, when Logan came in. It hadn't even been ten minutes since I'd left him in his room but he was already showered and dressed for the day. "I texted Aiden. He's on his way over."

My eyes shot open. "Aiden?" Then I winced at the pain in my throat.

Logan nodded as he buttoned his uniform shirt. "You've missed two days of work in the last eight years. That's including today. There is no way in hell I'm going to have you at home without someone here. It's Aiden or your mom."

I shook my head. "Don't call my mom. She'll drive me nuts."

Logan cackled at my protest. I loved my mom dearly, but the woman had no concept of boundaries. The last time she was here, she tried to do my laundry. I'd barely escaped her finding the bibs that Aiden had left on my bathroom counter when he and Logan had bathed in my tub. No matter how much the woman knew about me, I didn't want to have to explain why there were bibs in my laundry.

My mom was an amazing woman who'd accepted my sexuality without question when I came out. She was also the woman who'd spent twenty minutes telling me all about a kinky book she was reading. I'd cringed at the misrepresentation of the lifestyle, and when I'd snapped and begun to tell her all the ways the book was wrong, she'd listened carefully, asked engaging questions, and then managed to draw me up short when she turned the tables on me. "I'm glad we had this conversation. Now the way you bossed your brother and sister around growing up makes so much more sense."

I'd spit my coffee halfway across the kitchen.

There was no way in hell I wanted my mom in the house while I was sick. Since Aiden had been spending more time here I'd been finding toys stuck under things, and I'd found a binkie between the couch cushions a few days earlier. But Aiden's things weren't the only random items popping up. Logan, despite being one of the most organized men I knew, had been leaving toys scattered throughout the house as well. I had a feeling it had something to do with Aiden dumping them all out when they played and them slowly becoming scattered throughout the house. If my mom found a binkie or a dog toy, she'd have questions I definitely wasn't ready to talk to her about.

"That's what I thought, and that's exactly why I asked Aiden." He tucked his shirt into his pants before zipping and buttoning them shut. I'd been so focused on the skimpy rainbow briefs he'd been wearing I missed him moving closer to me and swiping my phone off the nightstand. "Your voice is all scratchy and keeps breaking. Open." He sat down and turned the flashlight on.

I opened my mouth and Logan winced. "Dude, that's strep

throat. It smells like an animal died in there." He scrunched up his nose and used the camera on my phone to take a few pictures. "We got that new remote doctor service with our insurance. You may as well use that. I'm sure Aiden will run and get you a prescription. If they won't diagnose you, though, you need to get to the actual doctor for a throat swab. That's gross."

"Yes, Mom."

Logan narrowed his eyes at me. "Listen to me. You're a stubborn ass. I'm going to tell Aiden that you need to get a hold of a doctor at some point today. If you haven't done so by lunchtime, I will call your mom."

"I'll make the call," I assured him. Truthfully, my throat felt like it was on fire and the fever I was fighting didn't seem to be letting up, even with the pain relievers in my system.

"Good." Then Logan leaned over and kissed my forehead. "Feel better. I gotta get to work now. See you tonight and don't overdo it. Love ya."

I couldn't stop myself from responding. "Love you too." Thankfully, Logan had left the bedroom without looking back because he would have found me red faced. I loved him, he loved me, and we couldn't do a damn thing about it. We were a mess. I took a deep breath, installed the app I needed, and made a remote appointment with the doctor. In twenty minutes, he'd confirmed—just by the picture—what Logan had told me, and I'd have a prescription waiting for me at the pharmacy when it opened.

[Logan] Aiden should be there soon. Have you called the doctor?

I rolled my eyes, but the smile that crossed my face told me I wasn't as annoyed with Logan as I wanted to be.

[Me] Called the phone doc. You were right, he says it's strep and already called a prescription in for me.

I could sense the smirk on Logan's face, but at least he refrained from an *I told you so.*

[Logan] I'll let Aiden know. He has the garage door code, so don't freak out if you hear it go up. Please let him know if you need anything.

I fought a smile as I clicked off the phone. His dream had brought a lot into focus for me and I could appreciate his concern even more. The two of us had been friends for so long I could easily forget that Logan showed he cared through being bossy and demanding. It made a lot of our interactions over the years feel a lot different. It sent a painful jolt of sadness through my stomach when I thought of the times we'd gone to DASH together in the past and he'd seen me play with other subs.

I flopped back on my pillow. If my throat weren't so sore, I'd have screamed in frustration. In my gut, I'd known that it hurt Logan to keep pushing me toward Aiden, but now I was looking at it through an entirely new lens. I couldn't think of a greater act of love than pushing me to find happiness no matter how much it hurt him.

I sighed, then winced. *Fucking sore throat.* Before I could get too far down a rabbit hole of thoughts, the garage door went up and a few seconds later I heard it go down. No one came up the steps, but about three minutes later my phone buzzed.

[Aiden] I'm here. Don't want to bother you. Logan said that you have a prescription that needs to be picked up in a few hours. Let me know if you need anything before I go to the pharmacy.

Aiden had effortlessly slipped into our group chats over the last few weeks. Knowing Aiden as a little first and an adult second, I'd been surprised at how easily he could take the ribbing of the guys and at times dish it just as well. The conversations had helped me get to know him as a person, and he wasn't a shy, quiet little. He had an opinion and wasn't afraid to let it be known.

[Me] Thanks, Aiden. I'm gonna try to get some sleep. But yeah, that prescription would be helpful.

I hadn't known if I was going to fall asleep or not, but I swore I blinked my eyes and three hours had slipped by and Aiden was knocking on my doorframe. I was shivering again, the Advil from earlier gone from my system, and my fever was once again climbing.

"Hey, uh, I got your prescription from the pharmacy and I brought you some Advil up, too. According to Logan, it should have been long enough that you can take more."

I gave him a weak smile and slid up in the bed so I was sitting up.

"You really do look like shit."

I tried to laugh but it hurt and instead I ended up wincing at the pain. "It's a good thing I'm sick."

Aiden came to stand by me. "Or what?" he teased as he handed me the pills and water.

Or what? I had no idea. I felt too crappy to think of an "or what."

Aiden's eyes were filled with laughter but he managed to keep his face blank. "That's what I thought. You need to sleep some more."

I grunted and took my pills. Thankfully, the next time I woke up, the Advil had kicked in and I was feeling well enough to shower. By the time I'd gotten out of the shower, I could hear Aiden in the kitchen. A glance at the clock told me it was past lunchtime. Since I felt well enough to head down the steps, I slipped on some clean sweatpants and a sweatshirt, grabbed my glasses and phone, and headed out of my room.

I made it as far as my doorway when my phone buzzed in my hand. Looking down, I noticed the group text had been active that morning.

[Travis] Caleb's got a meeting after work on Thursday, we're going to be about twenty minutes late

[Logan] Trent's sick. He's on an antibiotic and will have been for over 48 hours by then, but we'll have to see how he's feeling.

[Aiden] He's currently too exhausted to think of a comeback for me telling him he looked like shit.

[Larson] Oh, if he's too sick to at least threaten *something, he really must be sick.*

[Aiden] Right? I thought I'd at least get a swat.

My eyes shot open when I read the last line. What the hell were these guys talking about?

[Logan] Hell, he'd swat me for that!

[Merrick] How that man can live with you and not have you over his knee every day is a mystery.

[Logan] *evil cackle* That does nothing for me. Trent knows that.

[Caleb] Oh, spankings are nice.

Did they have any idea that this was the group chat? These guys were insane.

[Travis] That may be more than they need to know.

[Caleb] DELETE! DELETE! DELETE!

[Caleb] Oh god, I can't believe I wrote that.

[Caleb] I'm going to go hide now.

[Aiden] It's okay, Caleb. Logan just doesn't know how good it really is! ;-) I completely agree, it's amazing.

My phone slipped out of my hand and clattered to the hard-wood floor in the hallway.

"Trent? Are you okay?" I could hear Aiden making a move toward the steps.

I scrambled to pick up my phone, which of course continued to slide down the hallway and toward the steps. "*Fuck.*" I snarled as it slipped farther away from me and tumbled over the edge of the top step.

"Whoa!" Aiden yelped as the phone hit the third step. "What the hell is going on up here?" His head popped around the corner to find me a few steps behind my phone... the phone that was now in his hand. "How exactly is your phone three steps down and you're all the way back here?"

"It slipped out of my hand."

Aiden looked at the device he was holding. "Good thing you splurged on an indestructible case."

"Thanks." I shoved the phone in my pocket. "Logan bought me one a few years back, then we got into a shoot-out. The shooter had terrible aim and shot me in the ass, and he ended up hitting my phone."

CHAPTER 18

AIDEN

"Shot?" My voice only cracked a little in surprise.

Trent's eyes crinkled. "The case shattered, so did the phone, but it stopped the bullet enough that I only ended up needing two stitches in my ass cheek. I honestly think it was a freak thing, but Logan swears I need these big cases now. Listen, if Logan *ever* tells you something will be fine, do not believe him."

I blinked in confusion. I had no idea what the hell he was talking about.

"Custody dispute. Logan got shot in the thigh; I got shot in the ass. Logan, however, didn't have this handy-dandy case on his thigh."

I giggled at his sarcasm but it quickly faded, the weight of the words sitting heavy in my heart. There was a world in which that incident could have gone much, much worse and I'd never have met either of them. The thought made me far sadder than it should have. A memory tickled my brain and I reached for it as a distraction from my dark thoughts. "Wait, I've seen that scar. It's like a bubble, right below his hip." We'd made our way down the steps by that point and I was still keeping one eye on Trent as we headed toward the kitchen. He looked a little pale, though he was steady on his feet.

"That's the one."

"He just told me he'd hurt himself on the job."

Trent laughed. "Oh yes, hurt himself on the job alright. He swore he saw an opening. Don't tell him, but he did a good job that day. I'm certain that he saved that kid's life despite both of us getting shot."

It was the first time I'd ever considered how truly dangerous their jobs were. They'd both been shot on the same day. Thankfully, they were nothing more than what amounted to flesh wounds, but I still shivered. "Oh. That's scary, but I'm glad you were both okay."

Trent shrugged and changed the subject. "It smells great in here."

"I brought over stuff to make chicken noodle soup. I didn't know what you'd be in the mood for, and when I left the house, I didn't know it was your throat. Glad I chose to bring this stuff. It should be easy to swallow." I felt my cheeks heat. That sounded a lot dirtier than I had intended it to.

Trent was either feeling too crappy to notice or had intentionally ignored it, but either way I was thankful. I focused on dishing out two bowls of soup. I'd made rolls as well, but I didn't know if his throat would be up for it. "Uh, I made rolls. Would you like one?"

I saw a myriad of emotions flit across his face: appreciation, pain, and a resolve to suffer through it. I held up my hand. "I'll leave them and Logan can warm them up in a day or two when you're feeling better. They'll keep."

"Thank you, baby."

I had my back toward him at the moment and my eyes went wide at the comment. It seemed to have slipped off his tongue easily and I wondered if he'd even caught the slip. I'd teasingly called him Daddy and he'd just as teasingly called me baby a number of times. But that wasn't teasing—that had been as second nature as his calling me Aiden. My dick took an immediate interest in his words. I managed to croak out a, "You're welcome," and continued to get our lunches ready.

Trent swore up and down that he wasn't a Daddy, but no matter what he said or even thought, he was a natural caretaker. Logan and I kept joking that Trent had a sixth sense for when we were hanging out together because he seemed to show up at the house unexpectedly each time.

The first time, when he walked in on us in the tub, had been a shock. Looking back on it through adult headspace, he'd handled it with the grace of a caretaker. He'd even laughed at us when he could have flipped out that we were in the tub and had turned it completely blue. While we'd showered the body paint off, he'd scrubbed the tub, laid out towels, and had even managed a few smiles. Those were things a caretaker did.

The next time, Logan and I had been in their backyard playing. Logan had scrambled after a ball and in the process had knocked my tower over. Trent had appeared at the same moment, sighed, then knelt down to help me rebuild my tower. He'd then spent ten minutes throwing the ball for Logan so he didn't get too close to me. At least until Logan had tired himself out enough that he was ready to curl up at my side for snuggles.

Maybe he didn't identify as a Daddy, but I wasn't seeing the strict Dom that Logan told me about. I slipped a bowl of soup across the counter to him and Trent gave me a smile. "Sorry about that, Aiden. I didn't mean to make you uncomfortable."

I smiled down at my bowl of soup. "It's okay." How did I explain to him that the words hadn't made me uncomfortable, only the unexpected feelings they evoked that time? I was ready to curl up on his lap and do anything he wanted. "You didn't make me uncomfortable." Not really. Actually, he probably made me *too* comfortable. No more Daddy—teasingly or not.

Trent's eyes narrowed as though he was unconvinced. "I'll try to choose my words more carefully."

My eyes shot up. "Please don't. I mean, I don't want you to change. I mean, shit." I growled in frustration, sounding a lot like Logan when he got all protective of me at DASH. "What I'm trying to say is there's no reason to change. You didn't say anything wrong. My brain short-circuited for a moment."

Trent's smile was tentative, but he nodded. "As long as you're sure."

I nodded emphatically. I really didn't want to fuck up the friendship we'd formed by letting on how much my brain loved hearing him call me baby without any teasing or hesitation.

I'd get over it.

We ate in silence, though I kept watching Trent closely. Each bite, his eyes pinched slightly and I could see his throat work extra hard to swallow, no matter how much he chewed beforehand. Poor guy was miserable but putting on a braver face than I'd have been. I hated being sick and could easily empathize with how he was feeling.

Trent finished the soup and went to put his bowl in the sink. "I've got it. Go rest." I glanced over at the clock on the stove. "Actually, you could have some Tylenol now."

"We don't have Tylenol here. I'll have to wait another hour or so for some Advil."

I headed to the medicine cabinet I'd found in their kitchen and pulled a new bottle of medicine from it. "Correction, Sheriff." At least I could pretend things were normal between us. "You *didn't* have Tylenol here, but I picked some up when I was at the pharmacy." I pulled the seal from the mouth of the bottle and shook two into my hand, passing them over with a cup of coffee like Logan had told me. Black with just a little creamer.

"I'm impressed. You're very prepared."

Holy shit, that was way too close to *Good boy, Daddy's proud of you,* and my brain had no idea how to handle it. "I try." I clamped my mouth shut. The word "Daddy" had almost slid from my mouth and it wouldn't have been in the teasing, playful way it had been in the past. I'd covered it with an awkward cough and turned around to go to the schedule on their fridge and marked the time in red.

"What's that?"

"Oh, I've been keeping track of when I've given you meds. Blue for Advil, red for Tylenol. That way Logan and you both know when I leave."

Trent's eyes widened but he smiled approvingly. "Such a good boy."

Heat rushed to my face and I ducked my head, my legs suddenly feeling a little wobbly. He was going to kill me.

"Shit. Sorry. I'm really sorry, Aiden. I'm going to blame being sick. I really don't want to make you uncomfortable. Oh, did you see your bibs got put with your sippy cup in the cabinet? I didn't know where else to put them that you'd see them."

I burst out laughing. It was the only thing I could do. He apologized so sincerely for calling me boy and making me uncomfortable, then turned around and told me I'd left bibs and a sippy cup here. How had I not noticed I'd left things here? I went to the cupboard and opened it up to find three bibs folded neatly. I clearly had too many bibs and sippy cups if I didn't remember leaving them. At least Trent hadn't been to my house. At the thought, my face heated. I wasn't going to put too much thought into why I wouldn't think twice about letting Logan see my cupboards but would be embarrassed for Trent to.

Trent bit his lip. "It really hurts to laugh, but the look on your face is priceless."

My hand flapped around in front of my face like I was swatting at a bug, but really I was just trying to rationalize how I'd left three bibs and a cup here and not even noticed. "I can't figure out how I didn't notice I'd left them."

He cocked an eyebrow. "How many do you have?"

I ran a hand through my hair, chuckling at myself. "Too many, apparently!"

"Well, judging by how much food was on them when I found them, I'd say it's a good thing you have that many."

What could I say? I tended to pick at things with my fingers when I was little. Spills and messes were to be expected. There was nothing I could say that made it any less awkward, so I chose to channel my inner turtle and hide from it. I grabbed my cup—an adult one, not my sippy cup—of water and headed to the living room. "Want to watch TV? Or do you need more sleep?"

Trent seemed to weigh the options because his eyes glanced between the living room and the steps a few times before he came to a decision. "TV sounds good. Sorry again for making you uncomfortable."

"You're fine. I did it to myself." And I meant it. I really had done it to myself.

Of course, my embarrassment flared back to life in a hurry when we got to the living room and Hedge, my blanket, and my binkie were sitting on the couch cushion. Trent was looking right at them, so I knew he saw them, but he tried his hardest not to say anything, despite his smile.

I narrowed my eyes at him. I wasn't sure if I was daring him to say something or praying he didn't. "Don't say anything, Daddy." *Shit, and there I went.*

Trent snorted. "We're just going to pretend the last three minutes didn't happen."

"Deal."

"But you're not going to hide your binkie or your cuddlies from me."

I pulled my blanket over my head, which didn't help with the embarrassment I was feeling but at least I didn't have to see him.

"You know, it's cute you still have them."

I groaned and held a middle finger out.

Trent's laughter was light but genuine. "Dammit, brat, don't make me laugh. It hurts too much."

I couldn't help but giggle, making the apology I offered sound insincere at best. "Sorry."

"You really do need that spanking you like so much."

The laughter cut off in my throat and I peeked out from behind my blanket.

"Oh yeah, I read those texts. You're a naughty boy, aren't you?"

It was a good thing I was sitting down because I would have likely fallen over otherwise. "I—" My voice cracked and I cleared my throat. "I don't know what you're talking about." *Smooth, Aiden, real smooth.*

Trent chuckled. "Then maybe you shouldn't have said spankings are fun in the group chat."

Yeah, I was going to die of embarrassment. "I was just supporting Caleb."

"I couldn't believe he said that. He's probably never going to show his face at dinner again."

I liked Caleb. He was a little shy, but he was funny. And the way he looked at his Daddy was everything I'd always wanted. I'd been so shocked at his admission and then felt so bad that he'd been so horrified, that I volunteered that I also enjoyed spankings.

Trent tried to cough then wheezed a bit, making me uncover my eyes to make sure he was okay. "That hurts like a motherfucker. Listen, I'm teasing you a lot, but I really do appreciate you coming here."

"I already told you it's no big deal."

"You wouldn't have to be here if Logan weren't so paranoid. If it weren't for that, you'd be home, warm, dry, and with your stuffed animals and blankets."

"He lo-cares about you," I responded without much thought and found myself barely catching myself before telling Trent that Logan loved him.

Trent smiled sadly. "Yeah, I know he does." I played his words back in my mind. Did he know Logan loved him or did he just know that Logan cared about him? After a moment, he continued. "No matter what, it doesn't change the fact that he likely woke you up at six this morning to come over here to sit with me and be bored shitless until he gets home."

"I'm not bored! I ran to the pharmacy, I made lunch, and I have stuff in the fridge for dinner too. Soft stuff that won't hurt your throat too badly."

"Thank you, baby." He winced. "Shit, I'm not usually like this."

I was testing spontaneous combustion at that point. What had changed? He'd teasingly called me baby and boy a number of times. So what changed today? What made it no longer sound just friendly? Why were my emotions reacting so strongly? Some of it had to do with the fact that I had a binkie in my hand and a blanket still covering half my head, but that wasn't the only reason I was reacting to him like that.

Embarrassed, Trent made to stand up. "I think I'm going to head to bed."

Before my brain could tell me to let him go, I reached out and grabbed his hand. "No, no. It's okay. I know you don't mean anything by it." Even if my brain was wishing he did.

Trent's eyes narrowed but he sat back down. "All I meant to

say was thanks. I appreciate you giving up your day to come sit with a sick old dude."

"You are not old!"

"And you're not going to hide your stuff around me. Shit, Aiden, I already know you have it. I've known since the night I met you."

I couldn't help the groan that escaped. "This may be the most awkward friendship ever."

"And you're stuck with us. If the group texts are anything to go by, everyone already likes you."

We settled into opposite sides of the couch and I handed the remotes to Trent. As he searched for something to watch, I tucked Hedge in my elbow, covered up with my blanket, and slipped my binkie in my mouth. I had no problems curling up on the couch and watching TV until it was time to make dinner. Thanks to fall, a persistent drizzle outside, and a chill in the air, I was in no rush to be anywhere.

When my phone buzzed in my pocket I wasn't surprised to see it was Logan checking up on Trent. What I was surprised at was that he'd used the group text.

[Logan] How's Trent?

Before I could respond, the next text rang through.

[Merrick] If he missed work, he's probably dead.

[Trent] I am the model patient.

[Dean] You seem to forget we've known you since college.

[Logan] And you're a stubborn old shithead.

[Trent] Aiden just told me I'm not old.

[Travis] He's just being a kiss-ass.

I gasped when I read the words. "I am not."

[Trent] You're older than me!

They were nuts. There were no two ways around it, though I liked being part of their group. The chat with Logan, Larson, Dexter, and Caleb popped up.

[Larson] You doing okay with Trent?

[Me] We were just sitting down to watch a show when the crazies started chatting again.

[Larson] Cal, you okay?

[Caleb] Horrified. Trying to convince Daddy to not go to dinner on Thursday.

The poor guy was terrified but before I could remind him that I'd also admitted to the entire group that I liked spankings too, so I wasn't about to let him back out, Logan spoke up.

[Logan] You'll be fine and it's Travis's dad's bar. I'm pretty sure you're stuck. Besides, Aiden likes spankings too.

[Me] Don't you have work to do?

Trent's voice pulled me away from my phone. "You okay over there?"

"Yeah, why?" Had my voice squeaked?

"You're bright red."

I turned the phone off and pushed it onto the end table. "Oh, yeah. Fine." I wasn't about to tell him that I was turning red because I'd been reminded of my earlier admission. I'd said it only because Caleb seemed so mortified, but I'd actually forgotten for a moment that I'd been in the main group chat and not the smaller group. I hadn't thought about how many others would see it. I pulled my blanket over my head completely.

A moment later, the blanket got pulled back from my face. I blinked up to see an amused Trent looking at me. "You're really cute when you get embarrassed."

"Not helping."

With expert-level stealth, Trent found the binkie that had been dropped into my lap and pushed it into my mouth. "Time for a movie. And with your mouth occupied, I can choose whatever I want."

Did he have any idea how dirty that sounded?

CHAPTER 19

TRENT

"NEW PORN SUBSCRIPTION?" Logan's voice from the doorway of my office had me jumping nearly out of my skin.

I slammed my phone down on my desk and glared at him. "What the fuck are you talking about?" I was not going to have a heart attack at thirty-six.

Logan cackled as he bounced into my office. A quick glance at the clock on my computer told me that he should have been leaving for the day. I still had four hours left in my shift and felt a groan bubble up in my chest. "Whoa, the fuck?" Logan took a seat across from me. "I want to see it if it's that good."

"Wasn't porn." Though I wasn't going to tell him my dick was hard under the desk from the very *not* porn conversation I'd been having with Aiden over the course of the early afternoon.

The conversation hadn't been erotic at all, which was hard to rationalize with my dick. He'd texted me earlier that morning to see how I was feeling. He knew it was my first day back at work. My throat was still scratchy but it wasn't terrible. The fever had broken halfway through the day Wednesday and Logan had worried like a mother hen about me for half the afternoon.

Interestingly enough for me, Curious had come out shortly after my·fever started to break. Except the crazy hyper pup I knew was nowhere to be found. Instead, he'd curled up with me with his favorite rope toy in his hand and had laid his head on my lap. I'd stroked his head while I sweat what felt like buckets of fever out of my body. It had taken me twenty minutes to realize this was the side of Curious that Aiden always saw, and while I enjoyed it and could understand why Aiden liked the overprotective Curious, I missed the hyperactive pup I'd always known.

Despite enjoying the ability to snuggle with Curious for the first time, it made me feel more like I was dying than having a fever break. As I'd stroked his hair I'd thought about my time with Aiden and it had been hell on my emotions. Aiden had taken great care of me on Tuesday, but it felt strange having Logan being overly protective of me like he was. Then I ended up feeling guilty when I realized he was being so snuggly because he was worried about me.

Looking across the desk at his big blue eyes and wide grin, I felt horribly guilty for getting hard while talking to Aiden. They were friends, but something had changed between Aiden and me on Tuesday.

Logan looked at me in confusion. "What the hell? You've been staring at your phone every single time I walk by here all afternoon and you've had this shit-eating grin. You're either watching porn or you're..." He thought about it and then his eyes got wide. "Or you're talking to Aiden!"

My face gave me away before I could school my reaction. "Finally!" Logan grinned. Despite his outward excitement, I could see sadness in his eyes. "Took you long enough."

I steepled my fingers in front of my face. "Logan, listen to me carefully. I'm not going to get together with Aiden."

He blinked and his mouth hung open. "But, but... but he's perfect for you!"

I shook my head. "Logan, he's a sweet boy. There's no denying that. But there are too many things holding us back. First and foremost, I'm not a Daddy."

"Bullshit!" Logan jumped to his feet and shut my door, flicking the lock into place. "That's the biggest load of bullshit that has ever come out of your mouth, Trenton Sylvan, and you know it! I see the way you are around him. Hell, I saw with my own two eyes the way you were swooning at him when I got home Tuesday. You were watching him like a hawk and kept trying to step in to help him. You have this need to help him and nurture him, even sick and fevered."

I held up my hands. "Logan, I'm not arguing this with you. I'm not going to be his Daddy." Dammit, why were those words so hard to swallow? "I'm not right for him." At least that sentence hadn't sat so sour in my stomach. I could sense the attraction we had. I couldn't pinpoint the exact moment things had changed earlier in the week, but there had been an energy that had gone from friendly banter to flirtation. Logan was right —I'd been trying to step in and do things for him, sick or not. I wanted to bring that carefree boy that Logan spent so much time with to the surface. I'd wanted to hear the giggles and receive the tender smiles he so freely gave Curious.

"Why not?" Logan demanded.

"Because he's yours!" I barked, trying to keep my voice low so we didn't have the rest of the office at the door wondering what we were arguing about.

The admission drew Logan up short and he chewed his lip. "He's not mine, Trent. He *can't* be mine. Story of my fucking life! I'm not what people need." He turned and left my office. A moment later I heard him quietly tell Tammy goodbye, then the front door shut.

"Fuck." I growled. Any pretense of working I had for the day left with Logan.

I couldn't imagine how he must have felt, knowing that he cared so deeply for two people but feeling like he couldn't be enough for either of us. Wait, scratch that. Yes, I could. I knew exactly how it felt to love someone yet not be what they needed. I dealt with it every single day when I saw Logan. I felt it every time I pushed him to go to DASH or go out with Aiden. I knew what it felt like when I watched him texting with someone and smiling happily.

In the last few weeks, I'd been feeling that familiar pain even more than I ever had before. Logan spent evenings texting furiously and laughing frequently, but for the first time in I couldn't remember how long, my phone wasn't the one blowing up with texts from him and the group. Every time it happened, I wanted to know who he was talking to, if he was talking to the person who would finally replace me in his life. How would I feel the day it happened? Aiden had made me starkly aware that it was going to happen. Maybe not with Aiden, but one day Logan was going to find the person he needed.

[Aiden] Ugh, next week is going to suck.

While I'd been having an existential crisis, Aiden had still been talking about his job.

[Me] Why are you doing it if you don't want to? You've been nearly dreading this job since I met you.

[Aiden] It pays really well. But the director of the shoot is a total asshole. I wouldn't be surprised if this shoot took twice as long as it was supposed to. This is probably why I need a Daddy.

My fingers flew across the screen without input from my brain.

[Me] And what do you see your Daddy being like?

Oh shit, that sounded flirty.

Aiden had clearly thought the question out well before then

because the answer came faster than I could think of a way to backpedal my question.

[Aiden] Easy, he wouldn't be afraid to take control. I don't just mean in the middle of a scene. I want a guy who will help me make decisions about work... who will talk through if I'm taking too many jobs, or just remind me that this particular guy is an asshole and to skip the job because I don't really need that money. But even things like getting more sleep, or not minding that I'm kinda needy. He would like to be in charge. Lots of hugs, not afraid to spank me when I'm not following rules.

My dick twitched at the idea of taking control, but when I read the last sentence, it went from interested to rock hard. Holy lord, it was like the man was made for me. I really shouldn't have asked.

Bubbles appeared then stopped. Then appeared again. I waited for him to continue and I didn't have to wait long.

[Aiden] Most Daddies I meet online bolt when they find out I'm a little. And Curious scares them off at the club. He says it's because they aren't good Daddies for me.

Maybe it was because I knew Colt and Derek. Maybe it was because I'd realized Aiden was a little as soon as I met him. Whatever the reason, it didn't bother me. It fit what I knew about him.

[Me] If Logan doesn't like them, I'd trust his gut. His gut has kept us alive more times than I can count.

I rolled my eyes at myself. I couldn't go down that road, especially after Logan had just left my office so down.

[Me] As for the job thing, if he's an ass, you shouldn't have taken the job. That's just setting yourself up to be stressed out. A job isn't worth your sanity.

[Aiden] Stop it, Trent. Don't overthink it. It's money. I like money. It's just going to be some really long hours with a guy I really don't like much.

He already knew me too well.

[Me] You and Logan should spend some time together before then.

[Aiden] We were already planning on going to DASH.

I knew I should have been happy, but the knowledge only made me grumpier.

LOGAN and I were the masters of bottling emotions up. I was pretty sure our combined abilities to not address the elephant in the room were what had ultimately led to us being able to move past our short-lived relationship and still be best friends. However, I was starting to wonder if we'd actually resolved our feelings or had just learned to ignore them.

By the time I'd arrived home, Logan was acting like the discussion in my office had never happened, so I tried to push the memory aside as well. It worked until we were heading to Steve's and my big mouth had to go and say something. "Aiden says you're going to DASH this weekend?"

Logan's eyes widened then a smirk crossed his face. "Jealous?"

Jealous? No. Absolutely not. Not at all. "Curious, that's all."

Logan rolled his eyes at me. "Yeah, we're going to go this weekend. He's stressed out about work starting up next week."

"What do you know about this shoot coming up?"

Logan thought for a moment then shook his head. "Actually, not much. He hasn't mentioned much of anything beyond the fact that he doesn't like the director. The guy is at best difficult to work with from what he says. The last time he had to work with him, the shoot ran over by nearly a week. Aiden's worried about the jobs he has lined up afterward if the first one runs late. Well, that and the warehouse they are shooting at is not climate controlled."

"It's what?" I barked the sentence out, then winced at the volume of my voice and forced myself to quiet down. "What do you mean? It's October!"

Logan shrugged. "Trent, I don't have control over this. It's a vacant warehouse on the outskirts of Nashville. You know how October can be. Some days we need the heat, some the AC, and sometimes we need both on the same day."

I growled, which only caused Logan to laugh. "God, you have it bad for him."

My growl stopped and I glanced over at Logan. "Please stop pushing me toward him. He's sweet, there's no denying that, but there are way too many hurdles in our path."

"It's time for you to find someone, Trent. I can't even remember the last time you went to DASH. Well, went to DASH when you weren't there with me or because of me."

Had Logan actually sounded a little embarrassed by that? "Pup, I enjoy going with you. I like watching you be able to let go and just *be*. But for the last few years it hasn't been as exciting for me to go and have a scene."

Logan didn't miss a beat. "That's because you need something different. Something that Aiden could give you!"

"Logan!"

"Okay, okay, but what if you're looking for something different? What if you don't want to be the big bad Dom anymore?"

Yeah, what if? And what did that mean?

We pulled into the parking lot at Steve's before I could answer Logan, and he bounded out of the truck to meet Aiden before I even had my seatbelt unbuckled. I was so lost in thought it took Dean poking me in the side and leveling me with a stare before I blinked out of my confusion.

"What's up with you?"

I shook my head like it could clear the cobwebs from my

brain. "Logan said something in the car that has my brain in some crazy places right now."

Dean smirked. "Did he point out that Aiden has been looking at you like you hung the moon the last two times we've been here?"

"Huh?" My head snapped over to Aiden, who turned his head and nervously rubbed at the back of his neck while he flushed a pretty shade of pink.

"Jesus, Trent, you're a mess. You just need to ask the boy out."

My eyes widened. What the hell did Dean know about Aiden? I didn't know if it was the look on my face or if my thoughts hadn't been completely in my head but Dean laughed sardonically. "He screams boy. I've never pried about your personal life, but dude, you're a control freak. I don't know if you're kinky or not, but I can't see you being happy with someone who didn't need you to take control, at least a little—"

"A lot," I said without thought.

Dean chuckled. "Yeah. That's what I thought."

"It's not that easy, Dean."

Dean's face went soft; I could almost call it sincere. "Want to talk about it?"

I sighed. "It's too complicated to discuss here, and it's so complicated I can't really talk about it anyway."

A snort from beside Dean alerted me to the fact that Merrick had shown up unexpectedly. "You've gotten yourself in one hell of a mess, Trent."

I narrowed my eyes at the man across the table. "What are you doing here?"

"Finished up early. I've got an early flight out tomorrow to wrap something up at my last job, but afterwards you guys are going to be seeing a lot of me in the near future. Better get used to it!"

That started a conversation about where Merrick was working—he wouldn't tell us—and how long he'd be there—he didn't know—and just how much we could bug him—he claimed he'd kill us. Thankfully, the distraction was exactly what I'd needed to get my mind off Aiden and Logan.

CHAPTER 20

AIDEN

LOGAN HAD INVITED me over to his house again, but something didn't feel right, so I suggested we go to the club instead. At least at DASH I could escape the reminders of Trent. I liked them... both of them. They were great guys. If it weren't for the fact that the idiots were cluelessly in love with one another, I could have easily fallen for either of them. Logan, with his steady presence, or Trent, with the sweet side he aimed at me and the growly, stern side he had with Logan. And if I had gotten off to thoughts of Trent turning that stern, no-nonsense side on me, I wasn't going to tell anyone.

I just had to remind myself that it wasn't going to happen. Those two shared so many easy touches and laughs, I didn't think even they realized how affectionate they were. How in the hell could anyone miss how in love they were with one another? It should have been weird to watch it and then have one of them turn their attention to me and give me a hug, or a gentle kiss, or wash my hands and face after a meal. The passing of weeks didn't seem to be helping me sort out why it all felt so right.

It wasn't even that it felt right in the moment but looking back on it I felt strange. No, it had felt normal. Every time Trent went from scolding Logan for whatever he was doing to gently tending to my needs, I melted a little more for him. Hell, I felt comfortable around Trent. He'd seen me little, and instead of making a big deal about it, he'd treated me like it was completely normal. Those weren't the actions of someone who was uncomfortable with what he'd seen.

Logan never shied away from my little side either. No matter where we chose to play, DASH or his house, he watched after me and played with me. He made sure I had Hedge, and he double-checked that my bag was packed and I hadn't left anything behind. The day he held my hand while Trent drove me to my house on their way to pick up Logan's truck from DASH had been surreal. He'd walked me to my door with Trent, and neither of them would leave until they knew I was safely inside and the door was locked behind me. I'd watched from the front window as Trent placed his hand on the small of Logan's back and Logan had leaned into him as they made their way back to the truck. It was the weirdest, most perfect experience I'd had.

I'd gone from being mostly alone to having two best friends and a bunch of other guys who had effortlessly folded me into their group of friends. My phone had never pinged with as many text messages as it had in the last few weeks. Numerous. Multiple times a day. I still didn't know how these men got anything done.

As a person who never had been great at making friends, especially since graduating high school, I'd appreciated their easy acceptance of me. After focusing everything I had on my career for so long, any friends I'd had growing up had drifted far away from me. Gaining friends was still a bit foreign to me, but it felt nice. Hell, I'd even gained a friend who was a little. Caleb had slowly begun responding to my texts more often, which was how I'd found myself on the floor of my room coloring in my zoo animals coloring book on Sunday afternoon, texting with Caleb.

[Me] I shouldn't have bought a new box of crayons at the store.

[Caleb] Daddy bought me new crayons last week. Oh, and new coloring books!

He attached a picture of what he was coloring at the moment, a primary-colored dinosaur with spots that looked more like decorated Easter eggs. I noticed the shirt he was wearing matched my favorite unicorn onesie I'd bought a few months earlier.

[Me] Oh! I have that onesie!

[Caleb] Cool! Mine's actually a sleeper.

[Me] That's what I wanted, but they were out when I bought it.

[Caleb] Daddy bought it for me.

I was going to tell myself I wasn't jealous. Not only of the fact that Caleb had the unicorn pajamas I really wanted, but also because his Daddy was the one who had bought them for him.

[Me] Jealous!

So I lied. Wouldn't be the first time, and wouldn't be the last. I shut my coloring book with a sigh. It really was time for me to start getting ready for Logan to arrive and I was only wearing a pair of light blue ankle socks and a T-shirt with a race car on it that matched my training pants. As I thought about what to take to the club, I took a drink of water out of my sippy cup, then grabbed a warm pair of pajamas from the hanger. They were light blue with rainbows on them. It was cold enough that I'd probably want warm pajamas at the club that night.

[Caleb] You should ask Trent for a pair. He'd buy them for you.

I inhaled the water I'd just taken a drink of and ended up in a coughing fit. Why the hell would I ask Trent to buy me pajamas?

"What?!" I gasped, still trying to catch my breath.

[Caleb] A? Are you okay?

How long had it been since I'd responded to him? I looked

down at the phone and realized three minutes had passed and I hadn't been coughing for a while.

[Me] *Why would he do that?*

The bubbles below the message appeared immediately.

[Caleb] *Oh good, I didn't kill you. But you can't be that thick. Trent looks at you like he wants to jump you.*

[Caleb] *Then again, so does Logan.*

[Me] *They do not!*

[Caleb] *OMG, you really are that clueless. Oh, A... You three are so perfectly clueless, and I thought I'd been bad when Travis and I started dating.*

I stared at my phone. What the hell did he mean? I started and deleted at least five texts to him when the next one came through.

[Caleb] *Logan and Trent are goo-goo for one another. Now that I know Logan's bisexual I can see it plain as day. But I also see how much they both like you. I swear, if Daddy looked at me the way Trent looks at you, I'd melt on the spot.*

Did Trent look at me like that? I didn't know. If he did, I'd missed it completely. There was no way he looked at me like that because he gave those looks to Logan.

[Caleb] *Oh, I'm totally having a Dexter moment!*

I didn't know if I wanted to know. The little I knew about Dexter told me that he lacked a filter completely. The conversation about his neighbor tickled my brain. I couldn't imagine Caleb ever having a moment when he was as over-the-top as Dexter. Of course, that was until the next text came in.

[Caleb] *What if you, Trent, and Logan are perfect for one another?*

A conversation shortly after I'd met Logan flooded back to me. He'd explained that his best friend was a Dom. He'd gone into great detail about how they'd attempted to date but their different interests had prevented them from forming a long-term relationship.

Before I'd ever met Trent I'd known that, despite what Logan might have said, he still loved Trent. It showed bright in his eyes every time he talked about his best friend. Then I met Trent and I'd seen the way he interacted with Logan. Compassion and care that went far deeper than friendship was clear in his every action. The two would never be happy with anyone else.

What I still couldn't parse was the sweet, doting Dom Trent continued to show himself as, when I'd been expecting a strict one. Logan had always made it sound like his friend had been attracted to brats. He'd even mentioned floggings and canings he'd witnessed. No matter how hard I tried, I couldn't see Trent giving a submissive anything more than an openhanded spanking or maybe a light flogging.

Mmm. I wasn't a pain slut by any stretch of the imagination, but a light, thuddy flogging I could easily get behind. Or was that in front of? Either way, the thought made me wiggle as my training pants became too tight.

My hand snaked down to massage the outside of my race car-printed briefs, and I hissed at the contact. I could almost pretend that it was Trent's large hand rubbing me, making sure I was hard, aching, and needy before he laid me over his lap and pulled my undies down. The thought of having my ass bared while Trent spanked me had my erection straining to break free from the confines of my terry briefs.

Sinking down to the floor, my hand slipped into my briefs. I kept my legs pressed firmly together as I let my mind wander. I could see me bent over Trent's lap, my cock between his thighs as he methodically spanked me. The need to cum would build slowly as my skin heated. I stroked myself in time to the imaginary swats. He'd be thorough, making sure every inch of my exposed ass was reddened.

The fantasy was so real I could hear myself moaning, begging to cum between spanks. "Please." I was too far gone to care that I'd begun to voice my fantasy. My wiggles had pulled my underwear down below my ass cheeks, the rough carpet against my tender skin serving to drive my need higher. I frantically pumped my cock up and down, my hand struggling to find room to move in the snug underwear. The lack of room, the inability to fully stroke myself, kept my orgasm just out of reach. Then I rocked my ass and the carpet abraded my flesh.

One second, I thought I was going to be on the edge for the rest of the night, the next, cum was coating my hand and filling my training pants. Until that point, my fantasies always ended with my orgasm. That time, Trent's firm hand was replaced by Logan's big blue eyes peering into my face. He was so real I felt like I could touch him.

Sprawled out on the floor, my hand still in my undies as my dick softened, I couldn't bring myself to move. I could hear Trent's soothing words about what a good boy I'd been, and I could feel Logan curled up against me as I undoubtedly floated away in subspace. The fantasy was so vivid.

And so fucked up.

I was brought out of my reverie with a jolt. I'd been fantasizing about Logan and Trent, together, with me. They had a past that I didn't share, and I suspected they had a future together as well, once they figured their shit out.

At least reality finally had me able to move again. I forced myself off the floor and stripped out of my underwear. I'd just cleaned myself up and put a diaper on when I remembered Caleb. I reread the last text and that time, instead of insane lust, I saw it for as funny as it was and barked out a startled laugh so loud I was sure the neighbors heard. That was the most preposterous thing I'd heard in my entire life.

The doorbell rang before I figured out how to respond. And I was still standing in my bedroom in just socks, a T-shirt, and a brightly patterned diaper.

Fuck.

[Me] *Logan just got here. Gotta go.*

I ignored the pings on my phone as I headed toward the front door. Logan had seen me in less. He'd survive.

"Hey," I greeted Logan, stepping to the side so he could enter my house. It was a small rental I'd picked up a few years earlier, but it was perfect for me. The huge walk-in closet and the "room" with only one small window that abutted a densely wooded lot and was ideal for editing photos without annoying sun glare had sold me on it as soon as I walked through it the first time. The landlord, an octogenarian who kept the place in good repair but left me alone otherwise, was the icing on the good-rental cake. She'd liked me when I started asking about her feelings on my updating the house a little as time and money allowed. We'd worked out a great deal where she deducted the costs of any home repairs I did as long as I included my receipts with my rent payment.

"You okay? It sounded like you were yelling when I got out of my car."

Confusion creased my brow, then I remembered the bark of laughter from Caleb's text. "Fine. Caleb was being ridiculous. In his words, he had a Dexter moment."

Logan groaned. "Oh god, I don't even want to know. Dexter makes me look like a snuggly lapdog."

I leaned forward and pecked Logan's cheek. "You are a snuggly lapdog with me."

Logan smiled at me. "You seem to have forgotten to get ready." Then his eyes lit up. "Can I help?"

My flapping mouth and inability to form a sentence had Logan laughing. "Inappropriate?" he questioned.

I... I didn't know. Was it? Between the two of us? It probably wasn't. When I thought about it a moment longer, it felt natural for us. It wasn't a sexual or dominant thing. It was all very different than the feelings I got when Trent had cut up my pancakes or helped me rebuild my tower while throwing the ball for Curious.

I shook my head and offered a smile, then took Logan's hand and directed him to my bedroom. "Nah, come on." I'd already had some clothes laid out, but my toys had been more interesting and then... well, other things distracted me. Logan let go of my hand and glanced back and forth between the jeans and the snug pajama pants on my bed, then he tapped his chin while he examined me before finally coming to a decision. He scooped the pants off the bed, then crouched down. "It's cool enough that you can wear a coat into DASH. No one will see your diaper before we get there, and once we do it won't be a surprise."

I slid each of my legs into the openings while using Logan's shoulders for support. He stood while he pulled them up, making sure they were seated properly at my waist. A glance down told me my diaper was easily noticeable, but he was right—a coat would cover the majority of the bulge and DASH was in a remote area of downtown that was virtually unused on the weekends. Anyone around that area would be on their way into the club and wouldn't care if they noticed my less than adult attire.

Logan looked around my room, his head tilting to either side as he searched for something. I couldn't help but feel like I was looking more at Curious than Logan. "Is your bag packed?"

Shit. I knew I'd forgotten something. I shook my head. "Not yet."

Logan actually lit up with the admission. "Can I help?"

Yup, Curious was... curious.

Knowing Logan was more Curious than Logan, some of the more adult reservations I might have had slipped away. Just like when we were at DASH together, as Curious came more fully to the surface, I became more little than big.

I wondered briefly what Logan would think when I opened the closet. Sure, I had plenty of nice jeans and shirts for work and dates, but my onesies, sleepers, toys, and most specifically my diaper collection had grown exponentially since I'd moved in. I'd never shared my closet with anyone before. It was private, but Logan wasn't just any person. He'd seen me little and he'd seen me vulnerable and had never taken advantage of me in any way. Logan was my friend, but he was also so much more. He was my puppy, my guard dog, and like it or not, I had feelings for him.

I trusted him.

It wasn't hard to imagine Logan's tail wagging back and forth as I reached for the closet door. Why he was so excited to see my stuff was beyond me, but his excitement was contagious. I opened the door to my closet and flipped the light switch on. Logan didn't need his tail on for me to envision it wagging rapidly.

"I had no idea you had so much! This explains why I never see you in the same outfit. Oh, puppies and dinos." He tripped over his tongue on the last sentence from talking so fast.

Pangs of nervousness hit my belly. Was it going to be too much for Logan?

Then he surprised me again. "Look at all the toys!" His head shot over toward me so fast I got dizzy for him. "You never told me you had so many toys."

I didn't have that many toys. It was a shelf. And they were my favorites. Some dinosaurs, a few soft balls, and stacking toys. Then my eyes settled back on the balls. Curious noticed them too.

I picked a soft red-and-blue ball up. The fabric crinkled as I held it, and when I shook it, the bell inside jingled around. "Want to take this one to the club tonight?"

Logan—or maybe that was Curious—bobbed his head excitedly, then took the ball from me, tucking it safely under his arm. He focused back on the things in front of us. "If you keep distracting me with things that make noise, we're never going to get to DASH. How many diapers do you need for tonight?"

I thought about my diaper bag that was still by my bed. "Just one. There's one in there if I need a change while we're at the club."

Logan tapped his chin as he looked over the selection. I knew what he was going to pick, probably before he did. If he didn't choose the ones with the puppy patterns on them, I'd eat my left shoe. Sure enough, when his eyes fell on the stack of diapers with puppies, he reached out for one. "Perfect. What else do you need? Pajamas for coming home? Or different undies?"

It struck me how much Logan paid attention to me at the club. He knew I usually went home in warm pajamas, and he also knew that I didn't usually wear diapers on the way home. I tended to not be as little when we left as when we got there, so I normally wore a pair of training pants home.

I scratched my head in thought. When was the last time I wore any of my regular briefs? I couldn't even remember, which probably meant that it was sometime around my last job.

The thought of work soured my stomach and threatened to bring me out of the comfortable place I'd found. I had to force myself to focus back on Logan and his questions. "Yeah, I should take some undies. I don't think I have a pair in my bag. And I need a pair of pajamas for when we leave. I haven't restocked my bag from last time we played at your house."

Warmth pooled in my stomach as I thought about Trent helping me rebuild my tower, and his sweet smiles and the tender attention he paid to me. I was definitely harboring a crush on him, but one look at Logan—bubbly and excited—and I was feeling the same thing about him. What a fucked-up place my head was.

Logan was so engrossed in finding things for me for the evening that he didn't seem to notice all of my confusion. When I looked back at him, he had his phone out and was studying the weather app closely. "Okay. It's going to be pretty cold tonight. Warm pajamas it is." With that, he started looking at my longer pajamas and finally settled on a snug-fit plaid union suit. The thermal material would keep me plenty warm between the club and Logan's truck and from his truck back to my house.

Logan had already tossed them over his arm when he noticed the snaps up the seat. His eyebrows waggled and his blue eyes twinkled with mischief. "Easy access. These could be fun."

My cock started to thicken as I thought of all the fun Logan and I could have, especially if I wasn't wearing a thick diaper. Logan must have had the same idea because he didn't take nearly as long to pick out a pair of undies for me, and I noticed him trying to adjust himself as we left the closet.

The thought of naughty fun had us both moving in the direction of his truck. A bottle and a sippy cup as well as a few snacks for me were packed quickly into my bag. Logan found Hedge and my binkie in the living room, and helped me into my coat within minutes of leaving my bedroom.

We were barely buckled in when Logan's truck rumbled to life. He handed over Hedge and grinned. "To DASH we go."

CHAPTER 21

TRENT

I DRUMMED IMPATIENTLY on my knee as I waited for the phone to connect. It took me three rings to realize there was a phone ringing in the hallway that matched the pattern of the call I was trying to connect. Before I could call out, my friend Merrick turned the corner to my office, grinning wolfishly.

"Four missed calls from you in an hour. What's up with you? Someone die?"

I dropped my feet to the floor and blinked at the man in shock. Last I'd heard he was in some no-man's-land out west trying to turn a restaurant around. "What the hell are you doing here?" I demanded as my feet and brain finally started working together and I stood to envelop him in a hug. "I thought you weren't going to be back for a while."

Merrick slapped my back a few times before releasing me. "Got done in Nebraska early today. Caught the first damn flight out of there I could." The harsh overhead lighting in my office glinted off threads of silver in Merrick's otherwise dark hair as he looked around. "Oddly, I've missed this little part of the world. Not here, because this place has that jail cell chic vibe happening, but, you know, this part of Tennessee."

At thirty-six, I'd never lived away from Kingston Springs except for the four years I'd been at college. Even then, it was only thirty minutes away in Nashville. The desire to fly the coop, so to speak, had never been strong in me. Merrick, however, had graduated from a high school in some no-name town in Missouri, moved to New York and ended up as a flair bartender for a handful of years, then ended up in Tennessee for a few months to finish a business degree he'd started online. I'd met him in a class we had together and we became fast friends. By the time I met Merrick, I'd also met a handful of other guys who had wormed their way into my life to stay. After graduation, he'd used his connections to start a restaurant consultation business and spent the vast majority of his life on the road.

We were all good friends, but Merrick and I seemed to have a deeper bond than I had with the rest of the guys. We were close enough that he had figured out I was a Dom even before I'd figured it out for myself. Over the years, I discovered our close group of friends was a bunch of kinky fucks, and the older we got the more evident it became. I hadn't realized how dominant we were until it had taken Travis, Merrick, Dean, and me to get Logan out of the bar earlier in the year. At various points in the evening, I'd picked up on the exasperated Dom tones of all the men, as well as the stern looks they'd given Logan.

Shortly after that evening, I'd heard Travis's boyfriend call him Daddy. While it hadn't been as surprising to me as it would have been a few weeks earlier, it solidified that we all had secrets. It was nice to not feel the need to hide my own interests from our group, but I was still the most comfortable talking to Merrick about the things currently running through my head.

"Personally, I like it here. Wouldn't think about moving."

Merrick chuckled. "Obviously, you've made a nice life for yourself. I think I'm ready to hang around for a little longer this time myself. But you haven't called me four times to tell me you like it here. What's up?"

I sat heavily in my desk chair and gestured to the chair across from me before scrubbing my hand over my face. "I've managed to get myself into a sticky situation."

Merrick's body shook with the effort to not laugh at me. "Really? Trent Sylvan managed to get himself into a sticky situation. Wait, let me guess—Logan's involved too. Because if you're into something, Logan's usually right there with you."

My head hit the desk. "Fuck. My. Life. Yes, Logan's involved, but you have no idea how."

"From your reaction, I'm guessing this is something to do with you falling in love with him."

"What?" I yelped, unable to stop myself. No one knew. I'd always kept my body language and feelings toward him completely platonic around others.

"Bingo. So, Logan's not as in love with you as you are with him or what?"

I blinked my eyes, trying to figure out words. "Logan's not—"

Merrick held up a hand to stop me. "I swear to god, Trent, if you try to tell me that Logan isn't into men, I'm going to hit you with that stapler. Even if he isn't into men in general, he's been into you as long as I've known him."

"I've been in love with him since we were teenagers. When we broke up a few years ago, I realized he's the one, but... ugh." The word was more growled than anything else. "Our needs just don't align well."

The words stopped Merrick in his tracks. Any argument he was going to have fell away. "What?"

And just like that, the dam burst and I spilled everything for the first time. From meeting Logan at the football game when we were in high school to falling in love with him shortly thereafter. From trying dating and how it didn't work out to us falling into bed together every few weeks since then. I even threw in the part when Logan had told me he loved me while he was asleep.

Given that it was the first time I'd breathed a word to anyone about my feelings for him, it turned into verbal diarrhea. It seemed like every emotion I'd felt for Logan over the last handful of years was struggling to come out at the same time. I stopped short of telling Merrick about Logan being into puppy play, but I made sure to tell him that Logan just wasn't submissive enough for me.

Merrick sat quietly while he listened to me bare my heart and soul to him, but as my story ended he nodded. "You two are too fucking similar and stubborn as mules. You two would kill one another. I'm always shocked that you two have lived together for so long without one of you snapping. Now that I know you dated, I'm even more surprised. But I think it also speaks to the love you two have for one another. I've watched you two together for years. He balances you out nicely; you would be so stuffy and serious without him. He makes you laugh and be kind of immature and not take yourself so seriously. You guys are a perfect match in almost every way, but you're right—Logan doesn't want a Dom. Logan probably needs someone to focus on almost as much as you do."

Merrick held up a finger before I could cut him off. "I hear you, and I see that Logan isn't a Dom, or a sub, but he is like a kid on a sugar high. Does he ever stop in the office?"

My laugh echoed off the mostly empty walls of my office. "Logan has an inflatable dinosaur desk chair so he can bounce when he sits. It's supposed to be like one of those balance ball chair things, but it's a dinosaur." No, Logan never stopped. If he wasn't bouncing at his desk, he was pacing. I'd even come in one weekend and installed a basketball hoop out back, mainly for him to have something to do while he was on duty. He thought best while he was moving. Of course, he wasn't the only one who had benefited from the basketball hoop, but that wasn't the point at that moment.

Merrick was still chuckling to himself as he continued. "Dinosaur chair. Why doesn't that surprise me? See, Logan needs something to help him focus. It wouldn't surprise me if Logan ended up with someone he could pay a lot of attention to. Someone he could focus on without the expectation of needing to be the dominant partner." He was quiet for a moment. "You know, now that I think about it, he'd be great with someone like Aiden."

Aiden. Merrick hadn't meant to hit a sore spot, but he had.

"Whoa, Trent, what's that face about?"

"Aiden." If I'd groaned his name just a little, Merrick didn't react. "He wants a Daddy so badly, but I watch him and Logan together and they are so in tune with one another. I didn't understand it at first. Aiden told me that Logan was his..." I stopped myself before I said guard dog. "His protector. Kind of like his shadow. He said that Logan loves lying with him while he plays. Logan. Lying."

Merrick wasn't stupid. He was putting things together—I could see it in his eyes. But to his credit, he only pressed enough to see the bigger picture. His words were quiet and I suspected they weren't directed at me. It felt like he was working out the puzzle on his own. "Play what? If Logan is lying with him, I don't see this being active play. You said the guy wants a Daddy. Is he a little?"

I didn't say anything but felt my head nod as the memory of Logan and Aiden coming down the steps that first Sunday morning came to mind. Both of them holding hands and Aiden's eyes lighting up as he saw his breakfast. Then Aiden's big brown eyes when I caught him and Logan in my tub. I clearly remembered the way he instinctively moved closer to me the day I walked out back and found them playing together. And how could I forget the sweet blushes as we'd watched TV while I'd been sick? I hadn't been making that attraction up. Actually, that day was the day things had gone from a low-key crush to an infatuation. At least for me.

I couldn't forget, and I couldn't ignore. Things had changed; our interactions were different. I was willing to bet my left nut that I wasn't the only one who'd noticed the change either. As ridiculous as it sounded, even in my head, it was like we were magnets being drawn together.

"They met at the BDSM club. They have this amazing chemistry together. But Aiden is so sweet. I got to make him breakfast one morning a few weeks ago, and the way his eyes lit up—I would do it every morning if I could. He's screaming for someone to take care of him. Part of me is itching to be that man. I haven't been able to stop thinking about him since I met him. There's something about him that's telling me I could be that man for him. But I'm not a Daddy. I never have been. I have no experience. Besides, he's Logan's."

I blew out a breath in frustration and felt the sigh all the way down to my toes. What a fucked-up situation to be in.

"Okay, first things first. You're an idiot. If you really think that you can't be a Daddy, you're blind. I've never seen you fail at anything you've put your mind to... well, anything but book-keeping."

"Fuck you," I mumbled under my breath, causing Merrick to laugh at me.

When he finally got himself under control, he continued. "If you wanted to be Aiden's Daddy, there's no doubt in my mind you'd make it happen. You'd be great at it. You take care of everyone—Logan included. You never ask for anything in return. You are constantly making sure we have what we need. If you don't hear from us, you're calling. And holy hell, do you like order. You'd make a great Daddy. And it would be a perfect fit because Logan's not a Dom."

That was a lot to take in. But I was going to focus on what I didn't have to soul search on to answer. "They both say they know they can't be in a relationship."

Merrick's finger tapped at the top of my desk. "Let me get this straight. You're a Dom. You're in love with a man who is not a submissive but also not a Dom. That man is also in love with you, though he doesn't know you know that. The man you love found a submissive who wants a Daddy. And that guy gives Logan the ability to relax and be calm."

I nodded as Merrick spoke. "Fucked-up situation. Right?"

"So, what you're telling me is that Logan is attracted to a sub and to you. You're attracted to the sub and Logan. And the sub is definitely attracted to Logan, and you feel like there could be something going on between the two of you as well."

I deflated. "Yes."

"So what's holding you back from going after the sub?" Merrick asked the question like the answer was obvious, but it was anything but to me.

"Because the guy has a relationship with Logan. I'm not going to fuck that up."

Merrick pinched the bridge of his nose. "Trent Sylvan, listen to me carefully. Logan has a relationship with *both* of you. Why can't you have a relationship with both of them?"

"Huh?"

"I'm going to go out on a limb here and say that it sounds like the three of you each have something the others need. Emotionally, sexually, physically—you guys are all attracted to one another. So make it work."

I blinked. *Make it work.* "You mean like the three of us together?" I was going to ignore the way my voice rose as I spoke. The shock was making it hard to think.

Merrick rolled his eyes at me. "For being a kinky fuck, you're sure as hell oblivious to this. Yes, Sheriff, the three of you. Triads are legitimate, healthy relationships. A lot of research has happened over the last few years about how healthy it is to be in a relationship with more than one partner. Not only in a financial sense, but emotionally and physically. Look, I could go on, but by the way your eyes are bugging out of your head right now, I think I've managed to rattle you too much for you to process it all."

Yeah, my brain was rattled. I'd never thought of a triad before. In my head, I could have Logan or Aiden, and in order to have Aiden, I would have had to hurt Logan. I'd closed off the idea to the point that I was struggling to make sense of having one of them, much less both of them. Was it really as easy as Merrick was making it sound? Probably not. But the real question was if either of them would be interested in giving the three of us a go. Was I? At least I could answer that one with a resounding *Hell, yes.*

"Where's Logan, anyway? I haven't heard him."

Merrick's question brought me out of my thoughts. "DASH."

"With the sub." It wasn't a question.

I nodded. "Yes. They were going because he starts work next week and is going to be stressed out, and he wanted some time to relax before it got insane."

Merrick smirked. "And it's been driving you nuts that you can't do anything to help the boy relax. Or better yet, not work too hard."

My laugh was dry. "Fuck yes, it's driving me insane. He's a photographer, and his schedule for the next few weeks is absurd. But the biggest thing is the director of the first shoot is an ass. Doesn't Aiden know how to say no? Logan told me Aiden's doing fine with money. He shouldn't be killing himself for some asshole who doesn't respect anyone."

Merrick chuckled. "Down, boy."

"Why did he take the job?"

Merrick ignored my question. "When is your shift over?"

I glanced at the clock on my computer screen and cursed. "Twenty minutes ago. How the fuck have you been here two hours already?"

"Uh, because you felt the need to verbally spew your entire life to me after I got here?" He pointed to the door. "Go find your men. I'll show myself out."

"Asshole." But I got up and headed out of my office behind Merrick. This plan had the potential to backfire spectacularly, but I'd never know if I didn't try. First thing I needed to do was go find Logan and Aiden at DASH.

"GOOD EVENING, SYLVER." Alice greeted me as I entered the club, smiling as always. At least I didn't look as mutinous as I had when I showed up for that rope demo Logan was doing. *Fucking ropes.*

I handed over my membership card so she could scan it into the system. "Hey, Alice. Has Curious made it in?"

"Got here about an hour ago. Last I heard he was in the play-room with someone."

Aiden. "Thanks so much." I shot her a big smile as I headed through the door. I stopped at the small desk just on the other side to fill out my name tag: *Sylver, Dom, not open to play.* If I had taken a few seconds to think about it, I'd have been shocked that it was only the second time I'd put *not open to play* on my name tag, the first being that rope demo. With my name tag in place, I headed toward the playroom.

As I rounded the corner, my heart skipped a beat at the sight before me. Logan was curled around Aiden, just like Aiden had said he did, while he batted at a soft ball in front of him. Aiden had one hand on Logan's back while he focused on his coloring page.

I moved quietly and took a seat on the couch behind them. Watching the pair from afar felt wrong, but I couldn't bring myself to interrupt them. I'd seen Curious plenty of times. I knew what Logan was like as Curious, knew his mannerisms and his likes and dislikes. But Curious lying quietly was new. When I was with him at the club, he was usually going a mile a minute.

The boy lying on his stomach in a cute pair of pajamas was new to me, even from the few times I'd watched him with Logan at home. This boy had sunk further into his role. I couldn't see his face from my position, but his legs swayed back and forth in the air and his head tilted to the side as he colored.

When Aiden's hand stopped moving down Curious' back, Curious would bat the ball toward Aiden. Aiden would let out an exasperated huff, push the ball back, and resume petting Curious.

After about ten minutes, I started trying to picture the three of us in a relationship. Where we would each fit. Would one of us feel like the odd man out? Logan and I had sexual chemistry and shared love that I'd never experienced with anyone else. He could bring me out of my worst moods better than anyone else I knew. Even at his craziest, I didn't know anyone I'd rather spend time with.

My Dom side craved Aiden. I didn't have to know him as well as I knew Logan to know I wanted him. The way he practically melted when he saw his breakfast plate had me almost handing my heart over to him that morning. But as sweet as he was, he was also strong. I already knew that from how he'd held himself around Logan and how he so easily took charge when I was sick. When Logan panicked, Aiden hadn't been afraid to run to his side. He'd been worried but determined to stay with Logan until he was feeling like himself again.

Most importantly to me, Aiden gave Logan a peace that I'd never seen before. A sense of calm that settled over him and allowed him to rest. In all the years we'd known each other, I couldn't remember ever seeing Logan so at peace just lying down. For me to get him to that point, I had to either fuck him senseless or join him on a ten-mile run, then basically bear-hug him in bed until he fell asleep. I'd stopped the latter when it turned into a ten-mile run *and* shower sex before he was ready to pass out in bed.

Could I be what Aiden needed long term, though? Could I be the Daddy he craved? I'd always been a strong-handed Dom to bratty subs, but whether I'd known it or not, I'd figured out I wasn't looking to settle down with a brat well before I'd met Aiden. I just hadn't ever been someone's Daddy before. It was a huge responsibility, an undertaking even greater than my job as Sheriff Sylvan. If Aiden wanted a Daddy, and he saw me as fit to be his, I would have to be willing to put him first—well, tied with Logan—in everything I did. Was that a responsibility I was ready for?

My mind kept drifting back to Colt and his husband, Derek. Every time I saw them together, I accepted more and more that I wanted something similar to their love. Colt wasn't just Daddy to Derek in scenes, he was always Daddy. Colt couldn't shut it off, and Derek didn't want him to. Derek happily handed decisions over to Colt and Colt took every single one he could.

Sure, it was complicated for them. Derek was a country music superstar, and Colt was the sheriff of Kingfield. So Colt juggled being Daddy to a country musician and Dad to their three kids as well as his own demanding job. That had to be more difficult than juggling being in a relationship with two men, right?

The more I thought about it, the more I didn't care if it was more difficult. I was up for the challenge. I could easily see myself sitting with Aiden, going over his calendar and schedule, while throwing a ball for Curious.

Then Merrick's words came back to me. *Logan balanced me out.* He kept me grounded and from taking myself too seriously. Like it or not, Logan would also keep me from smothering Aiden. Because that was something I could easily see myself doing. For the first time, I truly understood why Logan and I never would have worked long term. Merrick was right—I was intense and he was easygoing. But with someone like Aiden, I could be intense. I could take control and help him find a healthy balance between work and life. And when I inevitably started to hover too much or butt in just a little more than was healthy, Logan wouldn't have a problem reminding me that Aiden was his own man.

Aiden's hand moving down Logan's back caught my eye and I watched for a moment. The farther down it snaked, the more intrigued I became. Finally, it ran over his ass, and Logan's hips rocked downward to hump into the floor. A whine escaped his mouth and Aiden did it again. That time, his hand slipped farther between Logan's legs. Logan spread them and whimpered.

My cock began to thicken as I watched Aiden's pets move from innocent to more erotic. He wasn't shy or hesitant. He knew exactly what he was doing to Logan. For his part, Logan was eating the touches up. Moans and groans and thrusts spurred Aiden's explorations on. The next time Aiden's hand moved over his ass, Logan spread his legs and arched into the touch. His heavy balls were noticeable, even beneath his sweats.

My men were hot together.

The thought made my eyes widen. At some point since I'd arrived, through all my thoughts and musings, I'd made up my mind. I wanted to give it a try. Three men in a relationship might not be the most conventional partnership, but we were perfect for one another. Besides, any relationship I'd be happy in wouldn't be conventional, so why not throw conventionality a little further out there?

I cleared my throat. If they were going to be mine, I needed to set some boundaries. Their getting off in the playroom at the club for anyone to see was not going to happen. The only person I wanted to be able to watch my men bring themselves to orgasm was me.

Possessive? Who me?

CHAPTER 22

LOGAN

THE THROAT BEING CLEARED behind us made me jump. The movement had me tagging myself in the balls and whimpering. But when my body spun around to see who was so rudely interrupting Aiden's explorations, I couldn't believe my eyes. The growl that had already built in my chest stopped in its tracks.

What the fuck was Trent doing here? In the playroom. At DASH.

I had never seen him in the playroom before, so why now? Before I could open my mouth to demand answers, Aiden let out a soft whimper beside me. It was decidedly not uncomfortable. He'd twisted around so he could see Trent, but his hand was still on me. "Daddy." Aiden's tongue traced his bottom lip for a moment, and when I looked into his eyes, they were hooded and focused on Trent. The "Daddy" that had slipped across his lips lacked any of the teasing it had in the past.

What was going on? I felt like I'd been pulled from ecstasy and crash-landed in a spiky bed of reality. A reality where Aiden was looking at Trent like he was a hot piece of meat.

Before I could fully process how I felt about Aiden looking at Trent the same way he looked at me, before I could become jealous because Trent could give him something I couldn't, he looked over at me. The same smoldering heat flashed in his eyes that he'd been giving Trent seconds before. I wasn't sure if it was shock from Trent's sudden appearance or just that Aiden didn't care, but his hand hadn't moved from my body. When I'd rolled over, it had gone from resting on my ass to resting on my very confused dick. I'd gone from rock hard and aching to cum, to soft in the blink of an eye. Now, I was half-hard and confused.

Trent's eyes were so intense it was hard for my cock to not take notice. Usually when he had that look in his eyes, I would be walking funny for a day. But given that Aiden was in the room and Aiden was exactly what Trent needed, I knew it wasn't directed at me.

Aiden smirked and palmed my dick. I moaned again, my confused dick deciding that it was more aroused than turned off. Trent's eyes tracked to Aiden and he growled low at the action. *What the fuck?* Aiden stared at Trent like it was a game they were playing before he slipped his hand below my waistband and found my cock. An involuntary shiver ran up and down my spine before Aiden moved his hand. When he finally stroked up the length of my erection, I couldn't help the whimper that came out of me. Aiden could send me tumbling over the edge faster than I could get myself off, and the way he twisted his fist and rubbed his thumb over my slit at the very top of the stroke had me dangerously close to cumming in my pants.

Trent shook his head, then narrowed his eyes at me like I'd done something wrong. "Is this what happens when you two come to DASH alone?"

I tried to remind him that this was in fact a BDSM club, but as I opened my mouth, Aiden flicked his thumb over the head of my cock, gathering the bead of precum that had formed. All that came out was a squeak before I forgot the question.

"Naughty boy, don't make the pup cum in his pants."

It was Aiden's turn to whimper, and by the way he squirmed,

he was likely closer to cumming than I was. The distraction from playing with my dick finally cleared enough so my brain could come back online and I was able to prop myself up on my elbows. "We're at a BDSM club—of course sex happens here. And yes, sometimes sexy things happen between us."

Trent's nostrils flared and his eyes hardened. He was pissed, but there was another emotion behind it, an emotion I struggled to identify. Trent's stride was measured as he made his way over to us. He got so close that Aiden had no choice but to twist his body around in order to see Trent. I almost sighed in relief as his hand left my pants.

Trent made it to my feet and crouched down, looking between both of us. And, nearly eye to eye with him, I knew what I was looking at. Trent was looking at Aiden with the same intensity he used to look at me. The look that screamed I was his. I felt my heart begin to break. I knew it would happen at some point, but to witness it with my own eyes hurt more than I'd originally thought it would. When he turned his gaze to me, the intensity in his eyes didn't falter. It was the same look he'd given Aiden. The emotion that welled up in me caused me to draw back.

Trent's eyes softened, concern etched across his forehead when I pulled my legs away. "Hey, pup, what's wrong?" The gentle tone, the true concern, the way he reached for me, it was too easy to picture him still being mine.

I forced myself to swallow the lump that had lodged in my throat as I tried to bring myself to stand up. "I should probably leave you guys alone."

Aiden grabbed for me as I slipped back, but my eyes didn't leave Trent's. I couldn't stay there and feel like a third wheel. Trent's eyes lost the gentleness they'd had. "Logan, stop." I might not have been submissive, but the finality of his command still caused me to still.

He didn't give me time to move farther back before he closed the distance between us. "You're spooked." His voice was back to gentle.

I tried to shrug off his concern. "I wanted to give you guys some time alone. You don't need me here."

Trent's chuckle was far from amused. "You're wrong about that." He gestured to the toys Aiden had in the room. "I'll help you guys clean up, then we'll go to one of the private rooms to talk without anyone overhearing."

Aiden looked confused, but his head bobbed up and down. "I don't want you to leave," he whispered quietly as Trent turned his attention to the small pile of items in the middle of the floor.

I didn't have a clue what was happening, but Trent seemed to be convinced that I wasn't leaving here and Aiden didn't want me to go. Instead of trying to make heads or tails of it, I adjusted my sweatpants and helped clean up the toys that were left on the floor. I tucked the red ball into the bag we'd brought with us as Aiden gathered Hedge and his sippy cup from the floor. Trent returned the coloring book and crayons to the shelf, then grabbed the diaper bag off the floor, slinging it casually over his shoulder. He held his hands out, an invitation for each of us to take one, and waited for us to move toward him.

Aiden looked at me, I looked at Aiden, and neither of us moved from our spots. This was the most surreal situation I'd been in, and that was saying a lot. Trent cleared his throat impatiently, shaking his hands slightly as if we'd forgotten what he wanted us to do. *Damn impatient man.* It was like Aiden and I had an invisible band linking us together because we stepped forward in unison.

Trent took the lead from there and closed the distance between us, grasping each of our hands. Possession, tenderness, love, worry—how I could feel all of those things in a simple touch was beyond me. Like he thought I'd bolt given half the chance, his hold was just this side of firm. His palms were sweaty, and I ventured a glance to his neck where I could see his pulse fluttering rapidly. *Nervous.* Trent was nervous. What the hell was going on?

He led us to a vacant room, pausing briefly to write our time in on it. The rule in the club was that there was a time limit on the room if we wanted complete privacy, so I knew Trent planned to shut the door. It also meant we would have an hour of complete solitude. For better or worse. For once, I wasn't going to fight Trent taking the lead. I had no idea what to expect, and I felt out of my depth. While I wanted to fall apart and mourn the loss of Trent in my life, there was something tickling my brain, urging me to be patient, because this moment didn't feel final.

Trent let our hands go as we approached the bed and he situated himself in the middle. He seemed to take forever to find a comfortable spot where his back was resting against the head-board and his feet were stretched out in front of him. "Come here, guys." He patted each side of the bed gently. Aiden went more readily, crawling straight over Trent's lap and adjusting himself so he was comfortably nuzzled into Trent's side. I took a bit longer to convince myself to climb on the bed. I only had to show the willingness to join them and Trent wrapped an arm around me and pulled me close. It seemed strange that Trent took longer making sure I was settled beside him than he had with Aiden.

Trent reached for my hood, then stilled. "Can I take this off, pup?" I gave a small nod and allowed him to gently remove it. "I want to be able to see your face tonight." He became concerned by whatever he saw on my face and used his thumb to smooth creases from my forehead. I hadn't known they were there, but his touch was making the muscles in my body relax. "Logan, you look like you're about to be sick."

I shook my head, though the movement was jerky and I didn't expect it was very convincing. Trent laced his fingers in mine and kissed my temple. "Please, I need to talk. With both of you. And I'm nervous as hell. I really need you to hear me out before you come to any conclusions."

There was no way I could walk away at that point. No matter how much I wanted to just leave and let the cards fall where they may, Trent had always been there for me. He'd been my best friend, sometimes my only true friend, since I was fifteen. If he needed me, I'd stay, even if what he had to say had the potential to destroy me. "Okay."

Trent's body relaxed slightly, surprising me with how much tension he had been holding. Even as his body relaxed, his hand tightened around mine. He took a deep breath and waited a beat before exhaling. "Listen, I think what I'm going to say is going to sound insane. At least it sounds insane in my head." He turned to Aiden, and while I couldn't see his face, his voice was kind though unsure. "Just like I need Logan to hear me out, I need you to hear me out too."

Aiden's face was more confused than anything else, but he nodded. "That's fine. Take your time."

Trent's shoulders relaxed a bit. "Thank you." Turning back to me, he studied my face for a long time. "When I got here tonight, I had a lot going on in my head. Merrick and I had a long talk this evening. I didn't fully understand what he meant at first, but I get it now." Trent's face showed amusement as he looked at my confusion. "Sorry, I'm not making a lot of sense, but just hang with me for a few. I'll get there. Promise."

Trent's eyes turned watery as he thought. "For years, I've been frustrated that we couldn't make it work. I fell in love with you when we were teenagers, and that love has always been there. It's been there since even before I knew you were bisexual, before we started to date, and it hasn't stopped just because we broke up. When we had finally decided to give dating a try, I thought my every dream was coming true. But we couldn't make it work. I've spent two years thinking that if I could find a way to turn off my need to be in control, we could be together again."

Hearing the pain in Trent's voice had my emotions fraying. "I've had similar thoughts. Except mine have been if I could find a way to give you more control."

Trent drew in a shaky breath and his chin wobbled slightly. "Watching you and Aiden together, paired with my talk with Merrick, I finally understood why the two of us hadn't worked as a couple despite how we feel about one another. You aren't submissive. Asking you to be submissive wouldn't be fair to you, just like asking me to be less Dom wouldn't be fair to me. I need to have control."

My eyes watered and a tear ran, unbidden, down my cheek. There it was, the end. He had figured out that we couldn't work on a basic level and we were done.

"No, no, please, don't." He brushed the tear from my cheek with the hand he'd been holding mine with. "Don't. I'm fucking this up. I'm sorry. Please hear me out." Trent sounded desperate for me to understand him, but I was on the verge of breaking down.

"You and I, as a couple, would be a disaster. But I think there's a way we could make it work, because..." His voice cracked. "Because, Logan, I can't imagine being happy in any relationship without you being part of it."

I blinked. I heard his words, they weren't impossible to understand, but what he was telling me made very little sense. How could we not work, but work?

"I'm intense. Too intense sometimes. I don't always realize how serious I can be, and how overbearing. The fact that you've tolerated me as a friend for all these years and even considered a relationship with me tells me how deeply you care for me."

Care, nothing—I was in love with Trent, whether he knew how much or not. I didn't tell him those words casually.

Trent swiped at his eyes. I hadn't made up that he looked emotional. Trent *was* emotional, and it hurt to see. "I need you. But," he turned to Aiden, "I think there's more at play than just Logan and me. You two together are beautiful. Aiden, you bring out something in Logan that I've never seen. You give him calm. Calm that I *can't* give him. Calm that he's searched for his entire life."

Aiden shot me a bashful smile, his cheeks tinted pink. "Really?" he mouthed.

I was certain I was just as pink as he was. "I've never been able to relax like I can with you. Spending time with you gives my brain, *and* my body, a chance to shut off."

"Exactly," Trent agreed readily. "You two need each other. But Logan, you can't give Aiden what he needs. You've both said that."

My stomach churned again, but I nodded in agreement. No, I couldn't give him what he needed. "He needs a Daddy. I have a hard time getting to work on time by myself. I couldn't help him organize his schedule or provide him what he needs for stability."

Trent kissed my nose. "And that's okay. Because I could."

I deflated. I knew it was coming, but it still hurt.

"Logan." Trent's voice was firm. "I can only do it with you."

I squeaked. "Huh?" That didn't make sense.

Trent softened as he looked into my eyes. "If Aiden will give me a chance, I think that I could be what he needs. But we both need you. We need you to be here with us."

"What?" Aiden and I spoke at once. A brief glance over at him, and I could see he was just as confused as I was.

Trent used a finger to point between the three of us. "We could work. I've given this a ton of thought. It will take a lot of communication. I don't expect it to be seamless, but I think we all need each other. I see where I can help Aiden; I could be Daddy. But by myself, I would drive Aiden away. Aiden is a strong man. He may want to give Daddy a lot, but he needs his autonomy as well. That's why I need you, Logan." He turned to face me. "I need you to be my anchor, to be there for Aiden when I'm too much, to be there for me when I need a reminder to back off. You need Aiden. He gives you something I physically can't. For whatever reason, he gives you the ability to stop moving, to stop thinking."

My mouth flapped open. "You... You really think that we, all three of us, could be in a relationship together?"

"I think we could be perfect together. But if either of you aren't willing, then we can't do it." He was looking directly at me. "Logan, you're just as important to me. You're vital for this to work."

My eyes darted between Trent and Aiden. "Aiden, what do you think?"

CHAPTER 23

AIDEN

WHAT DID I THINK? I thought it was the craziest idea I'd ever heard. Yet I could almost see what he meant. It seemed logical—logical to the point that I thought it might work. As insane as it was, I could see how much thought Trent had put into it, even if he'd just thought about it that night. Beyond that, I understood what he was getting at. We could each give things the others couldn't. I ventured a glance at Logan. He was wide-eyed. Hope mixed with concern, mixed with confusion. I probably looked the same.

"I... The three of us? Together?"

I could have Logan *and* Trent? Really?

Trent nodded slowly. "I've done a lot of thinking this evening. You two are beautiful together. But you both know you can't be everything the other needs long term."

He turned to Logan, speaking directly to him in a way I suspected he never had before. "Logan—you and I we're amazing together. I fell in love with you when we were teenagers, and that love has only grown. It grows every time I see you. Every single up and down life throws our way, I've come out the other side only more deeply in love with you. The hardest thing I've ever done hasn't been coming out as a teenager, it hasn't been burying friends too young, and it hasn't been being shot." His eyes sparkled with laughter at the thought, but then he turned somber again. "No, the hardest thing I've ever done is know that I loved you so much that I had to let you go before we crashed and burned. I've lost sleep over that decision for two years. I've spent nights pacing the length of my bedroom trying to figure out how you and I could make it work."

Logan sniffled, his eyes watering as Trent spoke, but he didn't even blink.

Trent continued. "I haven't been able to find a way, so I've pushed you to find happiness. I've pushed you to the club, hoping like hell you'd find someone who could give you what you need and want. Every single time I've told you to come here, I've felt like a part of my heart broke. And, lo and behold, I think you did find happiness. You found Aiden."

He turned to me and squeezed the hand he was still holding tighter. "And you, you helped him find peace. I've told you before it's something I've never been able to give him. I see it in your eyes; I see it in Logan's eyes. You two are happy together. But I also see the sadness there. The sadness you both have because you know you're not what the other needs. The way you look at Logan, it's the same way I do. The way he looks at you, he looks at me the same way. You guys are constantly trying to figure out how to be different people so you can be what the other one needs."

Okay, so Trent had hit the nail directly on the head.

"I know this is sudden. I know I don't know you as well as Logan knows you. I know that we've only known each other a few weeks. But we've talked, a lot. I feel something here." He turned fully to Logan, who still hadn't moved. "Merrick's right—"

"Wait." Logan's eyes went the size of silver dollars. "Merrick knows? About us? Why did you tell him? How much does he know?"

Trent held a hand up in surrender. "Whoa, easy there, tiger. He knows we dated. He knows I'm a Dom. He knows nothing about Curious, though. I started to deny that we dated and Merrick called me on my shit in a hurry. Apparently, we've not been great at hiding our attraction over the years."

Logan huffed but didn't interrupt again, so Trent continued. "Merrick's right. Separately, we're not any good for one another. We're two pieces of a puzzle, but we're missing the center. Aiden, he's the missing piece."

Logan's eyes darted back and forth between the two of us. I held my breath. This moment was so much bigger than me. This moment would require the three of us to all be on the same page. If Logan didn't agree, if I didn't agree, then I'd lose any chance of being with either of them. I knew well before that evening that I'd never do anything to get between Trent and Logan, and that hadn't changed.

Logan's eyes stilled and he focused on Trent. "You're serious. Aren't you?"

Trent nodded once. "More serious than I've ever been before."

Logan glanced in my direction, then back to Trent. "And you really think this could work? Because Trent, I don't think I can survive losing you again." His voice was small and unsure. He sounded vulnerable in a way I'd never heard from him before. "It doesn't matter that I know, logically, we would have resented each other if we'd stayed together. It hurt more than I ever let on. I... I can't lose you again, not like that."

Trent let go of my hand and wrapped Logan into his arms. "I'm sorry, Logan. I'm sorry I hurt you. However unintentionally. I hurt too. I understand that pain, and I never want you to feel it again." He kissed the top of Logan's head gently.

Logan made a sound in the back of his throat, somewhere between a sob and a whimper. Trent pulled back, cupping Logan's face in both of his hands. "Are you okay?"

The tenderness, the love that radiated from both of them, it should have made me uneasy. I knew I should have been jealous. Except I didn't feel anything like that. Seeing Trent show affection for Logan didn't even put a blip on my jealousy radar. If anything, it created a warmth inside me where I hadn't known I'd been cold before. I felt complete.

"It's a lot to process," Logan admitted. "What you've said, what you're offering—I want it." My heart soared for a brief moment until Logan found more words. "But Trent, I really don't think it's going to be as easy as it sounds."

Trent's ensuing laugh had a hint of smugness. "Oh, I know it won't be seamless. It won't always be easy. But if I didn't think this would work out, I wouldn't even be bringing it up with you guys. There's something here, but we're never going to know unless we try."

I wiggled around, excitement making it hard for me to sit still. I was ready to say yes. Trent felt me wiggling and placed a hand on my thigh to still me, though he didn't take his eyes off Logan.

Logan chewed his bottom lip in thought, then nodded slowly. "This may be the most insane thing you've ever asked me. I'm certain it's the most insane thing I've ever agreed to, but dammit, I want what you're talking about."

I squealed, nodding my head rapidly while Trent laughed. "That's quite a statement coming from your mouth, Logan Caldwell." He leaned forward and kissed Logan gently before he turned to me. "I am guessing that's a yes from you?"

"So many times over!" Alright, maybe I was a little too excited about getting to be with these two men, but my response broke the last bits of tension between Logan and Trent, and they both laughed.

"We aren't done talking," Trent reminded us.

To that, Logan rolled his eyes. "Shocking. You talk everything out. All the time."

"In this case, I think Trent's right. We're going to have to have a lot of conversations. This isn't going to be easy."

Logan's eyes fell. "I really just wanted an orgasm."

Trent sputtered in surprise at Logan's complaint. "Okay, not exactly what I was expecting, but I know that you wanted an orgasm."

"Yeah. You totally cockblocked me."

"Anything but that." Trent ran a finger along the crease of Logan's leg and he whimpered, the sound far closer to Curious than Logan.

Trent glanced up at the clock on the wall. "I think I'm going to let you two pick up where you'd been when I interrupted you. But you only have fourteen minutes until our time in this room is up." A wicked smile crossed his face. "And Aiden, you don't get to cum without permission."

My mouth flew open. "But Logan can cum? That's not fair!" Petulant? Who me?

Trent nodded. "I'm just his"—he pointed to Logan —"boyfriend." The happy grin Trent gave at the term proved to me how in love he was with Logan, and how happy he was to finally call him his boyfriend again. "We're going to have to sit down later and work on rules and expectations. But if I'm going to be your..."—he hesitated for a moment before finishing —"Dom, then I'm going to be in charge of your orgasms and so much more." The heated look he gave me turned me to putty in his hands.

Fair or not, it was hot. "Yes, Sir." That name wasn't going to do for long, but I didn't want to freak him out by calling him

Daddy not three minutes after agreeing to date. It would come, sooner rather than later, but not right now. Right now, I got to get Logan off while Trent watched.

Why was that so hot?

"Thirteen minutes."

Fuck. I crawled over Trent's lap and settled between Logan's legs. Trent had rendered Logan speechless, and he'd been sitting there with his legs splayed apart and his cock hard and pressing against his sweatpants. Leaning forward, I kissed Logan's nose. "Hey, Curious." When his eyes focused on me, I ran a finger up the length of his dick. That got his attention and I watched as his pupils dilated and his nostrils flared. There was my puppy.

I fought to contain the happy giggle that threatened to escape. *I had a puppy!* And a Daddy… but I needed to focus more on getting the puppy off than my new Daddy sitting beside us, watching what we were doing. *Oh, yeah, definitely hot.* I wiggled my hips, my diaper suddenly way too snug around my waist.

Satisfied that I had Logan's complete attention, I hooked the waistband of his sweats and pulled them down, exposing his erection straining against a tiny pair of briefs. Deciding how to get him off in the limited amount of time we had left was difficult. Did I use my hands? Did I use my mouth? Did I lay him out on the bed and grind against him? All had merits, but I decided to give Trent a show. I took a pillow with me as I shimmied down the bed so my mouth was level with Logan's crotch. Before uncovering Logan's dick, I push the pillow beneath my hips to give me something to grind against. If I was going to get permission to cum, I was going to be prepared.

Finally situated, I pulled Logan's underwear down to his thighs. He hissed as my cold hands ran down his outer thighs, but the hiss of surprise quickly turned to one of pleasure as I nosed at his groin before licking over his smooth balls, then up his hard length. My eyes fluttered closed as I wrapped my mouth around his dick. It wasn't like Logan and I had a long history of sexual encounters, but we'd had enough over the months that there was a comfortable familiarity about him and his cock that let all the insanity of what we were doing fade to the background. Yes, I was aware of Trent beside us. Sure, I heard his zipper slide down. And I'd have had to be deaf to not hear the sounds he was making. But my only responsibility for the time being was to make Logan cum. Okay, make Logan cum and not cum myself until I was given permission.

Logan had propped himself up on his elbows to watch me, but when I looked at him, I noticed he was holding tightly to Trent's free hand. "So good," I heard Logan murmur as I swallowed him down, the tip of his cock hitting the back of my throat. While I would have loved to take my time with Logan, I knew time was not on our side. If Logan didn't get off, I wasn't going to get off. This was not a challenge I was going to fail, so I pulled out every trick I'd gained over the years. Everything from sucking, to swirling my tongue around his tip, to dipping my tongue into his slit. Every move I made had Logan coming further apart. He whimpered, moaned, and whined.

My hips had begun to grind into the pillow each time I sucked him into my mouth, my own whimpers joining his and filling the room.

"You two are beautiful." Trent's voice sounded far away. "So gorgeous." There was a slapping sound that I vaguely registered as Trent's hand on his dick. I was too far gone on Logan's cock to peek and see what Trent looked like as he neared orgasm. Logan's balls were tight against his body, and I knew his orgasm was building. I ground my hips with more speed, my own orgasm close. "Not yet, Aiden." Trent's voice was thick. My hips stopped moving, but it took all the remaining effort I had in me.

I reached up and rolled one of Logan's nipple rings between my thumb and forefinger. His entire body came off the bed, sending his cock that much farther down my throat. He was so close I could feel his cock growing.

"Good boy. Logan loves that, don't you, pup?"

Logan whimpered and I hummed at the praise. The vibration of my throat sent Logan over the edge. Cum filled my throat, forcing me to pull back in order to swallow everything he was giving me. I looked up in time to see Logan's head thrown back with his mouth parted as his body shook, his dick pulsing in my mouth.

Logan finally collapsed back onto the bed, and his dick slipped out of my mouth with a lewd slurping sound. That had been enough to send Trent over the edge, and I got the added bonus of seeing him come apart. At some point, Trent had unbuttoned his shirt and it hung on either side of his body as cum painted his chest and stomach. He was so sexy, his eyes locked on mine as he came. I rolled my hips into the pillow, my cock overly sensitive and every movement almost pushing me over the edge. I made a noise in the back of my throat, desperate to cum but also desperate to wait for permission.

Even in the middle of his own release, Trent was able to grit out the words I was dying to hear. "Cum, baby boy."

I rocked my hips two more times into the pillow and came, muffling my scream in the crease of Logan's thigh. He squirmed at the feel of my light beard scraping against his tender skin.

The three of us lay there, panting for breath, all too tired to speak for a number of minutes. Eventually, Logan reached over and ran his finger through the cum on Trent's chest. "That was hot." He lifted his hand to his mouth and licked his finger.

"Fuck, Logan, do that again and we're going to need to find another room to take this to."

At least my mess was contained.

"We need to take it to the locker room and get Aiden changed. He doesn't like staying sticky for long," Logan responded, making me think I hadn't done a good job of keeping the thought to myself.

I raised my head and nodded my agreement.

"Come on, you two. Our time is just about up anyway. Let's go get ready to leave."

CHAPTER 24

TRENT

I FOUND myself leading Logan and Aiden back to the locker rooms for the second time, thankfully under very different circumstances than the first. This time, I had a small bag slung over my shoulder filled with Aiden's and Logan's toys. It wasn't the same cheerful bag covered in hedgehogs that I'd seen the last time, but it was still obviously a diaper bag and the colorful puppy patterns on it didn't leave much to the imagination. Logan was still loose and relaxed from his orgasm, all smiles and hooded eyes, while Aiden was making funny faces as he walked. Logan winked at Aiden, turning his body so he was almost sideways and effectively walking in a grapevine step but refusing to let go of my hand. I'd almost forgotten how easily Logan gave affection. *Almost.*

I also realized how much he'd been holding back on me and it felt like a punch to the gut. Thankfully, I must have hidden the pain well because neither man noticed.

Logan grinned at Aiden. "You can get changed in just a minute."

Aiden nodded. "It feels weird."

The conversation reminded me of how much they already

knew about one another. Instead of feeling daunted by the amount I still had to learn about Aiden, I felt excited. Logan had said Aiden didn't like staying in a sticky diaper, and watching his face as we moved through the club had been amusing. His nose was scrunched up and his eyes squinted like someone had put slime in his pants. Then again, it probably wasn't far from the truth.

Just like the last time, I held my hand out for the key and Logan produced it from his pocket. "Not fucking fair that it opens so easily for you," Logan mumbled as I turned the key and the lock popped open with ease.

"Patience is a virtue."

He snorted. "How long have you known me? I think you know I am not a patient man."

I placed Logan's bag on the bench and noticed a second bag, clearly Aiden's. The hedgehog pattern pulled my lips up into a smile and I felt a warmth spread through my chest. "Couldn't fit it all in one bag?" They both giggled and shook their heads, but neither said anything else. Aiden seemed more interested in the towel Logan handed him from his bag and scurried off to the back of the locker room where there were showers. Not even ten seconds later, I heard the unmistakable sound of adhesive being pulled away from the front of Aiden's diaper, then a shower being turned on. I processed what Aiden was doing on a subconscious level but had focused on Logan.

He was mine again. Well, not just mine this time, but he was with me. We'd only just discussed our relationship and were firmly in uncharted territory, but I couldn't ignore the part of my gut that told me this was how it should be. We, the three of us, were going to make this work. I searched through Logan's bag to find his clothes, but a hand came out and stilled mine. "Hey, Trent?" When my eyes met Logan's, his smile lit up his face. "I appreciate you wanting to help me, but I got this. Go take care of Aiden."

My mouth hung open and I tried to find a way to protest: It was too soon. I didn't want him to feel smothered. We hadn't talked about me helping him.

With Logan, I didn't have to talk about it. This was something I did after a scene when he was still a little fuzzy around the edges and wasn't quite ready to face the world again as Logan.

Logan shook his head. "I appreciate that you're worried about me, but I'm not Curious right now." He spoke like he had read my mind. "Aiden needs a Daddy way more than I need a handler. Go take care of your boy and I'll be here waiting for you two."

My brow furrowed. "Are you sure?"

Logan leaned forward and brushed a kiss to my cheek. "Absolutely." He reached into the hedgehog bag like he'd done it a million times, finding everything he was looking for with ease. A thick pair of training pants, a soft cotton shirt, and a matching pair of pants were placed in my hands. "Now go. He doesn't take a full shower, just rinses off."

I stared dumbly at the clothes in my hand before Logan bodily turned me and pushed me toward the back of the locker room. "Go. He needs you right now, whether you two realize it or not. *Go.*" He pushed at my shoulders and my feet started moving. Thankfully, they knew what they were doing, because —Dom or not—this wasn't something I was sure I should do.

The walk took no more than ten seconds—even with walking slowly to gather my thoughts—and I found myself outside of the only occupied shower. I wasn't any closer to figuring out what I should do, so I decided to tread lightly though portray confidence, and take my cues from Aiden. If he looked spooked, I'd step back. I placed the clothes on the bench and picked up the towel laid across it just as the shower turned off.

Aiden pulled the curtain back and his eyes widened for a brief second before he relaxed. "Hey," he said on an exhale.

"Hey, baby boy." I loved being able to call him that without worrying about how it felt. After he'd spent the afternoon with me on Tuesday, I had avoided calling him boy or baby because I'd seen how it affected both of us. Now I got to say it without worry and it was freeing.

I held the towel open, trying and failing to not look at his lean, hairless body. He managed to embody both masculinity and innocence, though the erection jutting out in front of him took some of that innocence away and replaced it with very naughty images in my mind.

Aiden stepped forward and I wrapped the towel around him, drying his arms, chest, and legs in short order. "Turn around," I instructed when I was convinced his front was drier than mine had ever been fresh out of the shower. He did as directed and I proceeded to dry his back in the same manner. As he turned around, I was aware of not having dried his dick.

Was it too soon?

I mentally slapped myself when I remembered Logan's words. Aiden needed his Daddy. Even if this aspect of caretaking was new to me, I was not a newbie Dom. This relationship just meant more to me than any new relationship I'd ever been in with a sub.

I reached down and dried his erection, making sure to get the underside of his cock as well as his balls and in the crease of his legs. Like Logan had assured me, Aiden hadn't taken a full shower and his hair was still dry, so I didn't need to worry about that. I could have thought over what I was doing all night, but instead I set the towel down and picked up the thick undies

Logan had given me. They were red and blue with bright space-ships all over them.

Aiden's cheeks flushed, but he steadied himself with my shoulders as he stepped into them. I pulled them up his legs and carefully tucked his erection into the front. We repeated the same process with the snug pants and then I helped him into the shirt as well. By the time he was dressed, Aiden was all smiles. "Thank you," he told me quietly. A ghost of "Daddy" hung in the air, but he closed his mouth tightly before it could slip out.

"You're welcome, baby boy. Now, let's go find Logan."

Aiden's eyes brightened. "Let's."

He gripped my hand as I gathered the towel and pile of clothes Aiden had left on the bench, and we rejoined Logan. He was propped up against the wall reading a book, looking relaxed and confident. "Do you want to follow me back to the house?"

Logan nodded, then looked over at Aiden. "You good with that?"

Aiden smiled. "Yeah."

I couldn't help the sigh that escaped me. "Great. Logan, why don't you take Aiden?" They probably had their own things to talk out, and I could wait to talk more until we got home. The space to sort my own thoughts out would probably be good for me anyway, even if I didn't want to let my men out of my sight so soon.

Logan agreed readily. "We'll meet you there."

CHAPTER 25

LOGAN

AT MY TRUCK, Trent placed a soft kiss to Aiden's lips and whispered something in his ear I couldn't hear, and Aiden blushed a deep red. Then he turned his attention to me and kissed me firmly on the lips. "Drive carefully. I don't want anything to happen to my men." The words wrapped around me like a blanket—his men. I was Trent's again. It was a day I hadn't expected to ever arrive.

He waited for us to both climb in and shut my door behind me. "I mean it, Logan. Drive safe."

Did he think I was Mario Andretti or something? Instead of rolling my eyes and driving him insane, I nodded at him. There would be plenty of time to drive him insane in the future, but today wasn't that day.

I watched as Trent walked three cars down to his own truck and climbed in. Aiden pushed my shoulder. "You've got the dopiest smile on your face." Then he sobered slightly. "You really love him, don't you?"

I nodded, an unexpected lump in my throat that I had to force words around. "More than anything."

Aiden squeezed my knee. "It couldn't have been easy the last few years. I'm sorry that you two ever broke up."

I blinked, forcing myself to focus on the road and following Trent. After I'd promised him I'd drive safe, the last thing I needed was to wreck because I'd teared up. "As much as I hate to admit it, Trent has a point. The two of us, we never would've worked long term. At least not alone. It may be insane, but I think he's right. I think we needed you."

Aiden chewed his lip. "Are you really okay with it?"

My eyes shot over to his. "Without a doubt. I've been struggling with the feelings I've had for both of you, knowing that I can't be everything to either of you. I can't be your Daddy and I can't be Trent's sub. But this way we can all still be together."

Aiden chewed at his lip. "What do I call him?"

I couldn't help the laugh that bubbled out of me. "Call him what feels right. I'd probably recommend leaving the name-calling to me, though. I think I can get away with calling him a stubborn, pigheaded, horse's ass better than you could."

Aiden let out the sweetest giggle. "Oh no, I'm not calling him that!"

"You say that now. Give him six months," I teased.

Aiden snorted. "How is he friends with you?"

"I keep his life interesting. He'd be a boring old man without me."

We kept a steady stream of conversation going until we pulled into the driveway, and Aiden let out a long sigh. "Wow, was it really only a few weeks ago that we were here together for the first time?"

"Under very different circumstances. You ready?" I laced our fingers together and brought them up to my lips to kiss his hand. "Part of me wishes that night had never happened, but a bigger part of me knows that without it, we wouldn't be here right now."

Aiden glanced at the house. "I'm glad I'm here with you... both of you."

Trent was at the front porch staring at us with a cocked brow. "We better get going or he's going to lose it." I cut the ignition and unbuckled my belt, Aiden following my lead. "He's a lot of bark."

"Hopefully, only the best kind of bite," Aiden teased.

Trent pulled me into his side when we joined him by the door, holding me to his body with a hand firmly around my waist. He held back from doing the same with Aiden, but I knew he wanted to by the way his fingers twitched at his side. Once Trent convinced himself that the three of us together was really going to happen and Aiden wasn't going to go anywhere, I knew he wouldn't hesitate to hold him the same way. "Thank you for driving carefully."

I wasn't going to preen at the compliment, but I did feel a smile tug at my lips.

He opened the door, guided us into the house, and took our coats from us, hanging them in the closet because he wouldn't be able to relax if he saw them sitting out. He fiddled with the hangers longer than necessary and tension radiated from him. He was nervous. The drive home had likely given him time to think. Think about all the ways the three of us could fuck this up, and the ways we wouldn't be compatible. If his mind was anything like mine, he had a nagging fear that we'd lose each other for good if we didn't make this work. I should have sent Aiden with Trent. I couldn't change the drive home, but I could step up and help him find his center.

I nudged Aiden and nodded my head toward Trent. "I'm going to go get us drinks. I think he could use a distraction." I'd leave *how* Aiden distracted Trent up to him.

Aiden chewed his lip in thought. "I can manage that."

"Great." Then I turned to Trent. "Sit your ass down. I'm going to go make coffee for us."

"Hot tea, please?" Aiden spoke up. "If I have coffee now, I'll never sleep tonight."

I personally thought there were far better ways to spend the night than sleeping, but I wasn't going to force Aiden to drink coffee. Trent and I, however, could drink coffee until our heads hit our pillows. "One tea and two coffees."

The living room was visible from the kitchen, and as I started the coffee pot and went about finding the tea bags in the kitchen, I kept an eye on Trent and Aiden. Part of me had expected Aiden to work on distracting Trent with kisses or something far naughtier. I certainly would have taken any chance I had to get my hands on him, but Aiden had taken Hedge over to where Trent sat and curled up beside him.

As I filled the kettle with water, I saw Trent's hand go to Aiden's hair and begin playing with it. Even from fifteen feet away, I heard the little sigh of contentment from Aiden. He was exactly what Trent needed because I wasn't one to sit stock-still and snuggle like that unless I was sick or about to fall asleep. A snuggly boy to cuddle with and help him relax after the world went to shit around him and an energetic pup to keep him on his toes. We were going to be the *best* partners for Trent.

With three mugs in hand, I headed to the living room. Trent had covered Aiden with the throw blanket from the back of the couch and had relaxed noticeably. He took the mug from my hand with a smile. "Thanks."

I settled into the recliner beside the sofa while we each sipped at our drinks. Trent needed to figure out where he wanted to start talking, so I let him think for a few minutes. Just as I was about to crack, Trent finally spoke. "I want to start by making sure that no one has changed their mind." He looked between the two of us, waiting for a response. After the insane orgasm I'd had while Trent directed Aiden, there was no way I'd be backing out, especially if it could always be that good.

We both shook our heads and Trent relaxed. Trent nervous made me nervous, so every line of tension in his body felt like it was directly connected to my own nerves. "Then we need to talk about what we each want and expect. I know it seems formal, but open communication is going to be key to making this work for us."

He'd probably spent most of the drive home running through possibilities and how to talk about our relationship. I wouldn't be surprised if he had a checklist of checklists already in his head. When he let go, he was still like he'd been in high school—loud, joking around, and even energetic—but he also had a tendency to let thoughts get into his head too much. Like right then.

I held my hand up to stop Trent from overthinking the issue. Knowing him as well as I did, he'd overthought every relationship dynamic the three of us could share. He'd want to know how we saw each of our individual relationships playing out as well as how we saw the three of us together. "Don't obsess over this, Trent. We're all going to learn things as we go along, no matter how much talking we do tonight."

Aiden grinned from his spot at Trent's side. "I, for one, am looking forward to that more than you know."

I snorted at his wiggle, and Trent's large hand popped Aiden's hip. "No getting yourself off without permission."

Thank fuck I wasn't his sub. That sentence alone would have had me noping the fuck out, but the way Aiden's eyes went wide and his nostrils flared, I knew he liked the idea. Even before he let out a needy whimper.

"Spankings are apparently on the list for you?" Trent questioned, an eyebrow cocked high on his forehead and a wicked smirk on his lips.

Aiden's head bobbed up and down without hesitation. "I like spankings. Maybe more? I don't know. I haven't tried anything else, but I'm not opposed."

I was pretty sure Trent stopped breathing for a moment before a smile spread. "Mmm, I can't wait to explore what you like. I also can't wait to get to know you better."

Aiden ducked his head. From anyone else it would look bashful, but on Aiden it looked purely suggestive. "I'm looking forward to that too."

Trent glanced at the schedule on the wall. "We'll need to have a date night soon. The two of us."

In the back of my head, I felt like the way Trent was looking at Aiden should have made me nervous. Part of me wanted to worry that if Trent needed that control... dominance... outlet... whatever it was, so much that his pants were already tight, and I'd have had to be blind to not see the bulge in his jeans, then how could I ever satisfy him? I tried to summon those feelings, that fear and uncertainty, and all I found instead was relief. I didn't have to be something I wasn't, and I didn't have to try to change. Trent wanted me to be Logan—he didn't want me to be his submissive.

"You're right." Trent was watching me with a soft smile on his face. "I want *you*, just as you are."

Shit, how much of that thought had come out? Instead of asking, I smiled and settled back into my chair. "I'm always right."

Aiden snorted into his cup of tea. "Oh my god, you're so ridiculous."

Trent rubbed his arm. "That's my Logan. All. The. Time." His eyes sparkled with an emotion I couldn't name. Whatever it was, it made my stomach flutter. I couldn't sit still any longer and got up to pace the length of the living room.

"Ants in your pants?" Trent asked as I bounced.

"Sitting too long tonight. I think my biggest question is sex and how that will work with us."

"Your mind must be a fascinating place to live in," Trent responded dryly.

Aiden wiggled in Trent's lap. "Oh, let's talk about sex. Because tonight was hot. And I'm really horny."

Trent threw his head back and laughed. I wished I was close enough to lick up his Adam's apple. The action never failed to give Trent chills and turn him on. Aiden, however, was close enough and had the same idea, though he didn't lick. The tease leaned over, wrapped his lips around the base of Trent's throat, and sucked. I watched as Trent's laugh turned into a moan and his hips jutted upward. That was hot. I didn't have to see Trent's cock to know it was just as hard as mine had gone.

Trent smacked Aiden's hip harder that time, and the crack echoed through the room. Aiden's entire body reacted to the contact, and that turned me on even more. Sex with the three of us wasn't going to be a problem.

"You guys ask questions, then *someone* tries to distract me." He narrowed his eyes at Aiden and Aiden batted his eyes innocently, like he couldn't figure out why he'd been naughty. "What have I gotten myself into?" I'd have been more concerned if Trent wasn't smiling so brightly.

I paced in front of them as I rambled. "I know what both of you like, sexually and otherwise. Don't forget, I've known Aiden for months. I've known you for two decades. I'm not getting into anything with either of you that I don't know already. The biggest thing I want for all of us is happiness, and however insane this relationship may be to the outside, Trent, I think you're right. I think this will work for us.

"Aiden being little has never bothered me before. Why would it start now? What I want is for him to find what he needs. I know I can't be a Daddy for him, but I can support him... and you, Trent. I don't have to be his Daddy to help him get ready to play. I don't have to be his Daddy in order to help care for him or *want* to care for him, for that matter."

Aiden's face split into a wide grin, but Trent eyed me suspiciously, as though he was trying to figure out if I was telling the truth. Whatever it was, he must have seen it because he reached out and snagged my arm, pulling me onto the couch and kissing the side of my head. "You are amazing."

I didn't know what I'd done, but I liked the compliment. Aiden leaned forward, almost sliding onto my lap. "The best." He pressed his lips to my cheek. "Thank you, puppy."

I chuckled at the term. No one had ever gotten away with calling me puppy before, but Aiden called me that frequently, and every time it made me feel special.

"We're three equal partners," Trent said with conviction as he stroked Aiden's back. "We're in this together, even if we all have different interests." I liked the sound of that. From the way Aiden hummed and wrapped his arms around Trent's body, he did too. "There's no one else but us three in this," Trent continued, his words sharp and final.

I rolled my eyes—I couldn't help it. "Jesus, it's taken us twenty fucking years to figure out how to be with one another. I don't think there's any way in hell we're finding anyone else."

"So eloquently stated." Then Trent looked at Aiden, who was laughing at my statement. "You don't get to talk like that. Do you understand?"

Aiden's eyes went wide, and he bobbed his head up and down. "Yes, Daddy."

"Thank you, baby boy."

Trent's nostrils flared with the word and I bit my tongue on wanting to scream that I'd told him so. I'd never seen his back stiffen with an urge to protect like I'd seen when he was around Aiden. From the way he hadn't wanted to leave him alone when

I'd panicked at the club, to how his eyes had taken in Aiden's pajamas when he came out of the bathroom, to how he went out of his way to make breakfast for him the next day. Trent was ready for it.

To a certain extent, Trent had been taking care of me since we were teenagers. He was always making sure I ate and drank enough, and made sure I was getting sleep—but it wasn't the same way he'd done so with Aiden.

Whether Trent had known it or not, he'd been overly ready to be a Daddy. Trent was a goner for Aiden. I waited for that part of my mind that screamed that Trent was mine and not Aiden's, but it never came. A part of my heart I didn't know existed seemed to open up and expand in that moment as I watched Trent bury his face into Aiden's neck, holding him tight.

There was only one thing bothering me about the entire arrangement and I hadn't even been aware of it until that moment. "Hey, Trent?"

His eyes flicked up to me. "What's up?"

I hated the uncertainty in my voice when I spoke. "If you're Aiden's Daddy, are you still going to be my handler if we play at the club?" Would he be able to play both roles? I loved snuggling with Aiden on the floor of the littles' room in the club, but I also liked my pup friends too. I was still most comfortable when Trent was my handler at those times.

If possible, his face softened even more. "I can absolutely be both your handler and Aiden's Daddy, even at the club, even if all three of us are together. I can be both at once." He directed me over to where they were sitting and situated me between him and the arm of the couch, pulling me close. I hated to feel vulnerable, but at that moment I was.

Trent was the first person I told when I discovered puppy play. He was the only person I ever asked to go to the club with me as my handler. He'd been the first person I trusted enough to fully let go around. I hadn't realized until I heard Aiden call him Daddy that Trent was now in a position where he had to wear three hats: boyfriend, Daddy, and handler. Even one of those hats was heavy. While I trusted Trent with Curious in general, I needed to hear from him that he could still handle Curious at the club.

Trent kissed my forehead and rubbed his hand up and down my arm. "Pup or Logan, you are important to me. And now that you're mine again, I hope you'd know that wouldn't change."

I felt myself relax into his grasp. His words made me feel better, but that moment of doubt reminded me why communication was going to be even more important for us. It wouldn't be hard for a small insecurity or doubt to multiply rapidly.

Trent held me until I started to wiggle. I didn't have the urge to get up, but lying so close wasn't going to happen either. Trent loosened his grip on me. I stretched out enough that I could move my legs easily, but then he poked my side. Judging from the giggle that escaped Aiden, Trent had probably done the same thing to him. "What else do you want to know about sex? Because I know that we all know how to have it."

Aiden and I both laughed and even Trent couldn't suppress his own laughter.

"You're his Dom. You get to decide when he cums." I pointed at Aiden, who was flushing deep crimson. I pointed at myself. "You don't get to control when *I* cum, though. So what happens when you're not around and I'm horny? Do we get to play together?" I gestured between Aiden and me. "Or do I only get to play with myself? Do the rules apply differently when it's just the two of us and Aiden can cum then? Likewise, will you guys be able to have sex when I'm not around?" A thought occurred to me. "And I don't want you two to leave the Daddy/boy stuff for when I'm gone. That isn't fair to Aiden, and I already told you that I'm okay with it." Maybe I'd thought about this too long.

Trent ruffled my hair, causing a growl to escape from my chest. "That's a lot to process. I think Aiden and I will have to have some more conversations on limits, but right now, I think I'm going to ask that Aiden text me if I'm not around and you two want to have sex. Sometimes, he may be able to cum. Other times, he might not be."

Aiden shivered. I'd lose my mind with someone telling me not to cum, but he loved it.

Trent continued. "As for Daddy/boy time, it will happen as it happens. If that means you're around, then you're around. It's not like we're hiding it."

"I wouldn't want to hide it from you. You're my puppy," Aiden spoke up as he used his socked foot to nudge at my thigh over Trent's lap.

"And as for sleeping, I think we can figure that out on a nightly basis." Trent looked over at the clock on the entertainment center. "Speaking of sleeping arrangements, it's getting late. Aiden, do you want to spend the night here or do you want us to take you home?"

He looked between the two of us. "All my stuff is already here." He held up Hedge. "He doesn't mind staying here tonight."

I hadn't ever expected to end up dating a little, but I had a feeling things like Hedge's opinions were going to be more common in my life now that I was. Trent's eyes twinkled with amusement. "Okay, baby boy, go get your teeth brushed."

"There's a new toothbrush in my bathroom, right where you found them last time."

Aiden shimmied off Trent's lap, and if Trent's expression was anything to go by, he'd gone out of his way to wiggle right over Trent's dick on the way. "Naughty boy. Go. Logan and I will be up in just a minute. We can sleep in Logan's bed tonight."

Aiden scurried up the steps like he belonged here. "We'll

figure out permanent sleeping arrangements later. But your big blanket is in your room, and no matter what you say about not being attached to it, I know you are."

"I am not." I might have sounded a bit petulant, but I wasn't attached to my blanket. At least not like Aiden was to Hedge.

Trent rolled his eyes so hard it looked painful. "Keep telling yourself that. You need to get ready for bed too."

I started toward the steps but turned back and motioned toward the diaper bag by the front door. "He likes milk." I winked and headed up the steps to get myself ready for bed.

"Huh?" Trent questioned, looking between the bag and me.

I laughed. "Open the bag, *Daddy*. You'll figure it out."

Trent growled at me and I hurried up the steps and into my bathroom.

CHAPTER 26

I will not kill Logan.
   I will not kill Logan.
   I will not kill Logan.
   What had I gotten myself into?

CHAPTER 27

AIDEN

LOGAN WAS GONE before I opened my eyes Monday morning, leaving me to wake up in Trent's arms, my face buried in his furry chest. It only took a few seconds to figure out Trent wasn't asleep. As soon as the fog cleared from my brain, I knew his chest was moving too frequently and there was no way he'd be rubbing my arm as he was if he'd been sleeping.

When I tensed slightly, trying to figure out what to say, he knew I was awake. "Morning, baby boy." He placed a gentle kiss on the side of my head.

"Morning," I mumbled into Hedge's fur, surprised for a moment that my binkie wasn't in my mouth. Then I remembered falling asleep halfway through my bottle. I hadn't bothered with my pajamas, and I'd left my binkie in my bag by the door. After brushing my teeth, I'd collapsed into Logan's bed in just my training pants... The training pants that were now tight around my morning wood. I thrust into Trent's thigh looking for relief, only to be met with a growl.

"Should my boy be doing that?"

It was way too early to pick that sentence apart. "Huh?"

He chuckled, but his voice was still stern when he answered.

"Good boys do not grind themselves against Daddy's thigh without permission."

His words did not help the situation in my pants or my desire to hump his leg. If anything, it made it worse. "I-I..." I took a deep breath, focusing harder on not humping Trent than on figuring out how to respond. "But..."

"No buts, Aiden." He angled himself so he could look me in the eyes. "Let's get up and I'll take you out to lunch. We can talk more about our limits and how the two of us see our relationship working."

"Lunch?" I just woke up. I glanced around the room. Yes, it seemed bright, but that simply meant it was somewhere between eight a.m. and six p.m.

He patted my butt, not helping the situation in my undies at all. "You slept straight through breakfast. It's already eleven thirty."

"Eleven thirty?" I clarified, looking desperately for a clock. My eyes finally settled on the one across the room. Sure enough, it read eleven thirty-one. "You let me sleep too long! And you didn't need to stay here with me all that time. I'm sure you have better things to do with your time than lie in bed."

Trent's chest went up and down a few times in silent laughter. "Aiden, I know very well what I have to do, but I can prioritize. You and Logan are my top priorities. Nothing is more important than you two. So if I want to lie in bed with my boy until nearly lunchtime, I can. And you said last night that you don't have to be at work until tonight, so I was happy to lie here until you woke up. Besides, you had a busy night last night."

I wanted to complain, but truthfully I felt better after sleeping so much. A lot better. The coming week had been weighing on me more than I'd allowed myself to believe. Being able to let go at the club the night before had let that stress fade away. The discussions we'd had as a couple... group?... had been extensive and left me exhausted. Happy, but exhausted. I had needed the sleep.

Trent extricated himself from my grip. "Go get a shower. I'm going to shower myself, then we'll get some lunch at Mable's."

My stomach rumbled. Food was not only welcome, but necessary at that point. It was all the motivation I needed to get up and showered quickly. Twenty minutes later, I was sitting at the island in the kitchen drinking a cup of coffee while I waited for Trent.

[Logan] Hey, how are things going?

[Me] Pretty good, waiting for Trent to get out of the shower so we can get lunch?

I couldn't figure out if Logan had used the speech-to-text feature or if he'd just typed ridiculously fast when a reply came in seconds later.

[Logan] Ohhhhhh. Shower at 11:50? Get up to something good? ~Eyebrow waggle~

[Me] If by good you mean sleep, then yes, great morning.

The next response came in more slowly.

[Logan] Seriously? Trent stayed in bed until nearly noon?

I took another drink of my coffee and could hear Trent heading down the steps. I tapped a reply quickly.

[Me] Yup, now we're heading to Mable's. And Trent's on his way down the steps. Have a good day.

The phone buzzed again, but I ignored it as I pocketed it.

Trent ruffled my hair on the way to the coffeepot to fill a travel mug. "Ready?"

I didn't answer with words but rather jumped up, placed my empty mug in the sink, and hurried toward the door to put my shoes on. Trent followed behind, chuckling to himself.

Twenty minutes later, we were sitting in a booth near the back of the local diner and he'd already been listening to me debate what to get for nearly five minutes. "Remind me to always have food ready for you when you wake up."

"It all looks so good!" I whined. "I can't decide if I want pancakes and eggs or a chicken sandwich with a salad... Ohhhh, I didn't see the chicken and waffles! Have you had them? Are they good?" Too many choices.

Trent hadn't even picked up his menu. "How about you let me order for you?"

I sighed. That sounded perfect. "Yes, please."

"Very nice manners. I like that."

I flushed. He hadn't called me baby boy or even alluded to it, but I could nearly hear it in his voice. "Thank you."

"Hey, Trent." A portly woman with graying hair approached our table with a great big smile on her face.

"Hi, Mable," he greeted in return. "Mable, this is my boyfriend Aiden. Aiden, this is Mable."

Mable's round face lit up with happiness. "Oh, Trent, I'm so happy for you! It's about time." Then she looked over at me. "You treat this man right. He's a great big sweetheart. I've known him since he was born. Don't let that hard candy shell scare you off—he's really just melty chocolate on the inside."

I couldn't help the flush that spread across my cheeks. "Thanks. He's pretty great."

"Don't tell all my secrets, Mable." Trent groaned playfully but gave Mable our orders. He ordered chicken and waffles for me, with gravy on the side, a fruit cup, and a side salad. I had no idea if I'd be able to eat it all, but I'd certainly enjoy trying.

When Mable was almost back to the kitchen, Trent shook his head. "I have no idea what she's talking about."

Reaching across the table, I took his hand in mine. "I have to tell you I think everyone but you has seen you're a big softie."

He growled at me and narrowed his eyes. "You better watch what you're saying. I just may show you how *not* soft I am."

I wiggled in my seat. His words had gone straight to my cock and it had begun to harden.

He cleared his throat, bringing attention to my movements and causing me to stop. "Sorry, Daddy," I whispered.

"If I didn't make this clear last night, I'm a little possessive. I don't want anyone to see my boy cum but me and Logan." He narrowed his eyes, and I could see the honesty and a hint of that strict Dom Logan had told me Trent had been for so long. "I will *not* tolerate you giving the diner a show."

I gasped. "I-I'm sorry."

He nodded sharply. "If you can't behave while we're out, there's no way you're going to get to have fun when we get home later."

The squeak I let out was highly unmasculine, but I felt myself nodding rapidly. I wanted an orgasm and that little hint of the no-nonsense Dom had me a little frightened—in the very best way—and a lot horny.

"We better change the subject before you misbehave."

That was a very good idea. Because I didn't know how much longer I'd be able to resist reaching below the table for some relief.

"Tell me more about your work."

"Work?" The thought of work had my dick softening almost immediately. I did not want to do the photo shoot with the crazy photographer later that week. I huffed and settled back in my seat. "I usually love my work..." I talked about the photo shoot, the crazy director, the even more insane schedule, and the fact that I would be shocked if it was done on time. While we ate, the conversation turned toward the things I loved about my job, and some of my clients.

"Really," I said as I swirled the last bite of my waffle into the gravy on my plate. "I love what I do. I've worked hard to make a name for myself, and I've got a nice life now. But I won't lie. I'm burning out."

Trent reached across the table and took my hand. "I'm sorry, baby boy. We'll get through the next few weeks, then figure out something that will work better for you. You can't burn the candle at both ends. Even if it's not all day every day, you shouldn't be working for weeks straight. Even I take time off."

A throat clearing from beside us made me jump. "No, you *have* days off. As in, your scheduled days off each week, that more often than not you work through at least one of them."

I looked up to see Logan smirking down at us. He slid into the booth and waggled his eyebrows. "So, what's up?"

CHAPTER 28

LOGAN

TRENT NARROWED his eyes at me as I sank down in the seat beside Aiden. I leaned over and kissed his cheek, then rubbed Trent's leg under the table, shooting him a playful wink.

When he got his surprise under control, Aiden beamed at me. "We just finished lunch. I saw a really yummy cheesecake in the display case."

Trent's eyes widened in surprise. "Where on earth are you going to put it? You just ate more than I did!"

Aiden patted his stomach. "I'm a growing boy."

"I could go for dessert." But I really wanted ice cream from the place next door. After the morning I'd had, I deserved it. It hadn't been particularly busy, but I'd put out a number of minor fires between local police departments and satellite departments, and even argued with a town council rep.

"I've grown enough for both of you," Trent complained, patting his belly.

I batted my eyes. "But I really want a black raspberry truffle ice cream in a dark chocolate dipped waffle cone from next door."

Trent's face scrunched up in disgust. "That just sounds so sweet."

Aiden's eyes lit up. "Ohhhhh, do they still have that chocolate Elvis flavor? It's my *favorite!* Banana, dark chocolate chunks, peanut butter ice cream, and if I ask nicely, they mix in graham cracker pieces... mmm."

That time, Trent actually had to hold back a gag. "That sounds repulsive."

I looked over at Aiden. "For being kinky... Trent's ice cream tastes do not get any more exciting than cookies 'n cream." Then I turned back to Trent. "Please?"

Aiden joined in. "Please, Daddy? Ice cream." He batted his eyes sweetly and I knew we were wearing Trent down.

"Yes. Pleeeeease, Daddy?"

Mable came to the table as Aiden and I begged for ice cream, our hands clasped together, faux angelic smiles on our faces, and batting our eyes. "I have no idea what I just interrupted over here, but *Daddy*"—she turned to Trent—"I think you need to take these two to get ice cream."

I'd never seen Trent turn so red. He handed over his card to Mable without looking at her or the bill, shaking his head. "You two are making a scene."

Mable was back before Aiden and I had stopped laughing. We'd fallen over so we were leaning against one another, tears streaming down our faces, while Trent glowered at us and hissed for us to behave. "Trent, I don't know what's going on here, but baby, you best start working out with Logan. Because if what I think is going on here *is* actually happening, then you're going to need the energy to keep up with them. Don't know Aiden well, but it sure seems like they'll keep you on your toes."

Aiden's laughter died in a heartbeat and even my own cut off as I stared up at her. Oddly enough, Trent seemed to pull himself together. "You may be right, Mable. You may be right. I better get them out of here before they cause any more of a scene." He narrowed his eyes at us, but even the stern set of his jaw didn't hide his amusement at the entire situation.

And we were getting ice cream!

Twenty minutes later, I swore we were going to roll out of the ice cream shop. Maybe the large waffle cone hadn't been the best idea, but it was so good I wasn't going to complain too much.

On the way to the cars, we debated who would drive together on the way home but eventually decided we'd all go in one car and I'd drive back with Trent to get my truck when he went to work.

Trent almost possessively guided Aiden and I down the street, his hands resting gently on our backs. He had parked down the block, and as we walked, his touch changed. At first, it was a hand right above the swell of my ass. We made it a few storefronts before it changed to a rub. I glanced over and was pretty sure I could see his hand working the same on Aiden's back as well. The way Aiden leaned into him was more confirmation.

But when Trent's truck came into view, he slid his hand into the back pocket of my jeans and squeezed a handful of my butt. The grope was hard enough that it made me wish there weren't any clothes separating my ass and his hand. The little gasp from the other side of Trent told me he'd done something similar to Aiden. I'd kept my groan in but my cock was responding to his touch.

"You know, public sex is against the law. If you keep this up, we're going to have to arrest ourselves," I muttered as we approached his truck.

Trent lifted his shoulder in a half shrug. "I'm not doing anything but holding my boyfriends close."

I could have reminded him that we were in Tennessee and even holding *one* boyfriend close could be a dangerous thing.

We'd arrived at his truck by that point, though, and the erection in my jeans was becoming more of an issue than what others thought of Trent having his hand in the pockets of two men.

We climbed in, and before I even had my buckle done, I unbuttoned my pants and pulled the zipper down, providing much-needed relief to my straining erection. Trent had helped Aiden into the truck and I'd caught him reaching over Aiden to buckle his belt into place, much to Aiden's embarrassment. "Hey!" Aiden protested when he saw my pants undone. "I want my pants down."

Trent glowered at me but shook his head at Aiden. "I will not have my boy exposing himself in the truck. I can't control what our crazy pup does." He was ridiculous, but I loved hearing him call me *their* pup.

Aiden looked around and huffed. "But the windows are tinted."

"Keep it up and you won't get relief when we get home either."

Aiden gasped in shock but didn't protest more. Thankfully, we were only ten minutes away from the house because I didn't know if we would have made it much longer without Trent either yelling at me or pulling the truck over to fuck us on the side of the road. I couldn't help that he was getting easily distracted by the way I was stroking myself through my briefs.

"Logaaan," Trent growled in warning about every half mile.

From the backseat, Aiden kept making little sounds of pleasure, encouraging me along. "More. Yes. Ohhh, your tip is so wet."

Trent finally gave up at the last stop sign before our house. "You two need to stop it, right now. Logan, you were worried about me squeezing your ass on the sidewalk through jeans, and you're practically giving us a porn show on the way home. And you, baby boy," he addressed Aiden, "are absolutely no better. You're encouraging him."

Aiden huffed. "But Daddy, he's so sexy!"

Trent threw his hands into the air, then pulled forward through the intersection. "Just let me get home."

I couldn't help but smirk at how insane I'd driven Trent. The smirk lasted until we parked the car and Trent turned to me. "I need to be inside of you. You better get upstairs and prep yourself."

I moaned, Aiden moaned, and Trent growled. I heard Trent asking Aiden something as I left the car, but I didn't wait to hear what. I rushed through my normal routine, taking off my shoes, locking my gun away in the drawer, then shucking my jeans, socks, and uniform shirt, leaving them in the laundry room. I ran through the kitchen and up the steps in just my briefs as the front door opened again.

By the time Aiden and Trent made it up the steps, I'd already been to the bathroom, done a record-breaking wash, and was on the bed, my hard cock leaking on my stomach, as I stretched myself open with my fingers. I looked at the doorway and smirked as the two of them stopped and watched me, mouths hanging open. Watching the two watch me was far headier than I'd expected it to be and I had to force myself to not grip my cock and stroke myself to completion before Trent even got inside me.

Trent managed to pull himself together and stalked over to the bed, running his hand up my thigh but stopping just shy of the crease of my leg and completely missing my balls. "So sexy. Keep stretching yourself while I get Aiden ready."

Aiden's whimper from the doorway had my eyes looking for him.

I heard the smirk in Trent's voice as he spoke. "Yes, pup. I'm going to use you to fuck Aiden."

My cock pulsed hard against my stomach. The thought alone was almost enough to have me cumming on the spot. Then Trent brought Aiden over to the side of the bed and began stripping him of his shirt and jeans. In seconds, Aiden was standing before us in only a pair of thick terrycloth briefs with a shark printed on the butt and the words "Baby Shark" scrawled above the picture. Despite my fingers in my ass, my cock begging for attention, and the two sexy men standing in front of me, I laughed... an odd sensation around my fingers.

Aiden's cheeks flushed when he realized why I was laughing, and Trent took the time to see what I was staring at. He smiled, warm and accepting, though I could see the laughter in his eyes. "You, baby boy, are adorable."

CHAPTER 29

TRENT

Baby Shark. I never thought I'd find a pair of training pants on a man both sexy and cute, but with Aiden I couldn't imagine him in anything else. They were just as sexy on our baby boy as Logan's barely there briefs had been on him.

"On the bed, baby." I needed to get my boy stretched. I'd been worried we were moving too fast for Aiden when I'd told Logan I wanted to be in him, but before I could even ask him about it after Logan rushed into the house, Aiden had grabbed my hand and started pulling me toward the front door with a "Hurry, Daddy. I need filled too."

My boy might have looked innocent, but he was far from it.

Peeling his snug briefs off, I took a moment to enjoy seeing him naked. Smooth skin, soft muscles—so different from the firm muscles that covered Logan's body but every bit as attractive. I leaned forward and sucked his nipple into my mouth, worrying the small bud between my teeth until it was hard and sensitive.

I'd been expecting to hear Aiden's voice, but instead it was Logan who let out a low moan. My eyes flicked up to see Aiden rolling Logan's nipple piercing between his thumb and forefinger. Logan was about to fly off the bed, and the color of his cockhead told me he was way too close to cumming. I released Aiden's nipple. "Baby, stop. You're going to make him cum."

Aiden craned his head around to look at Logan and his big brown eyes widened in surprise at what he saw. Releasing Logan's nipple, Aiden looked back at me. "Hurry, Daddy, I want Logan inside of me." The corner of my lip rose in a smile at knowing Aiden was on the same page as me.

Logan's head fell back on the bed when he realized what Aiden had said. "Yes, Daddy, hurry up, because *I* want *you* inside me." For all of Aiden's sweet, needy words, Logan's were frustrated and teasing. Mable was right—I was going to have my hands full with these two. But if I kept thinking about Mable, my erection was going to soften, so I dragged my thoughts back to the present. Two gorgeous men laid out on the bed in front of me, both begging to be filled. One glance at them and my cock —and my brain—forgot all about the owner of the diner.

I grabbed the bottle of lube lying beside Logan and coated my fingers, sliding the first one inside Aiden in one long motion. Aiden threw his head back and hissed at the intrusion but was able to relax quickly. He pulled his legs up slightly, allowing me easier access. "More," he whispered so quietly I almost didn't hear him. "More."

Who was I to deny my boy anything? I added a second finger. It took more work that time, but once I made it past the first ring of muscle, Aiden accepted me. He wiggled his ass to get more comfortable and in the process drove my fingers deeper inside of him.

"You two are gorgeous," Logan spoke from beside us. "So amazing."

I'd never had sex with two men before, and part of me had wondered how it would work. Not that I would admit it to either of them, but I'd spent time that morning while waiting for

Aiden to wake up watching porn with three men, seeing exactly how it had been done. Aiden might have thought I'd been bored waiting for him to wake up, but I'd used the time wisely. Logan and Aiden didn't seem to have the same concerns about the three of us being together for the first time as I'd had earlier in the morning.

I scissored my fingers apart in Aiden's ass, and he hissed out. Logan's cock wasn't anywhere near as thick as mine, so it didn't take long to stretch him. Someday, I'd take my time and drive him insane, but the three of us were all desperate to orgasm. I was still dressed and beginning to worry about the blood supply to my own dick if I didn't get it some room quickly. Removing my fingers from Aiden's ass, I smacked his thigh. "Up to the top of the bed, on all fours."

I began to strip my clothes off, unceremoniously throwing them toward the chair in the corner of the room. Heading toward the drawer containing the condoms, I toed my socks off and left them where they were, hoping I'd find them both later. With two condoms in hand, I tossed one to Logan as I began to rip mine open.

Logan grumbled as he removed the fingers he had in his own ass to open the condom while Aiden laughed at us both. Lube-slicked fingers and little foil wrappers were not compatible, and even after taking my clothes off, I was still struggling to get mine open. Logan hadn't even tried to open his condom packet, instead throwing it toward Aiden. "Help."

Giggling at Logan's predicament, Aiden gripped the condom packet and ripped it open at nearly the same time my own foil packet opened. Logan and I let out twin sighs of relief at having the condoms freed. I fumbled with my own, nearly cumming from the pressure of my hand on my dick while I watched Aiden roll the condom down Logan's erection. As soon as it was on, Aiden resumed his position on hands and knees, looking over his shoulder as Logan and I maneuvered ourselves into position.

"Don't move, pup. You are not going to enter Aiden until I tell you."

Aiden whimpered. He didn't have to use words for us to know he was telling us to hurry up. It took me a minute to get everyone set up, but when Logan was on his knees at the edge of the bed, his ass resting against my thighs with Aiden's ass at his groin in front of him, I finally gripped my cock and lined up with Logan's ass.

The sound Logan made as I slid into him was addictive. He'd done a great job prepping himself and I was able to slide in with one thrust. I didn't let Logan move until I was well seated and gripping his hips. "Okay, pup, get yourself into Aiden." I tried to keep my breath even and not let on how close I was to cumming already.

Watching Logan reach around Aiden and pull him slowly back as he lined up to enter him made the urge to cum even more unbearable. I pushed my hips forward, causing Logan to push into Aiden, who was watching over Logan's shoulder as he slid in. Grunts filled the room as Aiden adjusted to Logan's cock. After what felt like an eternity, Aiden nodded. "Good, god, so good."

Logan nodded as well. "Trent, fuck me hard. I'm not going to last. Don't care how slow you go."

I couldn't help but be thankful Logan was as needy as I felt. But when Aiden's head fell between his shoulders, I couldn't help but smile. This wasn't going to take long, probably for the best since I had to go to work in just under an hour, but I didn't want it to be over already either. I took a moment to regain my composure and then slid nearly out of Logan, pulling him back by his hips so that he slid almost out of Aiden before I thrust forward, sending them crashing together. I was thankful we didn't have neighbors near us because our noises through the open windows would have told anyone exactly what we were doing.

"Daddy, Daddy, ohhh, Trent," Aiden begged. "Need. More."

If I allowed him to wrap his hand around his dick, I knew it would be all over. It didn't matter that I'd barely broken a sweat or that we'd hardly been joined for more than a few minutes, we were all near cumming.

"Trent," Logan warned the next time I pushed him into Aiden. He was dangerously close and I wasn't going to be able to stop his orgasm.

"Wrap your hand around your cock, baby," I instructed Aiden as I pulled out of Logan. As soon as I pushed back in, Logan exploded, screaming and cursing his release into Aiden. I heard Aiden's hand working his dick hard and fast, and the way Logan's ass contracted around me, I knew I was going to cum.

With Logan releasing inside Aiden, his channel squeezing me tightly, I managed to growl "Cum" to Aiden just as my own orgasm overtook me. I slammed hard into Logan, pushing him even farther into Aiden and eliciting a long growl from Logan, his cock becoming sensitive as his orgasm faded. I came, biting my lip so I didn't roar into the room, instantly thankful for the restraint when I heard Aiden's quiet gasp as he came.

Moments later, the three of us collapsed onto the bed. I was holding Logan, who was holding Aiden, our hands not quite sure where to go or even who we were caressing, but I knew I couldn't stand to be separated from either man.

It was too early to be feeling so attached and I knew that, but I couldn't help the feelings swirling in my head and chest. I could see myself falling hard for Aiden. I didn't have to fall for Logan; I was already gone for him.

Even after disposing of the condoms, we lay together for a

long time, quietly enjoying the afterglow of the most amazing sex I'd ever had.

"That was perfect," Aiden finally whispered. "It sucks that I have to go to work in the morning."

Logan groaned and I couldn't help the annoyance I felt that he'd be leaving us, but he'd be back by Friday, Saturday afternoon at the latest. And we'd just have to make sure he knew how much we missed him while we waited for him to come back to us.

CHAPTER 30

LOGAN

WE'D HAD FAR TOO little time together with Aiden before Tuesday morning rolled around and Aiden was rushing about the house getting ready for his week. Trent had snipped and snapped all morning, something clearly bothering him, and I took the opportunity to confront him as soon as I knew Aiden was safely in the shower and out of earshot. "The fuck is wrong with you? You went to work last night happy as a clam and you arrived home grouchy as Oscar, slamming cabinets and growling. You look like you're ready to rip someone's head off!"

"I'm just sleep-deprived and frustrated that Aiden is going to be stuck in this photo shoot this week and he doesn't even like the guy he's working for."

I crossed my arms over my chest and propped my hip against the kitchen counter. "He's an adult and he both needs and enjoys money. Adults make decisions on how to best support themselves, and that's what Aiden has done."

Trent gripped the counter across from me so tightly his knuckles turned white. "But he's told us that this guy is an asshole!"

"So is the head of the Kingston Springs Town Council, but

we still go in month after month for their town meetings to remind him why our budget is what it is."

Trent groaned, that time not in frustration at Aiden's work but the reminder that it was once again time to go over the budget with Alistair Newcombe. Maybe it had been a low blow, but Trent needed something to get his mind off Aiden's work schedule. "Aiden has done this before. He's a perfectly capable man." I suspected he was talking to himself but I nodded emphatically just the same.

"See! Exactly!"

Aiden hit the squeaky step that Trent and I had both meant to fix since we moved in but we always seemed to have better things to do. We looked over in surprise. Seeing Aiden with his wet hair slicked back and his shirt slung over his shoulders but not buttoned had my cock thickening in my light gray sweats. Trent smacked me upside the head. "Behave. We do not have time to take him to bed."

Aiden walked toward us, casually buttoning his shirt along the way. He kissed me chastely. "Thank you, puppy." Then he kissed Trent. "I appreciate your concern, but I can't back out now." He looked over at our calendar on the fridge. "But maybe when the chaos dies down, we can sit down and look at my schedule going forward?"

Not even two days after we'd agreed to date, Trent had already proven why he needed me with them. Aiden, as strong and independent as he was, would probably smother Trent in his sleep if he didn't back off in a hurry. I leaned over and kissed Trent's cheek. "Don't worry, Aiden. I'll keep him busy while you're working." I winked.

Aiden giggled. "That's just mean. I have to leave here knowing you two are gonna have fun and I'm going to be at work."

I shrugged casually. "I'm just taking one for the team, that's all."

Aiden tapped his chin. "I better get pictures!"

Not even an hour later we drove Aiden home. We'd all forgotten until he'd gone to leave that I'd driven him to DASH Sunday night and we hadn't gone back to his house since. We watched as Aiden danced up to his door, leaving us to all do our own things for the week.

TRENT and I ended up working almost completely opposite schedules through Thursday. But when I ended up off at seven Thursday night and ready to torment Aiden with some sexy pictures, since he'd already ended up stuck at the warehouse late, I found Trent sitting on our couch looking at his tablet with lines of frustration creasing his forehead.

After putting my gun in the drawer and going upstairs to change into something more appropriate for the evening, I headed back down to find Trent. Work has not necessarily been stressful, but we'd had a number of calls and my head was swimming. I wanted a chance to let everything go. I'd put my harness on before getting dressed and grabbed the rest of my gear to take down with me. It had been way too long since I'd had my tail in and I couldn't wait for Trent to push it inside me... It would be a great time to torment Aiden with those pictures too.

I curled up beside Trent and craned my neck to see what he was concentrating on so hard. "What's up?" If he was that distracted, I'd never get to be a pup that night. I needed to get to the bottom of this, and fast.

He scritched my head like it would help him think. "I've never put a diaper on anyone."

"Okay?"

"How am I going to put a diaper on Aiden if I've never put one on anyone before?"

"There's got to be porn for that, right?" *Definitely the weirdest sentence out of my mouth all week.*

"There is! I've watched it until my eyes hurt. And I've read blogs. The blogs scare me the most. If you don't put them on right, they leak. They all say that the first few times are really hard to get it on properly."

I pushed the tablet down on his lap. "Aiden doesn't expect perfection the first time around. He's going to be happy that you're interested in learning."

"I need to be good at this!" Trent turned his head to look at me and his frustrated features softened when he saw my gear. "Oh, Curious."

My cheeks heated at the tenderness in his voice and I wished I'd put my hood on first. It had been so long since I'd heard the desire and need in Trent's voice when he saw me as Curious, I'd almost forgotten how good it made me feel.

Trent looked to the other side of me and saw the rest of my gear. "Need some playtime tonight, pup?"

I winked at him. "I thought we could torment Aiden with some pictures. He said he wanted them."

Trent kissed my nose. "Let's get you ready." He reached for my shirt, gripping the hem and lifting it over my head slowly. As his fingers traced my harness then slid down my chest, my abs fluttered. It had been so long since Trent had touched me like that, and a piece of me that had felt adrift for two years settled back into place.

I was Trent's.

My eyes drifted shut. We were at the point where the only thing I had to do was feel. I'd needed this for months. "Beautiful pup." Trent's arm reached across my body and grabbed my gloves. As he slid them on each of my hands, I felt some of the chaos in my head ease. I didn't have to worry about work or the constant thoughts that bombarded my mind.

Trent didn't need my direction. He guided me like we'd done this routine countless times or like we'd never stopped. Truthfully, he'd only helped me with this a few times during our short relationship. When he'd maneuvered me so I was standing in front of him, Trent loosened the drawstring on my sweats and let them fall to the ground. I hadn't bothered with underwear, so my nearly hard dick was at eye level with him. Instead of reacting, Trent grabbed the knee pads and helped me slip each one over my feet and settle them against my knees. "Down, Curious." He gently guided me onto all fours, rubbing my shoulders and my back.

I pressed my forehead into his stomach, seeking closeness and connection with him. I was so close to him, his contented hum sounded like it had emanated from his belly. When I moved back, he already had my hood in his hands. I settled onto the floor, my feet behind me and my ass resting between my legs with my hands resting on the ground in front of me. Trent lifted the mask and I ducked my head automatically. In seconds, it was pulled over me, and I already felt more like Curious than Logan. Trent pulled me closer to him by my harness and kissed the top of my head, then my muzzle. "Turn around, ass up, stomach on the ground."

My body reacted without question. Even I didn't normally sink this far into puppy space, but whatever was going on at the moment seemed bigger than pup and handler. We were finding each other again, we were putting the pieces back together, and the fluttery feeling in my stomach told me we'd be coming out of this stronger than we went in.

A slick finger grazed my hole, and instead of shying away from it, I pushed back, my body hungry for everything Trent could give me. "I'm going to get to take my time stretching you tonight, huh? You chose the big tail." The only response I could muster was a whimper and to try to present myself further for Trent. Thankfully, I knew he wasn't looking for words from me. One hand ran over my hip slowly, relaxing my tense muscles while the finger of his other hand swirled and eased my channel open.

I barely registered the second finger slipping inside me, but even with the extra lube, the third was the hardest to take. Trent's fingers were wide, and the stretch of three of them always felt as though they were splitting me apart when he first sank into me. I hadn't forgotten that part, but even the burn felt right. He didn't move until I arched my back, seeking more. Three large fingers would have been more than enough to ready me for his cock, but my plug was wide. I knew, even when he started to rock his fingers in and out of me and I felt my body opening up, it wouldn't be enough.

Face and chest pressed against the soft carpet—the same carpet Trent insisted we get when I discovered puppy play—ass in the air, I could have, maybe should have, felt exposed, but instead I felt safe and loved. Trent knew exactly how long to wait for me to relax before he attempted getting his pinkie in. A steady stream of precum was leaking from my slit as I rocked, but Trent wasn't in a hurry. When my hole fluttered, nearly begging for more, I heard lube squelch from the bottle and felt it drizzle down my backside.

My entire body sagged in the relief of knowing I would finally get more. His fingers left my ass for a brief moment before they slid back in, stretching me farther than I thought possible for a moment before my ass relaxed and the burn turned pleasurable. A long whimper escaped as my body was far more willing to accept the additional finger and I found myself rocking back against him in just moments.

"That's my good pup." Trent's voice was almost reverent. Then he eased out of my hole and I felt painfully empty. "Almost, Curious. Give me a second."

Without Trent's fingers inside of me, I began to feel exposed. Cool air from the house blew against my hole and over my skin where a fine layer of sweat had formed as he'd stretched me. Then they were back, soothing and warming me. "Ass high," Trent instructed, and I complied, immediately raising my ass higher. "Perfect, Curious." Then the blunt head of the plug was pushing against my entrance. Firm and thick, it always made me question if my body would take it at first. But Trent had prepped me well and I trusted him. He would move slowly, watching my body for any signs he was moving too fast.

Gentle pressure pushed at my entrance. Trent rocked and rotated the plug around my hole, waiting for my body to accept it. With a slight increase in pressure, the plug finally started to ease in, eliciting a moan from me and causing my ass to wiggle. I wanted more and faster, but Trent wouldn't force it beyond what my body could take. Inch by inch, the plug slipped farther into my body, stretching and filling me in a way that forced every thought from my head but the plug and Trent. My world had narrowed down to those two things, and there was nothing else that could draw my attention away from them.

Finally, *fucking finally*, the widest part of the plug breached my entrance and my body pulled it the rest of the way in. Once it was seated, there was nothing else that mattered to me. I was Curious... and where was my ball?

Trent gripped my harness and tugged me up to snuggle me tightly for a second. As I was buried against his chest, he rubbed my ass and jostled the plug. The zing of electricity that shot through my body when the plug pushed against my prostate was nothing more than a distant sensation I could easily ignore. "Let me get your toys, Curious."

I barked and looked toward the box by the fireplace where we'd always kept them. Trent headed over and I followed behind him, eager for him to throw the ball. I scrambled to see in the box when he got the lid off, but Trent gripped my harness and pulled me back gently. "No, Curious. Patience." I sat back in frustration and let out a yelp of surprise when I put pressure on my plug. Trent just laughed and shook his head while he searched for my ball.

The number of toys in the box had grown substantially since Aiden had been coming over to play. Every time he showed up at the house he had at least one more toy with him. "Ah-ha!" Trent held up my red ball and I let out another bark. It was by far my favorite toy. "I wish it wasn't nearly winter so we could take you out back to play. I liked throwing the ball for you outside when Aiden was here. How would you like to be outside right now? I bet the grass brushing your erection would drive you insane."

I probably should have been more aroused by the need in his voice, but all I could think of at the time was Trent throwing my ball. I felt like the dog in the old Beggin' Strips commercials. At least Trent had the decency to not roll his eyes at me if I looked as ridiculous as I felt. My brain was screaming, *Throw the ball, throw the ball*, but the words didn't come out of my mouth. My ass moved like it was going to propel me, my excitement built, but no words came. Then Trent threw the ball across the room and I was gone, chasing it as fast as I could on my hands and knees with my plug pushing deep inside me with each movement.

The ball wasn't easy to grab and slid away a number of times. Not that I tried hard to trap it. Chasing it across the room was half the fun. It gave Trent plenty of time to get me water and treats from the kitchen while I was distracted so that when I got back and he tossed me one of the graham cracker bones, I felt like I'd actually completed a difficult task and had earned the treat.

As I ate my treat, Trent pulled out his phone. "I'm going to take some pictures for Aiden." That was a purely naughty grin on Trent's face and it made me smile beneath my hood. I didn't shy away from the pictures and didn't care that Trent was taking them while I was naked aside from the hood. They were for Aiden and he'd love them.

I was vaguely aware of Trent texting as he threw the ball countless times. By the time I was done and climbed up onto the couch by Trent to signal as much, I was covered in sweat and panting. "You played hard, pup." He held out a squeeze water bottle and let me take a long drink before settling back onto the couch and rubbing my side.

As I calmed down, Trent seemed content to let me drift in and out while he scrolled through his tablet a bit more. I wasn't sure how long had passed before my head cleared, but when it finally did, I realized Trent was back to scowling at his tablet despite still running his hand down my back. He was so engrossed in what he was doing that he didn't notice I was looking at his tablet screen. He apparently hadn't forgotten his worries about not knowing how to diaper Aiden properly because he was deep into another blog.

"You can practice on me."

The tablet slipped out of his hand and tumbled to the ground, rolling over twice before coming to rest under the coffee table.

CHAPTER 31

AIDEN

I'D BEEN AN IDIOT. Someone needed to remind me again why I'd left Trent and Logan's house on Tuesday morning to come to this hell. Trent's irritation as I left the house had played on repeat in my head. He'd been genuinely annoyed that I'd taken this job. Then again, he'd been annoyed since Logan and I had spoken about it around him the first time.

I should have listened to him. Hell, I should have listened to my gut. And as if he heard me, my phone buzzed in my pocket. After pictures of Logan running around the living room with his hard cock hanging between his legs had shown up on my phone the night before, I made sure I was alone before I opened them. Those pictures were hot as hell, but no one needed to see my boyfriend naked but me... well, me and Trent.

[Trent] Any chance you're going to be done tonight?

The scoff I let out into the warehouse was so loud a few of the models and assistants looked around to see who had made the sound. I tried to ignore the looks as I tapped a reply onto the screen. It might have been the day we were supposed to finish up but there was no way in hell it would be done, even if we worked through the night.

[Me] No. This is torture.

[Trent] Do I need to pull the Sheriff Card out and call in some favors? I'm sure we could figure something out to get it shut down.

That time, I had to bite my lip to not laugh. I could see him and Logan doing something that ridiculous.

[Me] No. We're not at that point yet. Give us a few more days. No way I'm getting out of here by one. Not making it to your house tonight... again.

The following texts from both Trent and Logan were filled with frustration about the shoot. I couldn't blame them. It was already Friday, and we should have been done at eight. Done as in wrapped up and home in our beds, not to have to go back again, but it was already pushing midnight with no end in sight. At that rate, I was hoping to get home—my house, not Trent and Logan's—by two or three, collapse into bed, and sleep until seven or eight to start the entire thing over again the next morning. By this point in the week, Logan showing up with lunch for me on Wednesday felt like a lifetime ago.

He'd appeared at the exact right moment with a takeout bag and a large coffee in the middle of the afternoon and saved me from screaming at the director, Francois. As it turned out, I didn't function well without copious amounts of caffeine while working. We hadn't had enough time to do anything but eat quickly and have a few stolen kisses at his truck before Francois had come to find me, with another complaint about the last handful of shots I'd taken. He'd come face-to-face with a very overprotective Logan, who had growled low and stopped Francois in his tracks. I'd smiled at his shock, kissed my pup, and reluctantly went back to work after reminding Logan he could not arrest Francois for yelling at me.

The memory had gotten me through until Trent showed up tonight with dinner and chocolate milk for me. Francois had been pissed that I had disappeared for twenty minutes to eat.

He'd come storming out of the building to find me sitting on Trent's truck bed eating the sandwich he'd brought for me. Trent's shoulders stiffened, his chest and shoulders puffed out, and his eyes turned cold. "Is there a problem?" he'd growled at Francois even more menacingly than Logan had two days earlier. The badge, the gun, and the pissed-off sheriff surprised Francois so much he'd dropped his fake French accent as he mumbled an apology and ran back inside.

Trent hadn't found the interaction as amusing as I had, but I'd found it hysterical. Francois had a reputation for being an insufferable asshole to work with and everyone from assistants to models to photographers all knew the name and accent were a façade, but no one had ever seen it slip either. Trent's sudden appearance had proven, at least to me, that Francois was absolutely a Fauxcois and it had made me unbelievably happy. If I had to guess, I'd say he was a Midwestern boy through and through. I'd smiled the rest of my meal.

However, my smile couldn't hide my frequent yawns. My exhaustion worried Trent enough that he and Logan texted repeatedly for the rest of the evening. I'd finally promised to text them to let them know when we were done. When I texted after two Saturday morning that I was done for the night, my phone rang before I'd even made it to my Jeep.

"Hey, A." Logan sounded tired, but not quite as tired as I felt.

"Hey, Logan."

"Are you okay to drive home?"

I nodded first before I remembered that he couldn't see my nod over the phone. "It's only thirteen minutes from here. Given that it's night and no traffic, I bet it won't take more than ten."

Logan might not have been a Dom, but the growl he produced sent a shiver through my body. "That's not an answer."

"I'll be fine. Talk to me on the way?"

"Absolutely."

We chatted about the week so far and plans for the following day. Logan and Trent were both off work and had plans with their friends Saturday evening. "Not fair," I complained. I wanted to go out with everyone, but we were already behind schedule and I knew it wasn't going to happen. "I want to go with you."

"If things change, we've got an extra ticket." Logan sounded disappointed that I couldn't go and it almost made me throw in the towel and drive to his house. Unfortunately, that would mean an extra twenty minutes in the car and I didn't have it in me. I was already pulling into my driveway and I wasn't going to be safe driving farther that night.

"Thanks, puppy. I just got home." I hit the lock on my car and walked up the sidewalk to my front door. "And I'm walking into my house now."

"I'll wait until you're inside with your door locked, then I'll let you get to bed. Trent just texted and said to tell you to make sure to brush your teeth."

My laugh was too loud for my quiet house and it surprised me, but the fact that Trent was texting Logan as he was talking to me was funny. Actually, it was so sweet it made my heart clench and made my resolve to stay home waver. I was so tired my options had been laugh or cry and I'd chosen to laugh. "I will." I locked the deadbolt. "And I'm locked safely in my house. I'm going to go brush my teeth and head to bed. Tell Daddy thanks for thinking about me."

Logan smiled. "I will. Sleep well. What time do you have to be up in the morning?"

My moan was as dramatic as I felt at the moment. "Seven."

"Dammit, you need more sleep. Get to bed. Trent's already pissy about how little sleep you've managed to get this week. I need you to catch up on sleep before he really goes Daddy Dom and drives us both insane."

"I'm going, I'm going! Night, night, puppy." I'd almost said I loved him but had clamped my mouth shut. It had to have been my exhaustion because it was too soon to be in love with either of them, even Logan.

SATURDAY MORNING I woke to my alarm at five 'til seven and then my phone ringing at seven sharp. "Hello?" I answered groggily. I'd fallen back asleep and was beginning to think I could sleep for the next month.

"Morning, baby boy."

My eyes flew open. "Daddy?"

"You sound terrible. Did you sleep enough last night?"

When was the last time I'd had enough sleep? I hated that I'd worried him, but there was very little I could do about it, and I'd already slept longer than I should have. I was probably at the point that I'd have to risk not showering if I kept talking to Trent. "I slept."

"Is this your last day on this project?"

I didn't want to lie, but I hated to tell him that it looked like the project was going to go through the weekend. Instead of telling him the truth, I changed the subject. "What are you and my puppy up to today?" It hurt to roll out of bed. My shoulders ached from holding my camera and my knees ached from squatting down in awkward positions or kneeling on the ground. I hadn't hidden my hiss of pain as I rolled out of bed because Trent started quizzing me before I'd even gotten fully upright.

"Baby boy, are you okay?"

"Fine," I groaned a little as I stretched out. "Tense muscles."

"Have you taken anything for it?"

I rolled my eyes and bit my cheek to not laugh. "I just rolled out of bed."

"You should have taken something last night if you were sore."

Oh my goodness, he really was as overprotective as Logan had warned me. "I wasn't sore when I went to bed," I rationalized as I made my way to my bathroom to try to find a bottle of Advil.

He sighed loudly into the phone. "Logan and I are going out tonight. If you're not home by then, I'm sending you a message to take something to help you not feel like shit later on."

Having him thinking about twelve hours in the future and how I'd be feeling was strange. I'd been doing things on my own so long that it made weird emotions well up inside of me. I focused on his words more than how they made me feel. "Daddy said a bad word."

Trent laughed though he sounded tired. Then I remembered he'd worked the night shift, and he'd probably just gotten home. "I'm Daddy. I can say bad words."

"But I'm your boy, so I get to remind you that they are bad." I tried to tease, but my voice got choked with emotion. I had a Daddy, a Daddy that cared enough about me to sacrifice sleep after a night shift, to go out of his way to bring me dinner before his shift, and to remind me that I couldn't say bad words. I also had a puppy, a puppy who stayed up late to call me on my way home, who brought me lunch because he missed me, and reminded me how much he'd rather me be with him than away. I was a darn lucky boy. Lucky enough that it wasn't even hard to remember not to curse, even in my head.

Thinking about food made my stomach growl. I hadn't eaten anything since Trent brought me dinner. That had been fifteen hours earlier. Trent's teasing voice distracted me from my stomach's protests. "You can remind me all you want. It probably isn't going to change much at this point in my life."

I preferred the teasing and missing the opportunity to

shower to hanging up. "Then it's not fair to expect me to watch my language."

"Baby boy, I've got ten years on you. Ten more years of bad habits. And, just in case you forgot, I'm Daddy." There was a short pause and he sighed. "And as such, I need to tell you that you need to get off the phone and get ready for work."

The groan was out before I could stop it. My stomach joined in the protest as well. "I should probably eat breakfast at least. Dinner was a long time ago."

"Did you not eat anything after I brought you dinner last night?"

"No time."

He huffed into the phone, then I heard Logan in the background. "Trent! Leave A alone. He needs to get ready to go to work, and you growling and scowling at the phone like you're ready to break it is not helping him get to work on time. The sooner he gets to work, the sooner we get to see him."

If only it were that simple.

"Okay, okay, okay. Have a good day, Aiden. Promise me you'll eat better today. I'm not going to tolerate you starving yourself for your work. No matter how much you love it."

I really did love my job. At least most days. This particular project sucked.

"I'll eat." And I would. Just maybe not as much as he would have liked.

"Bye, Daddy. Tell the puppy I miss him too."

At least there was a smile in his voice when he responded. "Okay, baby. Have a good day."

In the background I heard Logan say goodbye before the call clicked off. I fought to hold back a sniffle at how much their concern touched me as I went downstairs for a quick breakfast before heading to work.

CHAPTER 32

LOGAN

BY ONE IN THE AFTERNOON, I was bored out of my mind. Aiden was supposed to be done with his shoot already, but he'd known it was going to run long even before it started. I'd known it was going to be a rough week, but I hadn't expected how difficult it would be on Trent and me, as well. I missed my boy. I missed spending time with him and seeing him. And maybe I shouldn't have been thinking of him as my boy because he was definitely Trent's boy, but part of me felt like he was just as much mine. He was part of me. And if I was his puppy, he could be my boy, *dammit*.

With Trent still sleeping and me feeling melancholy about Aiden's absence, I headed to the garage to run. I hadn't been in the mood for a full-out sprint like I often was, but I also needed to move. So I turned the TV on, found a movie on Netflix, and started to jog lightly on the treadmill. I'd gotten lost in the story line when I heard a truck back up our driveway, then a door shut. It took me a moment to realize it was a delivery driver.

I couldn't think of anything I'd ordered recently, and curiosity got the best of me after a few moments. I clicked the TV off and stopped the treadmill, then headed out the door and around to the front of the house. A box with a nondescript return address sat on the porch. It was addressed to Trent, so I took it inside, fully intending to drop it off on the counter and pepper him with questions about it when he woke up. I hadn't expected Trent to be standing against the counter drinking a cup of coffee like his life depended on it.

"Dude, you look like shit." I deposited the box on the counter and helped myself to coffee.

"Aiden sounded really tired this morning. It haunted me in my dreams. I hate that he's unhappy with this current project."

"It sucks that the guy he's working for is a total asshole. But he's a big boy—he can handle it. Also, this shoot was scheduled well before he'd even met you. It was too late for him to pull out. You can remind him not to book jobs like this one in the future."

Trent grumbled something about not being able to wait to get his hands on Aiden's schedule before his eyes fell onto the box. "What's in the box?"

I shrugged a shoulder as I poured myself a cup of coffee. "Don't know. Just got delivered and it's got your name on it."

Trent sat his coffee mug down and grabbed a knife out of our knife block to open the package. His face went from confused to amused as he opened the box. "Holy shit, those got here fast."

"What got here fast?"

He pulled the item out with a flourish, and I couldn't help the way my mouth hung open in surprise.

"Put this day on the calendar!" Trent announced as he grabbed the dry erase marker and started to write on our schedule. I looked over his shoulder as he wrote, then slapped him playfully. *Shocked Logan Speechless* was scrawled through the date.

"That was fast."

Trent looked nervous. "If you changed your mind, it's okay. I'm pretty sure they're Aiden's size anyway."

I shook my head. "Come on." I hadn't changed my mind, I just hadn't expected them to arrive so soon. We'd ordered the package barely thirty-six hours earlier, which might not have been enough time for me to mentally prepare myself for actually having Trent put a diaper on me. I'd held Aiden's diapers a number of times. I'd seen them on him even more often. But that was different; those were *his*. At least one of these was mine... well, meant for me at least.

Trent might have been anxious about how I felt about why we'd bought them, but I could see hesitation in his eyes as well. If I backed out now, he'd second-guess how prepared he was for Aiden. He'd worry about the first time he would diaper him. Trent didn't believe that it was okay to practice on Aiden, and this was something I could give him. I could give him confidence, and no matter what my brain said, I knew my heart would do anything to make Trent happy. If I helped Aiden find happiness in the process, it would all be worth it.

"Come on, let's go get this over with. You'll see—this will be easy and you'll have worried for nothing."

Trent shook his head at my false bravado. He knew me too well. "At least let me get dressed. My pants are in the laundry room. You came in before I made it there."

I took a moment to look at Trent. He was in the kitchen wearing only a pair of briefs. God, how had I missed that? "Hell no. If you're going to be putting a diaper on me, I at least get to see your sexy body while you do it."

Trent rolled his eyes so hard they disappeared for a moment. "You're full of shit."

I felt a growl form in my chest as I shook my head. "One day you'll actually believe me when I tell you that you're sexy. Come on, let's go upstairs."

We headed up the steps and straight into our room. I didn't know when his room had become our room, but I had only been in my room long enough to get changed since Sunday night. I stood at the side of the bed, waiting for instructions, all the while trying to ignore what we were about to do.

"There's still time to back out," Trent assured me as he ripped the bag open.

I shook my head again. I was going to give myself whiplash if I had to continue to emphatically negate his suggestions. "Absolutely not. You are worrying about this, so you're going to practice on me. No time like the present!" I waggled my eyebrows at him. "Undress me, Daddy."

The word sounded so absurd coming out of my mouth, and Trent started laughing at me but still went for my pants. This wasn't the first time he'd undressed me, and I was certain it wouldn't be the last. But this time it felt a lot different. He was undressing me to put a diaper on me. There was still a part of me that couldn't believe I'd volunteered for this. A small part of me kept saying there was no way I'd be doing this if I didn't love both of them so much.

I couldn't hide my apprehension when my pants were off and my cock remained flaccid against my balls. Trent swallowed twice, hard enough that I could see his Adam's apple bob in his throat. "Llama?"

I blinked a few times, not expecting the question from him. I started to shake my head but knew words were more important. "No, no safeword. I trust you, Trent."

He leaned forward and kissed me on the lips. No tongue, no pressure for more, just a silent thank you. When we finally pulled apart, he took my hands and directed me toward the bed. "Down you get."

I went willingly, settling myself in the middle, then reached up and grabbed my pillow and shoved it behind my head to watch what Trent was doing. He seemed to hesitate for a moment before a silent curse crossed his lips and he pulled one of the diapers out of the bag.

To break the tension, I worked on teasing gently. "First attempt. Show me what ya got, Daddy."

He leaned down and kissed the sensitive skin above my dick, causing my back to arch up automatically. "Let's get this over with. Lift up."

I planted my feet on the bed and lifted my hips so Trent could slide the diaper into place. When he bent down to get the diaper centered, his eyes were only a few inches from my dick and his breath ghosted over my skin, causing me to squirm and my dick to begin reacting. Satisfied with the position, Trent tapped my hip. "Back down."

I settled back onto the bed, but my dick was excited for more attention. It had filled and was pointing toward my hip. Trent blew out a breath of frustration. "Everything I read said it should be pointed downward."

My bark of laughter surprised us both. "That thing ain't going down. You're going to have to figure out how to work around it."

Trent's eyes darkened and the smirk on his face told me he was planning something. I had definitely not expected him to bend down and lick from my root to tip, or wrap his soft lips around my head and begin sucking. My hips shot off the bed like I'd been electrocuted. "Holy fuck!" I hissed, my breath already coming in ragged pants. "Dammit, Trent, you feel so good."

He knew every one of my hot buttons: a lot of spit, tongue in my slit, firm suction, and when I'd just about lost it, the gentlest graze of teeth along my shaft and I would explode in seconds. I didn't need someone to swallow my cock all the way down their throat. I actually preferred a tongue exploring more than a throat constricting.

All too quickly my orgasm began to build. I bit my tongue, I tried to think of anything but the wet heat enveloping my dick, but it was useless. In a matter of moments, I knew I wasn't going to last. "T-T-Trent! Close! Gonna. Ah!" I screamed into the room and began to fill his mouth. He'd been so surprised I heard him struggle to swallow the ropes of cum.

I collapsed back onto the bed panting and cursing under my breath about Trent having a wicked mouth and making me cum too soon. Trent seemed satisfied with himself, standing up and smirking proudly at his work, though his own cock was hard. "Want me to help you out there?" I croaked out as my brain began to function again.

"No. I'm good. This was all about you and getting your cock soft enough that I can put this diaper on you."

I'd forgotten all about the reason we were in bed until he mentioned it. Then I felt the thick cotton under my ass and heard the slight crinkle of the plastic. The waiting game for my cock to soften enough to get the diaper on was short. It only took a few minutes and I was soft enough that he could easily tuck my dick down and pull the diaper between my legs. Trent fumbled with the tapes a few times, lending credit to his claim that he needed to practice before he tried diapering Aiden, but eventually it was on.

"How's it feel?"

I wiggled around. It felt weird—thickness between my legs where normally only a thin layer of cotton covered. It wasn't terrible. "I mean, I guess it feels like a diaper?" With that I stood and watched in amusement as the diaper slid down on my hips. We both began to laugh. "It shouldn't do that, should it?" I gave a slight jump and felt it slide completely off and down to my knees.

As frustrated as I was sure Trent was, he was able to laugh his first attempt off. "See, this is why I needed practice."

I fell back on the bed. "Well, if at first you don't succeed."

In the end, it took us three diapers and as many blowjobs before he'd figured out how to get the diaper on so it stayed. Once he'd decided that the last one he'd put on me was acceptable, I was utterly spent. The last orgasm had been nothing more than a pulsation in my cock and a half spurt of liquid that hardly resembled cum. I curled up on my side of the bed, and Trent curled around me, pulling me close. "So three orgasms is what it takes to wear your ass out?"

"Well, three orgasms wears me and my cock out. As it rests"—I chuckled at my terrible joke—"my ass is ready to go... but later." I yawned and closed my eyes.

"How are they?" Trent asked me as he rubbed my back slowly.

"Eh." At some point, when I was functioning better, I'd try to explain to him that the constant pressure on my dick was damn near too much to handle, and not in a good way. Trent paying so much attention to my cock with every diaper he put on me was erotic as hell, and Trent's mouth made the blowjobs the best ever. But any thought I had required words that my brain simply didn't have the energy for.

At some point later, I woke up to Trent kissing my shoulder. "If we sleep any longer, we're going to miss the concert."

My cock responded automatically to his lips and the memories of the earlier blowjobs. I began to ask what time it was when I became starkly aware of the diaper still wrapped around my waist and my dick pressing against it. I yelped. "Whoa, time for this thing to get off!"

"Have to pee?" Trent smirked, already maneuvering his body to get between my legs to help take it off.

"Worse. I'm getting hard and it's uncomfortable."

Trent's eyes crinkled as he fought not to laugh. "Well, we can safely say you don't share the same fetish as Aiden."

"We knew that going into this, but this just solidifies it."

Trent grabbed the tabs on one side, I grabbed the tabs on the other, and we both pulled. I had no desire to orgasm, but just my cock having enough room to grow without being pinched was a huge relief. Sighing, I rolled over and gave Trent a lazy kiss. "Do we have to get ready to go? I feel like I could sleep for the next week. Love you," I mumbled as my eyes shut again.

"Love you too. Don't fall asleep on me. We need to get going." Despite his words, Trent didn't push, and I didn't feel the need to throw myself out of bed in any hurry.

CHAPTER 33

TRENT

IT HAD TAKEN AWHILE to convince Logan to shower. While coaxing him out of bed, I'd texted Aiden a number of times to make sure he'd eaten, taken painkillers, and was taking breaks. He'd texted back with a picture of a sad-looking sandwich buffet, told me he'd take Advil then, and simply laughed at the break comment. Logan finally reached over and took the phone from me. "Listen to my words. The more you bug him, the longer it will be until he gets back to us."

I hated when he was right. At least my impatience to talk to Aiden and make sure he was all right had Logan moving toward the shower. Of course, I ended up in the shower with him while we took the most platonic shared shower in history. He complained the whole time that I'd broken his dick with too many orgasms. I felt like it was another moment that should be marked on the calendar. Two in one day... that was calendar-worthy as well.

It was already pushing five when we finally got downstairs. Logan might have cum three times earlier in the afternoon and wasn't interested in sex, but I hadn't, and watching him in his very snug jeans was a constant reminder of my desire to drag him up to bed and fuck him. It was probably for the best as we were supposed to be meeting the guys for dinner before we went to the Hometown concert. I'd normally decline an invite to a concert, but when your close friend is the husband of the lead singer of a band, it's hard to get out of going. Thanks to Colt we had box seats... keyword being seats, because I really was that old now.

After helping Logan slip his arms into a lightweight coat, I slid my own coat on. Logan sighed regretfully as he bent to get his shoes on. "I'm actually kind of pissed that Aiden can't be with us tonight."

"What would we tell the guys?"

Logan's brows pulled together in confusion. "What are you talking about?"

"Most of them don't even know you're bisexual. They don't know we dated. They don't know that we're with Aiden. Would either of us be able to hide that we were with him?"

Logan looked uncharacteristically bashful. "Uh, that's not entirely true."

"What's not entirely true?""

"Well, Merrick knows about us. And Caleb and Travis know I'm bi. I'm guessing Dexter does too by now."

I blinked in surprise. "What? How? When?"

Logan ran his hand over the back of his neck uncomfortably. "Aiden and I may have run into Travis and Caleb somewhere one night."

My eyes popped open of their own accord. "DASH?" It was the only logical place that they could have run into Travis and Caleb for them to know that Logan wasn't straight.

Logan nodded slowly. "Yeah. Caleb and I talked a few days later. I'm sure Caleb talked to Dexter about it by now."

"So, you're okay with the guys finding out whenever they find out?"

Logan studied me closely, almost like he didn't know me. "I wanted them to know two years ago. I'm not going to hide one of us away. Dammit, I ran into Caleb and Travis at a sex club. How long are we all going to keep pretending we're completely vanilla? If they can't accept that the three of us are together, they weren't that good of friends to begin with."

I leaned forward and kissed him on the lips. Hard, firm, claiming. "You are amazing. You know that right?"

Before Logan could respond, lights came up our driveway and showed through the front door. When the vehicle parked and a figure appeared on the front porch, I was shocked to find Aiden walking toward the door.

"Are you seeing what I'm seeing?"

Logan's head bobbed up and down and he pulled out his phone. "Did he tell you he was on his way over?"

I pulled my phone out of my back pocket and shook my head. "What's he doing here?"

"We're not going to find out if you don't open the door."

My stomach flipped a few times as my hand reached for the door. I hadn't appreciated how much I'd missed Aiden until I saw him walking up the steps. His hair was mussed and not as perfectly styled as I normally saw it. His shirt was a bit askew, like he'd been tugging on it. It had been a long few days for him, but he was gorgeous. And he was here. At our house. My fingers wrapped around the door handle and I flung it open before he'd even managed to raise his hand to knock. If Logan's laughter from behind me was anything to go by, I wasn't portraying the calmest, most put-together Dom in history, but our boy was on the front porch. I couldn't wait to pull him into my arms and hug him.

He looked exhausted. Absolutely and completely drained. He blinked a few times when the door opened suddenly, followed by his face brightening up and his body relaxing like a weight had been lifted off his shoulders. "Am I too late?"

Logan's head cocked to the side and he looked confused. "Too late for what?"

"To go with you tonight. You said there was an extra ticket."

Logan's response was to turn and run from the room. I heard him clomp up the steps, and I turned back to Aiden. He looked as confused as I felt. "Why'd he run away?" Aiden asked as I gathered him in my arms.

"Does Logan ever have a reason for what he does? Did you finally wrap up the shoot?" We were going to have a conversation about him not texting at some point, but right then, I was relishing having my boy back in my arms. As he tucked himself under my chin, I breathed in deeply, allowing his scent to wrap around me like a blanket. Even after a nearly twelve-hour day, Aiden still smelled like coconut and sugar. It was a scent I'd forever associate with him, much like I couldn't smell the rain and not think of Logan and his bodywash.

I'd missed having Aiden in my arms, in our house. I'd missed his smiles and laughter and hadn't even known how lonely the house had been the last week without him there. He'd become an almost permanent fixture in our house, or at least common enough that his return brought into sharp focus how his absence was noticed.

Clomping interrupted us and Logan reappeared, hurdling the coffee table on his way through the living room to get back to us. I shook my head. "Logan, don't run in the house!" *Why was I saying that to a man over thirty-five?*

"Got the ticket! We can go now. Aiden can tell us about being here on the way to dinner. If we don't leave now, we're going to be late. I know you don't want that." He shot a saucy wink over his shoulder as he grabbed Aiden's hand and led him right back out the door and toward my truck.

I followed obediently, shaking my head while I locked up, then joined them at the truck. "Logan, you're being very pushy. Aiden, are you sure you're up for going to a concert tonight? You've had a long week." I made sure to watch Aiden carefully as I asked the question. He looked tired but not necessarily exhausted, more like he'd been stressed for way too long.

"As long as you guys will be there, I want to be there."

With a quick double-check to make sure his belt was fastened, I shut the door and climbed into the driver's seat. "Is your shoot finished?"

I caught the shrug of his shoulders as we pulled out of the driveway. "Dunno."

Logan's expression summed my feelings up well. "What do you mean you don't know?"

That time, Aiden ducked his head. "I know it was wrong. I know I shouldn't have. But I walked out."

I was glad I'd just coasted to a stop at the stop sign down the street from our house. "You what?"

"Good!" Logan said over me.

Aiden looked sheepish and focused more on Logan than me, like he couldn't quite bring himself to look me in the eye. "I was standing there, the wind was ripping down the alley we were shooting in, and I just kept thinking about you guys. We'd already been shooting longer than we were supposed to be. The director was barking at everyone. Daddy kept texting me to make sure I was taking care of myself. And all of a sudden, I had an epiphany. I didn't need to be there. My contract was through yesterday. There were no provisions beyond noon today... I need to remember to add a clause about extended time in my contracts going forward." He'd seemingly said the last part to himself. However, I made a mental note to remind him of the need for specific wording about a job going over in the future. He began to talk to us again. "But I was tired of being yelled at. I was tired of standing. I was tired of asking how high every time he barked 'Jump.'"

Logan's smile lit up the cab. "I'm so glad you're here. We were talking about how much we wanted you with us tonight."

"Are you in trouble for leaving?"

His eyes darted around the truck and his shoulders met his ears. "I don't know. Maybe? I sure won't be working with Fauxcois anymore."

I couldn't have heard him right. Logan was back to laughing too hard to ask the question, so I clarified. "Who?"

Aiden's light giggle filled the truck and I couldn't help but smile. "Francois. The director. You met him. He was the guy screaming that I was lazy when you brought me dinner."

"His name's Francois?" I clarified.

"He talks with a French accent and swears his name is Francois. The accent is fake. Everyone's always suspected as much, but when you surprised him yesterday, he dropped the accent. I wouldn't be shocked if his name was Frank and he was from Missouri. I've taken to calling him Fauxcois behind his back. But anyway, I'm sure he won't ask for me again. Not that I'm crying over it."

I wasn't going to cry over it either, but I couldn't miss the fact he hadn't looked me in the eye since he'd told me he'd walked out. I tried to get him to acknowledge me, at least meet my eyes in the rearview mirror so I could figure out what was going through his head, but he seemed intent on avoiding my gaze. "So why did you leave?"

Despite it being my question, he answered Logan. "I was standing there, the wind whipping around me, and I kept thinking about your texts. I hated this job before I took it. I knew it was going to be hell, but I took it anyway. But then you two came into my life, and you were here and I was there and I couldn't get away. Then the texts started about making sure I got enough to eat and that I should take ibuprofen so I didn't ache so bad. And I missed you guys. Both of you. Five days has never felt so long in all my life. I didn't want to spend the next god knows how long freezing in that damn—darn alley. I wanted to see you. I wanted to go to the concert with you. I wanted to crawl into bed with you tonight."

He sighed sadly. Far sadder than he should have been coming out of such a toxic job environment. "I finally get the men of my dreams and I have to leave them for five days. It just wasn't fair."

"So you walked out?" Logan spoke up.

Aiden gave a noncommittal grunt. "I mean, I didn't just walk out. I packed up my stuff first. When people realized what I was doing, they helped. Some of the models and the assistants actually clapped as I left."

As his Daddy, I probably should have encouraged him to stick it out because he'd given his word and I expected everyone to complete tasks they took on. However, I also expected any employer to not be an asshole. Francois, or whatever his name was, wasn't a reasonable employer; therefore, he got what he deserved.

"Good for you, baby boy."

Finally, Aiden met my eyes in the mirror. He couldn't have hidden his shock if he'd tried. "You're not mad?"

Ah, so that was what had him upset. "Absolutely not. First and foremost, you already said you fulfilled your duties. But even if you hadn't, you shouldn't have to endure verbal abuse to do your job. If there aren't provisions in your contracts for that type of thing, we'll work on getting them added in the future."

I could see stress leave his body as I spoke. It made me feel terrible that he'd been so worried about my reaction that it had stressed him out even further than the shoot had.

Logan vibrated with energy so much his leg bounced. "Now that that's out of the way, do we get to tell the guys tonight?"

CHAPTER 34

AIDEN

"TELL THE GUYS?" My voice cracked. "About us?" As in their friends? About the three of us?

The question knocked Logan down a peg or three. "Is that okay?"

Was it okay? I didn't know why, but I hadn't expected them to want to tell their friends. At least not right away. Sure, they had the gayest group of friends in Tennessee, and there were definitely some kinky guys in the group, but that didn't mean they'd accept three men dating. I had to trust that Logan and Trent knew their friends better than I did and if they were comfortable with them finding out about the three of us, then I was going to be okay with it too. Actually, I was at the point that I'd tell anyone willing to listen that I was dating two sexy men, but that didn't mean explaining our relationship to their friends didn't make me a bit nervous.

I didn't know if I'd have been at that point before I saw Trent and Logan standing in their doorway as I pulled up to their house. They'd been locked in a kiss as I'd turned the corner in their driveway. I'd seen into their house before they'd caught sight of my headlights. They looked so beautiful together and all

I could think about was joining them. I couldn't explain how I'd been lucky enough to find them, but I had, and the expressions of pure joy on their faces when they recognized me as I came up the steps reinforced just how right this was.

I'd been miserable at work that day, all week actually, but knowing that I had a Daddy and puppy waiting for me, missing me, gave me the courage to say when enough was enough. At any other point leading up to that day, I would have continued to suffer through it. Just knowing Daddy was there to run to, worrying about me while I was miserable, was enough to make me willing to take the potential fallout of leaving the job incomplete. It had been the most intense rush of adrenaline I'd ever experienced as I packed up.

Pulling into their driveway, it hit me that there was a very real chance I'd upset Trent when he found out. Even with his bright smile and the way he pulled me to him as soon as I got into the door, the chance was still there, and I instinctively resisted telling him that I'd walked out. That was why I'd talked to Logan—who had beamed with happiness from the moment he saw me—until Trent had told me he was proud of me for leaving.

If those four little words could make me feel so amazing, I knew that I'd do anything to make my men happy. And if telling their friends we were together was going to please them, I was more than happy to do so. "I'd love to tell them. As long as you think they'll be okay with it. I don't want to strain your friendships with them."

"Like Logan said to me before you got to the house tonight, if they can't accept us as a unit, then they weren't really our friends to begin with. But Merrick knows already and he wasn't just okay with it, he was the one that opened my eyes to us being together."

We were going to tell the group we were together, and I was

okay with it. Actually, I was excited. And like we had spoken the guys into existence, our phones started to vibrate.

[Caleb] We're ten minutes out.

Logan threw his head back and laughed. "Trent, you're going to be so excited. We're beating Travis and Caleb to the bar!"

Trent pumped his fist into the air. "Yes!"

[Merrick] If Trent is anywhere near the bar, he's going to be doing a happy dance.

[Dean] I just pulled into the parking lot.

[Logan] Trent is definitely celebrating.

[Me] We're only a few minutes away.

[Larson] Leaving the firehouse now, so you all will beat me.

I didn't know if there was anything about Trent and Logan that wouldn't make me giddy. Even the way they gloated about beating their friends to the bar was endearing. Trent pulled into the parking lot at Steve's with a giant grin on his face. "Victory is ours!"

This was the silly Trent that I'd heard about. I'd only seen glimpses of it before then, mostly at the park before he noticed me taking pictures of them, which reminded me that I needed to finish editing those pictures. Around me, Trent tended to be quite a bit more... Daddy-like. I loved his protective side, but the silly side was refreshing, and I liked that he was finally comfortable enough to let it out around me. I didn't need him to be a serious Daddy all the time.

Trent opened his door, then stepped back to get mine open. "Come on, let's get in there and find Dean."

The three of us walked through the parking lot together. Logan had threaded his fingers through Trent's and Trent had placed his other hand on the small of my back. There was no mistaking we were together—the touches were too natural. We were in a bar parking lot, and Trent had just claimed us both. It was perfect.

It was still perfect as he guided us to the table, still holding Logan's hand, still guiding me with his hand on my back. Warmth radiated through me and any remaining exhaustion I might have felt from the week seemed to evaporate before my eyes.

As we took seats around the tables Dean had pushed together, I noticed our positions changed slightly. I'd sat next to Trent and Logan sat next to me. As easily as he'd been holding Trent's hand as we walked through the bar, Logan placed his hand over mine on the table. Trent's hand went from resting on my back to resting on my leg.

Dean had been texting as we'd entered and didn't seem to notice anything out of the ordinary until the others started arriving. Caleb was the first to notice Logan's hand wrapped in mine. "Really? Finally? I thought you said you two were incompatible!" He beamed at the two of us. "See, Daddy? I told you!" His eyes widened and he threw his hands over his mouth in shock.

Travis chuckled and pulled Caleb close to kiss the top of his head. "Easy there, sweet boy. I don't know that it's your news to tell."

Merrick grinned knowingly, allowing Dean to take his time figuring out what was happening. Logan and Trent were so in tune with one another, they both squeezed me at the same time, and a glance to each side showed them both smiling genuine smiles. I was willing to say they were excited.

No one reacted to Caleb's slip. Whether they knew it or not, it made me a lot more comfortable telling them about the three of us. If they could accept the fact that Caleb liked spankings and called Travis "Daddy" without a second thought, there was a good chance they'd be okay with the three of us dating.

"Finally what? Who's incompatible?" Larson's deep voice drew our attention and the group greeted him happily as everyone took seats.

Caleb leaned across the table and bubbled over with questions. "When? How?"

"When and how what?" Poor Larson was confused.

Caleb gestured between Logan and me. "They finally got together!" He said the words like they were logical and Larson was being dense. Caleb's hazel eyes narrowed between us. "Does it work well?"

It was Logan who spoke up next. "It wouldn't work with just the two of us. For sure not."

Larson's eyes did funny things as he processed what Logan was saying. He'd gone from confused to surprised, back to confused, and his eyes settled at a point where one eye was scrunched up and the other one was wide. I'd never seen a face like it before and the harder he tried to school his features, the funnier he looked.

I fought not to laugh at Larson's expression, but the humor was still in my voice as I spoke. "I need someone more take-charge." I pushed at Logan's shoulder with my own. "This one isn't that way." Logan's head shook back and forth.

"He's right," he agreed readily. "I'm not... controlling enough for him, for lack of a better word. But he is." He tossed a thumb across my body and right toward Trent.

"I knew it!" Caleb exclaimed and clapped his hands together loudly enough that the entire table looked at us. "That's so perfect!"

They might not have figured out what Caleb was so excited about had Larson not put the pieces together at that moment and gasped. "The three of you are together?"

Dean and Travis looked between us in confusion. *Moment of truth. How were they going to handle it?* Logan and I nodded our heads. I was a little more hesitant than Logan, but we both confirmed it.

Dean's dark eyes darted between the three of us. "Wait, Logan *is* gay?"

"Bi." Logan said it confidently and without hesitation.

The table was quiet for a long few seconds before Travis spoke. "You never told us?"

Logan's cheeks turned a little pink and he spoke directly to Trent. "It really didn't matter until now. I met the perfect guy when I was in high school. By the time I realized I was bisexual, we weren't even living in the same state. We ignored our attraction for a long time, and then a few years ago tried to date for a few weeks. We were not compatible."

Dean's mouth hung open in shock. "You dated?"

Trent nodded. "We did, but quickly discovered that we needed very different things out of a relationship."

Logan jumped in at that point. "The sex was amazing, but it wasn't enough." He shot a naughty wink toward Trent and I couldn't help it—it shot straight to my dick.

Travis grinned at the three of us. "Yeah, sex definitely isn't everything, no matter how much we wish it to be the case. Oh, and Dean, you owe me twenty bucks."

"You bet on us?" Trent gaped at them.

Dean grouched. "You really need to ask that? Of course we did!"

Merrick shook his head. "You two have been shit at hiding your feelings over the years. Dean said you'd never figure it out. Travis swore it would just take time. I thought you'd been together since you were teens. At least on and off."

Trent shook his head but moved on from the bet. "We barely made it a month. I drove him nuts."

"Nuts is an understatement. Do you have any idea how many control issues this man has?"

"Trent? Never!" Travis joked in mock surprise.

"So what changed?" Larson questioned, finally finding his

voice. I didn't miss that he spoke more to Logan and me than Trent.

A soft smile spread across Trent's lips. "This one." He patted my shoulder with the hand that had been resting on my thigh. "He changed everything."

Dean blinked. Blinked again. His mouth opened and shut a few times, then managed a sound. "Huh?"

Since no one seemed shocked, I found my words. "I don't mind how controlling he is."

"But I keep Trent from going insane and barging into A's work and telling him to come home right now."

Trent nodded. "True story."

When the guys across the table from us laughed, I found more confidence. "And they're both really sexy."

At that, everyone laughed.

Merrick finally spoke up. "Are you guys happy?"

We all spoke at the same time. "Absolutely." "Yup." "Never happier."

"Awesome. I knew you'd figure it out."

Trent's lips curved upward. "Thanks for the push."

"Anytime."

And to think, I had thought that the three of us dating was going to be the biggest shock. So far, it seemed like Logan's sexuality was overshadowing that we were all together. Ten minutes, some bickering between themselves, and they all knew. They were happy for us.

CHAPTER 35

TRENT

WATCHING Aiden figure out who we'd gotten tickets to see was the best part of the night. When we'd gotten to the arena, Aiden had grinned widely. "I love Hometown!" He'd then gone on to explain how he knew the guys and loved working with them. He didn't know Derek and Colt like I did, but it was nice to know that they'd get along no matter what setting they found themselves in.

He'd gotten even more excited when we headed to our seats. We were in a box seat for the night, and as we'd taken spots, I pulled Aiden into my lap. The comfortable couches were more than ample to support the three of us. I sat down and pulled Aiden into my lap, and Logan slipped into the spot beside me and pulled Aiden's legs over his. Looking across the room, Travis had pulled Caleb onto his lap in a different chair. Apparently we were done hiding our proclivities now, and I wasn't going to overthink it regardless.

"This is the coolest thing ever," Aiden whispered as a server appeared with a tray full of finger foods and placed it on the bar behind us.

Being in the box seats, we were saved from the earsplitting

music and the screams of the crowded stadium, and were able to chat throughout the show. The thick windowpanes allowed Aiden to drift off to sleep before the concert began. His nap lasted precisely until Hometown took the stage, and even through the glass, the noise filtered in.

With Aiden awake and Logan becoming antsy, we stood at the window and watched the show. Aiden managed to sandwich himself between Logan and me as he sang along.

Colt made an appearance in the box halfway through the concert. He did a double take when he saw the three of us together, one of my hands having found Logan's pocket, the other draped around Aiden's shoulder and holding him close. Logan had been gripping Aiden's hand in front of us, but until Colt approached us, he hadn't been able to see that.

It was rare that Colt was shocked, but from the wide-eyed expression on his face, we'd done just that. His eyes darted between Logan, Aiden, and me quickly before he managed to school his features. His brother-in-law was in a triad relationship with two other men, a tidbit of information that had taken the media by storm when it came out, but Colt had been supportive of them from the moment he found out. The smile he gave us—once he'd gotten over his surprise—told me he'd extend the same acceptance to us.

"Good to see you. Now I know why you've been so elusive recently." He elbowed my shoulder and I couldn't help but grin over at him.

"I've got better things in my life now than BSing with you," I teased back with a wink.

Colt scratched at the five-o'clock shadow on his chin. "I'm calling Tammy to figure out your schedule next week. I think it's time I paid a visit to your office." His eyes narrowed at Aiden, then they popped open in surprise. "Hey, you shoot the cover photos for Hometown's albums, right?"

Aiden looked away from the stage and his eyes showed his surprise. "Oh, yeah, I do."

Colt reached out and shook his hand. "Good to see you again. Derek's looking forward to working with you again."

Aiden's smile was wide. "The band is great. I love working with them."

Colt excused himself at that point, swearing he needed to get back behind stage for when the show was over, but reminded me he would be at my office in the near future. As he disappeared through the door, Aiden looked up at me. "Small world, huh?"

If he only knew what I knew about Derek, he'd be even more shocked. Instead, I kissed his temple. "It sure is."

We stayed pressed together by the window until the end of the show. Even with the VIP parking tickets Colt had given us, it took us quite a while to get out of downtown and back home. Aiden's short nap had been enough to keep him awake through the concert and the drive home, but only just. Had we been in any more traffic, he'd have been out in the truck. As it was, he was drifting off to sleep as I parked and didn't make a move to get out of the truck.

Logan smiled as he looked in the back seat. "I'm going to go make him a bottle."

"We don't have bottles." The realization had me mentally kicking myself. I was already fucking this thing up.

Logan winked then squeezed my leg. "We didn't, but I ordered one earlier in the week. It's in the cupboard already."

Relief flooded me and I leaned over to give Logan a kiss. "I honestly don't know what I'd do without you."

"You'd figure it out; I have faith. Anyway, get A inside. I'll get his bottle ready for him."

With Logan hurrying toward the front door, I slipped out of the truck and opened the back door, reaching across Aiden and unbuckling his belt. "Come on, sleepyhead," I coaxed gently, then watched his eyes crack open. "We're home."

A sleepy smile spread across his face. "I like the sound of that."

I did too, but I wasn't going to distract us from getting him to bed. "Come on, baby boy, you need real sleep, in a real bed."

He nodded and took my hand, allowing me to guide him down to the ground. "My bag!" he said when we'd made it halfway to the door. "Hedge is in my bag."

"Where's your bag?" I asked, hoping like hell it hadn't been left at the shoot location.

"Behind my seat in my Jeep." He fished in his pocket and produced the key fob, clicking the button for the doors to unlock. Through an unspoken agreement, I went back for the bag and rejoined him, watching the lights blink as he relocked the doors. "Thank you, Daddy," he said from behind a yawn.

"Anytime, baby. Now, let's get you inside and into bed."

He nodded and headed toward the door and straight up the steps. "Trent's room!" I heard Logan call as I closed the door. "Your toothbrush is already in his bathroom."

Aiden mumbled something I couldn't quite understand. Logan and I both laughed as we watched him disappear up the steps. "Go, get him ready for bed while I finish up down here. He needs Daddy right now."

Logan was right. Aiden had barely managed to get tooth-paste on his toothbrush by the time I'd joined him in my bath-room. "Here, baby, let me help." He didn't even flinch, just handed the toothbrush over and opened his mouth, letting me brush his teeth for him. I had to fight a laugh as I thought of how much more difficult this would have been if it had been Logan. He'd probably end up biting the toothbrush instead of letting me work.

Once he'd spit and rinsed his mouth out, I helped him out of his clothes and directed him to the bedroom. Logan was walking into the bathroom as we walked out, and I watched as his eyes trailed up and down Aiden's naked body. His hungry eyes said enough and I bumped my shoulder into his. "Behave, pup. Our boy needs to sleep, not have sex."

Aiden groaned at the words and his cock began to fill. "Tell that to my libido."

"No sex," I insisted despite Logan's grunt of disagreement.

I pushed Aiden toward the bed and he flopped down on top of the covers. In his bag I found pajamas, Hedge, and a thick diaper. Given how tired he was, I decided a diaper would be appropriate for the night, so I grabbed it and took everything over to the bed. Aiden hadn't moved, and his erection hadn't softened any. If he stayed hard, it would be difficult to get the diaper on properly. At least the practice earlier made me more confident about getting Aiden diapered. I wasn't as worried that the diaper would slip off his hips as I had been with Logan, but that damn erection was not going to make it easy if it got any worse.

The problem was solved for me—and technically by me—when I accidentally brushed his balls with my cold hands. Erection gone, just like that. Of course, Aiden yelped and Logan called from the bathroom for me to be nice to him. If my hands warmed up any or if I wasn't fast enough, I knew Aiden wouldn't stay soft, so I worked as quickly as my hands would allow. Centering the diaper under him wasn't a problem, and neither was tucking his dick downward to smooth the diaper over his stomach. The damned tapes were tricky fuckers, but unlike the diapers we'd tried the night before, these had a Velcro strip across the front panel that the tabs stuck to rather than adhered to.

"So much better than tape," I mused as I repositioned the

bottom tape for the third time and it still stuck as though it was the first.

"Huh?" Aiden was looking at me with confusion and I realized I'd spoken the thought.

I chuckled. One day, Logan and I would tell him about the (mis)adventures of earlier, but for the time being I simply smiled. "Just muttering to myself."

Aiden didn't look convinced, but before he could respond, Logan came out of the bathroom in just a pair of green briefs with lemons and limes on them. "Wait, is that Velcro?"

"Yes!" Maybe my excitement was a little uncalled for.

Logan scratched at his light beard. "Huh, that's easier than the tape."

Aiden's eyes flicked between Logan's and mine, confusion written all over his face. "You guys aren't telling me something."

Logan smirked. "You're too young to know."

I snorted, Logan laughed, and Aiden groaned. "You two are evil."

Logan looked over at me. "You're still dressed. It's much too late to be dressed. Go get ready for bed. I can finish getting him ready."

I narrowed my eyes at them both. "Behave yourselves."

Something about the earnest expression on Logan's face told me I didn't have to worry. He was so excited to have us both in bed together, he wasn't going to try anything.

I brushed my teeth and peed in record time, all the while listening to Aiden and Logan laughing in the other room. Giggles and peals of laughter filled the room and I found myself smiling through my own exhaustion. Logan's deep laughter paired with Aiden's softer giggles while they chatted quietly was music to my ears.

When I stepped back into the bedroom, my hands were still

wet from rushing out of the bathroom without bothering to dry them. I stumbled over my feet as I rounded the corner into the bedroom. Logan and Aiden were both under the covers, Logan's hand resting protectively on Aiden's chest, and both men had heavily lidded eyes. I had no idea how any of us were still functioning at that hour, but I suspected it was mainly due to sheer willpower and stubbornness, at least if they were anything like me.

I swiped the bottle from where it had been left on my dresser and stopped at the foot of the bed to admire the two men. Logan's eyes cracked open farther and he lifted his hand from where it had been resting on Aiden's chest. "You. In. Now. Need you with us." Like I needed to be told twice? I hurried to my side and climbed in.

Aiden snuggled closer to me so that his head was resting on my shoulder. With my arm trapped, my fingers found Logan's head and I began to play with his hair while I brought the bottle to Aiden's lips. "Come on sleepy boy, open up."

Aiden's mouth parted and I slipped the bottle into his mouth. I heard more than saw as Aiden latched on, and a moment later, the rhythmic sound of milk being sucked out of the bottle lulled me into a light sleep. I woke when Aiden sucked air. As I pulled the nipple from his mouth he let out a light whimper. I found his binkie on his pillow and replaced the bottle's nipple with it, then clipped the end to his shirt. "Sleep well, baby boy." I ruffled Logan's hair again. "You too, pup. Sleep well."

He hummed sleepily. "Night, Trent."

Aiden reached up and pulled his binkie from his mouth. "Night, puppy. Night, Daddy."

CHAPTER 36

AIDEN

I WOKE up Monday morning feeling rested. Despite Logan having to work Sunday morning and Daddy working Sunday night, I'd been able to rest the entire day. My muscles were no longer sore, my head felt clear, and I was ready to face the world. What I hadn't expected was to wake to an empty bed at just after seven in the morning. Sure, Logan was an early riser, but I had thought Trent at least would be in bed by now.

The smell of breakfast and sounds of laughter filtered up the steps. My stomach rumbled at the smell and I wondered what my puppy and Daddy were doing in the kitchen so early. Grumbling because I didn't want to get out of bed, I knew I couldn't pretend to be sleeping much longer without risking missing breakfast.

I stumbled out of bed and headed toward the steps in just the T-shirt and diaper Logan had put me to bed in the night before. I'd thought it would feel awkward to have him diaper me before bed, but Daddy had made him promise to help me get ready before he left. It wasn't the same as Daddy changing me, but it hadn't been weird either.

Waking up in their bed without them felt weirder than

anything else. Hedge and I headed down the steps. I'd made it halfway when I heard their voices more clearly.

"Dammit!" I heard Logan's voice first. "How many times do I have to tell you that you can't walk out there looking like that? Running with a hard-on is not cool in the first place, but then you walk into the garage wearing those 'please fuck me' glasses and that thin pair of pajama pants. You're going to end up getting me killed!"

Daddy's laughter followed. "You shouldn't run so fast you could cause serious injury if you fell. I'm sure that's bad for you."

"I gotta get rid of these calories somehow. You make good breakfasts."

"All those muscles make me feel self-conscious."

I thought the two of them were perfect, though I'd been suspecting Trent didn't feel very attractive. He had a small layer of padding around his midsection that made him snuggly and handsome. Logan's muscles were gorgeous, but he never flaunted them needlessly. I was the one who felt rather plain around them.

I got to the bottom of the steps and saw Logan sitting on the counter drinking a bottle of water. "You're spoiling him." He was looking across the counter at something I couldn't see.

Trent's cheeks flushed. "I like getting things for him."

What had Daddy bought me?

Logan's voice was teasing. "He ticks every one of your boxes."

He'd been getting ready to drop a sausage link into the skillet and turned to face Logan. Trent waved the link in Logan's direction while he spoke. "You know damn well he does. Just like you do. If there were ever two men meant for me, it was you two."

"Why don't you let anyone else see that sweet, caring side you have?"

"I save it for my guys."

Logan's bottom lip stuck out in a pout as he thought of something. Trent chuckled. "Don't get that look in your eyes. You look like a sad puppy dog."

In return, Logan yipped at Trent, and he laughed so hard he dropped the sausage under the pan and into the flames of the gas stove. "Dammit, Logan." Despite trying to sound stern, he was laughing too hard to be mad. Though when the sausage started to smoke a moment later, I wondered if he'd actually get mad. "You're going to make me burn breakfast." He grabbed one of the metal grilling skewers to remove the flaming sausage from the stove.

I finally couldn't hide my laugh and walked into the kitchen. "What on earth is going on in here?"

Logan doubled over laughing so hard he fell off the counter. Trent began blowing the flaming sausage out but quickly decided it wouldn't work and headed to the sink to run it under water. "Blame your puppy."

"I will not take the blame for this one! You're the cook."

I looked between the two of them with skeptical eyes. It was easy to join in their banter. "Puppy, behave."

"Yeah, pup. Behave."

He huffed in mock offense then pushed the door of the fridge open and grabbed the sippy cup of milk and handed it to me.

I forgot about the conversation and the burnt sausage. "Thank you."

"Anytime."

I looked over at Daddy, who was still holding the charred, now soggy, sausage. "You are trouble, pup. Take our boy and get out of here so I can make breakfast without having to call the fire department."

Logan grabbed my hand and nearly danced out of the kitchen on his way to the living room. He swiped the Switch off its base and loaded the animal game we both played. We were lost to the game in seconds and played until a throat cleared behind us. "Breakfast is getting cold."

Logan's and Trent's plates looked every bit like a grown-up's plate should look: neat stacks of pancakes, a pat of butter on top, and a bottle of syrup on the side. My plate had my pancakes cut up into bite-sized pieces and syrup in a little divided section to the side of the plate. It was perfect to dip my pancakes into. I made it all of three bites before Trent jumped up and disappeared into the kitchen, only to return a moment later with one of my bibs. "You're going to be an absolute disaster." The bib saved most of my shirt but didn't save it all. By the time breakfast was over, it was going to need to be washed.

Logan laughed as he put his plate and cup into the sink. "Have fun with that, Daddy."

Trent growled low in his chest. "That's sweet when it comes from Aiden but not so much when you say it."

Logan cackled louder as he bent over to kiss me. "I gotta get ready for work and get out of here." He paused as he examined me. "Ugh, where do I kiss you that's not covered in syrup?" He settled on the top of my head then turned his attention to Trent. He didn't hesitate to press a deep kiss on Daddy's lips, a kiss that lasted far longer than the one he'd given me and was far hotter. My dick grew hard in my diaper as I watched them. By the time Logan pulled back, both their lips were swollen and red.

"Not fair." I pouted as he headed up the steps. "I only got a kiss on the hair and a hard-on from watching you two."

"That's because you're a sticky mess and your Daddy would have my head if I got syrup all over the house."

While Logan was upstairs, Daddy wiped down his spot at the table and took my plate and cup from me when I was finally done. It took three passes over my face and hands before he decided that I wasn't going to stick to anything. Then he went to the drawer and pulled something out.

Arriving back at the table, he laid out a new dry erase calendar, this one with three sections on each day. Instead of Trent and Logan like the current one said, the top spot was labeled Daddy, the next Curious, and finally Aiden. I almost cried when I saw the schedule. I knew it was a ridiculous thing to get emotional over, but it really did make me feel like part of them. The schedule was something that everyone who came over saw on their fridge.

"Okay, baby boy. We need to work on your schedule. I know you have the thing in Nashville this week and then the photo shoot with Hometown the following. I want to know everything else that you have planned. And I want to know how long each of your projects is going to be."

It took me a few tries to swallow down the lump in my throat. I was not going to get emotional over this. Once I started talking about my schedule, it got easier. I had four days solid of work the next week, and I'd need to work editing in at some point, but I had a few weeks to do that. Hometown's photo shoot wouldn't take long, but editing that one would be harder. We were at the mercy of the weather, and if it wasn't cooperating, editing could be a lot more difficult.

An hour later, well after Logan had left for the day, Daddy capped the marker. "This is your schedule. If something changes, you are expected to call me or Logan to let us know. I expect you to talk with me before you add anything to your schedule as well."

I nodded.

"You are a responsible man. I know that you've been making your own schedule for years, and I know that you've built a name for yourself. However, you've admitted that you have a hard time saying no. It's my hope that if you know you need to stop and call me before you agree to a job, it will give you the space to think about if you actually want the job. If you had taken a minute to think about it more, would you have taken the job last week?"

I almost nodded my head to say I would have, but stopped myself and thought about it. If I'd taken a minute, would I have taken the job? Probably not. I probably would have remembered how much I hated the guy and what a nightmare he'd been to work with. Slowly, I shook my head. "No, probably not."

Daddy looked pleased with my answer. "Thank you for answering honestly. I will have your schedule on my phone as well. Logan and I will share our schedules with you too. It isn't a one-way street. But for you, you're expected to run plans by me. Do you understand?"

I nodded, a giant sigh rushing from my body. It felt good to know I wasn't going to have to be responsible for every schedule decision. I had someone to talk it through with. I knew Daddy would help me. He'd make sure I wanted the job. He'd make sure I had time. He'd take care of it. It felt good to give up that responsibility.

"Good, now let's go get you a bath. I know I wiped your fingers and face down, but you have syrup in your hair. How did you get syrup in your hair?"

I blinked up at him with my most innocent expression. How was I supposed to know how syrup got in my hair?

Stripping me off left him making funny faces. Emotions ranging from repulsion to concern kept crossing his face and making me laugh. He was funny. One day, it would be fun to torment him and dance around while he filled the tub and got ready, but today, I'd behave myself. He helped me out of my pajama shirt and reached for my diaper. He seemed a bit surprised at how wet it had gotten. He looked up at me with amusement on his face.

I shrugged. "I've been up awhile." *And Logan had given me milk and Daddy gave me juice.* It was inevitable.

"Please tell me you need to be changed before you get this wet."

I wasn't that wet. It wasn't like I was going to leak or anything. But I nodded to placate him and was rewarded with a beautiful smile. "Alright, let's get you out of that diaper. Don't be a wiggle worm while I get the bath ready."

I stood as still as I could while the water filled and bubbles magically appeared in the water. So maybe I squirmed a bit, but bubbles! Daddy really needed to hurry up if I was going to be able to be good.

A deep chuckle made my eyes flick upward. "You're going to fall if you keep wiggling like that."

"Then you should probably get me undressed so I can get in the tub." *Duh.* I stopped short of saying that to him, though. I figured it probably wasn't the best idea to get snarky before my bath. Then again, he didn't like sticky so I'd probably still get a bath before any punishment. What kind of punishment would I get?

"What are you thinking about, baby boy?" Daddy's voice was definitely amused, and I focused my eyes on him. He wasn't looking at my face—he was looking at my dick, which had plumped up while my thoughts had wandered to being spanked.

My first reaction was to tell him I hadn't been thinking of anything. Denying it would have been a lot easier than admitting I'd gotten horny thinking about being bent over his lap. But I couldn't lie to my Daddy. Dammit, I was going to have to admit to the crazy in my head, like it or not. "I-I was thinking about what would happen if I got a little bratty."

His lip twitched like he was trying to suppress a laugh. "Exactly what were you thinking about?"

I groaned because I knew there was no getting out of it at that point. "Um, spankings?"

Daddy's answering groan was not out of embarrassment. Nope, his was pure lust-filled desire. The gold in his eyes darkened and his gaze turned heated. "Oh, someone has a naughty streak. We will definitely have to play around with that at some other time. For now, though, the bath is ready and I'm not about to let it get cold." His words said one thing, but the way he had to adjust himself, even within the loose confines of his pajama pants, said he liked the idea just as much if not more than I did.

He helped me into the tub, then upended a bucket I hadn't noticed before. A smattering of toys rained down into the tub and the sexual tension that had been simmering between us was forgotten for the time being. Toys dispersed in the water: a boat, sea animals, some blocks, and...

"Oh wait, not that." He scooped the tube of blue body paint out of the tub. "Definitely not that." He shuddered and it sent me into a fit of giggles. "I'm glad you and Logan enjoyed that, but I had a vision of owning the first ever Smurf Blue tub when I saw it. It's going to be a long time before either of you convince me that is a good idea."

Mean. Just plain mean. But the other toys were calling my name and seemed like more fun anyway. I lost myself in play. The few times I looked over, Trent was sitting with his back against the bathroom vanity either watching me or messing around on his phone. He seemed content to let me play but also not willing to let me out of his sight. I enjoyed it. It felt good to have him so close to me... even if I couldn't have the blue paint.

A throat clearing beside me had me looking over from where the submarine was exploring the cave the giant octopus lived in. Daddy had moved from the floor by the vanity to the side of the tub, with a washcloth and a bottle of bodywash in his hand. "Unfortunately, marinating in the warm water is not going to get the syrup off you. Especially not out of your hair." Daddy shook his head like he couldn't believe it even now. "I still don't know how you got it in your hair." He sighed like washing sticky hair could possibly be worse than things he'd seen as a sheriff. It just made me giggle harder, though the water being poured unceremoniously over my head made me stop quickly and hold my breath.

When I finally opened my eyes again, Daddy's had crinkled with silent laughter while he poured a generous amount of shampoo into his hand. "You're going to be a handful. I don't know what I did, but I'm glad I did it." It took a moment for the words to process, but when they finally did, I couldn't help but smile.

I didn't know if I should have been surprised or not that he washed me like he'd done it a million times before. Trent exuded a confidence, and I didn't fully understand where it came from, but no matter what I threw at him, he was ready. It was sexy, but of course that thought made it slightly uncomfortable to lift up when Trent was ready to clean the parts of me under the water.

I gave him credit for not reacting to my rock-hard erection, but the needy moan that slipped out of me when he ran the cloth around my length told him I was definitely interested in more. I wasn't sure what he'd do with the knowledge until he used the cloth to clean my crease and his finger brushed against my hole. My thighs shook with the effort to not sink back onto his finger and chase the pleasure. I wanted him inside me any way I could have him. I needed him.

"Gentle," Daddy murmured into my ear. The breath ghosting against my skin sent shivers down my body and my dick twitched. "I know what you want, baby boy. Daddy does, but if I'm going to make you feel good, you need to be good." *Mean Daddy.*

His lips brushed the side of my head. "Mmm, you smell so good. So fresh and clean. And not syrupy." As he spoke, the washcloth explored more of my ass and the underside of my balls. It was embarrassing how quickly I was becoming desperate to have his hand around my cock. The more noise I made, the more pointedly he ignored my dick.

Even when he brought a soapy finger up to trace along my balls, he avoided touching my cock. I growled in frustration, though Trent just chuckled at me. Even to me, my growl sounded needy, not menacing like Trent's or even playful like Logan's. Trent clearly found it cute, but my dick did not. "Please," I begged when I didn't think I could take more.

"Please what? What do you need?"

"M-more. More."

Fingers stopped their exploration and I almost collapsed in the tub. "I think I need to get you out of the tub before I risk you getting hurt."

"No!" I yelped the word so desperately that Trent paused.

Then his eyebrow cocked high on his head and he gave me a questioning stare that I was certain would make any criminal spill everything. "No? Are you really going to argue with Daddy that he doesn't know best?"

"N-no? I-I," I stammered nervously before swallowing. "I j-just want you to touch me more." I said the last part of the sentence so fast I didn't know if he'd be able to understand me, but I needed him.

That time a wicked smile crossed his face. "Oh, don't you worry, baby boy. I will be touching you plenty more, but I need you out of the tub before I risk you drowning. I don't have any breath play fetishes."

I didn't know if the right reaction was to melt into a puddle of happy goo because he wasn't done playing with me or pout because I was expected to move before I got more touches. One look into his eyes told me I needed to get out of the tub if I wanted anything more exciting than getting dressed. I heaved a giant sigh as I stood up. Trent reached his hand out and helped me dry off. He took his time, rarely saying anything more than to give me directions to either lift my arms or turn around. Finally, he hung the towel from the hook on the back of the door and looked me over.

"You're clean and dry, but I'm not sure the giant sighs and growls you've been giving me warrant a reward."

He tapped his chin while he thought and suddenly every sense in my body heightened. What I knew was that I needed to behave if I wanted a reward. "I'm sorry, Daddy. I'm just so horny and your touches on my... *your* lil' guy feel so good, I don't want you to stop."

And we were right back to Trent trying not to laugh. "My lil' guy, huh?" He looked back down at my cock that was jutting out in front of me, precum beading on the tip. "He's not so little." He licked his lips. "And he's definitely not as innocent as he's trying to be."

I chewed my lip and batted my eye. *Please, Daddy, please let me cum.* "He really needs your touches."

Daddy took a step closer to me so that we were nearly nose to nose and kissed my lips. "You beg very prettily, baby boy."

God, I hoped so. Daddy stepped back and air rushed between us, causing goosebumps to rise on my skin. Then his hand reached toward me, but before I could reach out and grab it, he wrapped it around my dick. "If *my* lil' guy wants to cum, he best follow me."

The pressure was just this side of painful and it did crazy things to my brain. I wanted to scream for him to stop and I wanted to beg for him to tug harder. In the absence of the appropriate reaction, I gasped and hurried to follow him. We'd need to revisit this moment sometime in the future when I had a clearer head.

We made it to his bed to find a brightly colored changing

pad laid out. The warring sensations of naughty and sweet, big and little, made the moment even more perfect. "Lie down, baby boy. I don't want my sheets to get all messy if you make a mess."

If I made a mess? Jesus, if he kept looking at me like that or guiding me by my dick, it was simply a matter of when. Sooner rather than later if he continued the way we were going.

I scrambled to get up on the bed, not wanting to lose my opportunity to cum. I'm sure it wasn't as graceful a maneuver as I would have preferred, but it got the job done. In seconds I was flat on my back, my dick in the air, and saying a prayer to any deity listening that I might get to cum soon.

Trent watched me, calculating his next move carefully. "Hands above your head. Grip the headboard."

I gasped and reached up to grip it.

Trent's hand hovered near my dick. "My cheeky boy. If you want Daddy to play with your lil' guy, those hands had best not leave the headboard."

Dead. I was dead. Where "lil' guy" had come from, I might never know. But the more Trent used it, the naughtier it became. With it, the need to cum increased and I was going to hold on to that headboard like my life depended on it. Of course, the first brush of his finger up the length of my dick had me nearly forgetting to hold on tight. I wanted to grab at the blankets. I wanted to grab my dick and jerk it hard and fast. Above all else, I wanted to make Daddy happy. I knew I could only do that by not letting go of the damned headboard, so I lay there, my hips bucking off the mattress while he laved my dick in the most maddeningly gentle strokes.

It didn't seem to matter how badly I wanted him to move things along, how much I needed him to wrap his hand around my cock, he was on his own time line. The bath he'd just given me was nearly rendered useless because sweat had broken out all over my body.

"Daddy, you're being mean!" I finally called into the quiet house. "I need to cum!"

I heard Trent's tongue click against his teeth but couldn't bring myself to open my eyes. There was every chance that I'd look at him and cum on the spot, and I hadn't been given permission yet. "Who does this lil' guy belong to?"

The possession in his voice almost did me in. He had to let up on the touches before words formed in my head. But at that, they were screams and staccato sentences. "You! You, Daddy! Belongs... ungh... You! Jesus, Daddy, need to cum!"

A large hand wrapped around my cock and I felt my entire body relax for the briefest of moments. Finally, I was getting the attention I desperately needed to cum. Then a terrifying thought occurred to me. What if he wouldn't let me cum yet? I didn't know how much longer I could hold off and I needed to be a good boy for my Daddy. My muscles started to quake and my stomach trembled. Then Trent growled the word I'd been dying to hear since he started washing me in the tub. "Cum."

And I came. All over his fist and my chest. Wave after wave of the most intense orgasm I could ever remember shook my body until I had nothing left to give. When the spasms stopped, Trent's hand and my chest were coated in cum and I was panting like I'd just run a marathon. When I finally collapsed, nearly boneless, onto the bed, a large thumb slid over my overly sensitive slit and I screamed out.

"Let go of the headboard, baby boy. Let me get you cleaned up."

I'd lost myself so far to the orgasm that I'd forgotten my hands gripping onto the headboard. My arms ached and my eyes felt heavy.

"You were perfect." A kiss was placed to my stomach, another on my hip, and a third next to my dick. "I'm so proud of you. But I need to get you cleaned up so you can take a nap."

"Good. Yes. Nap. Happy," I mumbled through a yawn.

Trent's laughter was rich. "Yes, you were a good boy. I'm very glad you're happy. You can nap as soon as I have new undies on you."

Mmm. Undies. Yes. I needed those—I just wasn't quite sure why.

CHAPTER 37

LOGAN

[ME] PLEASE TELL me you're going to be home soon.

Me, whiney? Never. No, I was just impatient.

Aiden had been working all week, still coming home to our house every night but then putting in extra hours editing pictures. It was a cold and rainy day, even by October standards. I was heading home from work, Trent had been home all day, and Aiden and I were supposed to be going out to dinner with Larson and Caleb that night. I had no idea what to expect with that. Thankfully, it wasn't for another four hours, but I missed Aiden.

[Aiden] The rest of today was canceled. The light sucks with all this rain. Nothing looked right. We're going to try again next week.

Before I could ask if he'd cleared it with Trent first, another text came through.

[Aiden] I already texted Daddy and we talked about it. It won't interfere with my Hometown shoot, and I already told the magazine that I'll need more editing time.

I didn't know if I should feel as proud of Aiden as I did, but I was. If I was proud of him for discussing his schedule with Trent and not overextending himself or overpromising, I was sure Trent was over the moon.

[Me] *Then I'll see you soon.*

Aiden's Jeep was already in the driveway when I pulled in. I let myself in to an almost silent house. No one even acknowledged my appearance as I hung my coat up, put my gun away, or headed up the steps. I figured out why that was when I got to our room and Trent was diapering Aiden.

The sight had become so common it didn't even warrant a reaction from me. I walked in, kissed Trent hello, shucked off my clothes, and climbed onto the bed to kiss Aiden. I could see he had already found little space and he giggled as my light beard grazed his cheek.

"Puppy!" he giggled, holding his hands out to me for a hug.

I humored him while also annoying Trent, though I didn't push too hard. I could see in his heavy eyes just how exhausted Aiden was. It had been four days filled with early mornings and late nights, and he desperately needed this time.

At the head of the bed, I watched both of my men carefully. The pinched lines Trent's eyes had held the last few days had all but completely vanished. We'd had puppy time the night before, and he'd fucked me hard on Tuesday afternoon before he headed to work. Both had been a good distraction for his frustration that Aiden was working so much, but neither had relaxed him as much as seeing his boy stretched out on the bed in front of him while he got him ready for a nap.

"Pup, can you go down and get Aiden a bottle while I get him dressed?"

That idiotic smile was back on my face. Despite my mind telling me that we'd make it work, part of me had worried that Trent would find what he needed with Aiden and wouldn't have a need for me anymore. Each time he asked me to do something, each time we crawled into bed together and Trent pulled me close, I felt that doubt ease more. Just being asked to make a bottle for Aiden made me excited and I hurried to do as he asked, making it back to the room before Aiden was fully dressed.

"Thank you, pup."

Aiden wiggled as Trent snapped his onesie shut. "Go snuggle your puppy. I'll be there in just a second."

Aiden didn't have to be told twice and nearly launched himself at me, coming to rest with his cheek pressed firmly against my chest. "Missed you, puppy," he managed to get out between yawns.

I kissed the top of his head. "Missed you too, A."

He hummed his approval as I rubbed his back while we waited for Trent to strip his pants off and join us in bed. As soon as Trent was there, Aiden slipped off my lap and curled so his torso was in Trent's arms and his legs were wrapped around mine. I handed Trent the bottle and grabbed my phone to catch up on the news, rubbing Aiden's feet and legs while he drifted off drinking his bottle.

An hour later, I was getting antsy but Aiden was still asleep, so I occupied myself talking to Trent. "Glad we're all home."

Trent agreed. "I like that this is home. It feels more complete when he's with us. You know he called me today to talk his schedule out?"

"He told me. I was really proud of him."

"Me too. He was so damn proud of himself too. He practically flew into my arms when he got here, thanking me for helping him make that decision."

I reached my hand over and squeezed Trent's. "I'm so glad you have him."

Unable to get closer to me, Trent squeezed my hand. "I'm glad I have you *both*."

My cheeks flushed at the sweet admission. "I know this all

seems new and crazy fast, but I can't imagine him not here. I started thinking about it at work today, and I realized that everything in our lives feels different with him in it. Not in a bad way at all. Just, kind of like we've waited for him to come along for so long and now we have him and I never want to let him go."

Trent's chuckle was more just a movement in his chest than sound. We were both barely whispering so we didn't disturb the boy lying with us. "I'm so happy you found him. Not just because he's now here with us, but because I see how much you adore him. You sleep better when he's with us. You are able to sit down more. He's so grounding for you. I wished for the last twenty years to give you what you have with him. I see how much you love him."

I looked down at Aiden. His hair had been messed up and had fallen over his eyes and was sticking up at odd angles. "Yeah, I think I do love him. I know it's way too soon, but I think I fell in love with him a while ago. I can't even put my finger on when."

Trent smiled. "I fell in love with him the day I saw you two in the playroom the first time. I knew that anyone who could give you that peace and calmness, that ability to sit still, was absolutely worth loving. I knew you loved him then too."

"I love you two, too. But I'd really like to be able to sleep."

Trent and I both gaped at Aiden, who hadn't cracked an eye open yet, hadn't moved a muscle, but had just told us he loved us back.

"Is he awake?" Trent whispered to me. I was trying to figure out the same thing. He'd been so still, I thought there was a chance he was talking in his sleep.

"Begrudgingly. I don't think I can sleep anymore. I was already debating opening my eyes when you two started talking about your feelings."

I reached over and pinched Aiden's side, causing him to

squeal and try to wiggle away. "You heard that but you didn't stop us?"

Aiden cracked his eyes open and stared between Trent and me. "Are you kidding me? The men I love start talking about how they fell in love with me, and you think I'm going to interrupt that? Come on, you can only say your first "I love you" once, and that was perfect."

We lay in bed another hour, chatting about our day, our plans for the evening, and even delved into our hopes for the future of our relationship. It wasn't until we finally admitted that Aiden and I had to start getting ready to go to dinner that I realized we hadn't even had an orgasm. I decided right then and there that love was a crazy thing. Crazy enough that I could stay in bed with two men for hours and not have sex.

Trent hovered around both of us as we got ready to go. As I got dressed, he helped Aiden into a pair of thick blue underwear with teddy bears on them and a clean pair of jeans. Then he followed us down the steps, reminding us to behave, to text him when we got there and when we left, and then proceeded to help not only Aiden on with his coat but me as well. It was cute for the night, and I knew the actions were helping him through all the emotions and feelings we'd talked through that afternoon; however, if it continued it was going to drive me nuts.

The trip to the bar only took fifteen minutes, and as we stepped out of the truck, it struck me that I had no idea what Dexter, Caleb, or Larson normally talked about when they went out. I didn't really know any of them all that well, which didn't say much for me since I'd known Larson for nearly a decade.

Aiden didn't seem to have the same reservations I did. He spotted the three sitting at a table toward the back and practically bounded over. I sank into the spot beside Larson while Aiden got lost in conversation with Caleb and Dexter.

"Holy shit, they are all the same age," I muttered to Larson as

I watched the three interacting and laughing about the latest dance challenge on social media.

Larson let out a belly laugh like I'd never heard from him before. "I always feel so old when I come to dinner with them. I'm kinda glad you're here this time. At least someone else can relate to the pop my knee makes when I stand up." I'd have liked to say I couldn't relate to that, but while it wasn't my knee, my left shoulder gave me hell.

I was nursing a water and Larson had a soda when Dexter turned the conversation back to Larson and me. We'd clearly zoned out from whatever the three were talking about because Dexter's green eyes were huge and he was grinning wickedly. "Puppy? God, that fits you so well!"

Larson blinked over at me. "I know Trent loves you guys, but I never thought I'd see the day you talked him into a puppy."

Well, if that wasn't a loaded statement. Not only had Larson admitted that he knew Trent's feelings toward us, but Dexter knew I was into puppy play now. Yup, I'd stepped onto the crazy train. "No, we didn't get a puppy. I'm the pup."

Larson's eyes narrowed in confusion for a second before they widened again in surprise. "Oh! Ohhhh. You're into puppy play?"

I lifted a shoulder. "Yeah, puppy play. It's... well, it's relaxing, I guess. Even when I'm playing hard, I get to relax."

"We got a puppy, finally!" Caleb announced proudly, looking directly at me. "I've always wanted to know a pup!"

Dexter patted his arm. "Cal, buddy, you may not want to announce that to the world."

"Oh, right. Sorry, Logan, I got excited."

Seeing Caleb smiling and happy was something I would never try to stifle, especially after the start to our relationship, so I shrugged a shoulder. "It's okay. I don't mind. Aiden introduces me to everyone at the club as his puppy."

Larson's eyes went wide. "Do you go to the fetish club too?"
Aiden and I both nodded.

"That's awesome." Larson's voice said one thing, but his eyes said something different. Was that sadness?

Dexter got lost in conversation with Aiden and Caleb. His red hair matched his arms flailing about wildly from every direction. I shook my head and focused back on the quiet giant beside me. "Tell me how you really feel."

Larson chuckled dryly. "No, it really is awesome. I..." He hesitated as he formed words in his head. "I'm really glad you have something like that. Knowing what I want and knowing it's not going to happen are difficult things to reconcile in my head."

Huh. That wasn't what I'd expected from him. "If you ever want to go with us, you're welcome to."

The flush in Larson's cheeks flared to a bright red and he ducked his head. "I, no. No, I couldn't. That would be hard."

I studied him closely, possibly for the first time in our friendship. Whatever Larson wanted, he had buried it deep. "I understand. I'm not submissive, but I'm into puppy play. Most people equate puppies with subs. It's really quite obvious when the handlers want a submissive pup who will listen, and I'm not like that."

Larson didn't look convinced by my words. "I see what you're getting at, but when you look like me, it's hard to find what I'm looking for. The Doms want someone with a body like Dexter, Caleb, or Aiden."

I looked between them. Dexter looked like a twink: trim, young, and I didn't know if he could grow more than stubble on his face if his life depended on it. Aiden had a beard, had more weight to him but was fit, and was still smaller than me. Caleb looked a lot like Aiden with a few extra pounds on him. I looked back to Larson. He was at least six foot four, maybe closer to six-six. He was the same age as me, with thick hair that covered his body, though he'd always maintained a smooth face. At first glance, he was a person to either run toward for protection or away from in fear.

I almost said something about it not being hard to find someone looking for a leather bear at a BDSM club, but a warning growl in my head that sounded a lot like Trent saying *Pup...* kept me from opening my mouth. He'd said the Doms were looking for people who didn't look like him. *Larson was a submissive.* I was at a loss. "Not all subs look like them." It was a weak response, but I couldn't come up with anything else. "And not all Doms want a twink or a twunk." That sounded a bit better.

Larson scoffed. "Thanks, Logan. I appreciate you wanting to help. It's okay. I'm not really meant for the lifestyle."

My heart hurt for Larson, but before I could come up with something reassuring to say, Dexter's voice caught my attention. "He's so damn sexy. He's got these steel blue eyes that are absolutely mesmerizing! He growled at me the other day. He was coming home and that perfect fucking pompadour hairstyle was all out of place, and his beard was a little longer than normal— like he hadn't shaved in a few days—it looked like he'd had the night from hell. But he's walking up the steps while I'm sipping my morning coffee on the porch swing, and I went to say hi to him and he growled. The sound filled the entire porch. I swear, I almost came in my pants!"

Caleb bounced his head off the table. "I do not need to know this."

"Like I needed to know your Daddy put you in dinosaur training pants before you left the house today?"

Caleb's eyes went wide and his nostrils flared like he was going to yell at him, but Aiden laughed. "Hey, my Daddy put me in teddy bear ones!"

Larson choked on the soda he'd been drinking. "God, is nothing sacred between you all?"

Dexter's confused look with his head cocked to the side reminded me of some of the puppies I'd seen at the club. "Should we hide things?"

"No. I think it's great that you all love each other that much, but really we don't need the entire restaurant to know what you're wearing under your pants."

My phone pinged and I pulled it out of my pocket.

[Trent] The charity football game is set for the third weekend in November.

With everything going on in my life, I'd forgotten all about the first responders' football game we had every year between Cheatham and Williamson counties. All the money earned at the game was split down the middle by the counties and usually paid off lunch balances, supported some after-school programs, and tried to offset the cost of back-to-school supplies for families in need. While the game did a lot of good, we all looked forward to a time when we could tease each other mercilessly and brag about winning the old Golden Donkey trophy. The hideous thing had been found at a thrift store decades earlier and had been the prized possession of our sheriff's departments ever since.

"Oh! First responders' game is the third week in November. Trent just told me."

Everyone but Larson looked at me like I'd grown a second head. Then I remembered that Larson was the only one who had ever been to one of the games. "Cheatham County versus Williamson County. It's a football game. This year it will be at Kingston Springs High School. Sheriffs, EMS, and firefighters from each county play against each other to raise money for the local schools. It's a lot of fun."

"Oh!" Dexter swooned. "Count me in! Sexy men running around and grabbing each other's butts!"

"Tag football, you perv," I teased him.

Dexter deflated. "Ugh, you take all the fun out of things. Oh well, I'll still go."

"I'll request the afternoon off tomorrow." Larson chimed in, making a note on his phone. "I'm still bitter that Davidson County isn't included."

I tapped my chin. "Hmm, maybe you all can be the cheer-leaders? I'm sure you'd look adorable in a short skirt."

Larson shook his head. "Never mind, sidelines are good for me!"

Talking about the game reminded me about something else. "Oh, while we're talking about it, Trent's birthday is in two weeks."

Aiden's eyes popped open. "Really?"

"Yup. We need to plan something."

Larson rolled his eyes at me. "Logan, we go to Steve's every year for everyone's birthday."

I poked Larson's arm with my elbow. "I wasn't talking about *you*. I meant me and Aiden."

Aiden grinned. "Confetti cake!"

Caleb nodded like Aiden had the best suggestion ever. "With lots of icing!"

"Chocolate frosting," Aiden agreed.

Caleb wasn't done adding things to the list. "With sprinkles!"

Now Aiden was into it too. "A doghouse!"

Wait, did they think a doghouse represented me? I did not belong in a doghouse. "Hey, I don't think I like that idea."

"And a doggy!" Caleb added excitedly.

Larson was trying to control his laughter but tears started to stream down his face.

"Think I could find a Daddy figurine?"

Caleb thought hard for a second. "A binkie! If there's a puppy and a Daddy, you need to be on there too."

Aiden giggled while he thought of the cake. "And candles!"

This was going to need to be a big cake, and I was a terrible baker.

Then Aiden's big brown eyes turned on me. "Please, puppy?"

Terrible baker aside, I couldn't say no to that face and found myself nodding. "Find the supplies." I'd do anything for the guy across the table from me.

Larson turned the elbow on me that time. "Never thought I'd see Logan Caldwell smitten."

CHAPTER 38

AIDEN

I ROLLED OVER. One side of the bed was cold; the other was also cold but pillows were stacked against my back. I blinked and tried to bring the room into focus without my glasses on. Then I remembered that Trent had to work at some ungodly hour, but that didn't explain why Logan's side of the bed was completely empty at... *did that clock say six oh five?* It was Logan's day off. He should have wanted to be with me, not out of the bed at some ungodly hour.

Once I forced myself out of bed, I tucked Hedge under Logan's blanket, then tried to remember the last time I'd spent the night at my own house. It had to have been the previous week when Logan and Trent both worked night shift and I'd had a client in Nashville early the next morning. It had just made sense for me to go to my place that night. I'd hated every moment of it.

My new routine was starting to become habitual. The first thing I did was check my phone and I was unsurprised to see a text waiting for me marked shortly after four in the morning.

[Daddy] Good morning, baby boy. Don't forget to brush your teeth this morning. I left something on the counter for you, please put

it on. Make sure to eat breakfast. I'm going to be home around 3:30 this afternoon. Text me when you wake up. Love you.

My grin was so wide it hurt. I was never going to get tired of hearing him say he loved me. Not only did he tell me multiple times a day, he also showed it. Since we'd talked about him taking a more active role with my schedule, he'd taken to it like a fish to water. Daddy knew my schedule better than I knew it and always made sure I didn't forget anything. Reminders were set on my phone, and he texted me frequently. And my stress level was lower than it had been in years.

[Me] Love you too. Just woke up. Logan's already up. :'(

Then I remembered what day it was.

[Me] Happy Birthday, Daddy!!! Promise you'll be home in time to celebrate your birthday?

I headed to the bathroom to relieve my bladder and brush my teeth. I was halfway through peeing when my eyes fell onto the thing he'd left on the counter.

"A cock cage?" I questioned the empty room. I didn't know how I felt about it, but my cock began to go hard even as I was peeing. "Bastard," I mumbled to my traitorous dick. He definitely liked the idea. My phone vibrated on the counter and I knew it was Daddy.

[Daddy] Did you find it?

I shook my dick of the last few drops of pee and washed my hands like a good boy before picking up my phone. My fingers flew across the screen faster than I thought possible.

[Me] Just saw it.

[Daddy] Can you get it on yourself? Or do I need to ask Logan to help you? He's working out in the garage and would be more than happy to help.

[Me] I can do it myself, Daddy. But really? A cock cage?

[Daddy] I have birthday plans for you. I want my present wrapped tightly.

Fuck. My. Life. My cock was hard. Very, very hard. Getting a cage on it right now was not going to happen.

[Me] *Keep saying shit like that and I'll never get it on. I'm hard as a rock.*

[Daddy] *Watch your language, baby boy.*

Fuck.

[Me] *Sorry, Daddy. I'm going to go calm down and get it on for you. Unless I can cum first?*

[Daddy] *Nice try, baby boy. No cumming. Send me a picture when it's on.*

"Fuuuuck." I was going to tell myself that it was okay to curse when he couldn't hear me.

[Me] *Yes, Daddy.*

I slid the ring around the base of my dick and worked my balls into it before I even tried to get soft. I knew I'd have a limited time to work on getting the cage on me before I got hard again. I'd watched enough porn to know the mechanics of getting the thing on, but I'd never had one on me, so I needed to buy myself all the time I could.

With the ring securely on me, I took the cage to the bed and tried to get my dick to go down. Eight minutes later, it finally began to soften. Three minutes after that, I was finally soft enough that I thought I'd have a shot at getting it on. I took a deep breath, grabbed the cage, and started working my dick into it. As soon as I touched myself, I felt my penis start to thicken. I'd severely miscalculated how long it would take to get hard. I had seconds to get this thing on and prayed I'd manage to succeed before I got fully hard again.

My hands shook slightly, making the task that much harder, but I managed to get the lock lined up, and with just a little pushing, the two halves of the device latched together. There was no key. I hadn't thought about how nervous a locked cage would have made me until I didn't have to lock it.

Breathing a sigh of relief at having the task done, I took a moment to decide how I felt about my cock being locked away. The plastic was heavier than I'd have expected but not uncomfortable. Trent had picked a cage that fit me well. Aside from the additional weight and the fact that my half chub could not get any fuller, it wasn't bad. We'd see how it felt once Logan came in from the garage.

[Daddy] Are you having troubles?

[Me] No. I just got it on. It took a while for your lil' guy to go down. He wanted to play. I was just lying here deciding how I felt about it.

[Daddy] Send me a picture of it. Then you can tell me all about how my lil' guy feels being wrapped up and waiting for Daddy to get home.

It didn't take until I saw Logan naked. I was officially horny and pissed off that I couldn't get hard. Frustrating was an understatement. I snapped a picture of my dick straining against the clear plastic and sent it.

[Me] At first, I didn't mind it. It's weighty but not heavy, and my cock was half-full but it wasn't annoying. Then I started talking to you and I'm really horny and can still only get half hard but I've filled up all the available space and it's so snug.

[Daddy] I'm proud of you for getting it on. My lil' guy looks so sexy in there, trapped and waiting for me. I need to get some work done, baby boy. I'll be looking forward to seeing you when I get home.

I was going to be looking forward to him getting home too. I doubted it would be for the same reasons, though. I was stuck until Daddy got home. Well, unless I used my safeword, but aside from knowing it was a possibility, I had no desire to use it. Instead, I got dressed in a pair of my training pants that had magically made their way into a drawer that just so happened to be totally empty in Daddy's dresser, and then finished getting ready for the day.

I'd barely made it into the kitchen when Logan came in, dripping with sweat and toweling his hair off. "Oh good, you've made it down here. Did you see what Trent left on the bathroom counter for you?"

I groaned because the cage was just as infuriating as I'd expected it to be when I saw Logan standing there. "I did. And you dripping sweat and not wearing a shirt is not helping me out at all."

Logan's grin was wicked as he started flexing his pecs. His nipple rings caught the light and I groaned. "Fucker."

"I'm gonna tell your Daddy that you called me a bad word."

I put my head into the pantry to hide my eye roll and smirk from Logan. I'd turned around with a box of crispy rice cereal to find Logan heading toward the steps. "I'm going to go get a shower, have a nice jack-off session, and then we can go to the store."

My brain had gotten caught on the jack-off session part of his list, so it took a minute for me to catch up to the rest. "Store?" I called to Logan's retreating back. "Why store?"

"It's Trent's birthday."

Oh! Cake! Logan and I had found a recipe online and were going to make Daddy a cake. I couldn't wait. Just thinking about surprising him made me excited. "Hurry up, puppy! You better make that orgasm fast!"

Logan's laugh drifted down the steps but the shower started a few minutes later.

[Me] Daddy, puppy is being mean. He's bragging that he can cum in the shower.

I set my phone down with a smile. If he was going to drive me nuts all day, I was going to drive him nuts too. I pulled one of my bowls down from the cabinet. It was smaller than the big breakfast bowls Logan used for cereal, but it was enough for me. Besides, mine had cute pictures.

My life had changed so much, all because Logan decided to try shibari. I had a Daddy *and* a puppy. I was happier than I'd been my entire adult life. Trent and Logan didn't have to be here with me, just seeing one of their names pop up on my phone screen sent a swirl of excited butterflies through my stomach. But every time I saw either, I still did an internal squeal.

I'd just put my bowl in the sink when Logan came down the steps. I hurried over to him and wrapped my arms around his waist, breathing in his fresh scent and soaking up the way he wrapped me tightly in his arms.

"Hey, you okay, A?"

I nodded my head against his shoulder. "I'm good. Glad to see you and excited to go get Daddy's cake stuff."

"Then let's go!"

CHAPTER 39

LOGAN

TRENT HAD BEEN BLOWING up my phone all morning. First to see if Aiden was awake. Then to worry if he'd overstepped by giving him the cock cage. It wasn't my dick, but I'd known Aiden would love giving Trent that control. Even if I hadn't been one hundred percent sure of it, Aiden's reaction when I'd seen him in the kitchen after my workout would have been answer enough. He loved it. I knew he did.

So I'd made sure to torment him a little more than needed. I'd also made sure to take longer than necessary upstairs so that he really did think I was jerking off. Truth be told, I was too tired to care about my dick. I'd worked out hard that morning and I knew that we had plans for the night. Trent had told me all about them and they sounded a lot more fun than a solo session in the shower.

But the clingy Aiden I came downstairs to was unexpected. And I kinda liked it. Of course, as soon as I reminded him that we needed to go shopping, he was ready to get his coat on and leave.

It would be a lot easier to leave if Trent left me alone.

[Trent] Is Aiden still doing okay with the cage?

[Me] Seriously? He has safewords. You need to chill out. A and I have plans today and you're going to foil them if you keep texting me. I can't safely text and drive. I'm guessing you want me to be safe, Daddy.

[Trent] Stop calling me that!

I cackled and turned my screen off, shoving the phone in my front pocket and heading out to the truck to find Aiden. He chattered the entire way to the store about what we needed. Thankfully, we'd talked about it enough that we knew exactly what we needed once we got to the store.

Aiden had decided it was a brilliant idea to do a homemade cake, despite my protests that a boxed cake would be just fine. Again, I was a disaster when it came to baking. It was too tedious. My brain didn't like having to read and measure things exactly. I was much better at cooking when I could just throw things together at random.

"How old is your flour?"

"Uhhh."

"Then we need flour too. What about the baking powder? If it gets old, it doesn't work as well."

"Which one is baking powder? Is it the stuff that comes in a little tin or an orange box?"

"Oh my god, you're hopeless!"

"A boxed mix would be just fine," I reminded him.

"It's the one in the tin."

"Then I don't know that we even have any."

Aiden searched the shelves, clearly looking for something. He was much more comfortable in the baking aisle than I'd ever been. "Ah-ha!" He grabbed a silver-looking can of baking powder. "I don't know how you two have survived this long without flour or baking powder."

"Hey! We have flour. It's just old."

"And probably riddled with bugs."

It was my turn to be shocked. "Bugs?"

Aiden shook his head in dismay. "Are you kidding me? Logan, wheat products get bugs in them... especially if they aren't sealed properly."

That was it. I was throwing away all the flour in the house. Eww. I did not want bugs in the house. My face must have shown something of my distress because Aiden laughed as he went back to searching the shelves. "Da—" he stopped himself when he noticed a middle-aged woman in the aisle with us. "Trent's cake needs sprinkles."

At least hearing him almost call Trent "Daddy" in the middle of the grocery store had me forgetting about the possibility of bugs in our house. I focused on the ingredients piling up in the cart and forced the pantry situation out of my head. Rainbow sprinkles, silver and gold edible glitter, sugar pearls, and happy birthday candles began filling our cart. This was going to be the gaudiest cake ever, and it would be perfect. Mainly because I was making it with Aiden and he was happy. God, I was stupid for this man. If possible, stupider for him than Trent... was "stupider even a word? It didn't really matter—I was happy.

Every so often, Aiden wiggled then groaned. No one else but the two of us knew that the cock cage was driving him insane.

[Me] *If Aiden doesn't explode before you get home it's going to be a miracle.*

[Trent] *What's wrong with our boy?*

[Me] *That damn cage is going to drive him insane.*

Trent was going to worry if I left it at that, so I quickly added:

[Me] *In the best possible way.*

We'd almost completed our shopping list when Aiden gasped. "I don't have a card for him!"

"You don't have to get him anything. Hell, we rarely exchange gifts at birthdays." Was that weird? It never had been for us, but now we were together. Maybe things were different for boyfriends? Should I have gotten something for him this year? Shit, I didn't know proper boyfriend protocol. It had to have said something that not one of my relationships had lasted long enough for me to ever worry about birthday gifts.

"Whoa, puppy, what's up?"

I blinked, blinked again. Aiden was looking up at me with concern in his eyes. "You look like you're about to pass out on me."

I needed to pull myself together and dragged in a deep breath. "Sorry about that. I started thinking about birthdays. I don't know if I should get Trent something. We're dating now."

To his credit, Aiden didn't look at me like I'd lost my mind. Going up on his tiptoes, he kissed my cheek. "We can look around?"

Aiden picked out a card that announced in great big letters *Happy Birthday, Daddy!* Then he looked over at me. "Okay, let's find him a gift." He was on a mission and started to go up and down the aisles, starting in the cards and working his way through. As we passed the stationary, I stopped and looked at the pens, a memory tickling the back of my brain. When I started to laugh, Aiden stopped in his tracks and looked back at me. "What's so funny?"

"When we were in high school, he was always bitching about losing his pencils. I just remembered that I used to buy him packs of pencils for his birthdays and for Christmas." I picked up the packet of pencils with sheriff stars on them. They were perfect. Aiden started looking around and quickly found erasers that matched. I chuckled the entire way to the checkout. It was stupid, I knew it, but buying the pencils felt right, like our relationship had truly come full circle.

As Aiden climbed into the truck, he moaned low.

"You okay?"

Brown hair flopped around as he nodded. "Y-yes. Th-the cage just moved, and it... wow, yeah, it reminded me it's there."

"Better you than me." Thank fuck Trent had Aiden. And by the look Aiden gave me—slightly glassy, blown pupils, almost lust drunk—he didn't mind the predicament he was in.

I pulled into the driveway and Aiden nearly flew out of the truck. He'd been doing a dance the last ten minutes home, complaining that he needed to pee. When I asked why he hadn't gone at the store, he'd looked at me like I was nuts. "I'd have to sit down to pee... and I am not going to sit down on a public toilet. *Duh.*"

So much sass. "Maybe you should have just worn one of your diapers. *Duh.*"

Aiden smacked his forehead with such force it echoed in the confines of the cab. "Shit, why didn't I think of that? Remind me next time."

I watched Aiden's retreating ass with a dopey smile on my face and pulled out my phone to text Trent.

[Me] I just want to remind you that it's your birthday and to not work all night. You might miss fun here.

Trent had a habit of missing his birthdays. He always bitched about getting a year older and not wanting to celebrate becoming old.

[Trent] Believe me, pup, I'm not staying here any longer than I have to. I have plans tonight that involve both of my men.

Dammit, my cock was getting hard in my pants and the front door opened a bit. Aiden's head popped out and he stared at me in confusion.

[Me] I need to get going. Aiden's waiting for me.

[Trent] Don't make our boy cum, pup!

I knew exactly how to drive Trent insane.

[Me] I'll try my best. Love ya.

As I clicked off the phone, I could almost hear Trent yelling at me. I could certainly *feel* the vibrations as he yelled at me over text.

"Everything okay?"

"Texting Trent." Simplifying the conversation seemed easiest. "He'll be home on time. He says he has plans for us tonight."

"Cake time!"

Aiden had lost his clothes at some point since we'd gotten home and he was standing in the entryway in only a diaper and socks. "Wasted no time, I see."

Aiden giggled, a sound I associated with little Aiden more than adult Aiden. That development could make the cake baking that much more interesting. How were we ever going to get a cake baked if the baker was little? "Diapers made more sense." He tugged at my arm, directing me through the house and directly toward the kitchen. "Daddy needs a cake! Come on!"

The things I did for these men.

Two hours later and I could honestly say that baking a cake from scratch sucked. Baking a cake from scratch with a little made it both much better and much worse. Aiden giggled every time something spilled, which was far more often than I cared to think about. There was a pile of flour next to the bowl from when I'd turned the mixer on too fast. Aiden had dropped an egg that I'd yet to clean up because I was so focused on following the directions. I did not understand how people baked for stress relief. My stress was through the roof.

I understood why it was called baking powder when I pulled the safety seal off of it and jostled the container and it looked like baby powder exploded in the kitchen. I'd given up on my black T-shirt after that. Fuck. My. Life.

Aiden made it better, though. He seemed to be having the time of his life. Every time I looked over at him he was either grinning from ear to ear or had his tongue stuck out in thought.

Of course, he'd insisted on testing the batter, then licking the beaters clean, then the bowl. By the time the cake was ready for the oven, Aiden had a ring of cake batter around his mouth and his fingers were sticking to the spoon.

I'd decided it was safer for me to put it in the oven and finally let out a relieved sigh, ready to clean up the kitchen. The first task was helping Aiden get clean. I could just see the sticky mess our faucet would be if I let him do it himself. Thankfully, washing his hands was easy, and a warm washcloth took care of his face. I ran it over his chest as well, just in case I'd missed something. Aiden giggled the whole time. "Thanks for your help, puppy!"

I yipped at him and he laughed harder. "Okay, all play aside, we need to clean up the kitchen."

Aiden's eyes went wide. "We need to make the icing!" I watched his diapered behind hurry over to the far counter where he'd placed the bricks of cream cheese when we'd unpacked the groceries.

"Wait, icing? We're hand making the icing?"

Aiden's face lit up. "The best icing is homemade."

"Okay, let's get it done with so I can start cleaning up the kitchen."

Aiden rushed around getting supplies. I felt like it was way more icing than we needed, but I wasn't the baker here. At least icing didn't have as many steps, though I did groan when he pulled out a large bag of powdered sugar. I'd already learned that anything with the name "powder" in it was bad, and this looked like it would be far worse than the baking powder. Aiden didn't have the same reservations I did and began adding the ingredients to the bowl. As expected, powdered sugar flew through the kitchen at one point, but overall, the process was far less daunting than I'd expected, and we had smooth, creamy icing in a matter of minutes.

Just when I thought it was safe to clean the kitchen, Aiden turned and booped me on the nose with a dollop of icing. The attack took me by such surprise, I yelped. "A!" My reaction sent Aiden into a fit of giggles, and soon I was laughing as well.

Then Aiden slipped on a pile of flour that had been left on the ground at some point. In his socks, he lost his balance, and I lunged forward to grab him. I managed to catch him before he hit the ground with any force, but I lost my footing and we both landed on the floor. Aiden's diaper hit my upper thighs and sent a poof of flour upward.

I worried for a moment that he'd been hurt, but the "Ohhhh" that escaped him was anything but pained. And when he started rocking against my crotch, sending all thoughts of injury out of my head, my cock responded to the attention. It couldn't have been comfortable with his cock locked up, but he didn't seem to care.

My hands went to his hips, digging in through the crinkly plastic wrapped around him as I rocked up into him. Somewhere in the back of my head, I remembered Trent's warning that we were supposed to text him if Aiden wanted to play, but he hadn't stipulated anything about if he *couldn't* cum... I was going to call it a loophole. Knowing Trent, he'd lock that loophole up iron tight as soon as he found out, but it was worth it to not pause what we were doing.

Fuck finding the phone.

Fuck stopping.

I rocked my hips upward, and the groan that began to escape me was covered up by a throat clearing above us.

CHAPTER 40

TRENT

I WALKED into the house and knew something was amiss as soon as my coat was off. I'd heard a bang followed by a laugh as I'd shut the door, but then there had been silence. I hung my coat up like I always did, but then I turned the corner and my eyes almost fell out of their sockets in surprise. The pristine kitchen Logan and I always worked hard to keep looked like a bomb hit it. There was a bowl with white stuff in it and a bowl that had clearly been dumped out but not cleaned. That wouldn't be so bad, but it was the coating of white stuff—all over the kitchen— that had me shocked to the core.

I never walked into the house with my shoes on, but this time, I couldn't bring myself to take them off. The white stuff coated everything. I was pretty sure I saw a smear of it on the pantry door.

What had they done?

Then there was a little grunt, and a sigh, then a small moan. I checked my phone; I hadn't missed a text. There had been no texts asking if Aiden could get off. I walked toward the noises. Thankfully, the floor didn't seem too bad as I got closer to the kitchen. I'd almost sighed in relief until I rounded the bank of cabinets that separated the kitchen and dining area. It was worse than I'd expected. A layer of white... dust?... powder?... flour? I guessed flour of some sort given that I was smelling something baking—something sweet—covered the floor and counters. My feet left tracks as I walked from the counter to the middle of the room. The state of the kitchen distracted me from the noises coming from below me.

A broken egg on the counter.

A pile of fluffy stuff by the bowl. Was that icing?

The mixer dripping onto the counter.

A spatula dripping batter onto the floor.

Logan and Aiden grinding together in the middle of the mess.

Wait, Logan and Aiden grinding against one another?

They were so lost in each other they hadn't noticed me standing there. They were definitely not supposed to be doing that. Well, Aiden wasn't supposed to be, but I had a clear memory of us talking about Logan helping Aiden follow the rules. I also distinctly remembered Logan agreeing to that.

I stood there, in the mess of flour, utterly perplexed. What had they been doing? Logan hated baking. Why would he be baking? From the mess, it certainly didn't seem like it had been something basic. Then I remembered my birthday. My chest felt tight and I couldn't help the smile that spread across my face.

I'd known Logan long enough to know this wasn't his idea. He was more of a "buy it already done" guy, not a "make it from a box" and definitely not a "make it from scratch" guy. For some reason, I already knew that Aiden hadn't had to try too hard to convince Logan to make it from scratch. I also knew it hadn't gone according to plan. And now our kitchen was a disaster and my men were rolling around on the floor, grinding against each other, *not* cleaning up... and not following the rules.

Part of me wanted to clean them up and drag them to bed,

demand that we continue there instead of on the floor, but it was the first time that Aiden had even pushed a boundary we'd agreed on. I couldn't let it go by without a consequence, and I had the perfect one in mind.

I let the two get a little more worked up before I interrupted them. When I saw Logan's forearms quiver, and watched as he rolled his hips upward to grind firmly into Aiden's diapered ass, I knew I had to stop them before he came. I wasn't worried about Aiden since I knew he was locked up, but I wasn't about to let Logan get the satisfaction of cumming like this.

Logan's mouth parted and I cleared my throat. They both halted immediately. Aiden raised his head, his eyes popping wide in surprise at my appearance and a little gasp escaped. "Daddy!"

Logan had to tilt his head backward to see me, and a wicked grin crossed his face. "Hey."

I glowered at Logan, trying to pour every ounce of stern Dom into it. I knew it wouldn't do much on Logan—hell, he'd seen it too often over the years to be affected by it—but Aiden shivered at the look, and that had been my goal anyway. "Do you care to tell me what is going on in here?"

Aiden's mouth opened and closed as he tried to figure out how to respond. Logan adjusted so Aiden slid down onto his thighs, then propped himself up on his elbow so he could see me from right side up. "We were baking."

I made it a point to look around the kitchen. "Believe me, I can see that. If this can be called baking." Honestly, I didn't know what a kitchen looked like after it had been baked in. I didn't bake. But I was pretty sure I'd never seen my mom's kitchen look anything near this, even two weeks before Christmas when she did all her baking.

"It's complicated." Logan tried to shrug, but it looked comically awkward from his position and I had to suppress a laugh.

"And let me guess. Aiden just slipped and fell on your dick?"

They both burst out laughing and their heads bobbed up and down rapidly. Aiden was giggling too hard to respond, and Logan snorted before getting words out. "Actually, yes, that's exactly what happened."

Why was it that I actually believed them? I wished we had security cameras because I'd have loved to figure out how they ended up in that position. I suspected the truth was even crazier than how they could explain it.

I closed my eyes and got my thoughts in order. "Pup, you were supposed to help Aiden remember to text me if he wanted to have fun with you."

Logan held up a finger. "No, actually, you told me if he wanted to cum he needed to ask permission. He's caged. He can't cum."

Loopholes. Fucking loopholes. "Logan, you knew damn well what I meant."

He shrugged. "You should have been more precise."

"Aiden, you were being naughty. You were trying to get yourself off on Logan, even with your cage."

Aiden's head tilted downward and he batted his eyes at me. He was fucking perfect. "Sorry, Daddy."

And damn if those words didn't go straight to my dick. I wanted to stretch him out on my bed and fuck him, but that wouldn't teach him anything but that he'd get rewarded for breaking rules. "I am sure you are, baby boy. But that doesn't change the fact that you were doing something you know you're not supposed to do without Daddy's permission."

Heat flashed beneath his hooded eyes but he stayed in character well. "I understand, Daddy. But puppy's fat cock feels *so* good rubbing against me."

Dead. I was dead. My boy might have looked innocent, but he was deliciously naughty and knew exactly when to pull it out. I coughed to hide the moan that tried to escape.

"I know his cock feels good, baby boy, but you can't use it whenever you want without Daddy's permission. You need to head upstairs and wait for me on the bed."

Aiden whimpered, the same sound I'd heard from him a few minutes earlier. Needy and desperate. "Did I earn a spanking, Daddy?"

Jesus, my cock was going to have permanent zipper marks at this rate. "Yes, baby. Now go wait for Daddy while I talk with your puppy about *his* consequence."

Aiden wiggled across Logan's dick as he worked to get off the floor, causing Logan to fall back against the ground. "You fucking cockblocked me," he groaned, rubbing at the front of his pants. He rolled himself so he could get up and brushed his ass off, sending a dusting of white powder around the kitchen. "Also, I'm not your sub—you can't give me consequences."

"Don't want to hear about cockblocking from you. Jesus, all I want to do is go upstairs and sink into him, but I'm going to have to spank him before anything else can happen."

Logan gave me a look that said he didn't feel any sympathy for me. "Such a hardship for you." He smirked and I knew he wasn't actually upset with me... that would probably change when I said the next thing.

"And *you* get to clean the kitchen while I take care of our boy."

Logan's face went slack. "What?"

I gestured around the kitchen. "Logan, look at this disaster!"

"Hey, A helped make this mess!"

I wasn't going to react to what a petulant child Logan sounded like at that moment, but damn, it was hard. "If you hadn't decided to ignore the rules that we *all* agreed on, then he'd be helping you out." I kissed his pouting lips. "You, pup, can come upstairs when it's clean. I'll have a surprise for you."

Logan huffed in annoyance, but I couldn't hide my smile. "I love you, pup."

He rolled his eyes but a small smile broke across his face. "Love you too, *Daddy*."

I would keep reminding myself I couldn't kill Logan. "The sooner you get done, the sooner you get your surprise." Before I could change my mind, I turned and walked out of the kitchen. I made it to the end of the flour disaster and slipped my boots off. I didn't need to track more flour through the house.

On my way up the steps, the timer went off and Logan cursed. "Shit. How do I know if it's done?"

He'd clearly been talking to himself, but I answered. "My mom always uses a toothpick. If it comes out clean, she says it's done."

Logan didn't respond and I headed up the steps to my room to find my boy. He was right where I'd told him to be. Sitting on the edge of the bed with his hands clasped in his lap. Hedge was tucked in his elbow, and if it weren't for the way his nostrils flared and how he wiggled every few seconds, I'd have thought he was going to burst into tears.

My body hadn't even cleared the doorway and Aiden's eyes shot over to me. "I'm sorry I was naughty, Daddy." He batted his eyes at me from behind his glasses and my resolve to be the tough, strong Daddy broke just a little more. I'd never had to force myself to be stern before, but with Aiden I was quickly discovering I was a big softy. *I hated when Logan was right.*

"I know you are, baby boy. But that doesn't mean that you are getting out of your spanking." *That we both knew he wanted.*

I strode into the room and headed to the bed and climbed up, settling myself against the headboard. I'd given countless spankings before. I'd bent men over a spanking bench and bruised their flesh with floggers, paddles, and whips. I'd reduced CEOs and police officers to tears on more than one occasion. But I'd never had a sweet boy draped over my knees.

This felt different. This was bigger. In this moment, I truly understood how special it was when someone like Aiden trusted me with everything. His pain, his pleasure, his happiness. My boy trusted me.

I patted my lap and opened my mouth to speak, but the words got stuck behind emotion in my throat. I swallowed hard and tried again. "Come here, baby."

Aiden scrambled up the bed to me, Hedge never leaving his body. As he spread himself over my legs, I knew I couldn't fuck this up. Nerves and excitement had him too keyed up to enjoy the moment, so I took some time to rub his back and shoulders.

"My boy needs to tell Daddy when he wants his lil' guy to feel good."

Aiden arched up into my touch. "I-I'm sorry, Daddy."

I hummed, focusing on Aiden's body. The distant noise of Logan cleaning the kitchen helped me center myself as well. Knowing he was there, even if he wasn't in the room, made this all feel right. My fingers snaked to the front of Aiden's diaper and I pulled at the tabs. He automatically lifted up slightly and spread his legs to make it easier for me. "Good boy. You already know that spankings can't be over diapers."

I should have thought further ahead. With Aiden already over my lap, I couldn't inspect his cage to make sure it wasn't rubbing him. I'd do that after his spanking. But there was enough room between him and my lap for me to get my hand in there and cup the cage and his balls. His balls were heavy and I could feel how full he'd filled the cage, though he was nowhere near fully erect.

Aiden rocked down into my hand. "Daddy!"

It couldn't have been bothering him too much if he was so

needy. However, I couldn't have my boy rocking against me like that. The swat I landed on his hip had him gasping. It wasn't a spank, and it didn't even turn his skin pink, but it was enough to make him stop.

"Your lil' guy belongs to Daddy. You'd be wise to remember that."

He damn near melted into my lap at that point but managed to bob his head up and down in acknowledgment. "Yes, Daddy, I understand."

"I'm glad to hear that because that's why you're over my lap right now in the first place. You didn't let Daddy know your lil' guy wanted attention." Aiden's body was limp and relaxed, and I'd reminded him why he was over my lap. It was the perfect time to land the first true spank on his unblemished skin. The first one wasn't hard, barely enough noise to fill the room and only a faint pink filled the area I'd made contact with. I needed to slowly build speed and strength to find Aiden's limits. That point where pain and pleasure mixed to an intoxicating level.

Aiden drew in a breath but didn't so much as flinch. He could take more. The next slap came down on the other cheek. It was harder, but Aiden arched up to meet my hand. "Mmm, yes, Daddy."

I methodically spread the next few spanks around the globes of his ass, making sure to cover from the top to the bottom of both his cheeks so they were an even pink color. By the time I'd finished working my way around, I could feel his precum making my pants wet. My boy was handling his first spanking beautifully, and through the course of the warm-up, I'd gained a good deal of confidence myself. So when the next spank came down harder, I knew he could take it. Even when the loud crack filled the bedroom and Aiden screamed out in shock, I knew he was fine by the way he pushed back, searching my hand out.

Somewhere in the kitchen, I heard Logan drop a bowl and

curse. I smiled, wondering how long it would be before Curious was up here checking on his boy. My hand came down over and over again on Aiden's backside. Each time he arched up and moaned, then came back down and rocked into my thighs.

"No rubbies on Daddy's leg." I'd said some variation of that phrase so many times over the course of the spanking, I felt like a broken record. Aiden would only gasp, then arch right back up into the spank and start the process all over again.

His skin had turned a beautiful shade of red, but I was confident I hadn't bruised or hurt him. He was still begging for more with each spank, but if we kept going, there was a very real risk of him being left with something more than a delicious ache in his backside. If that happened, *my* reward would never happen. So I gradually changed the pace of the spanks just as Logan hurried into the room. He'd broken a sweat in his rush to clean the kitchen. Hell if I knew if it would actually be clean or not, but he was in our room, kneeling directly in front of Aiden's head and looking between the two of us. I knew he'd want to reach out and touch Aiden, but he also knew better than to do that in the middle of a spanking. So he waited patiently as the swats slowed to gentle caresses.

I'd never seen Aiden acknowledge Logan's presence, but his hand went out and reached for Logan's. When Logan joined their hands, I saw Aiden's muscles flex as he gripped it. Logan squeezed back, then turned his head to smile up at me.

Aiden didn't look anywhere near moving in the near future, and when he didn't react any further, I knew I'd lost him to subspace.

I was thankful I hadn't chosen the middle of the bed when I was able to reach over and run my hands through Logan's hair. He whimpered, and I knew it was time to start the second part of my birthday surprise.

CHAPTER 41

AIDEN

I BLINKED the world into focus. I had no idea how long I'd been sprawled across Daddy's lap. One minute, I'd been chasing all the feelings I could: more, harder, faster, orgasm. I'd have taken it all. The next minute, I had a strong body wrapped around me, and a bottle of water between my lips. The deep chuckle sounded a lot like Daddy's but the body felt like Logan's.

I sucked a few times, the cold water helping to ease my parched throat and lift some of the haze that had settled over my brain. I remembered the spanking, a fleeting memory of Daddy checking my cage and pronouncing it fine, then nothing until that moment. The fog cleared enough that I knew I was no longer over Daddy's lap. I was in bed, my head on a pillow, sandwiched between two warm bodies.

"There's our boy." That was Daddy's voice, in front of me.

That meant Logan was wrapped around me. But I didn't feel cotton or even naked skin at my back. There were hard bits and spongy parts resting against my shoulder and back. Then a quiet whimper sounded and I couldn't help the grin that spread on my face. "Curious!" In my head the word was almost shouted in excitement—what came out was a sleepy, kind of dazed sound.

So I wasn't fully awake yet.

Daddy's rumble of laughter in his chest finally pulled my attention to him and I forced my eyes to open. He was looking down at me, his eyes shining with love. I smiled around the bottle's nipple.

"I see how I rank in your life. I send you flying and you're just excited to see the pup." He was grinning widely, so I knew he wasn't upset.

"Hi, Daddy." The words were slurred due to the nipple still in my mouth. "How long was I out?"

Long enough that Logan finished the kitchen and was now Curious.

"About forty minutes."

"That long?" I couldn't believe that much time had passed. It shouldn't have surprised me because I knew how long it took Logan to get ready. It wasn't a quick process, especially if he was wearing his tail. Judging by the wiggles and the hard cock pressing into my back, I'd guessed that he had it in.

Trent leaned forward and kissed me on the nose. "That long. And now that you're awake, my birthday can continue."

Daddy's birthday. I'd totally forgotten about it after my spanking.

"Cake!"

Logan groaned behind me, but I couldn't figure out why, and Daddy laughed. "I don't think Curious is ready for cake... yet. To be honest, I'm not either."

It spoke to how foggy my brain still was that I'd forgotten that Curious was curled up behind me. As if to emphasize the point, Curious yipped, and it sent me into giggles. So my brain was very ready for little time.

"I'd love to get my boy ready to play, and I know Curious is anxious to play too."

Curious' muzzle poked at the back of my neck and he yipped again. He was definitely ready to play, which just served to make me wiggly and excited. I wanted to play too. I went to roll over and my butt rubbed against the sheets.

The sheets were soft but my butt was sore, and I hissed at the sensation. Damn, how had I almost forgotten why my brain was foggy and we were cuddling in bed in the middle of the day? The sting was going to remind me I belonged to Daddy for the rest of the day. The thought caused my dick to twitch, then I groaned when it grew just large enough to hit the edge of the cage. Fuck. The hiss followed by a groan had been the wrong choice because it sent Daddy's worry sky-high. "Was I too rough, baby boy?"

How did I explain that it was the most perfect pain in the world? Instead of trying for words, I rolled back toward Daddy and kissed him. "No. Thank you, Daddy." I hoped those words were enough to ease his fears.

He kissed me back, though it wasn't lust filled or passionate, just a gentle brush of lips before he pulled away. "Good, I'm glad. I'll put cream on you before I put your diaper on."

That sounded perfect. It would have been better if I could have gotten fully hard and maybe gotten some release, but I knew it wasn't even worth asking.

Daddy slid out of bed but the puppy stayed, still snuggling my back. I hadn't even realized Daddy was gone until he returned with a diaper and one of my onesies. "Okay, baby boy, let's get you ready to play. Your diaper will help your butt feel better." He hooked my legs, lifted, and pulled me down.

The sudden movement surprised me and I let out a gasp. "Daddy!" But he had me settled so that my legs were over the edge of the bed and my ass nearly touching his legs.

"Much easier to take care of you from this position." Without another word, he set to work diapering me. Curious slid off the bed. I kept feeling him brush against my leg and I watched as he'd knock into Daddy's side, sending him off balance.

"Curious," he'd admonish from time to time when his knee would buckle from being hit. The only response would be a bark and he'd start the circuit again. After the third time, Daddy held up a finger. "Don't pee on the bed," he warned as he left me lying there to go find something.

He was worried about me peeing? Daddy was funny.

He took a few steps across the room and stopped by the chair next to the window. When he turned around, one of Curious' rope toys was in his hand. From the corner of my eye, I watched as my puppy plopped down on his butt, then whimpered as his plug likely nailed his prostate.

Daddy chuckled and threw the rope toy out to the hallway. "Maybe that will keep him busy for a few minutes." He'd been mostly talking to himself but I still giggled as I watched Logan scurry after the toy, pausing to shiver every few feet. He was so going to cum at some point if he was that keyed up already. I almost laughed at myself, for once thankful for the cage. If I didn't cum without permission, I'd get to cum later... hopefully.

"Okay, baby boy. Let's get you ready to go downstairs and play."

Now that sounded like a plan.

I'd never seen Trent as a hard-nosed Dom despite what he and Logan both said. Maybe it was the circumstances that we'd met under—he'd been so concerned about Logan and his protective instincts had been through the roof—or maybe it had just been something about the way the two of us clicked together. Knowing he'd never been a Daddy and had little experience with regression, having him put a diaper on me felt huge the first time. After weeks of his getting me ready for bed, it felt natural when he diapered me at night or undiapered me in the mornings.

We worked together, though we were interrupted a number of times by Curious dropping his rope toy on the floor or the bed next to Daddy. Daddy would smile down at him then toss the toy away and heavy clomping would follow the toy. He sounded about as graceful as a bull mastiff, but it made me smile.

By the time my diaper was on and Daddy had helped me into a onesie, I was wiggly and ready to go play downstairs with Curious. Daddy knew it too because his eyes were crinkling up in the corners while he watched me watching Curious. "Playtime, baby boy."

"Yay!" I hopped off the bed and ran toward the steps, forgetting all about my trapped cock and my spanking from earlier. The pain was nothing more than a slight tingle as the diaper rubbed against my skin, reminding me with every step that I was Trent's.

"Walk!" Daddy called before I could hit the hallway. I huffed, Curious rolled his eyes, and we both headed—carefully—down the steps.

CHAPTER 42

LOGAN

LAUGHTER FILLED THE HOUSE. I didn't think I'd ever heard so much laughter. I'd been able to sink into Curious just about any time I'd needed since I'd discovered puppy play. Trent had been by my side in some form or another nearly every time. Actually, f it hadn't been Trent, it had been Aiden. With all three of us, it felt so much different.

Aiden had been playing with blocks and cars in the middle of the living room for quite a while, then abandoned them at some point and was crawling around after me. He wasn't going for my toys as he had plenty of his own strewn across the living room, but he seemed to be having the time of his life as he rushed after me. Thanks to my kneepads and mitts I was faster than he was, but he was still trying.

Trent had been splitting his time between tossing various toys my way, rubbing my belly, and scritching my head, and praising Aiden, snuggling him, and making sure he wasn't getting into trouble. It looked exhausting to me. I had no desire to be in his shoes, but even as Curious I couldn't help but notice the way he smiled more, the way tension had completely left his body, and the way he laughed more easily. Rarely seen smile lines appeared around his eyes and mouth. Even around our friends he didn't relax this much. Trent was happy, truly happy, for the first time in years.

I was part of that happiness. Aiden and I together had given him that happiness. Oddly enough, no sex I'd ever had gave me the same high that seeing Trent that happy did. Then I glanced back at Aiden chasing me, dragging Hedge with him as he crawled, and laughing like it was the best game in the world. The moment was perfection.

Not thinking, I stopped chasing the ball Trent had thrown and Aiden crashed into me, throwing his arms around me and laughing. "Puppy!" We ended up in a heap on the floor with Aiden on top of me and Trent standing beside the couch laughing at the two of us.

I was panting too hard to even bark. How long had we been going in circles around the living room?

With Aiden on my stomach, my plug pushing against my prostate, I felt Curious start to get fuzzy around the edges. As it turned out, it was hard to stay fully in puppy space with a sexy-as-fuck man on top of me.

The position was oddly reminiscent of the scene in the kitchen earlier. Aiden on top of me, his diaper rubbing against my crotch. Only this time, I had no clothes on and a large plug nailing my prostate. Given that Aiden kept rocking his hip against me, I figured the position had pulled him out of his little space as well.

Trent hadn't been too interested in what we were doing beside the couch until I whimpered. The sound had surprised me as much as it had drawn Trent's attention to us. It wasn't quite pup, it wasn't quite human, but it was all desire.

Once again, a throat clearing from above us had us stilling. We looked up to see Trent standing there, arms crossed, trying to look stern, but the arousal in his eyes was impossible to hide. "Baby boy, should you be playing with Curious like that?"

Aiden batted his big brown eyes, his mind working hard. "I was just getting puppy ready to have fun tonight. He wants it."

"Hey!" I yelped. "Don't get me in the middle of this. I mean, you *can* get me in the middle, but only if it's in bed. I will not be held responsible for you trying to get me off."

Aiden's theatrical gasp broke me. "I was doing no such thing! I was helping Daddy out!"

I dissolved into laughter so hard my sides hurt. He was sweet, wicked, naughty, and perfect. There were still times I felt like I needed to pinch myself to believe he was real, and beyond that, ours.

"Baby boy, I feel like you're trying to drive Curious nuts."

He shook his head. "Oh no, Daddy. I would never do that. My bum is still tender from earlier and *your* lil' guy wants to cum tonight."

Trent examined us closely. "You'll get to cum tonight, but I don't know if it's going to be how you expected."

Aiden's eyes darkened even more, turning them nearly black. He couldn't have hidden the desire in his voice if he'd tried. "Take me to bed, Daddy." Then he turned to me. "Take me to bed, puppy. I need you, both."

I glanced over at Trent and could see all the ways he was planning on ravishing his boy... and me. Those honey brown eyes were almost midnight the way his pupils dilated. "Upstairs, baby boy. On the bed." His hand swatted at Aiden's diaper and he wiggled off my lap, rushing toward the steps.

"Hurry, please," Aiden called over his shoulder as his feet hit the steps.

When his footsteps faded, Trent helped me to my feet, then grabbed my harness on either side of my chest and pulled me closer. His lips pressed against my temple, and even through the neoprene hood the spot heated. "I love you, Logan Caldwell."

I nuzzled against his neck for a moment. "I love you too, Trent Sylvan."

He held me tight for a moment before Aiden's voice broke our comfortable silence. "Are you two going to get up here to fuck me or not?"

We both smirked. "Coming!" we called as our feet moved toward the steps.

The teasing in Aiden's voice as he responded had us both moving faster. "You better not be cumming yet! I want at least one dick in my ass first!"

CHAPTER 43

TRENT

Logan and I fought to get up the steps the quickest. Without a large plug in my ass I made it to the steps first, though I was impressed with how close the race had been. We were up the steps in record time and skidding to a halt just outside the bedroom door. I didn't know why Logan was waiting, but I knew I needed to get myself under control and not look like a teenager getting ready to lose his virginity as I walked into the room. I had to take a few deep breaths while Logan sauntered into the room oozing sex appeal and making his hips wiggle more than should have been possible with his ass stretched so far around that plug.

A needy whine broke from Aiden as he watched Logan walk in, his thick cock swaying between his legs as he approached. Maybe not forcing Logan to get dressed for the evening had been a bad idea. His erection was the only thing either of us could focus on while he moved toward the bed. From the twinkle in his blue eyes, Logan knew it too. He exaggerated the sway of his hips, causing his cock to swing more. The bead of precum on his tip was nearly hypnotizing.

I had to shake my head to break the spell. "Get yourself over here, pup."

That was the only thing I needed to say and Logan nearly launched himself onto the bed, coming to rest beside Aiden on his hands and knees. He used his head to nudge Aiden's cheek and barked playfully at him.

Aiden's laugh wasn't the soft giggle he had when he was little but a rich belly laugh that settled deep in my stomach and made me smile. "Let's get that diaper off you, baby boy." He might not have been little, but I would never look at him and not see my boy.

Aiden flopped backward on the bed with a giant sigh. "Thank fu—"

I shot him a glare and he quickly changed the word. "Thank goodness. I need to be filled by one of you."

Logan remained perched on the bed, ass in the air, forearms resting on the bed, his head cocked to the side as he watched what we were doing, occasionally clenching his ass muscles so his tail wagged. Each time he did it he'd whimper. It couldn't have taken more than two minutes to get Aiden's diaper off and his skin wiped down, but there was already a puddle of precum on the bedspread below Logan.

Logan's tail wagged more furiously when he finally got a good look at Aiden's caged cock. "I don't know why I find that so fucking sexy, but you were right. That's a good birthday present for you."

I tossed the diaper in the trash can in our room, then turned my attention to Logan. "Come here, pup. Let's get you out of that gear."

Logan crawled over to me. The soft bed, blankets, and his bulky kneepads and gloves caused his movements to be a bit jerky and uncoordinated, but he made it and sat back on his feet, waiting for me to remove his gear. I loved this part nearly as much as I loved seeing him slip into Curious. Watching him go from Curious back to Logan was something I'd fallen in love with the first time I'd gotten to see it, and it hadn't gotten old.

I started by removing his hood, then toweling his short hair off from the sweat that had gathered there while he'd played. I didn't miss the way Logan leaned his head into my hands as I worked and my heart soared. Logan didn't let anyone do this for him but me. I'd always cherish these moments. Even knowing Aiden was lying there watching our every move, even with my persistent erection begging for attention, I wouldn't rush the process.

Satisfied that I'd dried him off well enough, I pulled gently at his harness and kissed him on the lips. I didn't resist when his tongue came out and he deepened the kiss. We explored each other's mouths, my tongue sweeping behind his teeth and over the roof of his mouth, all the while I worked to get his gloves off. The leather was bulky and stuck to his hands but protected his knuckles while he played on the floor.

"It's like a private porn show, but I can't get fully hard. This is not fair!" Aiden's protest had us laughing.

"Oh dear, our boy is feeling left out," I mentioned to Logan as we glanced at Aiden. His cock had filled the cage as far as it could, leaving him to wiggle but not find relief.

Logan flipped around and began to trail kisses down Aiden's body. He'd begun at his chin and jaw and worked slowly down. Little red splotches appeared on Aiden's chest as Logan's stubble grazed a trail downward. He gripped one of Aiden's nipples between his teeth just as I slid the first kneepad off his leg. From my vantage point, I was able to watch as Aiden's back rose from the bed and his cock twitched futilely. The bead of precum that dribbled from the slit of his cage told me he wasn't hating the cage at all.

I worked to remove Logan's other kneepad as Logan laved

Aiden's other nipple with attention. The first one had turned a dark caramel color and had pebbled under Logan's administrations. I had no idea Aiden's nipples were so sensitive, and filed the information away for later.

With Logan naked aside from his tail and both men in front of me distracted for a moment, I took the time to strip. Aiden had complained that Logan and I had been a porn show, but he wasn't able to see how sexy he and Logan were. Logan hadn't even made it to Aiden's belly button and Aiden was a mess of pleas, sweat, and stubble burn. Logan's balls were full and I knew he'd cum with very little stimulation to either his cock or his prostate, but that wasn't my goal at the moment.

I headed to the nightstand and grabbed a few condoms, the lube, a cock ring, and a vibrating prostate massager. In the last few years, my sex life had been rather dull, actually nonexistent, but looking at the items and the men on the bed in front of me, I knew those words would never describe it again. I stretched the cock ring and fitted it around my length, knowing that I was going to need all the help I could get to not cum too soon. Then I took the condoms, plug, and lube to the foot of the bed and knelt in front of Aiden without him even noticing me.

I pumped a squirt of lube onto my hand then rubbed it around before finally sliding my finger into Aiden. I hadn't given him much warning. The intrusion caused him to cry out at first but it turned into a pleasured sigh just as quickly. He rocked down onto my finger, trying to drive me farther into him. His body accepted me hungrily, and after only a few circles, Aiden gripped the blanket on either side of him and raised his head to look me in the eyes. "More, Daddy. I need more fingers. Now. Please."

"Well, since you asked so nicely." I removed my first finger just enough that I could line my middle finger up with it and drove into him. Aiden screamed his agreement before collapsing back on the bed. I watched him, pleasure and desire radiating from his head through his toes that curled and stretched over and over again.

"Daddy!" he began to call out just as Logan captured his mouth in a kiss.

I'd miscalculated how needy Aiden would be after a full day locked in his cage. His body swallowed my fingers as soon as I slipped the second one in, his ring of muscle offering almost no resistance to the intrusion. I swirled, scissored, and rotated for a few minutes longer, purposely avoiding his prostate with every movement before I added my third.

Aiden screamed around Logan's mouth, the kiss unable to hide his calls. "Daddy, so good. So. So. Daddy!"

The cage twitched and jerked with every twist of my fingers, and I watched Aiden's abs quiver and ripple as he tried to rock his ass down on my fingers, desperately searching for contact with that spot deep inside him. Then my fingers were gone and Aiden's head flew up so fast he knocked into Logan's forehead.

"Please don't give Logan a concussion on my birthday, especially before I've had a chance to be inside either of you."

Logan moaned at my words but Aiden rubbed his forehead, his eyes searching for why I'd removed my fingers. I knew he was hoping for my cock, but I pulled the plug from beside Logan's hip and slathered it with lube. Aiden's mouth made the most adorable "O" shape. I watched as he mouthed *Fuck me* over and over again, but since no words came out, I couldn't scold him for cussing.

The plug slid in with almost no effort. My three fingers were larger than it was, and I'd clearly done my job. With it seated securely inside him, I pushed the button on the base, the pulsation low enough at first that he didn't notice it. A few seconds later the light lit up brighter, indicating the pattern had intensified. Aiden didn't miss it, shock running across his face followed by pure bliss. "Daddy!" he gasped, trying to catch his breath as the vibrations nailed his prostate in a staccato beat, not enough to let him cum, yet enough to send jolts through his body.

"Oh, that's just mean, Daddy." Logan smirked while he watched Aiden's body jerk as another pulsation vibrated deep inside him.

I reached down and grabbed Logan's hips, maneuvering him so that his ass was lined up with my cock. "I expect you to keep Aiden distracted, pup." My words came out gravelly as I worked to open the condom I'd swiped off the bed. My hands were too slippery with lube to get it open without the help of my teeth. As I brought it to my mouth Logan reached out and swiped the packet from my hand.

He ran it over the blanket to dry it, then pulled it open with ease. "Patience, Trent."

Without input from my brain, my hand made contact with his raised ass cheek. I went to apologize for getting wrapped up in the moment, but to my surprise Logan moaned. His reaction made me smile, but I wasn't going to push my luck. Instead, I gripped his tail and began to rotate it around, loosening the muscles that were holding it securely in place. "Keep Aiden distracted, Logan. I want him ready for me when I'm done with you."

"Oh, holy fuck," Logan groaned. I wasn't sure if it was my words or the fact that his plug began sliding out. His mouth went to Aiden's neck and latched on, causing Aiden to call out. The plug slipped from Logan and I watched his hole as it pulsated, begging to be filled again.

Pressing gently on his hips, I pushed his ass so it was lined up with my cock, then slid in. Logan hissed and rocked back, taking me inside him in one fluid motion. "Oh my god. Trent, fuck me hard. Please. Please fuck me. Make me cum." Logan was already on the verge and I hadn't even begun to move. I wasn't going to complain because I still fully intended to sink into Aiden after Logan came.

I moved my hips, pulling almost completely out of Logan before sinking back in. Logan rolled forward, dragging his chin along Aiden's chest. "Logan needs more, baby boy. Can you help him?"

Logan's head fell between his shoulders. "Oh, fuck me."

I chuckled as I wrapped my body around his back. "I already am."

"Smartass." I was impressed with Logan's ability to speak while so close to the edge.

Our banter seemed to bring Aiden back from his own edge, and I watched his eyes roll. "You two are ridiculous."

Logan sucked one of Aiden's nipples between his teeth and nipped lightly before looking up at him. "And you're stuck with us."

But Aiden had the last laugh because he reached between Logan's legs and grabbed his dick. I couldn't see his hand, but Logan's entire body stiffened and the laughter in Logan's voice cut off suddenly. "I'm not gonna last," Logan warned as I watched Aiden's arm pump up and down Logan's dick.

"Good." I adjusted my angle to the point where I knew I'd hit Logan's prostate and began pounding into him. "Cum for me, pup."

Logan drove back into me as I pushed forward, pushing my dick inside of him as deep as he could. Seconds later, I felt his ass contract around me, squeezing me so tightly I was certain I was going to lose my own orgasm inside of him. "Cumming!" he warned needlessly. Had I missed his ass squeezing my dick for all it had, I wouldn't have missed the sound of Aiden's hand gliding through Logan's cum as he made sure Logan was totally drained.

A few seconds later, Logan collapsed onto the bed, puddle of cum be damned. He'd collapsed so fast, I'd barely had a chance to grab the base of the condom as he separated from me. "Nice. Thanks. Good."

Aiden licked his fingers clean of Logan's release, then patted Logan's ass. "That didn't make sense, puppy."

"Later. Sentence. Bad."

I pulled the condom off and tossed it into the trash can. "I think we broke him. Give him a few minutes. But I think someone else needs attention now."

CHAPTER 44

AIDEN

WAIT, my turn? Was it bad that I'd forgotten about my desire to cum as I'd watched Trent fuck Logan? My own orgasm and need to release had been put so far out of my mind that I'd assumed Trent had cum too. Except he was standing in front of me, his cock hard as a rock, as he sheathed his dick in a new condom. *Holy hell, he hadn't cum.* That might be hotter than Logan flying apart only a minute before.

Beside me, Logan looked up at me and smiled. "Soon. I'll help, soon." He reached a hand out and placed it on my stomach. It was like he knew Trent was preparing to pull the vibrating plug from my hole at that exact moment and he wanted to keep me in place. As my back arched upward, Logan's hand pressed down firmly, keeping me where I was. "Fuck him," Logan said through a yawn.

I watched as Trent reached out and ran his hand down Logan's spine. "I will—don't worry."

My hole pulsated as the plug slid from me, begging for more attention. Now I knew how Logan felt when his puppy tail came out. I was empty and needy, and I needed to be filled. "Daddy!" I hardly recognized my own voice pleading for something I didn't yet have. "Daddy, I need you in me."

Trent grinned and Logan managed to lift his head enough to look between the two of us. "Yes, Daddy, fuck him. You both need it."

Trent lined his cock up to slide in as Logan's hand moved from my stomach down to grope my caged erection. *Shit, the cage.* The realization must have crossed my face because Daddy's naughty smile was back. "You can cum when you need to. But you're not getting out of that cage until morning if you don't cum before I do."

Brain. Fried. Nothing worked right. My thoughts collided in my brain so fast I couldn't keep them straight. My dick twitched inside my cage. I should want out. I should want to cum with a hand wrapped around my cock and Trent's dick in my ass. Yet there was a challenge there and something incredibly erotic about Daddy fully controlling my orgasm. I'd been frustrated by the damned cage all day, and now I was frustrated in a whole new way. Frustrated that I couldn't touch, that I might not get off, frustrated that it sounded amazing and perfect and I couldn't think of a better way to spend the evening.

"Make me cum." The words hardly sounded like I'd spoken them. My voice was deeper than I'd ever heard it, and the threads of need that had woven through it were evident.

Trent raised his eyebrows in challenge. "We'll see."

Logan's hand squeezed. "His balls are really tight and so full. I bet he'll cum, then be super frustrated because his dick's going to be spent but he's not going to feel completely satisfied."

If Trent wanted to be inside my ass when I came, he was going to have to talk a little less and act a lot more. The crazy thoughts I had going through my head at the moment were nearly enough to send me over the edge. Trent's fingers ghosting over my stretched hole and Logan's hand groping my aching balls were nearly sensation overload. Just when I thought it was a lost cause, that I would cum before being breached, I felt the blunt head of Trent's dick pressing against my opening.

Reminding myself to relax, I took a deep breath and felt his cock slip into me with ease. Three big fingers and the massager had prepped my body well—all I had to do was lie back and enjoy. Big hands wrapped around my hips and pulled me farther down the bed so my ass was resting mostly on Trent's thighs while he worked in and out of my body.

"He's not lasting long," Logan warned as he watched Trent's cock disappear into my ass again.

Trent managed to hum his agreement, but no words came out.

Logan had reenergized enough to torment me: a finger rolling my hard nipple, his hand massaging the tender place right behind my balls. I'd waited all day to cum, but I didn't know if I'd be able to now that I had the permission to. To say I was keyed up was an understatement, but I felt like I needed more.

Just as I began to accept that I was going to be spending the night horny and in a cock cage, Trent adjusted his hips and nailed my prostate. The sound that tore through me was part animal, part desperation. He knew exactly what he was doing and continued to nail my prostate over and over. Trent's cock was magical and I was pretty sure something along those lines spilled from my lips with each thrust in.

I was teetering on the edge just as Trent's movements sped up. He was going to cum and I was so close I could feel it, but I needed something extra. Logan must have known it was time to pull out all the stops. "A's close."

"Help our boy cum, Logan."

Logan wasted no time and leaned forward to lick up the crease of my leg. The area had never been particularly sensitive, but it was exactly what I'd needed in order to tumble over the edge.

My cock tried hard to break free of the cage as I emptied my load. It wasn't a hard spurt that hit my abs. It ended up being a number of small spasms that sent cum trickling down my balls and into my crease. I was vaguely aware that I was likely being fucked with my own cum, but the thought was chased away when Trent gripped my hips and thrust hard into my ass one last time, stilling as his cock pulsated in my ass.

Sweat trickled down his forehead and chest, his breath coming in hard pants, but a happy smile played across his face. "You're perfect," he whispered, then turned to Logan and repeated the words.

Logan slipped off the bed and pecked Trent's cheek. "You're not so bad yourself. I'm going to go get a washcloth to clean us all up with. Our blanket needs to be replaced too. It's a crime scene tech's wet dream." He was laughing to himself the entire way to the bathroom, but when the water started, my attention drifted back to Trent and my dick. Just like Logan had predicted, I felt totally spent but like my orgasm had only half happened. My balls were drained but the sensation, the completion of my orgasm, hadn't come—no pun intended. For the first time in my life, I had firsthand knowledge of what a ruined orgasm was, and oddly enough, it was perfect.

"Love you," I whispered to Trent when I was sure my voice would work again.

He beamed. "Love you too."

"You guys are so sappy." Logan had returned with warm washcloths for both of us. He'd had time to recover from his orgasm, but Trent and I weren't working quite as fast. Trent took one cloth from Logan as he slid his dick from me with a hiss. The condom got tied off, and he used the cloth to wipe his forehead and chest before flipping it over and cleaning his cock.

"We love you too, Logan."

Logan tried hard to hide his smile but it didn't work well. "I love you two weirdos too."

Logan finished wiping me down as Trent reached for the cage. "That was really hot."

I nodded, my brain still too tired to form words. I'd do that again, but having my cock out of the cage for the first time in nearly twelve hours was nearly as good a feeling as an orgasm.

Trent and Logan were already working together to get a new blanket from the closet and remove the soiled one from the bed. I reluctantly rolled off, taking Hedge and Logan's blanket with me.

Five minutes later, we'd curled up in the bed. Logan was under his blanket with a glass of water beside him; I had my binkie, Hedge, and a bottle of water; and Trent had found *Scooby-Doo* on the TV across the room. The position was nearly identical to the first night we'd spent together after the disaster at DASH. The main difference was we were in Trent's room instead of Logan's. Well, that and now we were dating.

My life had changed so much I could hardly believe it. I had two amazing men—a Daddy and a puppy—and they accepted every part of me. Little or big, it didn't matter to them. I was their boy and it felt right.

I hummed as Trent's hand ran through my hair. "Hmm. I'm glad you made it home early today, Daddy." With a jolt, I remembered *why* he was home early. "Daddy! Your birthday cake!"

"It will be there when we get downstairs."

"But it might go stale!" I couldn't let his birthday cake go bad.

Trent squeezed my shoulder gently. "If that's the case, we can make another one... or there's always next year."

The cake might be inedible by the time we got to it, but my gift for Trent would stay good no matter how long it took to get it to him. I'd spent every free moment I could editing the pictures I'd taken at the park. Calling in a favor, I'd had a friend of mine print a few of my favorites on canvases at the last minute. They were beautiful and I knew he'd appreciate having them. But they could wait a little while longer. The bed was comfy and the thought of dragging the box from the closet was too daunting at the moment.

I settled deeper into my spot. There was always next year. And the year after that. And the year after that. I fully expected to be in the same place decades from now, celebrating Daddy's birthday with my puppy at my side.

EPILOGUE

TRENT

"GO LONG!" I yelled to Logan when I had the football in my hand.

Logan's blond hair was visible despite the knit beanie on his head as he ran down the field. I was staring a bit too intently at his perfect ass as he ran because I almost missed Colt coming at me from my left side and his deputy, Zander, barreling at me from the right. I had to remind myself this was just flag football, and I hoped they remembered it too.

Colt was in his midforties. He shouldn't have been so quick or agile, but he was running at me with shocking speed. I forced myself to wait as long as I could before I stepped back a half step and let the ball fly, trusting Logan would be where he needed to be. I watched the ball soar for about a half second before realizing Colt and Zander were closing in on me too quickly for comfort.

"Not tonight, boys!" I teased as I jumped back and out of their paths.

"Shit!" I heard from either side as the men discovered they were moving way too fast and were on a collision course with one another. I watched them try to apply the proverbial brakes as they collided in the spot I had been just a moment before.

I looked up in time to see Logan running toward the end zone, four of Colt's deputies and a firefighter from Kingfield hot on his heels. A few of my deputies, James included, as well as a couple of the EMTs from our county went running down the field after them, trying to block as many people as possible from catching Logan.

"Run!" I screamed across the field while simultaneously trying to avoid laughing at my friends who were at my feet watching the action from the grass. "Don't let them get him, James!"

"Get him! Come on!" Colt yelled over me.

Zander sighed dramatically and flopped back onto the grass as Logan crossed the line into the end zone just as time ran out.

The half of the crowd cheering for the home team erupted into cheers while the other half of the stadium grumbled. We always had a great turnout for the game. This year's game felt different, and not just because Cheatham County was ahead. Logan's victory dance had me laughing, and I could see Aiden's floppy brown hair from behind his camera. For the first time in my life, I felt complete. It really hadn't mattered what the outcome of the game was. Win or lose, I'd be heading home with my men that night.

Of course, Colt's team had won last year's game by a point, so this win felt just a little sweeter. We'd be going home with the ugly golden donkey trophy back in our possession.

After we'd shaken hands with everyone on the field, the masses in the stands began to file out. As soon as it was just our core group of friends left, Aiden barreled at Logan and me, practically launching himself into my arms. "Congratulations, Daddy! Congratulations, puppy!"

Merrick snorted as he walked up to us. "You guys really need to watch it. News is going to travel through here like wildfire. The sheriff's not just gay but with two men. That's going to have the old biddies at the salon clutching their pearls."

I flipped him off and looked toward the sidelines to see Caleb, Travis, Larson, Dean, and Dexter heading over with Derek. Anyone still hanging around the stadium would be more interested in Derek Westfield than who Sheriff Sylvan was dating.

James gasped as the group approached. I turned to see if he was okay and found him looking pale. *"Him,"* was all he said, staring at the group approaching.

Logan and Aiden were just as confused as I was, but the confusion was quickly rectified when Dexter's eyes lit up as they got closer. "It's you."

The two knew each other, and they were both shocked to see one another there.

"Are you stalking me?" James demanded, drawing Colt's and Zander's attention.

Dexter's mouth opened and shut a number of times, the first time in nearly a year I'd ever seen him speechless. Then pieces started falling into place. James' new neighbor. His new house, the place he'd moved into shortly after Caleb moved in with Travis. Dexter was the person driving James insane. I couldn't help it—I laughed.

Logan had also put the pieces together and was trying hard to get an introduction out before he lost his ability to speak. "James, meet Dexter. Dexter, this is James. I think you two already know each other, though."

"You know him?" Was that a crack in James' voice? Sure, Dexter was loud and excitable but he'd always seemed as harmless as a fly. James' dismay seemed unnecessary.

I swallowed my humor and filled the confused men in on who everyone was. It struck me that, for the first time, James was officially meeting the group of guys Logan and I hung out with. He'd met them in passing but had never spent time with them. I hadn't ever thought about the fact that I kept them separate from one another. "James, this is Larson, Merrick, Dean, Travis, and Caleb. Dexter is Caleb's best friend, and Caleb and Travis are together."

James let out a long-suffering sigh. "Oh."

Aiden sensed the tension in the group and changed the subject quickly. "Mable's?" Before we left that morning, I'd promised him dessert if he was a good boy. I'd left the definition of "good" undefined. If we hadn't gotten dessert, Logan would have melted down. Mable's was a tradition and Logan looked forward to it every single year.

"Pie!" Logan cheered excitedly from beside me.

Mable had been giving us odd looks since the day Logan had shown up while Aiden and I were eating there. She definitely knew we were together, but oddly, news hadn't spread across town yet. "Yeah, Mable spoils the hell out of you, doesn't she?" I ruffled Logan's hair like I would Curious'. I wouldn't have thought much about it until he let a quiet growl out. Caleb and Larson both laughed hard enough that I knew they'd heard. Larson had been coming out of his shell more and more over the last few weeks, and I couldn't help but wonder if my boy and pup had something to do with it.

Logan looked over at Colt, his husband Derek, and Zander, who were the only three from Kingfield left at the field with us. "Want to join us for a slice of pie before you head back to Kingfield?"

"Winner buys," Zander shot back with a grin.

I nodded like it made perfect sense. "It's only right."

Derek's eyes went wide. "In that case, Mom and Dad can watch the kids a little longer!"

Colt leaned over and whispered quietly into his husband's

ear. "I saw you drink at least two hot chocolates during the game. Do you really think you need more sweets?"

Derek looked like an injured puppy. "But, Daddy, pie!"

I thought I'd been the only one close enough to hear the remark, but Aiden's eyes widened and he tugged at my hand, mouthing *Daddy?* The football field wasn't the place to discuss Colt and Derek's relationship. I'd have to double-check with Colt that it would be okay to share that piece with Aiden no matter what.

Later, I mouthed back, then made a mental note to talk to Colt.

Unaware of our silent conversation, Colt sighed and I could tell Derek was going to get what he wanted. His boy had him wrapped around his little finger. "I'll make you a deal. Milk or water only, and then you can have a piece of pie. No ice cream."

Derek's face scrunched up like he'd eaten a lemon. "No ice cream?"

Colt's face turned stern. Derek wasn't going to win this argument. "Or we could just go home if you want to push it."

Derek deflated. "Fine, no ice cream."

They were funny, though I resisted laughing at them because I'd end up having an almost identical conversation with Logan before long. A glance to the side found Dexter and Caleb in a hushed conversation while a glance to my other side showed Logan guiding James toward the exit. The others might have been concerned with keeping their voices down in the empty stadium, but Logan didn't have the same reservations. "No, you're coming to Mable's. It's good for you to have a friend. Besides, he's your neighbor—you can't ignore him forever."

James' voice carried back to us, though not quite as loudly as Logan's and I didn't think that Dexter could hear anyway. "I can try. I could move."

Logan patted James on the back. "Hate to break it to you, but you signed a year lease. Dexter's not all that bad." Aiden came up beside me and kissed me on the cheek. I squeezed his hand and we began to follow James and Logan to the parking lot while listening to them chat. "Besides, he basically worships you. I've heard so much about your tattoos and muscles the last few months. Come to think of it, I should have put it together sooner."

James tripped, nearly falling on his face. This would be an interesting meal. I would have to make sure Logan behaved himself during dessert. Then Aiden skipped ahead to catch up with James and Logan. He slipped his hand in Logan's and Logan took a step toward our boy.

Aiden turned and flashed me a huge smile, then used his free hand to gesture for me to follow him. "Come up here, Daddy. You promised me dessert."

James only shook his head. "Too much information about my bosses. Too much." He'd said the words with a smile and I knew he wasn't offended. He had more on his mind than what Logan, Aiden, and I were up to in our spare time. He'd just figured out that Dexter was not only Caleb's best friend but that Dexter thought he was hot. That information was enough to fry the brains of any straight man, and James was no exception.

I jogged ahead to take Aiden's free hand and watched as he and Logan both beamed at me. This wasn't where I'd seen my life two months earlier, but thanks to my curious pup getting in over his head, I now had a pup and a boy and I'd never been happier. It had taken Logan and I twenty years to figure out we were missing Aiden, and Aiden had given us more than he'd ever know when he agreed to date us. We were stronger as three, and I never saw that changing. I had no idea what the next week or month would hold, much less the rest of my life, but what I did know was that whatever I faced in life, I'd have Logan and Aiden by my side.

ALSO BY CARLY MARIE

Finding Home Series

At Home, Finding Home Book 1

Be My Home: An At Home Valentine's Day Novella Book 1.5

Coming Home, Finding Home Book 2

Close to Home, Finding Home Book 3

Already Home, Finding Home Book 4

Undisclosed Series

Undisclosed Desires, Undisclosed Book 1

Undisclosed Curiosity, Undisclosed Book 2

Untamed

Untamed

Untamed Christmas

Worth the Risk

Worth the Risk

Audio Books

At Home, Finding Home Book 1

Coming Home, Finding Home Book 2

Close to Home, Finding Home Book 3

Already Home, Finding Home Book 4

Undisclosed Desires, Undisclosed Book 1

Untamed

UNDISCLOSED DESIRES

A LOOK AT BOOK 1 OF THE UNDISCLOSED SERIES

Travis

THE LAST PLACE I wanted to be that morning was a physical therapist's office. I needed to get to a jobsite, but after having surgery on my ankle following a nasty fall, I had to be there to get rid of a persistent limp and hopefully the dull ache that was beginning to plague me on a daily basis. I'd done the basic PT through a different office, but their schedules never seemed to line up well with my work, so I decided to try a place with earlier appointments for the more intensive therapy I now needed. I just hoped the physical therapist would be able to help me along quickly so I could waste as little time as possible.

My phone was vibrating like crazy with text after text from a jobsite foreman relating to an issue with an order we were trying to track down. It had started with a few missing cabinets for the kitchen and had snowballed to missing pieces and parts for the entire house. The supply company was trying to figure out what had happened to the shipment, and in the meantime, our completion date was shot to hell.

The constant texts and added stress were making it impossible for me to focus on filling out the necessary paperwork for the therapist, and I could already tell this was going to be the Monday from hell. Was it possible to go back to bed and start the day over? Maybe with two or three more cups of coffee before leaving the house.

Ben: Hey, boss, sorry to bother you. I've been making some calls. Finally got the owner of Canter's on the phone. Seems at least part of the order was shipped to another jobsite... not ours.

Me: Fuck! What about the rest?

Ben: No clue. But the stuff that was shipped to the wrong place can be recovered tomorrow. He's got a new person in the ordering department, he figures there was a mixup with that.

I sighed and ran my hands through my short hair that seemed to be getting grayer at an alarming rate recently. It was now more salt than pepper and it was making me feel every day of my forty-one years. It was probably a good thing I was in physical therapy for a bum ankle and not complications due to a heart attack with the amount of shit I'd been dealing with lately.

Me: Keep on him—

"Mr. Barton!" a high-pitched voice called from the doorway of the waiting room, interrupting my text before I could send it. I shoved my phone into my pocket and plastered on a fake smile, hoping it looked genuine. My nerves were already shot and if I had to listen to this mousey-voiced woman for an hour, I might end up on blood pressure meds by the end of the morning.

As I joined her, limping along and wanting to curse my sore ankle, she smiled up at me. "I'm Lisa. I'll be taking you back to see Caleb. He's going to be your therapist."

First good news of the day—my physical therapist was not the woman who barely looked like she was out of high school. As we entered the therapy space, there were only a few patients working at different machines so, thankfully, the place wasn't absurdly loud.

Lisa walked me to a chair at the side of the room. "Caleb is running just a minute or two behind. He'll be with you shortly. If you haven't had a chance to finish the paperwork, feel free to do so now." She shot a pointed look at my mostly blank packet as she walked away.

From the small room beside me, two voices could be heard disagreeing... arguing maybe. It took me a moment to hone in on the conversation but once I did I couldn't help but smile to myself. The deeper of the two voices sounded exasperated. "They aren't toys!"

The other voice scoffed before responding. "Cal, your desk is covered in dragon toys! I'm pretty sure this one came from a Happy Meal."

"Leave Puff alone! He didn't do anything to you. And leave my desk alone."

The second guy was gasping for air as he laughed. "Cal, dude, they're named! You've named the toys on your desk."

Voice one sounded irritated when he responded. "It's Puff from Pete's Dragon you imbecile."

My phone buzzed again and I zoned the two out. I needed to figure out what the fuck was going on with my supply shipment and how I was going to get things where they needed to be to avoid further delays. We were into spring and I couldn't afford to fall behind on even one job because work was stacking up faster than I cared to admit. I'd never been so thankful to have someone like Ben working for me. I pulled my phone out and finished my text to Ben.

Me: *Keep on him. We need to figure out where everything is. I'll be at the office as soon as this damn appointment is over.*

Ben: *If you keep limping around the office bitching about your ankle, the guys are going to force you to take leave. I recommend focusing on your PT.*

I cursed but picked up the incomplete paperwork and began

to fill it out. I didn't get far before the conversation from the office beside me caught my attention again.

"Shut up, Dex. I'm late for my appointment because of you. *Get out of my office, now!*" the voice huffed.

A tall ginger-haired guy in his mid-twenties was pushed out of the office just ahead of a muscular man an inch or so shorter than the redhead. The office door slammed shut and the muscular guy crossed his arms and stared at his co-worker. There didn't appear to be any malice in his eyes, so I figured they were friends, though I thought the redhead might be pushing his luck given the stern expression on the muscular guy's face.

The redhead held up his hands in surrender and walked away shaking his head. "We're going to talk about your little obsession later, Caleb."

The muscular guy appeared embarrassed by his friend's words and turned pink while he shook his head in frustration. "Ugh! You're impossible. I'm going to lunch with Lisa!" For some reason I suspected the threat was empty.

The redhead shook his head again as he walked across the physical therapy floor and into another small office before shutting the door behind him.

The muscular guy turned his head toward me with a faint pink blush still staining his cheeks. "You must be Mr. Barton." He held out his hand and flashed me a bright smile that was clearly trying to push his discomfort away. "Sorry to keep you waiting. I'm Caleb Masterson. It seems you're stuck with me for a while!"

I bristled at being called *Mr. Barton*. That always reminded me of my dad and made me feel old. "Please, call me Travis."

Caleb smiled. "Nice to meet you, Travis. You can call me Caleb. I hear you've recently had surgery on your ankle?" he probed, quickly glancing down at my work boots. He was likely judging my choice of footwear. I hadn't thought much about it when I'd left the house that morning. It had been over two months since my surgery, and I was annoyed that the recovery hadn't been quicker, despite the surgeon telling me it was going to take time. I wouldn't own a top-rated, custom home building and remodeling company if I weren't stubborn and impatient. My ankle, however, didn't seem to realize I had deadlines and projects that needed my attention.

"Yeah. I need to get this thing back in shape. I really don't have time for a weekly appointment."

"Twice weekly," Caleb corrected, fighting a grin.

I balked. "Twice a week?" *When had I agreed to physical therapy twice a week?*

Caleb nodded while looking at the small laptop in his hand. "Yes, it was confirmed when the appointment was scheduled."

Ben. I'd left it to him to find me a new physical therapy place when the last one wasn't working out. It was a good thing the guy was a hard worker and knew his shit because I wouldn't normally take too kindly to this type of surprise. I had to concede that Ben also knew me too well after working for me for over two years. If he'd told me I was going to be coming here twice a week for the foreseeable future, there would have been no way I'd have come to the first appointment. But now I was here and stuck.

I sighed. There was nothing else I could do. "Alright, we might as well get a move on. What's first?"

Caleb shook his head. "You're clearly used to being the boss, but here, I'm in charge. So you can just sit yourself down on the table and take your highly-inappropriate-for-physical-therapy boots off so I can see where we're starting."

Big hazel eyes glanced over the clipboard that I'd set beside me. I watched as he looked at the incomplete paperwork on it and shook his head.

"Well, since you didn't get this all filled out, tell me how you managed to land yourself here when you'd, clearly, much rather be working."

I gave him the condensed version of events, avoiding an explanation of *how* I'd broken my ankle, while he focused on my ankle and the scars on either side from the surgery I'd had. "This is my busy season, and I need to get this ankle back into shape quickly. The last physical therapist I was at couldn't work with my early morning schedule."

"Well, the only way you're going to get it there is to put in the appropriate time in therapy and do the exercises I give you. Oh, and don't do more than you're ready for. I can already see you're likely one who will push through the pain and end up injuring yourself more." He sighed and shook his head. Apparently, I wasn't the first stubborn patient he'd had to deal with. "So, what did you do to yourself, Travis?"

I couldn't help the exasperated huff I blew out at my own stupidity. "I was coming down a ladder, missed the last rung, and landed on my ankle. Not one of my finer moments."

Caleb fought a grin at my expense. I couldn't deny he was adorable as he tried to remain professional, but the twinkle in his eyes gave away a playful personality just below the surface. Even if I wanted to be frustrated with him, the little dimple that appeared in his left cheek was enough to wear me down slightly. "Sounds like a freak accident. It's going to help if you wear tennis shoes here, though." He was rotating my ankle and shifting his attention from my ankle to my face, likely watching for any signs of discomfort.

He squeezed and turned and rotated it more than my doctor had at the last appointment. He seemed to be making mental notes of every tight spot, slight pop, and anything he perceived as discomfort from me. After a few minutes, he went to my right ankle and repeated the process. It felt like it took ten minutes before he'd compared every movement.

Caleb finally opened his laptop and began typing rapidly. The tip of his tongue stuck out slightly as he worked, making him look younger. When he was done with his notes, he asked me all the questions I hadn't answered on the paperwork and by the time we were done with all that, our time was almost up.

He shut the laptop and smiled at me. "Well, unfortunately, we didn't get much done today. The good news is, we've got all the boring stuff out of the way, so we can get right down to fixing you up on Friday."

The last thing I wanted to do was spend another hour each week in physical therapy, yet I had a feeling Ben was right—boss or not, the guys were at the end of their rope with me. I was going to find myself persona non grata at my own company if I didn't start taking physical therapy more seriously.

"Yes, see you Friday," I agreed reluctantly.

Caleb smiled and nodded like he'd won a battle. "Have a good week, Travis. See you Friday."

A NOTE FROM CARLY...

Dear Reader,

Thank you for reading *Undisclosed Curiosity*. If I'm a new-to-you author, I want to say thank you for giving my book a try. If you've been waiting for Logan and Trent to get a story since *Desires*, I appreciate your sticking this journey out with me. These guys were a challenge to write—often times leaving me frustrated, sad, and questioning my own sanity. When Aiden entered their story, I knew I'd finally found what they were missing.

Without the continued support of everyone from friends and readers, to fellow authors and editors, this book would have never come together the way it did. I can't thank everyone enough for their support, suggestions, and sometimes simply being a shoulder to cry on.

Deep breath And with that, it's off to start the next book!

With Love,

ABOUT THE AUTHOR

Carly Marie has had stories, characters, and plots bouncing around in her head for as long as she can remember. She began writing in high school and found it so cathartic that she's made time for it ever since. With the discovery of M/M romance, Carly knew she'd found her home. She was surprised to learn not everyone has sexy characters in their heads, begging for their stories to be written. With that knowledge, a little push from her husband, and a lot of encouragement from newfound friends, she jumped into the world of publishing.

Carly lives in Ohio with her husband, four girls, two cats, and more chickens than she can count. The numerous plot bunnies that run through her head on a daily basis ensure that she will continue to write and share her stories for years to come.

Connect with Carly!
　　Mailing List: Carly's Connection
　　Website: www.authorcarlymarie.com

　　　　　　　⬤ instagram.com/carlymariewrites
　　　　　　　⬤ goodreads.com/CarlyMarieWrites
　　　　　　　⬤ bookbub.com/authors/carly-marie
　　　　　　　⬤ amazon.com/author/carlymarie

Printed in Great Britain
by Amazon